Charman Coleman

The life of John J. Crittenden

With selections from his correspondence and speeches

Charman Coleman

The life of John J. Crittenden
With selections from his correspondence and speeches

ISBN/EAN: 9783337278502

Printed in Europe, USA, Canada, Australia, Japan

Cover: Foto ©Raphael Reischuk / pixelio.de

More available books at **www.hansebooks.com**

OF

JOHN J. CRITTENDEN,

WITH SELECTIONS FROM

HIS CORRESPONDENCE AND SPEECHES.

EDITED BY HIS DAUGHTER,

MRS. CHAPMAN COLEMAN.

IN TWO VOLUMES.

VOL. I.

PHILADELPHIA:
J. B. LIPPINCOTT & CO.
1871.

I DEDICATE

𝕿𝖍𝖊𝖘𝖊 𝖁𝖔𝖑𝖚𝖒𝖊𝖘

TO MY GRANDSONS WHO BEAR THE NAME OF

JOHN J. CRITTENDEN,

HOPING THAT THIS RECORD OF A NOBLE LIFE MAY INSPIRE THEM TO UNSELFISH PATRIOTISM AND ACTS OF LOVE AND KINDNESS.

"MAY ALL THE ENDS THEY AIM AT BE THEIR COUNTRY'S, THEIR GOD'S, AND TRUTH'S."*

---

* " May all the ends thou aimest at be thy country's, thy God's, and truth's," were among the last words spoken by Mr. Crittenden, and they are engraved upon his tomb.

PREFACE.

IT may not seem appropriate that the life of so great and good a man as Mr. Crittenden should be written by the feeble hand of a woman. There was, however, danger in delay, as many of the records necessary for such a work were being lost or obliterated. The consciousness of this fact impelled me to the effort I have made, and now submit to the public. My heart has failed me many times since I commenced the work, but I have been again encouraged by words of cheer and kindly interest from more than one who knew and loved my father.

Many distinguished men make preparation, during their lives, for handing down their names and reputation to posterity. Mr. Crittenden had repeated applications, from persons acquainted with political events, and capable of writing his life, for information necessary for that purpose, but he always declined. I heard him say once, in reply to such a request, "I have promised a friend that if there should be anything in my poor life worthy of record, he shall record it." The name of that friend I have never been able to ascertain. My purpose has been to let my father speak for himself through his letters and public speeches, only endeavoring to link together these scattered fragments, and give such recollections of early days in Kentucky as would have interest in connection with him in his social and political life. Of the mass of letters in my possession, addressed to him during forty years of his public life, I have selected such as I thought would have a general interest, being in themselves historical,—a partial history of the times, and characteristic of the eminent men who adorned them. I have also ventured to introduce a number of family letters. It has always seemed to me that a man's character, his "heart of hearts," is most surely displayed by such letters. My father was not a demonstrative man in his daily intercourse, most certainly he was not demonstrative in his family circle, but his letters to his wife and children are the exponents of his grand, simple, and loving nature. I have but few of his political letters; my application to distinguished men, or their executors, for his replies to their letters now in my possession, have been almost in vain. His correspondence with Governor Letcher, Orlando Brown, and A. T. Burnley, I have been fortunate enough to secure. He considered Governor Letcher the "prince of correspondents," and I have thought it best to publish many of his letters, as they give, in a familiar form, the views of a man of great discernment and inimitable humor. This correspondence alone is in fact almost a political history of Kentucky during the time which it embraces.

These volumes contain a statement of Mr. Crittenden's views and position on all the important questions before Congress from 1819 to 1863, and extracts from many of his speeches. This seemed to me to be the only mode of doing him justice, and placing his opinions as a statesman beyond the reach of controversy.

CONTENTS OF VOL. I.

(ix)

CHAPTER VII.

CHAPTER VIII.

CHAPTER IX.

CHAPTER X.

CHAPTER XI.

CHAPTER XII.

CHAPTER XIII.

CHAPTER XIV.

CHAPTER XV.

CHAPTER XVI.

CHAPTER XVII.

CHAPTER XVIII.

CHAPTER XIX.

CHAPTER XX.

CHAPTER XXI.

CHAPTER XXII.

CHAPTER XXIII.

CHAPTER XXIV.

CHAPTER XXV.

CHAPTER XXVI.

CHAPTER XXVII.

CHAPTER XXVIII.

CHAPTER XXIX.

LIFE

OF

JOHN J. CRITTENDEN.

CHAPTER I.

1787–1811.

Birth — Parentage — Education — Study of the Law — Admission to the Bar —
Appointed Attorney-General of the Territory of Illinois by Ninian Edwards—
Appointed Aide-de-Camp by General Shelby, in 1813, for the Campaign into
Canada—Letters from Chancellor George M. Bibb, General Samuel Hopkins,
General Shelby—Anecdote of his Legal Practice in Logan City.

JOHN JORDAN CRITTENDEN was born in Woodford County, Kentucky, on the 10th of September, 1787, and died at Frankfort, on the 26th of July, 1863. His father, John Crittenden, who held the rank of major during the Revolutionary War, was a farmer of moderate means. He was killed by the fall of a tree, and left a family of four sons and three daughters. His ancestry on the father's side were Welsh, and his mother was a descendant of French Huguenots.

Mr. Crittenden was sent from home to school in 1803–4, in Jessamine County, Kentucky. J. J. Marshall, T. A. Marshall, J. Cabell Breckenridge, Hubbard Taylor, Francis P. Blair, etc. were among his schoolmates. Every one of these men became distinguished in after-life. I think this could have been no accidental coincidence; their teacher must have had much to do with the rich development of character and intellect which made of these boys both great and good men: his name should be known and his memory honored. One of these gentlemen told me that Mr. Crittenden's delight in the study of the Latin language, and his facility in mastering it, was a subject of surprise and comment among his companions, and they believed that his own natural powers of eloquence were greatly aided by his study of Cicero's works.

Mr. Crittenden's cotemporaries in his own State were most remarkable men; it was indeed a proud honor to be distinguished among such brilliant competitors. The names of Jesse Bledsoe, Robert and Charles Wickliffe, John Pope, John Rowan, John Boyle, Ben Hardin, Richard Menifee, John Adair, William T. Barry, Robert Letcher, Governor Metcalf, F. Grundy, and Joseph H. Davis will live in history.

These men were educated in the wilds of Kentucky,—"the dark and bloody ground." There was then but little social intercourse, even between the neighboring States, books and schools were scarce,—in fact, it was not possible to obtain the accessories and advantages now considered indispensable to a finished education; and yet as lawyers, as politicians, as orators, they were unsurpassed. I have heard it stated that the Kentucky bar was at that time superior to the bar of any other State. This was, perhaps, attributable to the fact that every acre of ground in the State was covered over by conflicting law-claims. In social life, these men were full of originality of wit and humor, and although differing widely on legal and State questions, each one of them was the personal friend of Mr. Crittenden. He was a man of strong and ardent feelings, but his opponents were invariably met by him with a marked courtesy.

Mr. Crittenden commenced the study of the law under the judicious and kind counsel of Judge G. M. Bibb,—in fact, he was a member of Judge Bibb's family, residing at this time near Lexington, Kentucky. He completed his law studies at the ancient college of William and Mary, in Virginia, and commenced the practice of law in 1807 in his native county of Woodford, Kentucky. He did not continue there many years, however, but removed to Russellville, in Logan County, this location seeming to offer more inducements to promising and enterprising young men than (what was then considered) the old settled part of the State.

Soon, by his attention to business, his eloquence and ability, he obtained a good and lucrative practice, and inspired the entire community with confidence in his sincerity and honesty of purpose, and whenever he chose to be a candidate for any office in his native State, he was elected without difficulty. In 1809 he was appointed attorney-general of the Territory of Illinois, by Ninian Edwards, then governor of the Territory, and in 1810 he received a commission as aide-de-camp from Governor Edwards.

In 1811–12, Mr. Crittenden was elected to the Kentucky legislature, and during an intermission between his public duties and the courts he dashed over to Illinois and acted as volunteer aide to General Hopkins, in an expedition against the Indians. The same year he was appointed aide-de-camp, by Governor Charles Scott, in the first division of the militia of Kentucky.

In 1813 he was selected by Governor Shelby as an "aide-de-camp," and associated with Adair and Barry in the campaign into Canada. He took part in the battle of the Thames, where, under Generals Harrison and Shelby, the British under General Proctor were captured, the Indian force defeated and dispersed, and the Northwest Territory, which had been lost by Hull's surrender of Detroit, was recovered. His conduct in the campaign was favorably noticed in General Harrison's report, who long afterwards manifested his regard and confidence in Mr. Crittenden by appointing him attorney-general in 1841, this being the only cabinet appointment Mr. C. was ever willing to accept.

(Hon. George M. Bibb to John J. Crittenden.)

Senate Chamber, April 16, 1812.

Dear John,—We have been waiting for a respectable force to be embodied. The Kentuckians are impatient, Congress firm ; their ultimate acts will not disappoint the expectations of a brave people, determined to be free and independent. The truth is, the Secretary of the War Department is too imbecile ; he has neither the judgment to concert, the firmness to preserve, nor the vigor to execute any plans of military operations ; his want of arrangement and firmness is now so apparent, that he cannot longer remain at the head of the War Department. The President and majority in Congress have already suffered much by having such a man in that position. He must be dismissed by the President, or an inquiry of some kind, touching the conduct of the department, will be introduced. With a proper minister of war we might now have been prepared for war. If Eustis should be removed, we could soon be ready. Expecting that another man will be called to direct our military arrangements, I hope that a declaration of war will be made before the expiration of the period for which an embargo has been laid. I obtained a commission of first lieutenant for Thomas Critten-den; have been informed that he will not accept. How is Butler coming on in his electioneering campaign? I long to see him among the *natives*, " courting the sovereigns." Are his friends active? He must be elected. We want no wavering, time-serving, insincere politicians here; we have but too many already.

Yours truly,   GEORGE M. BIBB.

(General Sam Hopkins to Mr. Crittenden.)

FRANKFORT, August 24, 1812.

DEAR JOHN,—I arrived here, agreeably to the orders of his excellency the governor, to-day, by an express from Detroit. Certain it is Hull has retrograded, and is now in Detroit, sur-rounded by the British. He has twice attacked their post at Brownstown: the second attack, in which the gallant Lieu-tenant-Colonel Miller, of the 4th United States Regiment, com-manded, was successful, and the enemy beaten, though the post was not taken. The Ohio cavalry refused to charge; their provisions nearly expended, and no supplies can arrive till Brownstown is taken.

Hull's situation is precarious; the troops from Kentucky are on their way to relieve them,—say upwards of 2200. Michila-makinaw is taken, and I fear Chicago has met the same fate; in fine, everything in that quarter is gloomy. To-morrow a council, consisting of Messrs. Clay, Johnson, Governors Scott, Shelby, Harrison, and myself, are to meet and consult upon the best means of defending the country.

The Indians are not friends. This reverse will no doubt settle them hostile. Ten other articles could be recounted I hate—I *can't* be the author of anything worse, yet I fear I have worse to tell you the next opportunity.

Yours truly,   SAM HOPKINS.

J. J. CRITTENDEN.

FRANKFORT, August 20, 1813.

DEAR SIR,—Your favor of the fifteenth has been duly re-ceived. I had been casting my mind about, for a day or two past, for my second aide-de-camp. Among others, you had passed through my mind, but I feared that the distance between us and the short time I had to make my arrangements, would not afford me an opportunity to address you on this subject. Having, however, received your letter, expressing your willing-ness and desire to be one of my family on the present campaign, I embrace the earliest opportunity to assure you that you shall be my second aide-de-camp. General John Adair is already appointed the first.

I shall, therefore, look out for no other gentleman to fill that station, and beg you will be so good as to acknowledge the receipt of this letter, and apprise me of your determination by the returning mail. I shall forward a duplicate of this letter to Bowling Green, to guard against possible disappointment should you have left that neighborhood.

I have the honor to be, most respectfully,

Your obedient servant,

ISAAC SHELBY.

CAMP AT LIMESTONE, November 2, 1813.

Major J. J. Crittenden having acted as my second aide-de-camp on the late expedition into Canada, I cannot, in justice to his merits or my own feelings, take leave of him without expressing my warmest approbation of his whole conduct during the campaign, and the great obligations I feel for the attachment shown to my person, and the zeal and promptitude with which he always executed my orders, particularly so in the battle of the fifth of October last, on the river French.

Given under my hand, ISAAC SHELBY.

A number of young men in Russellville, Kentucky, raised and equipped a volunteer artillery company, in 1816, of which Mr. Crittenden was selected captain ; he was commissioned as captain by Governor Shelby, and attached to the 23d Regiment of militia on the 18th of May, 1816. This company continued its organization under successive captains until the late war. Many years after Mr. Crittenden removed to Frankfort, he visited Tennessee, and returned home by the way of Russellville. The morning he was to start home, this old company paraded before the door and informed him that they intended to escort him some distance, with banners flying and drums beating. Mr. Crittenden, who was a modest man and always shrank from anything like exhibition or display, was, at first, very reluctant to be made so conspicuous ; he soon recovered himself, however, and, after this flattering and touching attention, he parted with his old comrades of the company with heartfelt thanks. Only a day or two before his death, one of the members of this old Logan County command was seated by his bedside, when suddenly his mind reverted to those far-off times, and he asked about the company and the name of some member whom he had partially forgotten.

There are, perhaps, people now living in Logan County, Kentucky, who remember Judge Broadnax. He was a stately, high-toned Virginia gentleman, who dressed in shorts, silk stockings, and top-boots; he had an exalted sense of the dignity of the court, and a great contempt for meanness, rascality, and all low rowdyism. Mr. Crittenden used to describe, in his most inimitable manner, a scene which took place in the court-room, in Logan, where Judge Broadnax presided. A man had been indicted for biting off another man's ear, in a street brawl. This was a penitentiary offense, and Mr. Crittenden was engaged to defend the prisoner.

Judge Broadnax was a warm friend and admirer of Mr. Crittenden, but he railed at him fiercely for taking fees of such *low rascals*. The judge was, at heart, an aristocrat.

In this case, after great difficulty and delay, eleven jurymen had been obtained. Many respectable-looking men had been summoned, and rejected by the counsel for the prisoner, and both the judge and sheriff were much exasperated. At last an ill-looking fellow, with a tattered straw hat on his head, half the brim being torn off, a piece of his nose gone, and his face bearing many other evidences of drunken brawls, was brought in. After looking at him a moment and asking him a few questions, Mr. Crittenden said, "Well, judge, rather than be the cause of any *more delay*, I'll take this man."

The judge, who had been looking on angrily, could no longer control himself. He sprang to his feet, exclaiming, "I knew it; yes, I knew it!—the moment I laid my eyes on the fellow I knew you would accept him." Then, taking a contemptuous survey of the jury, he exclaimed, aloud, "Did any living man ever see such a jury before?"

Mr. Crittenden quietly replied, "Why, your Honor, I pronounce this a most respectable jury."

After that speech of the judge, Mr. Crittenden said his mind was at ease about his client; he knew he would be acquitted, and he was.

CHAPTER II.

1811–1814.

WHEN Mr. Crittenden was first elected to the House of
Representatives from Logan County, Kentucky, he
took his wife to her brother-in-law's, Mr. Sam. Wallace, in
Woodford, Kentucky. From this point he rode to Frankfort
on horseback, and was joined on the way by an old gentleman.
They were utter strangers, but conversed pleasantly together,
and when they reached Frankfort they separated, not even
knowing each other's names.

The House met the next day, and, after some other nominations had been made, the same old gentleman, Mr. Paine, of
Fayette, nominated J. J. Crittenden, of Logan County, for
Speaker of the House. Mr. Crittenden rose and protested
against the nomination in a modest but impressive speech, and
positively declined the honor. Mr. Paine replied that the
speech itself removed all doubt as to the expediency of electing
Mr. Crittenden. He persisted in his nomination, and Mr. Crittenden was unanimously chosen Speaker.

In 1811, Mr. Crittenden was married to Sallie O. Lee,
daughter of Major John Lee, of Woodford County. Major Lee
was a descendant of Hancock Lee, the elder branch of the same
family from which General R. E. Lee descended.

Mrs. Crittenden died in 1824, leaving three sons and four
daughters,—George, Thomas, and Robert, Ann Mary, Cornelia,
Eugenia, and Maria. The eldest son was a graduate of West
Point: he became a colonel in the Federal army, resigned during

the late war, and served for a time as major-general in the Confederate army.

Thomas L. Crittenden was aid to General Taylor in the battle of Buena Vista. He was afterwards sent by General Taylor as consul to Liverpool. He entered the army during the late war, and was promoted to the rank of major-general, resigned before the close of the war; but soon after its close, he was again commissioned, with the rank of colonel. Eugenia Crittenden died unmarried, at the age of twenty-one. Ann Mary, the eldest daughter, married Chapman Coleman, of Kentucky, and has been a widow for twenty years. Cornelia married Rev. John C. Young, President of Danville College, Kentucky, and is now a widow. Maria Crittenden married Dr. Edward Watson, of Frankfort, Kentucky, and is also a widow. Robert Henry, the youngest son, has always been engaged in commercial pursuits. On the occasion of Mrs. Crittenden's death, Mr. Crittenden received the following letter from Mr. Clay:

ASHLAND, 17th September, 1824.

MY DEAR SIR,—Although I know how utterly unavailing are the condolences of friends, however sincere, and that nothing but time can assuage the grief which is excited by a loss so irreparable and afflicting as that which you have recently sustained, I cannot deny to myself the melancholy satisfaction of expressing to you my deepest sympathy for your heavy bereavement.

In the lamented death of Mrs. Crittenden, I do not merely recognize the loss of the wife of a friend, but that of a friend herself. I knew her, I believe, before you did, and although her residence in another and distant part of the State prevented my seeing her for many years, I never ceased to feel the respect and esteem for her which was inspired by my early acquaintance. Although thus early deprived of a mother's care and a mother's tenderness, it must be some consolation to you to know that your children will find their mother's place supplied, as far as that is possible, in the affections and attentions of Mrs. Wilkinson and Mrs. Price.

One would be almost inclined to think that our State in these last years had lost divine favor; its afflictions by death have been numerous and extreme. I have myself had a slight fever.

With best wishes, I remain, faithfully, your friend,

H. CLAY.

On the 15th of November, 1826, Mr. Crittenden married Mrs. Maria K. Todd, daughter of Judge Harry L. Innis, of Franklin County, Kentucky; she died in 1851, leaving two sons,—John J. Crittenden and Eugene. John died at the age of twenty-two, and Eugene is now a major in the Federal army.

On the 27th of February, 1853, Mr. Crittenden married Mrs. Elizabeth Ashley, who is now residing in New York.

Thinking of Mr. Crittenden's early life and its surroundings, I recall many curious customs in Kentucky which have, no doubt, passed away. At that time ladies were in the habit of attending criminal trials, and I have gone with them to the adjoining counties for this purpose. Mr. Crittenden was born in Woodford County, about twelve miles from Frankfort, and the admiration and love cherished for him there was unsurpassed. Every man in that county felt that he had a sort of right in Mr. Crittenden, and criminals from other counties were always trying first to engage him to defend them, and then to have the trial transferred to Woodford, well knowing that a jury could scarcely be found in the county that could resist *his* arguments and eloquence. Indeed, there were many old men there who declared they could not conscientiously serve on the jury with John J. Crittenden as counsel for the prisoner; they were so completely fascinated by his eye and voice that justice and the law were lost sight of. I remember something of a famous trial for murder in Woodford which I will endeavor to relate. The name of the man who was murdered was, I think, Cole. Court-day is a great day in small inland towns in the West. All business to be done in the towns is, if possible, deferred until that day, and the plowing, planting, and reaping are stopped without remorse. The plow-horses are fastened to the long lines of fence, and the yeomanry gather in groups about the taverns and court-house. Any important trial brought together the prominent speakers, and the chance of announcing and spreading one's opinions, by a lusty fight or two, was an ever-new delight.

Mr. Cole and a friend named Gillespie, of the like calibre and tastes, rode into the little town of Versailles on court-day. Everything was propitious: they drank, played cards, and were merry. Late in the day they rode most amicably, side by side, out of Versailles, going home together. Unfortunately they had both *cards* and whisky in their pockets, and of the latter they partook freely. They rode slowly, and were benighted. Passing a dismantled log cabin by the wayside, they determined to stop and rest, tied their horses, struck a light, and concluded to play "High, low, jack, and the game," and take a little grog from time to time, by way of refreshment, till the morning.

As might have been expected, they grew quarrelsome and abusive. It is a short step from words to blows. Gillespie struck at his friend Cole with a knife, and killed him instantly. The sight of the blood and of the dead man, his friend from boyhood, sobered him fully, and his sorrow and remorse were indescribable. No thought of concealment of his crime or flight from justice was in his heart; he sprang on his horse, and galloped to the nearest house, told his story with groans, lamentations, and tears, and gave himself up to answer for his deed of blood and violence. There was, of course, no witness, the testimony rested upon his simple statement. Mr. Crittenden was employed to defend him, and he was acquitted.

Mr. Crittenden's speech was pronounced a masterpiece of oratory. Almost the entire assembly was moved to sobs and tears; the attempt was made to invalidate or set aside Gillespie's testimony; he acknowledged the murder, and his statement of the circumstances was the single point in his favor. Mr. Crittenden's reply to this effort on the part of the prosecutor is all I can recall of his speech. In fact, I remember but the sentiment he expressed; the voice, the eloquent lip, the living eye, it is impossible to portray.

"Can any man in his senses, with a throbbing heart in his bosom, doubt this man's testimony? No, gentlemen of the jury, the truth gushes from his burdened heart in that hour of agony as pure as the water from the rock when smitten by the hand of the prophet."

Mr. Crittenden seemed inspired, and his aspect and words carried conviction with them, not only to the sympathetic audience, but to the stern jury.

I think it was of this man Gillespie that I once heard

Mr. Crittenden say, "Yes, I begged that man's life of the jury."

On one occasion, when Mr. Crittenden was engaged in defending a man who had committed a capital offense, he closed an elaborate and powerful argument by the following beautiful allegory: "When God in his eternal counsel conceived the thought of man's creation, He called to Him the three ministers who wait constantly upon the throne,—*Justice*, *Truth*, and *Mercy*,—and thus addressed them: 'Shall I create man?' 'O God, make him not,' said Justice, 'for he will trample upon thy laws.' Truth said, 'Create him not, O God, for he will pollute thy sanctuary.' But Mercy, falling upon her knees, and looking up through her tears, exclaimed, 'O God, create him; I will watch over him in all the dark paths which he may be forced to tread.' So God created man, and said to him, 'O Man, thou art the child of Mercy: go and deal mercifully with thy brother.'"

When Mr. Crittenden closed, the jury were in tears, and, against evidence and their own convictions, brought in a verdict of "Not guilty."

When I was about sixteen, I went with two or three other young girls to the house of my aunt, Mrs. Raleigh, in Versailles, Woodford County, to attend a trial for murder.

A young man from one of the Southern States, a student of Transylvania College, in Lexington, Kentucky, in a sudden brawl, killed one of his fellow-students. There was no charge of previous malice; but the circumstances were aggravated, and the feeling of the community seemed against the young Southerner. So great was the local excitement about Lexington, that a change of venue was demanded and granted. The trial was removed to Woodford, and Mr. Crittenden was counsel for the prisoner.

The youth of the parties excited the interest of all the young people in that part of the State, and many prominent lawyers, not employed in the suit, made a point of being present to hear the arguments.

I remember now, with a glow of satisfaction, the bright array of native talent which I saw congregated on that occasion. General Flournoy, an eccentric, but clever and kindly lawyer, belonging to that part of the State, had volunteered to assist the prosecution. I can never forget his appearance, and the effect he produced on the court and audience, when he entered the room to make his speech. He was at that time a middle-aged man, tall, thin, and angular; he had many personal peculiarities; among other eccentricities, he always dressed in green, and the proverb "in vino veritas," he had changed to "in vino mors;" this motto he wore about him always in some form or other. He was an old bachelor, with the peculiarities of that rigid class stamped upon him unmistakably in every line and lineament; he was ambitious to be a *beau*, but the girls laughed at him and ran away from him. He was a man of truth, integrity, and intelligence, but, nevertheless, he had a hard time of it with the youth of his day.

The general wanted to be very confidential, even when he had absolutely nothing to say. When he desired to be especially kind and flattering in his attentions, he would fix his eye steadily and bear down upon you from a distant point; then, bowing over you, he would seem to whisper something in your ear; at times you would hear a confused and almost inaudible sentence; at others something of about this importance, "*Miss Crittenden, I see you.*" These little confidences of his were a source of unending amusement to the young ladies.

General Flournoy entered the court-room on the occasion referred to, dressed, of course, in green, and followed by a stalwart negro man, bearing a market-basket; not the *pitiful thing* now dignified by the name of market-basket, but a basket in which Falstaff might have been concealed.

This was filled with ponderous law-books intended for reference during his argument. This spectacle produced a variety of emotions in the minds of the spectators. There was, naturally, some shrinking terror at the thought of the ordeal before them on a hot summer day; but the grave dignity of the gentleman in green, the grinning, panting negro, who seemed to appreciate the situation, the solemnity with which the general removed the books from the basket and arranged upon a large table before him as many as the table would hold, was too much for the crowd, and there was a burst of laughter, in which, I think, his Honor joined.

The general was not a graceful orator: his arms were too long; he threw his head and neck forward, and described a half-circle first with his right arm, and then with his left, in regular rotation; he made a long speech, read many voluminous extracts from the *law library* before him, and was often so violent as to be unintelligible. He had not learned the lesson, "that in the very torrent, tempest, and whirlwind of your passion you should acquire and beget a temperance that might give it smoothness."

When General Flournoy concluded, Mr. Crittenden rose calmly, and passed his hand several times over his eyelids, as one half asleep is accustomed to do. "Gentlemen of the jury, I have either slept and dreamed, or I have had a vivid waking dream, which I can scarcely dispel. I thought I had gone out on a whaling vessel, the winds and waves were high, and the mighty waters were roaring around me. Suddenly the sailors cried out, 'All hands on deck, the whale is upon us, she blows!' I looked, and there indeed was the monster of the deep; its tail was flying through the air and the surging waves, till we were enveloped in mist. I am stunned, confused, and your Honor must grant me a few moments to recover my self-possession."

Mr. Crittenden then commenced his argument. I remember only its close. The counsel for the prosecution had made a strong point of demanding an example, spoke eloquently of the lawlessness of the times, and the necessity of maintaining the majesty of the law. On this point Mr. Crittenden said, "The counsel against the prisoner demands example. Yes, I agree with my stern and learned friend, we should make examples from time to time, even among the young and thoughtless, to check the heat of youthful blood and the violence of ungoverned passion; but, my countrymen, let us take that example from among our own people, and not seize upon the youthful stranger, who came confidingly among us, to profit by the advantages of our literary institutions, to learn to be a man in the best sense, honest and capable and cultivated. We have, I am grieved to say, frequent opportunities to make example of our own sons, in our own borders. Let us do this, then, when the occasion offers, but let us send this broken-hearted, trembling mother [pointing to the prisoner's mother, who was present], and her dear, loved son, back to their home in peace. He has been overtaken in a great crime, but an acquittal, in consideration of his youth and other extenuating circumstances, will be honorable to our great State, and do no damage to the laws."

The jury retired for a few moments, and the prisoner was acquitted.

General Flournoy left the court-room enraged against Mr. Crittenden ; he was standing on the street near a pump (pumps were the great rallying-points on court-days), denouncing Mr. Crittenden to a group of amused listeners, when Mr. C., approaching silently, struck Flournoy on the shoulder, and said, "How are you, old whale ? I know you are dry, after all that blowing ; come and take a drink."

Mr. Crittenden's voice and manner were like the sunshine after the early and latter rain. Flournoy grasped his hand forgivingly, and they went off arm in arm to settle their differences over the punch-bowl.

Mr. Crittenden was so often electioneering in Franklin County for a seat in the Kentucky legislature that he knew personally every man in the county. No one ever had warmer friends ; indeed, he was idolized by the older men of his party. Among these was Bob Collins, a sturdy yeoman of powerful frame, who had always a shoulder for the political wheel when it required putting in motion. Bob was a man of good common sense, clear judgment, and healthy, jovial nature, and he almost adored Mr. Crittenden. In some question which arose in Kentucky, either as to the old and new court, or Jackson and Adams, Bob's personal attachment to Mr. Crittenden and his political tendencies were unfortunately at variance. He was a man of considerable influence in his neighborhood, and as it was well known that he would carry a number of votes along with him, Mr. F. P. Blair conceived what he himself calls the *mad idea* of winning him completely away from Mr. Crittenden by a little well-applied flattery and *political dealing*. He accordingly visited Bob Collins in his humble home, and proposed a pleasant little social walk and chat ; he adroitly introduced small insinuations against Mr. Crittenden, said he was a man greatly overestimated, not the man Collins took him for, etc. At this point, when Mr. Blair thought he had made considerable headway, they passed a large pond. "Stop there, Blair!" cried Bob Collins, angrily. "Look at that! that's a frog-pond and full of frogs, and the *varmints* often make such a hell of a fuss the whole neighborhood is disturbed. Every frog thinks himself the big man of the lot, and each one tries to screech louder than the others; but, Lord bless you, they take no notice of each other. You see, each one knows in his heart that the other is *but a frog*, and scorns him. Presently a little boy from the village comes along and thinks to himself, Ha! my fine fellow, I'll put a stop to this. He approaches the edge of the pond, and hollows out Wh-i-s-t! wh-i-s-t! and every dirty little fellow drops down to the bottom of the pond, disappears as it were from the face of the earth, and prudently holds his tongue : they know the little boy has *stones in his pocket*. Well, just so it is with you and your set. When you get together in a safe place, you make a mighty fuss and abuse John J. Crittenden ; but let the fine fellow come along, and say Wh-i-s-t! wh-i-s-t! and your heads drop down, and you slink away to a safe place. Hurrah for John J. Crittenden, say I !"

I have heard another anecdote connected with Mr. Crittenden and Bob Collins, which is interesting, as going to show the characteristics of the people of Kentucky in that day, and Mr. Crittenden's influence over them. Bob professed to be an enthusiastic Baptist, although not a member of any church. There was a Baptist church in his neighborhood, over which he ruled despotically, founding his claim to *dictate* upon the fact that many of his slaves were members of this church. He used to consult with Mr. Crittenden about the interests of *his church*, giving him an account of baptisms, etc. Bob took great interest in these proceedings, and whenever one of his own negroes was to be baptized, he superintended the whole affair; nothing would have induced him to allow one of them to go down into the water supported by the preacher alone. Bob took the candidate for baptism by one arm and the preacher took the other, and as they descended into the river, old Father N. exhorted at every step, and Bob cried out, "Amen!" most devoutly. On one occasion Bob came into town to give Mr.

Crittenden an account of a misfortune that had befallen him.
A large, stalwart negro man of his had been baptized. Bob
was filled with zeal on that occasion: to *own another* member
of the church, gave him, he thought, a new right to control
the congregation. The convert was valuable, and Bob was so
anxious about his safety that he forgot to lay aside his watch,
which was almost ruined. As they came up out of the water,
the preacher was exhorting and commending the new brother
as a model of piety and zeal to the assembled crowd. Bob
declared he was completely carried away by the discourse, and
exclaimed, "Yes, yes! a model! a model! I wish I had a
thousand such." He professed to be hurt on perceiving that
this was not regarded as altogether a pious ejaculation. The
church members got into some difficulty among themselves,
which he attempted to settle in a very summary manner; they
resisted, and he entered the church by force, in the midst of the
proceedings, broke up the assembly, scattered them ignomi-
niously, and barred up the house. For this act of violence
they brought suit against him, much to his righteous indignation. He employed Mr. Crittenden to defend him. The suit
was talked about far and wide, and was the occasion of many
merry jests. A great crowd assembled at the trial. Mr. Crittenden made one of his best speeches, and placed the character and conduct of his client in the most favorable light. In
conclusion, he stated that he had not been able to do his friend
justice, but had employed an assistant in the defense, whom
he would now call up to conclude the argument. To the
amazement of every one, Mr. Crittenden now summoned Bob
Collins to speak for himself. The call was wholly unexpected,
but he came forward instantly,—in fact, he was as fully convinced
that he belonged to Mr. Crittenden as that the church belonged
to him. The speech was, as you may suppose, original, and
brought down the house. Even the judge and jury gave way to
the merry spirit of the hour. At the close of a short speech,
Bob said, "If their Honors would only call upon his friend
John to do '*the finishing!*' before he had spoken five minutes
they would think they heard a pint of bullets rattling over a
shingle roof." I do not remember how this suit was decided,
but expect Bob carried the day.

Mr. Crittenden and F. Preston Blair were playmates, school-mates, and personal friends through life. In early manhood they were also united in politics, but when the question arose in Kentucky between the pretensions of Jackson and Adams for the presidency, they differed, and finally separated. Political feeling ran high in old Kentucky (in those days men, women, and children were politicians), and as parties were nearly equally divided, such a condition of things always led to great effort and excitement. Mr. Blair and Mr. Crittenden were opposed to each other, each making speeches in further-ance of his views in Frankfort and the vicinity. Mr. Blair tells this anecdote in connection with that period:

A few days before the election was to take place, an appoint-ment was made for a political meeting in the neighborhood. Mr. Blair reached the ground first, and made a violent speech, in which he brought many charges against Mr. Crittenden's political course, and abused him personally. He was greatly excited. Ashamed of his course towards his old friend, and afraid of the lashing he knew was in store for him, he had, during his tirade, been looking round anxiously for his oppo-nent, and found his flashing eye fixed steadily upon him. He closed his speech, and a rather cowardly impulse took posses-sion of him to steal off and escape the scourging, the mere anticipation of which weighed heavily upon him. He reached the outskirts of the crowd, when, hearing *that voice* which always thrilled and, in a measure, controlled him, he turned back almost involuntarily and gave himself up to justice. As he found he was not personally alluded to, he drew nearer and nearer, with some feeling of security. Mr. Crittenden took up the charges with which he had been assailed one by one and refuted them; managed to cast a furtive glance from time to time upon his adversary, but did not call his name or allude to him. At first, this rather pleased Blair; then, as he became convinced that "John" meant to pass him by silently, he was humiliated and ashamed.

A few days afterwards Preston Blair was seated in one of the clerks' offices in Frankfort, when Mr. Crittenden entered; he advanced to Mr. Blair with extended hand, and a kindly greet-ing: "Well, Preston, how are you?" Mr. Blair, greatly embarrassed, stammered out a few words of salutation, and then, feeling that something more must be said to break the silence, remarked, "You had a son born in your house yesterday, Crittenden,—what do you intend to call him?" A cloud of mingled feelings passed over Mr. Crittenden's speaking countenance. After a moment's pause, he said, "I have been thinking, Preston, of calling him by that name which you have been trying of late to dishonor."

"That," with the kind and sorrowful glance which accompanied it, "went straight to my heart," said Mr. Blair. "The fountain of my speech was dried up, and this was the only reproach Mr. Crittenden ever made me."

CHAPTER III.

1814–1820.

(General Isaac Shelby to J. J. Crittenden.)

April 8, 1814.

MY DEAR SIR,—Your favor of the 18th came to hand when I was absent from home, and since my return a letter from the Secretary of War has been received, informing me that the appointment of officers has been made for the corps of riflemen to be raised under the late act of Congress. This letter was an answer to one of the last which I had written to him, in favor of some of my friends who wanted to enter the service, and assures me that Kentucky has had her full share in those appointments. I have, therefore, deemed it unnecessary to trouble the Secretary in favor of Captain H. R. Lewis, whom I well recollect, and of whom I formed a good opinion upon the late campaign.

I am very apprehensive that we shall have peace by the mission to Gottenburg, if the affairs of Europe do not prevent it. Perhaps it may be well for us if we do obtain peace. The war is a ruinous one. We are, literally, " a house divided against itself." And, although we may not fall, the war, if carried on, will finally exhaust the best blood and interest of the nation; none others will embark in it unless with a view to *mar* its success. This is lamentable, *but true!* and unless we can cure the evil at home, defeat and disaster will attend the efforts of our best patriots. I may in confidence confess to you, that I lament over my country,—that she has in her very bosom a faction as relentless as the fire that is unquenchable,— capable of thwarting her best interests, and whose poisonous breath is extending to every corner of the Union. There is but one way to cure the evil, and that is an awful and desperate one, and in the choice of evils we had better take the least. Were we unanimous, I should feel it less humiliating to be conquered, as I verily believe that the administration will be driven to

(31)

peace, *on any terms*, by the opposition to the war. We have no news from our Eastern armies, nor do we know that the fleet at Ontario has left its winter-quarters.

I wish Niagara was near to Kentucky, it should not remain long in the hands of those blood-hounds! to be given up for *Malden*, as no doubt it will on a general peace. Will you come to Frankfort this winter? If the war continues, the country will want her best friends in the legislature, and I shall be glad to see you.

The Eastern mail has this moment arrived, and brings information that the President unquestionably recommended the repeal of the embargo and non-importation acts. This looks like giving way to the clamors for commerce. What is to become of our new manufactories and young merinoes? It will afford me great pleasure to hear of your happiness and prosperity.

Your obedient servant,
ISAAC SHELBY.

Hon. J. J. CRITTENDEN.

(George M. Bibb to John J. Crittenden.)

WASHINGTON CITY, April 24, 1814.

DEAR JOHN,—The court-martial sentenced Hull to be *cashiered and shot*, but recommended him to the mercy of the President, who, I understand, intends to remit the sentence of death. What weakness! If cowardice such as Hull's, which surrendered a fortress, an army, a territory without firing a gun,—which surrender was followed by such loss of lives and treasure,—is not punished with death, but pardoned by the commander-in-chief, what can we expect? No military officer hereafter can be punished but by loss of commission for cowardice. A negotiation is going on between an agent on our part and General Prevost, for an armistice. Prevost is willing to an armistice on land; our government wishes it also by sea. The negotiation may, perhaps, terminate in an armistice on the land, the lakes, and on our seacoast, leaving our coast to be blockaded, and the war upon the ocean to progress,—that is to say, that no expedition on land, nor any enterprise against towns or forts, shall be attempted,—such an armistice to be continued for a limited time, or until our negotiations at Gottenburg are broken off, or until either party shall give reasonable notice that it shall cease. I speak of the probable issue from what our government would agree to, and what it may well be supposed the British government would not agree to. The maritime superiority of Great Britain she will not yield by an armistice.

Your friend, as ever,   GEORGE M. BIBB.

I found among Mr. Crittenden's papers a letter from Mr. Blair, from which I make the following extract:

WASHINGTON CITY, 1831.

DEAR CRITTENDEN,—Eliza sends her love; she has ordered the *Globe* to be sent you, that you may have the advantage of her hemisphere, which she promises to make interesting. The black side—that is, my side of the paper—you need not look at. I presume you believe all you see in the prints of Old Hickory; if you do, you know nothing of him: he is as full of energy as he was at New Orleans, and is to his cabinet here what he was to his aids there. He is in fine health, and nothing daunted at all the plots, conspiracies, and intrigues of which some hope he is to be the victim. In a recent conversation with me about the Seminole affair, he spoke of you as "his friend Crittenden." I suppose he refers to the past. Give my wife's most affectionate remembrances to Mrs. Crittenden, and if you can make my offering of good wishes and sincere respects acceptable to her, let me hope that you will tender them. I shall be glad to hear of the prosperity of the young gentleman who received last year a name that you seemed to think "*I was trying to make one of little credit to him.*" God knows you did me injustice *in that* at least. If ever I had a kind heart, it is for you; but, as Tom Church says, "although I love you, I don't love your ways."

Yours, in everything, politics excepted,

F. P. BLAIR.

Tom Church was a Franklin County man, one of the Bob Collins order, and a man of influence in his neighborhood; he was a personal friend of Blair and Crittenden, and when they separated politically, they were both anxious to secure him. Mr. Crittenden heard that he was wavering, and walked out to see him, and "*straighten him up.*" At parting, Church said to him, "Well, John, I think I must go for Preston. I love you, John, but I don't love your ways." This phrase became from that time onward a sort of conciliatory "by-word with the old friends."

Many barbecues (called in some parts of Kentucky, bergoos) were given in the State, at that time, for electioneering purposes. Men, women, and children assembled for miles around the place of meeting to dance and sing, speak and listen to speaking, eat, drink, and be merry. From the time I was twelve years old, I used to go and dance on the hillside for hours.

A long arbor was generally erected, covered with green branches from the trees; under this rough planks were set up for a table, and upon them the baskets of provisions were emptied, and the "good things" spread out before us.

Some of these occasions dwell most pleasantly in my memory. The dogwood and the redbud, quivering in the sunshine, formed a charming roof over our heads, the merry groups scattered around under the trees, the speakers' stand, the laughter, the applause, the songs, the voices of children,—even babies, too young to be left at home, joined in the chorus,—all this is indelibly impressed upon my heart.

I remember an amusing little incident connected with a barbecue given near Frankfort. Far and wide the people had come together. In those days there were no operas, no concerts, no Grande Duchesses, no Belle Hélènes. Barbecues were the order and the dissipation of the day. A young woman was thought to have more than mortal strength if she resisted successfully the temptation of a barbecue in her neighborhood. Young mothers with young babies were the most at a loss *what could* be done with their children,—too young to take, too young to leave at home!

A pretty young country mother, with a baby perhaps a month old, suffered terribly with doubts and perplexities on this subject. At last, she resolved to *take the baby* and take the consequences; she knew she would have to play nurse, could not dance, and could only be a looker-on. Nevertheless, she determined to go! In the height of the entertainment, Mr. Crittenden's eye fell upon her sorrowful countenance, and he resolved to devote the time that our old Virginia reel would occupy to her amusement. He took his seat by her and tried to make himself agreeable; he soon saw, however, that she gave him but a languid attention; eye and ear were given to Yankee Doodle and the dancers. Suddenly, in the twinkling of an eye, before he had time to see his danger or to remonstrate, she sprang up, plumped the baby down in his lap, exclaiming, "Oh, Mr. Crittenden, human nature can't stand that!" Before the last words were finished, she was whirling away in the reel, to the great consternation of Mr. Crittenden, who had a mortal fear of babies, and the infinite amusement of the bystanders. The rival candidate and his party considered this a very good joke, and used to tell it, with great gusto; but there is no doubt that Mr. Crittenden's exemplary discharge of his new duties gained him many votes.

In 1816–17 Mr. Crittenden was Speaker of the House of Representatives in Kentucky, and was elected in 1817 to the Senate of the United States.

There is an anecdote connected with his maiden speech which Governor Barbour related with great spirit. The subject was worthy of Mr. Crittenden's patriotic eloquence, being the first attempt to grant pensions to the soldiers of the Revolution, and to his memory belongs the glory of that achievement. On rising to speak, Mr. Crittenden was greatly agitated (this was a trait which marked his ablest efforts in after-life). His embarrassment became so intense that his friends apprehended a failure, and Governor Barbour, who had often been delighted by Mr. Crittenden's powers of conversation in social life, *looked* his anxieties to Mr. Clay.

Mr. Clay gazed steadily and confidently at his young friend for a moment, and then replied to Barbour by a whisper (yet loud enough to be heard throughout the senate-chamber), "Never mind, he will be all right." And soon, indeed, Mr. Crittenden's magical voice rose to the occasion, and he electrified a listening Senate with an eloquence which no first effort had ever before effected.

During this session, as chairman of a committee to whom a bill putting fugitives from labor on the same footing with fugitives from justice was referred, Mr. Crittenden reported it back with several amendments, one of which provided that the identity of the fugitive should be proved by other evidence than the claimant's.

December 8, 1817, Mr. Crittenden submitted this amendment:

Resolved, That all persons who were prosecuted and fined under the sedition law, approved the fourteenth day of July, 1798, entitled An Act for the Punishment of certain Crimes against the United States, ought to be reimbursed, and indemnified out of the public treasury.

Mr. Crittenden said:

I consider the sedition law unconstitutional, not only from a defect of power in Congress to pass such a law, but because its passage was expressly forbidden by the Constitution. The sense of the nation had unquestionably pronounced it unconstitutional, and that opinion being generally entertained, it ought to be solemnly confirmed by the legislature, in order that history and the records of the country may not hand it down to posterity as a precedent for similar acts of usurpation. If a reversion of the proceedings in that case was important in a public point of view, it was certainly so as it related to the individuals who became the subjects of prosecution under that act. To every citizen of the United States the Constitution guaranteed certain rights, which had been violated under this law. This guarantee entitled them to indemnity in all cases where those rights were violated; of this indemnity the courts ought not to deprive them; if they did, there was no redeeming power in the Constitution. Legal sanctions cannot vitiate constitutional provisions. The judiciary is a valuable part of the government, and ought to be highly respected, but it is not *infallible*. The Constitution is our guide, our supreme law. Blind homage can never be rendered by freemen to any power. In all cases of alleged violation of the Constitution it was for Congress to make just discrimination. When the Constitution forbids a law, it will not hesitate to interpose for the relief of those who suffer by its inflictions. The case of Matthew Lyon, now before the Senate, was a fair case for the interposition of Congress. It had a peculiar character. Lyon had a right to remuneration: this right ought not to be sacrificed to contingencies or speculative opinions. We may not do wrong that right may come of it! Justice to the individual, to the country, to the Constitution, all required this course. Let us add new defenses and guards to the Constitution on this assailable point. Let us secure it, as far as possible, from future infractions on the ground of precedent.

The Senate, on Friday, December 29, 1819, resumed the discussion of the bill prescribing the mode of settling controversies between two or more States. Mr. Crittenden said:

The same course had been pursued at the last session which was now proposed, and if this motion prevailed it must be considered as a rejection of the bill. The State of Kentucky had addressed a memorial to Congress in favor of such a measure as was proposed by this bill, and I deem it a duty to submit the reasons which occur to me in support of it. Under the Constitution, power was given to Congress to make the provision contemplated in this bill. Why tremble at the exercise of this power? There must be authority somewhere to settle disputes between States, and where would it be so safely lodged as in the national judiciary? I believe no ground of alarm exists. The greatest and proudest States in the Union would cheerfully submit to the decisions of that tribunal every litigation between them. The States would be sued by their consent: as they had given their consent to the provision of the Constitution authorizing this law, they would not therefore complain of any violation of their sovereignty and independence. I deem it essential to the perpetuity of our Union that this power should have been given, and that it should be exercised. The objections came from those States likely to become defendants under this act, and from the great and powerful State of Virginia. This provision was meant to protect the small States against the populous and powerful. Have we come to this, that such States threaten resistance to the constitutional laws? I hope such threats will not terrify us into an abandonment of this power. I appreciate the high and honorable motives of the gentleman from Virginia, but think his apprehensions unfounded and visionary. I believe the judgment of the Supreme Court, as now limited, executes itself silently and effectually,—there was no danger of the necessity of employing military force. The States would not settle their disputes amicably among themselves, without the mediation of a disinterested tribunal. Virginia and Pennsylvania had almost come to war on a territorial difference; was this the "suaviter in modo" which ought to be pursued in settling boundaries? Such a dispute would not now be settled between these potent States so easily. Suppose, in this difference between Kentucky and Tennessee, Kentucky should give up her claim rather than come to open war, would it be right for the general government to see her stripped of her rights? Kentucky had no alternative but to do this or appeal to the sword. Would it be just or magnanimous to refuse to exercise this power and thus permit such wrongs to be done? Though justly proud of my State, I should not deem her disgraced by being made a defendant under this law, or by submitting to the judgment of the Supreme Court. I wish such a high tribunal could be erected to settle all disputes between nations, and oblige proud and ambitious people to submit to just and equitable terms of settlement. Should we, of one flesh and blood, quarrel among ourselves when so easy a remedy is in our power? New Jersey has had her disputes, Rhode Island has had hers, and if wrong has been done, is there any honorable gentlemen who would not wish to see wrong righted?

Mr. Crittenden made a speech on the 18th of February, 1819, in support of the bill for the sale of public lands. He said, in conclusion :

Mr. President, I acknowledge that I feel a particular partiality for this bill, independent of the reasons I have had the honor of submitting to you. I am influenced by reasons somewhat of a personal character, to desire its passage. It is the work of the honorable gentleman (Mr. Morrow) of Ohio, who is so soon to be finally separated from us : he has long been our Palinurus in everything that relates to this important subject; he has steered us safely through all its difficulties, and with him for our helmsman we have feared neither Scylla nor Charybdis. We have followed him with increasing confidence, and have never been deceived or disappointed. The bill now before you is perhaps the last and most important act of his long and useful life. If it should pass, sir, it will identify his name and his memory with this interesting subject: it will be his.

A noble monument, which, while it guides the course of future legislation, will perpetuate the memory of an honest man. Sir, if the ostracism of former times prevailed with us, I do not know the individual whose virtues would more certainly expose him to its envious jealous sentence. The illustrious Greek himself who claimed such unfortunate distinction from that ancient usage did not better deserve the epithet *Just.*

Mr. President, I do not intend to flatter the gentleman from Ohio. Flattery is falsehood. I burn no such incense at the shrine of any man. The sincere homage of the heart is not flattery. I have spoken the spontaneous feeling of my own breast. I am confident, too, that I have spoken the feeling of the Senate. But yet I ought perhaps to beg pardon of the honorable gentleman. I have much cause to fear that the gratification I have had in offering this poor tribute of my respect is more than counterbalanced by the pain it has inflicted upon him.

Mr. Crittenden resigned his seat in the Senate in 1819, and resolved to give himself up wholly to local politics and the practice of his profession. He was poor, and his family large, and he felt its claims to be paramount.

One of Mr. Crittenden's most intimate friends has written to me that this period, from 1819 to 1835, passed in the arduous duties of his profession, and in the legislature, was the most interesting, and probably the happiest, of his life.

The three following letters, two from Mr. Clay and one from James Barbour, show the regret of his cotemporaries at his resignation, and the political aspect of affairs at that time.

(Henry Clay to John J. Crittenden.)

WASHINGTON, December 14, 1819.

MY DEAR SIR,—We have just heard of your resignation, which has occasioned general regret here. On the public account, I regret it; on yours, I do not! Tell my friend Mrs. Crittenden that I congratulate her on the just triumph she has obtained over you. You will have seen the correspondence respecting the Florida treaty, and you will have read it, as I did, with mortification, for, with the *worst cause*, the Spaniards came off victorious in that correspondence. Forsyth has acquitted himself very badly; he appears to me to have been furnishing evidence at Madrid, and certainly not of the most courtly kind, to refute an insinuation I once made at Washington against him of partiality to the King of Spain. I think our eagerness to get the ratification has probably lost it. What shall we do? These people will put me in the opposition whether I will or no! I wanted to go with them respecting our Spanish affairs; but how can I join in such a foolish course? Instead of resorting to the natural expedient of taking possession of our own, they ask us to take (on the ground, too, of right) what does not belong to us! Thus, in regard to the Patriots, all the premises of the President point to the conclusion of recognizing them, and yet, strange to tell, he concludes by recommending further laws to enforce our neutrality!—in other words, further laws against the Patriots. I shall be glad to hear from you,

And remain faithfully yours,

H. CLAY.

P.S.—Tell Bibb that he and you must make out your joint instructions to me, relative to Florida, and which, as I acknowledge the right of instruction, I shall of course obey, or *disobey* under my responsibility.

(From the same to the same.)

WASHINGTON, January 29, 1820.

DEAR SIR,—I received with very great pleasure your favor of the 9th instant, and thank you for the valuable information which it contains. I think Tennessee ought to give us an equivalent beyond the Tennessee River for our land which she holds on this side; yet it is so important to have the dispute settled, as well for its own sake as in order to enable the legislature to dispose of the land south of that river, that I shall not regret a determination to accept of the proposition of their commissioners, especially as if we were to obtain the equivalent, it may be questionable whether we should acquire more than the naked sovereignty. Your friendly advice is received in the same spirit of kindness which dictated it. I came here anxious to agree with the administration whenever I could, and particularly desirous to concur with them in regard to Spanish affairs. This wish sprang from that retirement on which I had determined and to which I still look forward; but how is it possible for me to lend myself to such a crooked, unnatural, untenable course as that recommended by the message? To give up what we have a good right to for the purpose of seizing that to which we have none, and this, too, when what we propose thus wantonly to sacrifice is confessedly of more intrinsic value than that we hone after; to consider a treaty as obligatory which has been executed by one of the two parties only; to limit the measures of our redress to that treaty when the American negotiator of it acknowledges that Don Ouis was authorized by his instructions to grant us more than we get! And to do this, when, if the views of the President be correct, Spain, by her failure to ratify the treaty, has taken a position most decidedly disadvantageous to her. If, as you seem to suppose, it was contemplated to take Florida without the abandonment of Texas, one could consider of the scheme, possibly unite in it. But *that* is not the intention of the President; he wishes us to take the former and renounce the latter, and moreover to assume the payment of five millions of dollars to our citizens. Should we adopt this course and seize Florida, what would be the nature of our title to it? Would it be conventional, or one of conquest? Now, I cannot, in my conscience, go along with the President in these his views. I mean to propose the recognition of the Patriots and the seizure of Texas. These two measures taken, and Florida is ours without an effort. I might, indeed, be induced to comprehend Florida also in the self-redress which I think we are authorized to take; but if I am reduced to the alternative of subjecting ourselves to the obligations of the treaty whilst Spain remains free from them, *or* taking Texas, I must prefer the latter! The Missouri subject monopolizes all our conversation, all our thoughts, and for three weeks at least, to come, will occupy all our time. Nobody seems to think of or care about anything else. The issue of the question in the House of Representatives is doubtful. I am inclined to think that it will be *finally compromised.* No idea exists here of any issue or modification of paper to relieve the country. The prevailing opinion is that the only effectual relief for its embarrassments is in the hands of the people *themselves.* We regret very much the measure to which you have thought yourselves constrained to resort at Frankfort. The Secretary of the Treasury said to me that he thought, from the exhibit which he had of your affairs, there was no sort of necessity for it, and he added, "that he could no longer give any sort of credit to your paper." I would be obliged to you to inform me what amount of paper you may issue, and what is the price of stock since the suspension, and whether *any* period is thought of when a resumption of specie is contemplated. To give us even as much money as before, you must put out an amount equivalent to the depreciation, which again will occasion further depreciation, and so on *ad infinitum.* Tell Bibb he is *a lazy fellow,* but lazy as he is, I must subscribe myself his and your

Faithful friend,
HENRY CLAY.

(James W. Barbour to John J. Crittenden.)

WASHINGTON, February 6, 1820.

DEAR SIR,—I sincerely regret that your private affairs made it necessary for you to leave the Senate. Among our regrets to which this life is subject there are few more unpleasant than those resulting from sudden and unexpected separations from those whom we delight to call friends. I hope it is unnecessary for me to state that my regard for you justifies me in telling you that such were my feelings on hearing that we were probably to see each other no more. You have, however, been relieved from one of the most irksome tasks I have ever experienced,—the discussion of the Missouri question. Who could have thought, last session, that the little *speck* we then saw was to be swelled into the importance it has now assumed, and that upon its decision depended the duration of the Union? *The dissolution* is one of the alternatives spoken of, rather than submit to the spirit of aggression which marks the course of our antagonists. A proposition has now been made for a compromise,—the amendment proposed by Thomas, which, I believe, unpleasant as it is, will be acceded to, as a lesser evil than either dividing the Union, or throwing it into confusion. The *great movers* of this question are against all *compromise*, leaving strong suspicions that they look to it as a means to acquire power, and unless speedily adjusted, such will be the result. I have been laboring incessantly on this subject, and if I can have industry enough to write out my remarks, the delivery of which cost me the best of two days, I will send you a copy.

Accept assurances of the most friendly regards.

J. W. BARBOUR.

JOHN J. CRITTENDEN.

Mr. Crittenden's house in Frankfort was a straggling, old-fashioned house on the corner of Main Street. The front door opened immediately on the street, and led into a wide hall which separated the dining-room and parlor. In fair summer evenings, the custom of the family was to take tea some time before night, and then assemble at the front door, which was only elevated about a foot and a half above the level of the street. The house was entered by two broad stone steps, and opposite these, on the outer edge of the pavement, were several massive marble steps, half circular, which had formed originally the base of some of the stone columns of the old capitol, burned down in 1826. Upon these steps the family and the guests (for there were always guests) seated themselves, the old folks on the sill of the door and the house-steps, the boys and girls (as Mr. Crittenden continued to call his children as long as he lived) on the steps opposite. The neighbors and friends would soon gather in and join the group at the front door. One of the *boys* would make his way with difficulty into the house, and hand out chairs through the low windows. Stragglers taking their evening walk would pause for awhile, and take part in the conversation, then move on, and others would take the vacant seats. Often the group assembled would be so large that the pavement would be filled up, and those who did not wish to pause would pass by on the other side.

There is no feature of the family life, as connected with Mr. Crittenden, more indelibly impressed upon my mind than these evening gatherings. Mr. Crittenden's cordial and kindly greeting, his warm sympathy and interest in all that concerned the welfare of his friends and neighbors; his inimitable style of telling an anecdote and detailing the news of the day could not be surpassed; his quick appreciation of even an attempt at wit encouraged the timid to do their best, and sent every one home between ten and eleven satisfied with himself and admiring and loving him more than ever. First in the order of the day or night, on these occasions, were family news, kind inquiries for the sick and the absent, little narratives of the wonderful children everybody had or supposed themselves to have, then politics in the largest sense, local and general.

Every man in Kentucky was a politician, and felt that he had the might and the right to be a public speaker, if he chose, and the women and children generally thought the same of themselves. In early times, I recollect a row of tall Lombardy poplars, all along the front of the house; they were grand old trees, "growing ever upward, having neither fruit nor flowers, and giving no shade;" they were considered cumberers of the ground, and were cut down and replaced by locusts. I remember them with regret. The tree has grown out of fashion, but whenever I see one it brings back misty recollections of the past and of the old home-life. Mr. Crittenden had a real affection for his trees; his locusts were topped from time to time, and watched over with great care. He had a habit of talking to himself with animation. He came down generally before breakfast and walked in front of the house. If alone, he talked and gesticulated earnestly, to the amusement of the children, who were peeping at him through the window. Strangers, guests in the house, would sometimes catch a glimpse of him, and say, "Why, who is Mr. Crittenden talking to?" They would be highly amused when the thing was explained, and join the children at their post of observation. The old corner tree, which was twisted and gnarled and unsightly to every other eye, was his especial favorite; he would stand by it every morning, tapping it with his cane, and holding with it, seemingly, an animated conversation. These seem trivial things to recall, but the *old Frankfort people* will be gladly reminded of them, and these simple facts will bring back with them other memories of Mr. Crittenden: his cheerful "good-morning," his ready sympathy, his unostentatious hospitality, and all the nameless charm of manner, which not even his political opponents could resist. Mr. Crittenden was, indeed, hospitable in a grand old way, not as many men are with their superfluity, for, in his whole life, he never knew "*that thing.*" It was his custom to entertain the senators and members of the Kentucky legislature every winter, giving about three dinners a week, and thus entertaining, before the session closed, every member more than once. These dinners were of the simplest character. In early days "old Bourbon" figured largely at the feast, but later, when times grew hard and money scarce, it was dispensed with. A big fish and a saddle of venison were the principal dishes, and vegetables of old Kentucky growth the only addition. In those days, I am confident that French peas and asparagus would have been looked upon with suspicion and avoided. I believe that a merrier and wittier set of fellows were never assembled around any table than those Kentucky lawyers and politicians.

CHAPTER IV.

1820–1823.

MR. CRITTENDEN did not return to the Senate till 1835; during the period from 1819 to 1835 he was elected to the legislature of Kentucky repeatedly, and made Speaker of the House.

This was a most exciting period in Kentucky. The Old and New Court question, originally called Relief and Anti-Relief, was agitating the State as no other question has ever agitated it.

This was altogether a local question, but as Mr. Crittenden was greatly interested and took a prominent part in the dissension of the day, it may be well to give a sketch of the rise, progress, and defeat of the New Court party.

The termination of the War of 1812, with Great Britain, was followed by financial distress throughout the whole country, but particularly in Kentucky; the people were greatly in debt, and not content to trust to industry and economy for relief, they cried to the legislature for aid. Carried away by the force of popular feeling, the legislature of 1820–21 assembled and passed first a sixty-days' "stop-law," of all legal process of collection of debts, and then a two-years' replevin law, in connection with the establishment of the Commonwealth's Bank, which issued and loaned to the people, in every county, three millions of paper money. This currency soon became worth only fifty cents on the dollar, but the legislature required the creditors to receive it in full payment, or to wait two years for the specie. The law was pronounced unconstitutional by one or two of the Circuit Court judges, and their decision sustained by the Court of Appeals, composed of Boyle, Owsley, and Mills. A violent excitement throughout the State was the result. The following legislature repealed those judges out of office, and reconstructed the Court of Appeals, making it to consist of four members, of whom William T. Barry was chief justice. Amos Kendall was the editor of the *Argus*, published at that time in Frankfort, and this paper was the organ of the Radical party.

A condition of public feeling followed in Kentucky only less violent than civil war. Private friendships were broken up, and danger of strife and bloodshed was imminent. The Old Court party contended that the Court of Appeals was established by the Constitution; was intended to be, and was, in fact, independent of legislative control; that its repeal was a legislative usurpation of power, and a practical overthrow of one of the co-ordinate departments of the government; that liberty itself lay prostrate at the foot of a legislative majority for the time being; that the Constitution intended the three departments— legislative, executive, and judicial—to be co-ordinate, independent, and reciprocal checks. True liberty could only consist in this arrangement of power.

After several years of bitterness and strife, the Old Court party prevailed, the old judges were reinstated, and the New Court decisions were set aside.

Order and peace were restored, but the New Court party became, almost without exception, Jackson Democrats, or Red Republicans, and the Old Court party, Whigs, or Conservatives. These two parties, their leaders and followers, have continued with but little variation to the present time. Mr. Crittenden belonged to the Old Court party,—was, in fact, its leading spirit. He was made president of the Commonwealth's Bank, and continued to fill that position for some time.

Among the many private friendships interrupted by this embittered state of feeling, Mr. Crittenden numbered two devoted and cherished friends,—George M. Bibb and Francis P. Blair. Every man who knew Mr. Crittenden remembers *how* he loved his friends. A friend once found was, indeed, "grappled to his soul with hooks of steel." Under no doubtful or suspicious circumstances was he ever given up. This characteristic of his was so marked, that many of those who loved and admired him considered it a weakness and reproached him for it. Judge S. S. Nicholas, of Louisville, Kentucky, told me that he was at one time so exasperated with F. P. Blair for the unjust aspersions he had cast upon Mr. Crittenden, that he resolved never again to recognize him as an acquaintance. Being in Washington about this time, he entered one of the departments to visit Mr. Crittenden; found several gentlemen present, and among them Preston Blair. True to his purpose, Judge Nicholas straightened himself up and passed by Blair without even bowing. Mr. Crittenden received the judge with that kindly greeting and cordial grasp of the hand the magic charm of which many will remember; then, with some little embarrassment, he turned the judge around hastily, in front of Preston Blair, and said, "Here, Nicholas,—here is our old friend Blair. I know you will be glad to see him." There was no resisting *this*, said the judge: "I could but speak to Blair. As Mr. Crittenden would not resent Blair's conduct to himself, I could not very consistently do so."

(J. W. Barbour to J. J. Crittenden.)

BARBOURSVILLE, May 31, 1820.

DEAR SIR,—I had intended to have written to you by Judge Logan, who left us before the adjournment without any anticipation, on my part, that he meant to do so. I most cordially wish that you may very soon realize your golden prospects, as well for yourself as for your country. Take care, however, that your limits do not recede as you advance upon them. Enough has never yet been accurately bounded. Independence is a jewel of inestimable price, and should be forever kept in view, at least by the head of a family. In pursuing it, you give high proofs of prudence. That you will soon reach it I have no doubt. The session closed with the catastrophe of the tariff; not quite as important as the Missouri question, but probably the undisputed progeny of the policy that seeks to promote the interest of one portion of the Union at the expense of another. Deprived, however, of much of its consequence, from the circumstance that it was not so sectional in the support given it. Had Tompkins been elected governor of New York, there would have been considerable commotion among the aspirants to the two great offices. His defeat was a perfect damper. They are, for the present, in the language of diplomacy, placed "*ad referendum.*" In a year or two they will be, like Falstaff's reasons, as thick as blackberries. The old Revolutionary generation has passed away. The new presents so many who are really equal, or think themselves so (which is the same thing), that every section of the Union will have its claims, except Virginia. She, by common consent, is to repose on the recollection of what she has done. I fear, however, that the slave question will be revived in all its fury, and will be sufficient to bar the door against either a Southern or Western man. Time, however, will decide these things. It is not my nature to anticipate evil. I inclose you thirty dollars, as the fee in my case. Let me hear from you as soon as possible after its decision, or in the mean time, if convenient.

Your friend,   J. W. BARBOUR.

Mr. Crittenden was appointed one of the Commissioners to settle the boundary line between Tennessee and Kentucky, and the following is his report:

To the Honorable the General Assembly of the Commonwealth of Kentucky, on the Boundary Line of that State.

The undersigned, one of your Commissioners, respectfully reports: That the two Commissioners appointed for that purpose, in pursuance of the act of Assembly, approved the 1st instant, proceeded to confer and negotiate with the Commissioners of the State of Tennessee for the settlement and adjustment of the disputed boundary between the two States.

It may, perhaps, be necessary, for the more clear understanding of this report, to trace very briefly the origin and grounds of this dispute.

By the original charter of Virginia, granted by James I., in the year   , she would have included in her boundaries considerable extent of territory southward of the parallel of north 36° 30′ north latitude. This charter, however, was repealed in the year   ; and afterwards, in the year   , the charter of Carolina was granted, by which the territory of Virginia was restricted on the south, and a line to be run on the parallel of latitude above mentioned, "throughout the land from sea to sea," was, in effect, established as the boundary of the territories of Virginia and Carolina, and was, by both of them, regarded and considered as the limit of their respective sovereignty and right. As the population of those States, then provinces, advanced westward, and as convenience and policy required, this scientific line of division was ascertained and marked, and some time previous to the year 1778 had been extended, and marked by Jefferson and Fry as far as to a point on Sleep Rock Creek, about sixty miles east from Cumberland Mountain. About the last-mentioned period settlements began to be so far multiplied, west of the mountains, that it became necessary, for the purposes of government, that the line of division between the territories of the two States should be still farther extended. Many circumstances rendered that measure necessary. The governments of both States had sold and issued, and provided for the selling and issuing of land-warrants to individuals, to be located by them on the vacant land of the West. It became, therefore, the duty of both States, by a demarkation of their boundary, to avoid, as far as possible, all conflict between the claims granted by the one and the other, and to put it in the power of every individual to know where to locate his warrant with certainty and security. Influenced by some or all of these considerations, it was agreed between said States that the boundary line between them should be extended and marked from the point on Sleep Rock Creek, where the line of the former Commissioners, Jefferson and Fry, terminated, as far westward as the Tennessee River. And, accordingly, Walker and others on the part of Virginia, and Henderson and others on the part of North Carolina, were appointed Commissioners by their respective States, for the purpose of so extending and marking said line. The Commissioners met at Sleep Rock Creek, and having ascertained the point of beginning and made the necessary observations, then commenced the running and marking of said line. Before they reached the eastern foot of the Cumberland Mountain, the Commissioners of the two States differed about the latitude of the line they were to run,—Henderson's observations inclining him to go farther north than Dr. Walker's. The parties being unable to come to any agreement upon the subject, finally separated. The North Carolina Commissioners returned home, the Virginia Commissioners went on ; ascertained, as they supposed, the true latitude, and marked the line, with some intervals, as far westward as where it strikes the Tennessee River.

This line was made in the years 1779 and 1780, and is the same which has ever since been so generally known and called by the name of " Walker's line." In the year   the District of Kentucky became an independent State, and entitled to all the territorial rights of Virginia, west of the line which separates Kentucky from that State. The territory which forms the State of Tennessee was ceded by North Carolina to the United States on the   day of   ,   , under the authority of a law of that State, passed   ,   , and Tennessee was admitted into the Union as an independent State in the year 1796. It follows from this statement, either that " Walker's line," or a line upon the parallel of 36° 30′ north latitude, is the coterminous boundary of the States of Kentucky and Tennessee. The Assembly of Virginia, in the year 1781, passed an act which recites that, " *Whereas*, a considerable part of the tract of country allotted for the officers and soldiers,

by an act entitled, etc., etc., hath, upon the extension of the
boundary line between this State and North Carolina, fallen into
that State, and the intentions of the said act are so far frus-
trated," and then provides that other lands, therein described,
shall be "substituted in lieu of such lands so fallen into the said
State of North Carolina."   By another Act of Assembly of the
State of Virginia, passed on the   day of   ,
1791, it is recited by way of preamble, "that official information had been received by the General Assembly that the
legislature of North Carolina have resolved to establish the
line commonly called "Walker's line," as the boundary between
North Carolina and this Commonwealth, and it is judged expedient to confirm and establish the said line on the part of this
State."   And it was then enacted, "that the line commonly
called and known by the name of 'Walker's line,' shall be, and the
same is hereby declared to be, the boundary line of this State."
The Commissioners have not been able to find the act or resolution of the legislature of North Carolina, which is alluded to
in the preamble to the last-recited act of Virginia, or to obtain
any other information of it than what is afforded by that preamble.   Nor does it appear, from any researches which your
Commissioners have been able to make, that any communication or agreement had taken place, or been made, between Virginia and Carolina, in relation to "Walker's line," antecedent to
the Virginia act of 1791, and the resolution of the legislature of
Carolina therein alluded to ; but from various acts of the North
Carolina legislature, passed in the year 1781 and 1786, and
between those periods, it appears pretty strongly that, even at
that time, they regarded "Walker's line" as the boundary
between them and Virginia.   In several of those acts, passed
for the erection of new counties, and containing a description of
their boundaries, there are calls for the "Virginia line;" and in
some instances the position and locality of that line are
described in such a way as to leave little doubt but that
."Walker's line" was intended.

The States of Kentucky and Tennessee having been formed
respectively out of the Western territories of Virginia and North
Carolina, are entitled each to all the territorial rights of its
parent State.   And of course the coterminous boundary of those
Western territories of Virginia and Carolina, whatever it may
be, must be the true and proper line of division between the
States of Kentucky and Tennessee,—and whether "Walker's
line" is to be considered as their proper coterminous boundary,
or whether that boundary is to be sought for and established
now upon the chartered latitudinal line of 36° 30' north, is the
question in controversy between the States of Kentucky and

Tennessee. It is deemed unnecessary to enter into any detail of the proceedings of those States in relation to this subject. Too much excitement has prevailed between them. Some of their acts have been precipitate and inconsistent, others rash and angry,—the remembrance of which can only be useful as a means of guarding against their repetition.

It is only necessary to remark further on this branch of the subject, that the line run by Walker has ever since, whether rightfully or not, been observed and regarded as the actual boundary of jurisdiction by all parties, and that this question of boundary never became a subject of legislative attention or of dispute between the two States now interested till about the year ——. Till about that time it is believed that the general opinion of those who thought " Walker's line" erroneous was, that it was south and not north of the proper latitude of 36° 30'. It has, however, been since ascertained, beyond any reasonable doubt, that " Walker's line," or a very great proportion of it, is north of the proper latitude, and that as it extends westward from the Cumberland Mountain, it gradually diverges farther and farther from the parallel of 36° 30' north latitude. The experiments made during the last summer by Messrs. Alexander and Munsell demonstrate this divergence. They ascertained the latitude of 36° 30' north on the Mississippi River, and found it to be seventeen miles south of where " Walker's line," if extended, would strike the same river. They then ran a line eastward on that latitude to the Tennessee River,—a distance of about sixty-five miles,—and at the termination of their line found that it was only about thirteen miles from " Walker's line." If this line of Alexander and Munsell be correct, and should, if extended, continue to approximate " Walker's line" in the degree, it is very evident that these two lines would not only converge to a point, but would cross each other some miles on this side of the Cumberland Mountain, which, according to Walker's mensuration and report, is about two hundred and forty-seven miles from the point at which his line intersects the Tennessee. Such is the general history of the origin and grounds of the dispute between Kentucky and Tennessee, and of the most important facts which relate to it. Your Commissioners proceeded to the task assigned them with a deep sense of their responsibility, and of the high importance of a subject involving directly the interest and harmony of two States, forming parts of one common country united by local situation and political ties, and almost identified by sympathy of feeling, congeniality of character, and the still more endearing ties of consanguinity.

In the course of our negotiations your Commissioners submitted to those of Tennessee the following propositions : First, that " Walker's line," from Cumberland Mountain to the Tennessee River, should so far form the boundary of the two States; that for all the lands lying between that part of " Walker's line" above described and the line of latitude 36° 30' north the State of Tennessee is to give to Kentucky an equivalent in territory, to be laid off between the Tennessee and Mississippi Rivers, on the south side of and adjoining to the line which was run during the last summer by Alexander and Munsell, and to be included in a line to be run from the one to the other of said rivers, and parallel to the said line of Alexander and Munsell; and that the line, including said equivalent, to be run as aforesaid from the Mississippi to the Tennessee, and thence down the latter to the termination of " Walker's line," should be also established as completing the boundary between the two States.

The second proposition was, that the said line of Alexander and Munsell, from the Mississippi to the Tennessee River, thence down that river to the point where " Walker's line" strikes it, thence with " Walker's line" to the point where it approaches nearest to the mouth of Obed's River, and from that point due north or south to the parallel of 36° 30' north latitude, and thence eastward on that parallel of latitude to the eastern extremity of this State, should form the permanent boundary between said States.

Both these propositions were rejected by the Tennessee Commissioners, who had submitted to us the following propositions: That " Walker's line" to the Tennessee River, thence up the same, on the western bank thereof, to the line of Alexander and Munsell, and thence with that line to the Mississippi River, should form the boundary between said States, and that reciprocal engagements should be made for the confirmation of certain claims granted by the States of Virginia and North Carolina, respectively, and which had been located south of " Walker's line," and north of Alexander and Munsell's line. And this proposition, submitted by them as the basis of a compromise and settlement, was declared to be, in substance, their ultimatum. The two propositions submitted by your Commissioners were rejected, and the propositions submitted by the Tennessee Commissioners remained as the only basis on which a settlement and compromise could probably be effected. On these propositions your Commissioners were divided. Mr. Rowan was entirely opposed to the boundary which was proposed, and refused on that account to accede to the terms offered. The undersigned was willing to have accepted the proposed limits with a slight modification, making the Tennessee River, instead of its western bank, the boundary of the two States, and giving to each a common and concurrent jurisdiction over it. Your Commisssioners disagreeing upon this principal and important point, did not much consider or discuss the incidental propositions which related to the claims of individuals. The undersigned entertained some doubts about the power of the Commissioners to enter into stipulations concerning those claims. But, if stipulations were to be made on this subject, he thought that those proposed by the Commissioners of Tennessee ought to be modified. Your Commissioners informed those of Tennessee of their disagreement upon the propositions submitted to them, and that, of course, no settlement could be made upon those terms. And in the same note which communicated that result, they proposed that the matters of controversy between the two States should be referred to the decision of such distinguished men as might be mutually agreed upon, and who should neither be citizens of Tennessee or Kentucky, Virginia or North Carolina, or of any other State formed out of territory which belonged to either of the latter States. This proposition was also declined by the Tennessee Commissioners.

And here terminated our negotiations with them. In addition to the above statement, and in order that the legislature may have the amplest information, it may be proper to remark that the Tennessee Commissioners expressed their perfect readiness to accede to any modification of their propositions that should not essentially change them, and particularly that they would agree that the Tennessee River, instead of its western bank, should be the boundary; and that it should be subject to the common jurisdiction of both States; and that they would make any modifications in their propositions which related to private claims, which should render them more satisfactory, or make them more equitable and reciprocal; or, in fine, that if it was preferred by Kentucky, they would waive all stipulations or engagements about private claims, and leave individuals without prejudice to assert and pursue their rights in any lawful way they might think proper. And upon the whole, the undersigned has no doubt that all other matters might have been satisfactorily arranged, if your Commissioners could have agreed upon the boundary of the two States as proposed by the Commissioners of Tennessee.

In differing with his more able and enlightened colleague, the undersigned has experienced the deepest and most sincere regret, and he feels so sensibly how much the burden of his responsibility has been thereby increased, that although he will not presume to attempt an elaborate argument upon a subject with which your honorable body is so well acquainted, he yet hopes that, without being considered obtrusive, he may be allowed to suggest some of those views which have influenced his conduct.

The only question of difficulty between the two States is, whether "Walker's line" should be established, as Tennessee insists, or whether the line of division shall be sought for and fixed, as Kentucky has contended, upon the latitude of 36° 30′ north. The undersigned has not so much considered on this subject what was abstractedly right or abstractedly wrong, but what was the best, the most politic, the most equitable, the most magnanimous that could be expected or done. And in this aspect of the subject he was willing to have concurred in the boundary proposed by the Commissioners of Tennessee. Upon the question of dispute between the two States, the undersigned did believe that in strictness the mere right was with Kentucky, and that there had been no such mutual and direct confirmation of "Walker's line" as would render it obligatory upon Kentucky in a court of law. But there are many circumstances that are calculated to mitigate this right, that address themselves strongly to us, and plead against a rigorous assertion of it.

Walker's was a line of demarkation made by our own parent State. In the year after it was completed that same parent State, by the act of 1781, before referred to, recognized it in the most emphatic manner as the limit of her territory. And again, by her act of 1791, before Kentucky had become an independent State, while she yet formed a part of the "Commonwealth" of Virginia, and before the authority of that State, as expressly reserved by the act or compact of 1789, had ceased over this country, she, in the most solemn manner, confirms and establishes "Walker's line," and acknowledges that she had previously received "official information" that North Carolina had also "resolved" to establish it. But it is said that this resolution of North Carolina and this act of Virginia were entirely inoperative because, some short time previous to the said act of 1791, North Carolina had ceded her western territories, according to their "chartered" limits, to the United States. Admit this argument to be conclusive, but let us ask if this transaction was so understood by the States of Virginia and North Carolina? Did they consider their act and resolution as mere nullities? And did they yet enact and resolve, as it appears they did, from the above-recited act of 1791? No, they most certainly did consider themselves as then competent to fix the boundary of their western territories, and Virginia did, in all probability, consider her act of 1791 as effectual and conclusive upon that subject. If, then, the States of Virginia and Carolina so considered and understood their own acts, does it best become their descendants, Kentucky and Tennessee, to apply to those acts rules of construction which will entirely defeat and frustrate their effect, or to observe them, according to the understanding of the original parties, and in the same spirit of amity and conciliation?

"Walker's line," since the year 1780, and for about the space of forty years, has been observed as the line of division and jurisdiction. North Carolina, the United States, and the State of Tennessee have each in succession, as they were the sovereigns of the country, exercised jurisdiction on the south up to "Walker's line." That line for the same period has limited the jurisdiction of Virginia and Kentucky. Counties and county towns have on both sides been established with reference to this line. And with very few exceptions it has guided and regulated individuals, claiming under Virginia or Carolina, in their locations and appropriations of land. The effect of a change of this boundary for one a few miles farther south, will be to confound and endanger individual rights, to disturb and derange the municipal regulations, the counties and other sectional divisions of both States, and to coerce a reluctant people into subjection to our government. Ought all these considerations to be sacrificed to the acquisition of a strip of territory a few miles in breadth, along our southern border? or do they not rather strongly prompt us to a forbearance of our right and to the establishment of an old and long-respected boundary? Is, this little acquisition necessary to the dignity and consequence of Kentucky? Surely it is not; and it does appear to the undersigned that the annexation of it to this State would be much less beneficial to us than the dismemberment of it from Tennessee would be injurious to them.

But suppose that all these considerations avail nothing; suppose that Kentucky, regardless of consequences, determines to insist upon her right to the disputed territory, and to compel its reluctant inhabitants to a state of vassalage, or, what is the same thing, unwilling submission to her government,—by what course is she to effect it? Tennessee has possession, a possession which has continued uninterrupted forty years. There is no tribunal before which a reluctant State can be arrayed. Congress has repeatedly refused, though urged in the strongest manner, to pass any law authorizing the Supreme Court of the United States to take cognizance of controversies between States. If their negotiation and compromise fail, where is our remedy? What is the value of our naked and abstract right —"a right without a remedy?"

There may now be some magnanimity and generosity displayed in sacrificing it to the peace and harmony of the two

States. We shall thereby also obtain a peaceable and quiet possession of all the territory which we claim, west of the Tennessee, and which would, in all probability, otherwise become the scene of active controversy and dangerous collision between the two States. Upon the whole, then, the undersigned could perceive no advantages likely to result to Kentucky from a protraction of this disagreeable controversy. He considered it as worse than useless to hold up "in terrorem" a *barren right* to be brandished a few years longer in vexatious contest, and then to sink into that oblivion to which time will inevitably consign every right which is not accompanied with its proper remedy.

Influenced by these circumstances and considerations, the undersigned was willing to establish "Walker's line," and to accede to the terms proposed by the Commissioners of Tennessee, with such modifications as they afterwards expressed themselves ready to allow. And in so doing, he trusts that he should in naught have committed either the interest or honor of Kentucky. For anxious, as he is willing to acknowledge he was, to see all matters of difference amicably settled, and proud as he should have been to have been instrumental in the humblest degree in removing every obstacle to the peace and harmony of two States so united, so allied, and so congenial in character, yet all these feelings are subordinate to that superior attachment and love which binds him to the interest and honor of his own native State. And in acceding to the proposed terms of compromise, he trusts that he has in naught committed either her honor or her true interest.

The undersigned begs leave to tender his sincere acknowledgments for the honor conferred on him by your honorable body by placing him in this important commission. And although he and his colleague have failed, he yet hopes that the superior wisdom of your honorable body may devise means for the accomplishment of the desirable object you had in view.

J. J. CRITTENDEN.

Mr. Crittenden assisted General Shelby in the preparation of his defense against the charges brought by Colonel Preston against the old hero.

The following letter from General Shelby to Mr. Crittenden with relation to Ferguson's defeat, will no doubt be an object of interest :

DANVILLE, June 16th, 1823.

MY DEAR SIR,—You have no doubt before this seen the replies of both General Preston and his son to my publication.

Colonel Preston proposes to establish for his own father the merit of planning the expedition which led to Ferguson's defeat.

I have examined the subject in my own mind in every point of view, and cannot, in the remotest manner, discover wherein General Preston could have had any agency in this exploit. I lived nearly one hundred and twenty miles from him, in a different State, and had no kind of communication with him on the subject, and from every recollection, I am convinced that the statement I gave you is indisputably true. I recollect, however, that Major Cloyd, with three hundred men from the county of Montgomery, commanded by Colonel Preston, fought an action with the Tories at the shallow ford of the Yadkin River, nearly one hundred miles north of King's Mountain, about two weeks after the defeat of Ferguson. It has always been a mystery to me as to Cloyd's destination, or that of the enemy whom he encountered. I have only understood that they met accidentally in the road, and that the enemy was composed of the Tories in the neighborhood, and of the Bryants, of Kentucky, some of whom were killed in the fight.

If Ferguson was Cloyd's object, he was too weak to effect anything, and besides, Lord Cornwallis, with the British army, lay directly in the route between them. My convictions are so clear on this point I have no fear that General Preston can render my statement doubtful. He proposes, too, to invalidate the testimony of Moses Shelby. I will, for your own satisfaction, give you a short sketch of his history. Moses was in his nineteenth year when he left his father's house to join the expedition against Ferguson, and had never before, to my knowledge, been more than forty miles from home. It is well known that our march was too rapid for a youth of that age to trespass in any manner, the army having marched two or three hundred miles, and fought the battle in twelve days, three of which we were detained on the road from different causes. Moses was severely wounded at the Mountain, and the bone of one thigh being fractured, he could be carried but a short distance from the battle-ground, where he lay on his back nearly three months, and was only able to ride out a few days before General Morgan came up into the district of Ninety-Six. He joined Morgan but a day or two before the battle of the Cowpens, on the 17th of January, 1781. Here he was wounded more severely than at the Mountain, and lay, until March or April, under the hands of a surgeon. When Colonel Clarke, of Georgia, came on with his followers to commence the siege of Augusta, his wounds were still sore and open, but at the warm solicitations of Clarke, Moses joined the expedition, and was appointed captain of horse. It is well known that the siege lasted until May or June following, in which Moses was actively engaged, and Clarke asserted to many that he made several charges on the enemy, who sallied during the siege, which would have done honor to Count Pulaski. Moses returned home shortly after the siege, and never crossed the mountains again during the war. The next year, 1782, he, with other adventurers, went to the new settlements, then forming where Nashville now stands, where he continued off and on until he married, two or three years afterwards. As the settlements progressed down the Cumberland, he was always among the foremost of the pioneers. He finally settled in what is now called Livingston County, Kentucky, where, at the unanimous solicitation of the inhabitants, he was appointed colonel of the new county, about the year 1793. He had the command for a number of years. And after the acquisition of Louisiana, he removed to that territory, and now resides on the west side of the Mississippi, two miles below New Madrid, covered with the scars of thirteen deep wounds, received in defense of his country, from which he is too proud to receive a pension, always disdaining to apply for one. In his youth he was of a warm and ardent disposition, always ready to risk his life for a friend, and profuse of his property (of which he had a considerable inheritance), even to a fault. It would exceed the bounds of a letter to give you a statement of the many hair-breadth escapes and imminent dangers through which he passed. Soon after his marriage he became impressed with religious sentiments, joined the Methodist Church, liberated his slaves, and, so far as I know and believe, has always supported a good character in that county.

It is possible, while at the South, in 1780–81, from his ardent disposition and the prevailing excitement of the times, that he may in some cases have acted imprudently. The war between the Whigs and Tories was carried on with the utmost rancor and malice, each endeavoring to do the greatest injury to the other.

Colonel Willoughby, whose affidavit has been published, swears to no point. He lived three hundred miles from the scene of action, and his information may have been very erroneous.

If, however, General Preston proves *apparently* anything more, he shall be answered.

I have made this hasty sketch for your own satisfaction.

I remain, dear sir, very respectfully, your friend,

ISAAC SHELBY.

JOHN J. CRITTENDEN.

(Henry Clay to J. J. Crittenden.)

ASHLAND, September 13, 1823.

DEAR CRITTENDEN,—I received your letter by Mr. Davis. I participate most cordially with you in the just solicitude which the dispute between Messrs. Breckenridge and Wickliffe awakens. When it was first mentioned to me, considering the peculiar circumstances and the character of one of the parties, I feared that all private interference would be unavailing, and that the best course would be an appeal to the civil authority, with its chances of delay,—cooling of the passions, and possible ultimate accommodation. Supposing the intercession of the civil power, would not Mr. W. be relieved from the necessity of having the interview, and Mr. B. be stripped of any ground to carry into effect the alternative, which it is said he menaced? There is, however, no incompatibility between the two courses, which may be tried in succession, or simultaneously, according to *circumstances*. I have therefore prepared and, on my own part, signed a letter addressed to the parties, and which may be signed by *both*, or *either* of you, and the governor. If the relations of one of them to your brother should induce you to withhold your signature, that of the governor may be affixed without yours. I would advise a copy of this letter to be delivered to each of the seconds; and considering that it is uncertain where they *may meet*, I would suggest that one of the judges of the Court of Appeals or Circuit Courts be applied to for a warrant to bind the parties. The public rumor of their intention to meet will form a sufficient ground for his action. One of the motives which took me to Woodford was to see you. The melancholy event which occurred there of private affliction to you (on which I offer you my sincere condolence) deprived me of that pleasure. My health is not re-established, but is improving, and I begin to feel that I see land, or rather, that I may not *get under it*.

I am faithfully yours,

HENRY CLAY.

HON. J. J. CRITTENDEN.

CHAPTER V.

1824—1829.

(George M. Bibb to J. J. Crittenden.)

WASHINGTON, March 8, 1824.

DEAR JOHN,—That there are men who will ascribe my actions to any motive but a reasonable one, I know, but that any should suppose that I have come to Washington for the purpose of electioneering against Mr. Clay is an extravagance that I did not anticipate would have been charged against me. My great motive in coming here was to get a hearing and decision in my suit for the land at Falmouth; in this I have succeeded. The opinion is delivered, and is in my favor. I endeavored to lay a contribution on other suitors in the court to help pay expenses of the trip, but the people of Kentucky are not drilled to paying fees to the lawyers. They pay in promises. As to Mr. Clay, he has broken the cords of friendship which bound me to him; they can never again be tied. I have no desire to interfere with your friendship for him, nor to trouble you with complaints of his conduct to me. Beware of such sunshine friends! As to electioneering upon the subject of President, I am as far removed from it as Washington is from Kentucky. I have heard a great deal; said little. I am not a member of Congress, and have, therefore, no right to go to caucus or vote in caucus, nor have I a vote when the question shall come before the House of Representatives. A listener, who hears all parties, is perhaps better able to form his opinions than those who are heated, busy, bustling managers. The grand Harrisburg Convention has decided, with but a single dissenting voice, for Jackson. Roberts was the only man who did not, upon the first vote, declare for Jackson. This has given a new impetus to him. The anticipation that Pennsylvania would declare for him gave him great advantages. The undivided voice of the Convention at Harrisburg has surprised the friends of all the other candidates,—save those of Calhoun,—they looked for it after the meeting in

the county of Philadelphia, for the purpose of choosing a delegate to the Convention at Harrisburg. It seems that the people
of North Carolina are taking up Jackson, as Pennsylvania did,
against their politicians and of their own mere will. So it is in
New York. The majority of the Senate are disposed to keep
the appointment of electors in the legislature,—that is their calculation for Crawford; but a large majority of the House of
Representatives of that State are decidedly opposed to Crawford. Adams is the most *potent* there. With the people, Jackson is next to Adams, and should the election go to the people
Jackson may prevail in that State. The indications in Maryland are for Jackson. Tennessee and Alabama, Mississippi,
Louisiana and Missouri, for Jackson. All New England for
Adams. As for Indiana and Ohio, it is difficult now to say for
whom their vote will be. The most knowing say that the
substantial controversy is now between Adams and Jackson,
and by a union of the slaveholding States with Pennsylvania
Jackson may be elected. Unless Clay gets the votes of New
York he cannot be one of the three from whom the House of
Representatives is to choose. What revolutions in the electoral
votes may take place before the time of choosing the Electoral
College, should the friends of Crawford find out what everybody
else seems to have found out (that *he* cannot be elected either
by the people or the House of Representatives), cannot be foreseen. Jackson's ticket is every day acquiring new friends.
Since the Convention at Harrisburg his pretensions are placed
before the people by means of newspapers that were devoted
before to other candidates. So much for politics. The great
case, between Jersey and New York as it is called, upon the
constitutionality of the law of New York, giving to Fulton the
exclusive right to navigate the waters of New York by steam-
boats, is decided against New York. In this cause, I heard
from Wirt the greatest display that I have ever heard at the bar
since the days of Patrick Henry. His legal argument was very
strong ; his peroration was beautiful and grand. I did not hear
Webster, nor Oakley, nor Emmett in this case, but all are said
to have exhibited great talents. I have heard Webster, Sergeant,
and White, of Tennessee. Wirt, Webster, White, and Ogden
are the ablest lawyers, and Walter Jones should also be ranked
among the first. Emmett I have not heard, but his reputation
is high. After all, I have not been convinced that the bar of
Kentucky does not contain as much talent and force as any
other bar in the Union.

March 17*th.* I have heard Wirt in another great case, opposed
by Clay and Harper. Wirt rises with the occasion and the
opposing force. The bill for putting the choice of the electors

of New York to the people has been rejected by the Senate, so
that it cannot now be foreseen how New York will be.   The
majority of the Senate for Crawford, the majority of the House
of Representatives against him.   Mr. Clay's prospects there,
feeble as they were, *are gone*.   We may now begin to settle
down between Jackson and Adams.   I can have no hesitation ;
my voice is for Jackson.

Monroe is here, *our Tom*, and is charged with a speech.   I
have no mission in view ; I expect to be a pleader of causes as
long as I am able to follow the profession.   I had not, in coming
here, any other motive or prospect.   This day week I expect to
be off to Kentucky.

Yours, as ever,
George M. Bibb.

(Henry Clay to J. J. Crittenden.)

Washington, August 22, 1825.

Dear Crittenden,—Upon my arrival here, yesterday, I found
your agreeable favor of the 7th instant.   Although it is a moment
of severe affliction with me, I cannot refuse myself the satisfaction of addressing a line to you.   I rejoice most heartily in
the event of our elections.   I rejoice in *your election*, to which I
attach the greatest importance.   I rejoice that the vile and dis-
gusting means employed to defeat you have failed, as they
ought to have failed.   Your presence in the House will be
highly necessary.   The *pruning-knife* should be applied with a
considerate and steady hand.   The majority should dismiss
from their minds all vindictive feelings, and act for the good and
the honor of Kentucky, and for the preservation of her constitution.   You will have some trouble in preserving the proper temper, but you should do it ; *nothing* should be done *from* passion
or *in* passion.   Undoubtedly restore the constitutional judges,
repeal bad laws, but preserve good ones, even if they have been
passed by the late dominant party.   When you have the power of
appointment, put in good and faithful men, but make no *stretches*
of authority even to *get rid* of bad ones.   Such would be some
of *my rules* if I were a member of the G. Assembly.   I hope
we shall preserve the public peace with Georgia, notwithstanding the *bad humor* of her governor.   Nor do we intend that the
treaty with the Creeks shall be executed before the time fixed
by its own stipulations for its execution, which, *happily*, will
again bring that instrument in review before Congress.

Your faithful friend,
Henry Clay.

Respects and congratulations to Harvey.
John J. Crittenden.

(J. J. Crittenden to Henry Clay.)

FRANKFORT, September 22, 1825.

MY DEAR SIR,—Your letter has been received, and I thank you for your friendly congratulations on my election. You are pleased to attach more consequence to it than it deserves. The general result of our late elections is a triumph, and a just subject of congratulation among the friends of constitutional government. It is my misfortune that so much is expected of me. I speak it more in sorrow than in vanity. The " Anti-Reliefs" and the " Reliefs" both have their eyes fixed upon me. The former expect me to *do* a great deal, the latter to *forbear* a great deal. My situation will be delicate, and I fear I shall not be equal to it. The party ought to do nothing from passion, nor in passion. We must retrench, and we must have a short session, must avoid every act of indiscretion which would turn from us the public feeling. It is not certain what course the new judges will pursue. They have not resigned; some of their party talk of their holding out to the last extremity. Supposing them to take *this course*, and supposing the governor and Senate to defeat the passage of a bill for the repeal of the act under which these new judges were created, ought not the House of Representatives to declare, by resolution, that *act* to be unconstitutional, and that Boyle, Owsley, and Mills are the only constitutional judges? Ought they not to resume their functions and *coerce* the redelivery of the records that were wrested from their clerk by the new court? Would it be better to leave the new court in possession of the records and appeal again to the people at the next election? The subject is perplexing, and I should like to hear your views.

Yours, etc.,
J. J. CRITTENDEN.

(Henry Clay to J. J. Crittenden.)

WASHINGTON, March 10, 1826.

DEAR CRITTENDEN,—Robert Scott informs me that there are several cases of the estate of Colonel Monison on the docket of the new Court of Appeals. I should be glad if they were anywhere else; but, being there, I must beg that you will not allow the estate to suffer for the want of counsel. If you do not practice in the new court and believe that counsel may be nevertheless necessary there, be pleased to engage for me some one who does. I have absolutely not had time or health to keep up my private and friendly correspondence during the past winter with any regularity. With respect to politics, from others and from the public prints, you have no doubt received most of the information which *I* should have been able to communicate. In the House of Representatives members and talents are largely on the side of the administration. In the Senate matters do not stand so well. There are about sixteen or seventeen senators resolved on opposition at all events, seven or eight more are secretly so disposed, and indulge in that spirit, as far as they can, *prudently.* When these two sections unite, they make together a small majority. Neâr three months ago a nomination was made of ministers to Panama. That subject has been selected for opposition, and by numerous contrivances, the measure has been delayed to this time, and *may* be for some days to come. On all collateral questions, these senators who are secretly disposed to opposition, vote with the Macedonian phalanx, and thus making a majority procrastinate the decision. Nevertheless, that decision is not believed by either party to be doubtful. The measure will be finally sanctioned by a small majority. The Vice-President (your particular friend) is up to the hub with the opposition, although he will stoutly deny it when proof cannot be adduced. One of the main inducements with him and those whom he can influence *is*, that they suppose, *if* they can defeat, or by delay cripple the measure, *it will affect me.* I am sorry to tell you that our senator (Mr. Rowan) is among the bitterest of the opponents to the administration. He appears as if he had been gathering a head of malignity for some years back, which he is now letting off upon poor Mr. Adams and his administration; he is, however, almost *impotent.* As for the *Colonel*, he is very much disposed to oblige all parties, and is greatly distressed that neither of them is willing to take him by *moieties.* If the Relief party should decline (as Jackson's cause seems to be giving way), the *Colonel* will be a *real*, as he is now a nominal, supporter of the administration. The President wishes *not* to appoint a judge in place of our inestimable friend, poor Todd, until the Senate disposes of the bill to extend the judiciary, though he may, by the delay to which that body seems now prone, be finally compelled to make the appointment without waiting for its passage or rejection. It is owing principally to Mr. Rowan that an amendment has been made in the Senate, throwing Kentucky and Ohio into the same circuit, and his object was to prevent any judge from being appointed in Kentucky. He told me himself that he wished the field of election enlarged for a judge in our circuit. Give my respects to Blair, and tell him I mean to write to him soon,—not, however, on Kentucky politics. Say to him that I should be very glad to gratify him if I could, by expressing an opinion in favor of *the* —— or *a* compromise, but I would rather oblige him in any other matter. I mean to *abjure* Kentucky politics, not because

I have not the deepest interest in all that concerns her character and prosperity, but—it is not worth while to *trouble you with the reasons.*

I am faithfully your friend,
H. CLAY.

HON. J. J. CRITTENDEN.

(Henry Clay to J. J. Crittenden.)

WASHINGTON, May 11, 1826.

DEAR CRITTENDEN,—I have received your acceptable favor of the 27th. The affair with Mr. R., to which you refer with so much kindness, was unavoidable (according to that standard, my own feelings and judgment, to which its decision exclusively belonged). I rejoiced at its harmless issue. In regard to its effect upon me, with the public, I have not the smallest apprehension. The general effect will not be bad. I believe it is the only similar occurrence which is likely to take place here. As to McDuffie and Trimble, the general opinion here is that Trimble obtained a decided advantage, and in that opinion I understand some of the friends of McDuffie concur. You will not doubt it when you read Trimble's speech, who really appears on that occasion to have been inspired. Mr. Gallatin is appointed to England, and there is general acquiescence in the propriety of his appointment. Our senator, Mr. R., made a violent opposition to Trimble's nomination, and prevailed upon four other senators to record their negatives with him. He is perfectly *impotent* in the Senate, and has fallen even below the standard of his talents, of which, I think, he has some for mischief, if *not* for good. The judiciary bill will most probably be lost by the disagreement between the two Houses as to its arrangements. This day will decide. My office is very laborious. Amidst sundry negotiations and interminable correspondence, I have, nevertheless, found time during the winter and spring to conclude two commercial treaties,—one with Denmark and one with Guatemala, which have had the fortune to be unanimously approved by the Senate. Publication deferred till ratified by the other parties. I am rejoiced at the prospect you describe of the settlement of our local differences. It will be as I have ever anticipated. I think, with deference to our friends, there has been all along too much doubt and despair. On the other hand, you should not repose in an inactive confidence. I believe with you, that some of the Relief party have been alienated from me. Not so, however, I *trust with Blair*, to whom I pray you to communicate my best respects.

Yours, faithfully,
HENRY CLAY.

(J. J. Crittenden to Henry Clay.)

FRANKFORT, September 3, 1827.

MY DEAR SIR,—I have received your letter of the 23d of July last, and cannot hesitate to give you the statement you have requested. Some time in the fall of 1824, conversing upon the subject of the *then pending* presidential election, and speaking in reference to your exclusion from the contest, and to your being called upon to decide and vote between the other candidates who might be returned to the House of Representatives, *you declared* that you could not, or that it was impossible, for you to vote for General Jackson in any event. This contains the substance of what you said. My impression is, that this conversation took place not long before you went on to Congress, and your declaration was elicited by some intimation that fell from me of my preference for General Jackson over all other candidates except yourself. I will only add, sir, that I have casually learned from my friend Colonel James Davidson, our State treasurer, that you conversed with him about the same time on the same subject, and made in substance the same declaration. Notwithstanding the reluctance I feel at having my humble name dragged before the public, I could not in justice refuse you this statement of facts, with permission to use it as you may think proper for the purpose of your own vindication.

I have the honor to be, yours, etc.,

J. J. CRITTENDEN.

HON. HENRY CLAY,
    Secretary of State.

(Henry Clay to J. J. Crittenden.)

WASHINGTON, Feb. 14, 1828.

MY DEAR SIR,—I have delayed answering your last favor under the hope that I might have it in my power to communicate to you some more certain information than I am able to transmit respecting public affairs. In regard to New York, the late caucus nomination of General Jackson was the mere consequence of the packed elections to their legislatures last fall. So far from discouraging our friends there it is believed that good will come out of it. They speak with great confidence of a result next fall that will give Mr. Adams a large majority of the electoral vote of that State. Our prospects are good in Pennsylvania and Virginia, and especially in North Carolina. If our friends, without reference to false rumors and idle speculations everywhere, do their duty, the issue of the present contest will, in my opinion, be certainly favorable to Mr. Adams. All that we want is a tone of confidence corresponding with the goodness of our cause. Is it not strange that no member of the court, nor any *bystander*, should have given me any account of my trial before the Senate of Kentucky, with the exception of one short letter before it began, and another after its commencement, from a friend residing some distance from Frankfort? I have received no satisfactory information about the extraordinary proceeding. Of the result I am, as yet, unaware. I hope if I am to be hung I shall be duly notified of time and place, that I may present myself in due form to my executioner. But to be serious, was it not a most remarkable proceeding? I never doubt the good intentions of my friends, but in this instance I am afraid their zeal and just confidence in my integrity have hurried them into some indiscretions. By admitting the investigation, have they not *allowed*, what no man of candor and of sense believes, that there may be ground for the charge? At this distance it is difficult to judge correctly, but it seems to me that it would have been better to have repelled the resolution of General Allen with indignation. I make, however, *no reproaches*. I utter no complaints. Resignation and submission constitute my duty, and I conform to it cheerfully. I perceive that Mr. Blair refused to be sworn. I persuade myself that his resolution was dictated by honor and his personal regard for me. Still, I fear that malice will draw from his silence stronger conclusions to my prejudice than could have been done if he had exhibited my letter. Should that appear to *you* and *him* to be the case, I should be glad that you would have the letter published,—there is nothing in it but its *levity* that would occasion me any regret on account of its publication. The public will, however, make a proper allowance for a private and friendly correspondence never intended for *its eye*.

We shall have the tariff up in Congress next week. I anticipate a tremendous discussion. The Jackson party is playing a game of brag on that subject. They do not really desire the passage of their own measure, and it may happen in the sequel that what is desired by *neither party* commands the support of both.

I am, as ever, cordially your friend,
H. CLAY.

Hon. J. J. CRITTENDEN.

(Governor R. P. Letcher to J. J. Crittenden.)

WASHINGTON CITY, March 15, 1828.

DEAR SIR,—I answer your favor of the 4th without a moment's hesitation. You ask me whether I have any recollection of writing to you during the pendency of the late presidential election, requesting you to see Mr. F. P. Blair and get him to write to David White, your *representative* in Congress, to *encourage or induce him* to vote for Mr. Adams, informing me at the same time that Mr. Blair, in a recent friendly conversation between him and yourself, alleged such to be the fact. Now, sir, *you* nor no other gentleman ever received such a communication from me. How could I have made such a request? What necessity was there for it? Mr. White never, to my knowledge, expressed any doubt in relation to his vote for Adams. On the contrary, he was determined, positive, and decided in his feelings against General Jackson from the moment he knew between whom the contest would be. I knew him too well to suppose he needed any stimulants to vote for Adams. His anxiety on that subject was superior to mine. I have no doubt if Mr. Blair and yourself will, in that free and friendly intercourse which always existed between you, call upon White, the mistake which you allude to can at once be corrected as far as my name is concerned. Let Mr. Blair look into his letters to Mr. White, and their dates, and he will at once perceive from the whole tenor of his correspondence that it would have been worse than idle on my part to ask *him* through *you* to induce White to vote for Adams. White showed me several letters from him early, I think, in January, 1824, advising him in the most persuasive language to vote for Adams, saying, "he was much the *safest chance of the two.*" I saw similar letters of Mr. Blair to Mr. Clay. I speak from recollection, but it is probable Clay and White have both preserved their letters, by which Mr. Blair can satisfy himself. I have no doubt he will be very much surprised when he looks into the whole of his letters at the great solicitude he manifested in behalf of Mr. Adams in 1824. I have said nothing about these matters. I have interfered less with the vile charges made against others and *myself also* than any other man who has been implicated, having resolved as long as possible to keep myself out of all newspaper controversies. I believe I can satisfy you how the mistake *has* occurred between you and Blair. I wrote very few letters during the pendency of the presidential election to any one. I wrote *two* to you, neither of which contained more than ten or twelve lines. The first was written about the middle of January. In that letter I said that Mr. Bibb (I had just understood) had obtained, or perhaps was the bearer of many private letters to Mr. White, informing him that his district was in a flame at the idea of his voting for Adams, and that Kentucky would burn every man in effigy who dared to vote against Jackson. . . . I think I inquired if such was the fact, and whether you had any reason to believe

Mr. Bibb had such letters, and suggesting that *if he had*, they contradicted all the information which had been communicated by you, Blair, and others in relation to public opinion. Whether you read this letter to Blair I *can't tell*, neither did I care whether you did or not,—it *contained no treason.* You never answered my first letter, or my *second*, which bore date the day of the election for President, and in which I informed you of the result. I have given you a hasty, but I believe a correct, account of our correspondence in 1824. This letter is not intended for publication. Should you and Blair get into a paper war, and I am called upon to make a statement, I will endeavor to do justice to both, but should regret to form any part of it. I will apply to Clay to see the whole of Blair's correspondence with him in 1824, by which I can ascertain *facts* and dates.

With great respect, yours,
R. P. LETCHER.

Hon. J. J. CRITTENDEN.

Mr. Crittenden has been charged with inconsistency in his political course in early life, more particularly in relation to General Jackson. It is said that he was originally a Jackson man, and abandoned him for Mr. Adams without cause. This was at the time when the cry of "bargain and corruption" was brought against Mr. Clay. In this connection I will give a letter written by Mr. C., in 1825, to the Hon. Mr. White, and another to Ben Taylor:

DEAR SIR,—All compliments aside, I am really much obliged to you for your regular correspondence. The information you give me concerning the presidential election dissatisfies me more and more with the course pursued by our legislature, in instructing you to vote for Jackson. Without reasoning much about the matter, my preference was for Jackson; but that preference was unmingled with any condemnatory or vindictive spirit towards those who should take a different course. I felt that it was a subject of deep and vital consequence, and that there were many considerations which rendered it important that you should be left with entire liberty to act and represent us on that occasion. I was totally averse to the instructions given you, and desired that you should be guided by your own discretion and sense of responsibility. You were as well acquainted as the legislature was with the sense of your constituents, and they ought to have been satisfied that you would support Jackson, but for some sufficient reasons which might arise out of facts and contingencies which they neither did or could know. The fact is, our legislature had taken it for granted that Jackson was to be the President, and they were ambitious of having a hand in the matter, *discharging* their duty, and having the seeming honor of conferring the Presidency.

From what I have said you may readily conclude that you have no cause to expect my condemnation for any course you may think proper to pursue, nor do I believe you have anything to apprehend from your district. I am told that your senator, Charles Allen, was violent against the instructions. It is true I am an advocate for the right of instruction, and it is moreover true that I prefer Jackson to Adams, but I prefer my country to either, and I do not consider a request of the legislature as a binding instruction on a representative of the people. Preferring Jackson personally, I still feel that many considerations might arise which would lead me to forego that preference, and the request, or even instructions, of the legislature with it. I would not hesitate to give my vote for Mr. Adams, if it was necessary to prevent a failure in the election. Of all the results that would grow out of this contest, none would be more obnoxious, or more to be deplored, than that of devolving the chief magistracy upon the Vice-President. The people expect a President, and will not be satisfied with a subaltern. It will be a reproach to the republic, and an ill omen for the future, if it shall appear that we have already become too disunited, too factious, to agree upon a chief magistrate. I would do almost anything to avert this! Again, as much as I like Jackson, I know that he has not that knowledge of politics best calculated to qualify him for the discharge of the high and arduous duties of the Presidency. The character of his administration would depend greatly upon the qualifications of his cabinet or counselors. Thinking, as I do, of Mr. Clay, of his great integrity, his consummate ability, and his lofty American spirit, I believe it to be highly important to the public interests that he should occupy a distinguished position in the executive department. Under all circumstances, my first wish, dictated by my personal partialities and considerations of the public good, would be, that Jackson should be elected President and Clay should be his Secretary of State. I really do believe that the common good is more concerned in Clay's being Secretary of State than in the question between Jackson and Adams.

My letter is so long I scarcely know what I have written. Of this I am sure, it contains a quantity of hasty, trashy politics which I would not willingly have any but a friend look upon. In your last letter you express some friendly apprehensions that you might have given me pain or offense by what you said of Calhoun. Dismiss all such fears. Mr. Calhoun has seen, but does not know me, and I know but little of him. He cares nothing for me; and I, as old Lear says, "owe him no subscription." I voted for him as Vice-President; I thought he was the abler man. Had I believed that Clay's interests would have been advanced a hair's breadth by my voting against Calhoun, it would have been done. It is *dark;* I cannot read over what I have written. Write to me frequently.

Your friend,
J. J. CRITTENDEN.

(J. J. Crittenden to Henry Clay.)

FRANKFORT, Dec. 3d, 1828.

DEAR SIR,—Though recent occurrences have greatly depressed my spirits, my principles forbid me to despair. I have a strong confidence "that truth is omnipotent and public justice certain," and that you will live to hail the day of retribution and triumph. Your political enemies render involuntary homage to you by their apprehensions of your future elevation, and your friends find their consolation in looking upon the same prospect. The combination formed against you will dissolve,—its leaders have too many selfish views of personal aggrandizement to harmonize long. Your friends will remain steadfast,—bound to you more strongly by adversity. You will be looked to as the great head of the mass that constitutes the present administration party. This spirit is already visible, and I am sanguine of its final result. What an excellent philosophy it is which can thus extract good from evil, consolation from defeat! You will, of course, go on with the administration to the last moment, as though Mr. Adams had been re-elected, and with all the good temper and discretion possible. But what then? That you should return to your district and represent it again in Congress seems to be the expectation of your friends. It is certainly mine. Our judges of the Court of Appeals, Owsley and Mills, have this day delivered their resignations to the governor. This will deprive the agitators of one of their anticipated topics. I think they will both be renominated. Owsley will be confirmed, Mills will be strongly opposed,—he is, unfortunately, very unpopular. As to the Federal judgeship, to which you say I have been recommended, I have only to remark that if it should come to me, neither the giving nor the receiving of it shall be soiled by any solicitations of mine on the subject. The kindness of those friends who have recommended me is doubly grateful to my feelings, as it was unsolicited. I have never been guilty of the affectation of pretending that such an office would be unwelcome to me, but I have certainly never asked any one to recommend me. I wrote to Judge Boyle that I would not permit myself to be thrown into competition with him ; but he informed me that he would not have the office. I have violated all rule in writing so long a letter to a Secretary of State, and will only add that I am his friend,

J. J. CRITTENDEN.

Hon. HENRY CLAY,
    Secretary of State.

(Letter from Mr. Crittenden to Ben Taylor.)

DEAR SIR,—I have this morning casually learned that in a conversation, held by you in Versailles within a few days past, on the subject of my removal from office, you declared it was justified, if for no other reason than upon the ground that I had written two letters to different gentlemen at Washington,—one expressing a wish that General Jackson might "beat the Yankee," the other "that Mr. Adams might be elected." I may not be accurate as to words, but the above is the substance of your declaration, as stated to me. The letters alluded to were, I presume, those written by me to General Call and to David White. They have been published, together with my remarks and explanations in relation to them. That publication, I persuaded myself, ought to have satisfied every impartial man, who took the trouble to read and to consider it, that the charge of inconsistency made against me was groundless, and had been propagated by those who did not or would not understand the case. I felt, indeed, that I might treat it with disdain. Judge, then, of my surprise and astonishment that you, at such a time and under such circumstances, should be the first to renew such an imputation. My enemies I can defy! But your multiplied kindnesses forbid me to regard you as an enemy; and I was not prepared for such a blow from the hands of a friend. Believe me that I write to you "more in sorrow than in anger," and that if I had regarded you less I should not have troubled you with this communication. I do know and feel that you have done me injustice, unintentionally, I hope; but this consciousness will no longer permit me to look upon you as my friend so long as your conduct is unexplained or unatoned for.

I have thought it due to frankness and to the relations which have heretofore existed between us to make this communication to you.

In conclusion, I have only to assure you that I do not feel the least concern at my removal from office,—that no sensation of chagrin mingles with my emotions on this occasion. I care nothing for the office, and nothing for the removal,—it is your imputation alone which wounds me.

J. J. CRITTENDEN.

BENJAMIN TAYLOR, Esq.

In 1827 Mr. Crittenden was appointed Attorney of the United States for the District of Kentucky by President Adams.

In 1829 he was removed by General Jackson, and John Speed Smith appointed in his place. The same year Mr. Crittenden was nominated, by President Adams, to fill a vacancy on the bench of the Supreme Court, occasioned by the death of Judge Trimble. A partisan Senate resolved not to act on the nomination during that session of Congress. I give below two letters from Henry Clay on this subject; one written on the 6th of January, 1829, the other on the 27th of the same month, and letters from other friends:

DEAR SIR,—I received your letter of the 27th with its inclosures, which I have sent, through the post-office, to their respective addresses. They arrived in time to produce all the good they are capable of effecting. Your nomination was made to the Senate, agreeably to the intimation I gave you in my former letter; it has ever since been suspended there, and its fate is considered uncertain by your friends. It was referred, I understand, to a committee, which is not a very usual thing with original nominations. The policy of the Jackson party will be to delay, and ultimately to postpone it altogether.

I believe it is contemplated by some of our friends to move to have the committee discharged, and the nomination taken up in the Senate. Such a motion will probably be made in a few days. As soon as the result is known I will inform you. In the mean time you need not to be assured that I will do everything in my power, consistently with propriety, to promote your success.

I remain, with constant regard, cordially
Your friend and obedient servant,
H. CLAY.

January 27, 1829.

DEAR SIR,—I received your letter of the 16th. I was not aware of the neglect of your friends to write to you. I do not think that you have any ground for apprehending that they have, in other respects, neglected your interests. I believe, on the contrary, that all of them have exerted themselves to get your nomination confirmed. Fletcher has employed the most active exertions for that purpose, direct and indirect. Should your nomination be rejected, the decision will be entirely on party grounds, and ought, therefore, to occasion you no mortification. I understand that the Senate is considering a general proposition, that they will act upon *no* nominations during the present administration, except perhaps in some few cases of great emergency. I need not comment upon the exceptional character of such a proposition. It amounts, in effect, to impeding the action of the whole government. If the Senate were to resolve that they would not, during the rest of the session, act upon any business sent from the House of Representatives, such a resolution would not be more indefensible. What will be the fate of the proposition I cannot undertake to say. There is no doubt that it is principally leveled at the appointment for which you have been nominated. Besides the general party grounds, there are two personal interests at work against you,—one is that of Mr. Bibb, the other, that of Mr. White, of Tennessee. If General Jackson has to make a nomination, I think it probable that the Tennessee man will get it. I wish I could afford you some certain information as to the probable issue of your nomination. I regret to be obliged in candor to tell you that the more prevailing impression is that it will be rejected. If the above-mentioned proposition should be adopted, it will not be specifically acted upon; but if the question shall be directly put on the nomination, I cannot help *thinking*, perhaps I ought rather to say hoping, that it will be approved. Tyler, McKinley, Smith of South Carolina, and Smith of Maryland, have all, I understand, been repeatedly spoken to. I had a conversation with Tyler and Smith, from which I concluded that they would vote for you, whilst a directly contrary impression has been made upon the minds of others by the same gentlemen. I was told this morning, positively, that Tyler would not vote for you! So uncertain is everything, you see, here. The best course, perhaps, for you, is not to let your feelings be too much enlisted; cultivate calmness of mind, and prepare for the worst event.

I remain, with constant regard, your faithful friend,

H. CLAY.

WASHINGTON ACADEMY, May 22.

MESSRS. WHITE AND CRAIGHILL, Federalists,—As all the news which I have to write will not, at the most liberal calculation, be worth more than the postage of one letter, I have judged it proper to address you both in the same epistle. I believe you were the last of the students who went away during the vacation. Nearly all the old students have returned, except the Archers, who, Richard Powell informs us, will not come back. Isaac Booth has not yet arrived, but I suppose there is no doubt but he will return. It is supposed the students will be more numerous this session than formerly; there are between forty and fifty here now, and I think if you two were here we should be a complete phalanx. All your old friends concur with me in wishing your return. I should have written to you long since had it not been for lack of something to write; but surely the same excuse will not do for you, who should have written us certainly whether you would return or no, and likewise change of place would have given you an opportunity of seeing and hearing a great many things. I should like to know how you employ yourselves; for my own part, I am studying belles-lettres and mathematics, which occupy all my time. Nothing hostile has happened of late between the students and their enemies. I hope you will be regular and faithful in your correspondence. Although it is not my custom, however badly I write, to ask forgiveness for my inaccuracies, yet this letter will need your utmost partiality. Adieu.

Yours,
J. J. CRITTENDEN.*

P. CRAIGHILL AND J. WHITE.

---

* This letter Mr. W. N. Craighill found among his father's papers, in 1844, and sent it to Mr. Crittenden as a pleasant reminder of his college days in Virginia.

CHAPTER VI.

1829–1832.

IN 1829 Mr. Crittenden was removed from the office of Attorney-General for Kentucky. At the time congratulations
and testimonials of confidence and admiration poured in upon
him from every quarter. The following letter came from " Old
Logan," where he commenced his career:

Dear Sir,—The undersigned, a committee authorized in
behalf of the citizens of Russellville and Logan County, invite
you to a public entertainment during the summer. A visit to
this quarter of the State would insure them heartfelt satisfaction.
They cherish with pride and exultation the recollection that
in the town of Russellville and in the county of Logan those at-
tractive and endearing qualities of the heart, candor, sensibility,
and generous magnanimity, and those powerful, diversified, and
commanding talents that seize upon the mind and sway the
human soul, were first felt and properly rewarded. Here you
began your practice at the bar, which has since been to you a
field of honor and renown ; here the citizens of *Old Logan* took
you by the hand and sent you to the legislature, where your
genius and eloquence won for you the brightest honors of the
statesman. The people of Logan rejoice that your talents and
impassioned eloquence, and your private and political virtues,
commanded and still command the affection and admiration of
the people of Kentucky. Their motive, however, for wishing to
give a marked expression of their kind feelings on the present
occasion is not limited by the sentiments of respect and love
which they cherish for you,—they are influenced by views of a
more general nature.

They have learned with indignation that the hand of arbitrary
power *has* reached you, that you have been rudely hurled from
the office of Federal District Attorney, conferred by the disinterested patriot Adams, because of the virtues and qualities you

are known to possess, and for the necessary, prompt, faithful discharge of the duties incident thereto.

The reason of your removal is obvious to all who have noticed the signs of the times and the wanton abuse of power. You had the independence to think and act for yourself and your country, and voted for that distinguished and much-abused statesman, John Q. Adams. You had a heart fitted to appreciate and a mind to acknowledge and generously sustain the private worth and public virtues and patriotism of your persecuted friend, Henry Clay. This was offense enough in the eyes of him who now guides the destinies of these United States,—a sin never to be forgiven by him, whose desperate acts evince a settled determination to destroy the liberties of this country, to fetter the human mind, and to bribe and corrupt the press by official largesses.

A new standard is introduced to decide qualifications for office. The question is not now, as in the days of the republican Jefferson, "Is he honest? is he capable? is he faithful?" No! the only questions now propounded are, "Is he a true *Swiss?* did he vote against my competitor? has he fought for me? has he echoed my slanders against Henry Clay?" You did not suit the powers that be, hence your dismissal from office. Your friends here are anxious to declare to the world, in a suitable way, their estimation of your worth and their detestation of the wanton outrage committed against the spirit of our institutions by your removal from office. They believe you to be incapable of an unworthy act, they know you have always had an eye to the public good.

With these views and feelings, they invite you to this festival. In the event of your acceptance, will you please advise with Mr. Clay, and let us know the time agreed upon?

With sentiments of personal regard, respect, and esteem, we remain your humble servants,

THOMAS RHEA,	A. R. MACEY,
THOMAS PORTER,	ARCHIBALD CAMPBELL,
D. L. SMITH,	DUDLEY ROBINSON,
JOHN M. SHIRLEY,	RICHARD BIBB,
BEN PROCTOR,	ROBERT EWING,
W. STARLING,	ALEXANDER HULL,
JAMES WILSON,	JOHN B. BIBB,
E. M. EWING,	A. P. BROADNAX,
W. L. SANDS,	B. ROBERTS,
M. B. MORTON,	GABRIEL LEWIS.

This tribute from "*Old Logan*" was more grateful to Mr. Crittenden than any other he could possibly have received.

Mr. Clay and Mr. Crittenden accepted this invitation, and

their progress through the Green River country was an ovation. The tariff was the burden of their speeches.

In 1829 Mr. Crittenden was Speaker of the House, and the ardent advocate of internal improvements and the common school system.

(Letter of Mr. Crittenden to Albert Burnley.)

DEAR BURNLEY,—I was gratified by the receipt of your letter of the fourth. With *proscription* on one side of me and politics on the other, I have been compelled, in a measure, to take refuge in the latter. I became a candidate but three weeks before the election. You have heard, before now, that I have been elected. It is a great discomfiture to some folks here. They can never forgive me for the *injustice they have done me.* There are, thank God, but few of these, however. Very many of those who voted against me are well satisfied with my election. They have a story on Charles Bibb, that after voting for Richmond, he jumped immediately off the block and huzzaed for Crittenden! I believe it is true; and I hear it is complained of by our more *faithful* and *zealous patriots.* As I have stepped so far into politics I must go a little further,—I must be Speaker of the House of Representatives. I don't wish to make this public, but I confide it to you, to be used according to your discretion. Mention it to Griffith, and such others as you may please, in your own way, and give me what aid you can. Unless I am very much deceived, I think I shall have but little difficulty in attaining my object. It is the only sort of revenge I feel and seek against my proscribers. I want them to see how much I am indebted to them. Remember me most kindly to all the family, and believe me to be as ever,

Your friend.

(W. S. Archer to J. J. Crittenden.)

WASHINGTON, Feb. 2, 1829.

DEAR SIR,—I derived sincere gratification from the evidence afforded by your letter of the 26th, of your participation in the lively impression I have always retained of our early regard. We have now lived long enough to know the estimate which ought to be put on those regards as compared with those of later formation, in which interest in some form has inevitably so large a share. In our estimate (if I were to judge from your letter) of the reciprocal rights and obligations connected with early amity I should think we differed very materially if I did not know that your sentiments would be the same with mine were our situations reversed and I the person to stand in need of service. Were I even your enemy, or separated by *irreversible* lines of party, you would have had a right to require of me *as much as you have done*, to speak of *you as you are*, and I should hold myself bound as a man of honor to comply with the requisition. Your early associate has thought that the duty resulting from ancient friendship bound him to *far more*. I have forborne answering your letter from the desire that my acknowledgment of it should be accompanied by something further than the mere general expression of my willingness to serve you. I wished to be enabled to give you information concerning strong presumption of the result of the affair in which you are so deeply interested. I have chosen to wait till I have no doubt. I have now *none*. It is understood that the Senate have had your case under consideration for several days. *You will certainly be rejected!* If the decision had turned on the mere consideration of personal character, you would with the same certainty have been *confirmed*. When I last saw you, you were, I remember, the friend of General Jackson, and I was violently opposed to any proposition for his advancement in civil life. I have the testimony, therefore, of my own consciousness to assure me of the entire uprightness of the change of attitude you have exhibited in this respect, I having been the supporter of the general's election in the last contest. I now regret separation from you, which I would do under any circumstances, the more as it has been connected with the loss of the desirable situation to which you have been nominated. I have during this winter undergone no little mortification in the inefficiency of my zeal in relation to the service of two of my earliest friends, yourself and General Scott. The general will to all appearances *share your fate*.

I am going to be connected to a certain extent with a triumphant party. If I can be of any service, not to yourself personally, but to any one in whom you are interested *for whom you can ask me to exert myself* (you know that this description refers to the *faith* I shall repose in your declaration), rely upon me to do so.

I need hardly say (if my appreciation of you, founded on ancient recollections does not deceive) that you will give credit to the sincerity of this profession. If you have heard anything of me of late, you will believe of *"thine ancient comrade"* that he has not permitted political life and party feeling to *dry up* or freeze over the heart with which you once had acquaintance.

I am sincerely your friend,

Hon. JOHN J. CRITTENDEN. W. S. ARCHER.

(Letter from John Chambers on the subject of Judgeship.)

WASHINGTON, 1829.

DEAR CRITTENDEN,—My constant hope has been that I would be able to relieve your suspense, but the impenetrability of the senatorial conclave has baffled all our curiosity and kept us suspended between hope and fear for the fate of your *nomination*. I believe the die is cast! They have to-day refused to vote upon the nominations,—this decides nothing but a refusal to act for the present; but the committee have made a report upon the nominations referred to them (observe this is confidentially communicated), in substance "that because there are several propositions for a change of the judicial system now depending, and *because the administration of the government is about to change hands,* it is inexpedient to advise and consent to the nominations now." What a set of corrupt scoundrels, and what an infernal precedent they are about to establish! My opinion is that your friend Johnson has *gone over,* has not firmness enough to resist or disregard the proscriptions of his party. Amos Kendall is quartered upon him, and although the poor fellow seems to struggle occasionally for a little self-control, they hold him down, and he will be compelled to yield. You have some very zealous friends in the Senate, particularly in Johnson, of Louisiana, and Chambers, of Maryland, but they almost despair, not alone of your nomination, but of all the others made by Mr. Adams. We are all doing worse than nothing here, and I am tired to death of it. We have a rumor that General Jackson is dead, but it is not credited, and I hope it is not true; I would rather trust him than Calhoun!

Mr. Clay is quite unwell. "The Old Quill," however, is in perfect health, and keeps the machinery in motion, says, "How do, sir?" to everybody that calls on him, and gives his friends a very cordial pump-handle shake of the hand. The moment anything conclusive is done about your nomination I will write to you again. Rest assured that your friends here, powerless as they are, are neither silent nor idle, but take care to be prudent in the midst of their zeal. We have received letters communicating the rejection of Judge Robertson's nomination to be Chief Justice. Ben Hardin is just the man I took him for.

Your friend,
JOHN CHAMBERS.

(J. J. Crittenden to his daughter, Mrs. Coleman.)

FRANKFORT, November 18, 1831.

MY DEAR DAUGHTER,—I have been long intending to write to you; that I have not done so is not because I have not often and tenderly thought of you; and notwithstanding the excuses with which I am furnished by the almost continued occupation of my time by courts, the legislature, and visitants, I yet take to myself some reproach for not having before written. I have not only thought of you often, but anxiously. You are now in the most interesting and critical period of your life,—a young, married lady. Your own welfare and happiness, and that of your husband, depend much upon yourself, and your early adoption of those rules of conduct that are suited to your situation. I have never seen a wife who made her husband happy that was not happy herself. *Remember this*, and remember also that the reverse of it is equally true. Kindness and gentleness are the natural and proper means of the wife. There are wives who seek *to rule*,—who make *points* with their husbands and complain,—ay, scold. To love such a woman long is more than mortal can do, and their union becomes nothing more than a dull, cold, heartless partnership, yielding only discontent and wretchedness. As to your intercourse with and deportment in the world, I feel assured that the delicacy of your feelings and your good sense will dictate to you the proper course. There is a certain dignity and reserve that should always mark the conduct of a married lady; *just enough* of it to proclaim that she is a *wife*,—that she knows what is due *to her* and *from her*, and to repulse and rebuke, without a word spoken, the fops and triflers, and their petty flatteries and familiarities. The wife who would desire to be the pride and happiness of her husband, who would desire the real esteem and respect of society, should never lay aside this reserve and dignity. Esteem and admiration will follow her steps, if her qualities entitle her to them, and she need not seek after them. There is nothing more repugnant to my feelings than a sort of admiration-seeking, beaux-hunting *married woman*. Such conduct shows want of sense and want of taste, if *nothing worse*. I have seen married ladies who had their friendships with particular gentlemen, who visited them with more than common freedom and familiarity. In this there is nothing criminal, but it is wrong,—very wrong. Be not extravagant. You have a husband disposed to indulge you in all things. Show him that you know how to estimate and take care of his interest, and when his kindness and affection should prompt him to any little extravagances on your account, you should kindly check him. Show him that you know how to practice the economy of a lady. Take care of your health, and do not sacrifice it to fashion or amusements. The lacing now in use among ladies would kill you; I pray you not to destroy yourself by such a *petty sort of suicide!*

But enough of this homily for the present. When *this is reduced to practice* I may add something more. You seem to have been chagrined at my not being elected to the Senate! I *could* have gone to the Senate; it was but for me to express the wish and Mr. Clay would not have been the candidate. There was no *collision*, no rivalry, between us. All that was done was with my perfect accordance. I hope I shall always be found ready to do what *becomes me.* I have done so on this occasion and am satisfied.

We are all well, and wish much to see you. Write to me.

Your father,
J. J. CRITTENDEN.

Mrs. A. M. COLEMAN.

Mr. Crittenden's warm and constant attachment to his friends, and his prompt and frank appeals to them when any seeming estrangement, or apparent cause of mistrust arose, will be exemplified by the following letter to Governor Letcher:

SIR,—In a handbill, published by Mr. James Love, under date of 31st of July, 1831, and addressed to the voters of your congressional district, he represents you as having stated to him "that I was not entitled to the confidence of the party." These terms certainly admit of no favorable or friendly construction, and are calculated to convey imputations altogether derogatory to my character for candor and integrity. From the relations which had long subsisted between us, I had hoped that you would promptly, and without solicitation, have tendered to me some disavowal, or some explanation of the charge and imputations which you had been so publicly represented as having made against me. In this hope, though waiting long, I have been disappointed, and it has now become my duty to ask you for some disavowal that may reconcile my *feelings* and my *honor.* Another reason why I did not make this application to you before now, and before you left Kentucky, was the fear that it might, in its possible consequences, lead to some exasperation, or renewal of the quarrel between Mr. Love and yourself, a result I should have greatly deprecated. That quarrel was to me a matter of deep regret; of its merits I may say I *know nothing,* and it is my wish to remain ignorant. I have known Mr. Love long, and esteemed him as a friend and man of honor; but I may still entertain the hope that he misunderstood your language and meaning in reference to me. I will further hope that your answer to this letter will be so full and satisfactory as to efface from my mind every unpleasant reflection and remembrance of the subject; such as will permit me honorably to resume and cherish those feelings of friendship I had so long indulged towards you. It is right, perhaps, that I should add that I did *not* receive from Mr. Love the handbill alluded to, nor was it through him that I became aware of its contents.

Yours, etc.,
J. J. CRITTENDEN.

(R. P. Letcher's Reply.)

House of Representatives, April 10, 1832.

Sir,—To your letter of the 1st, this moment received, I respond with pleasure. The statement imputed to me in the handbill of the 31st of July last, of having declared that you were not entitled to the confidence of the party, is without any foundation. With this disclaimer, I might perhaps stop; but from the kindly relations which have so long and uninterruptedly subsisted between us, and which have, on my part, always been cherished with pleasure, combined with the fact of the active frankness and propriety of your communication, I feel justified, in the same spirit of frankness, in saying, as an act of justice to you as well as to myself, that I never entertained such a sentiment, and am not aware that it was *ever entertained* by any one of your personal or political friends. Of the unfortunate differences which sprang up at the last election I shall say nothing ; but I will say the only incident connected with it in any degree, for which I reproach myself, is in not writing you a letter, containing, in substance, what I have now written ; but the truth is, I conversed with some five or six of our mutual friends, with whom you were in the habit of constant and intimate intercourse, particularly with a view of making known to you my disavowal of the expressions referred to, and had supposed this had been communicated to you. I should regret exceedingly to do anything, or to *omit anything*, which would alienate a friend, or inflict the slightest wound upon his feelings. I think I may say of myself, that I am not wanting in attachment, in zeal, or in fidelity in friendship, and I do, therefore, reciprocate sincerely the hope expressed in the conclusion of your letter.

With great respect,

R. P. Letcher.

During the sixteen years in which Mr. Crittenden was absent from Washington, between the resignation of his seat in the Senate in 1819 and his return to Washington in 1835, he was almost constantly engaged in the diligent practice of his profession,—this was, indeed, his principal means of support. During this time a murder was committed in Frankfort, where he resided, which led to great bitterness and excitement. Sanford Goins was the name of the prisoner, for whom Mr. Crittenden appeared as counsel,—I have forgotten the name of his adversary. These two men had grown up in the same town, and had, perhaps, been acquainted all their lives ; but there was *bad blood* between them, produced, no doubt, by small and insufficient causes in the beginning. I doubt if they could themselves have accounted for their animosity. Matters grew worse and worse between them, and finally Goins heard that his enemy had threatened his life. From this time he was forever on the watch, and found himself dogged and waylaid at every corner,—at morning, at noon, and nightfall: whatever corner he turned, or street he entered, the man stood before him. Exasperated and half crazed by this, Goins came out of his house at a very early hour one morning, and the first object he saw was his adversary on the other side of the street, opposite his house. Completely carried away by passion, Goins seized a stick of wood, pursued and caught up with him, and being a much more powerful man, he literally beat him to death with the wood. These are the circumstances of the murder, so far as I can remember them, but their accuracy is not very important. Goins was tried for murder, Mr. Crittenden defended him, and he was acquitted, and is, I believe, still living. The case, and Mr. Crittenden's argument in favor of the criminal, were much discussed at the time. The most effective ground taken by him in favor of the prisoner was, "that a man had not only a right to live, but to be happy," and that for many months Goins's life, so far from being a blessing to him, had been an unspeakable torment. There had been no moment, night or day, free from the apprehension of sudden and violent death. He could not enter his own door at night without finding this, his enemy, skulking around the corner; he could not leave his wife and child, with the sunrise, to go to his daily work, without seeing this terror before his door. Was it any wonder that he had been driven to frenzy and to a deed of blood by such a life? Prejudice was, I think, very strong against Goins in the beginning of the trial, but under the influence of Mr. Crittenden's eloquence and the masterly manner in which he pictured the horrors of Goins's life, during the months which preceded the murder, public opinion veered round completely, and Goins was not only acquitted, but received back into the community with sympathy. This may seem rather a trivial detail and Mr. Crittenden's argument of but little value, but it made a great impression on the audience and the jury. In my after-life, when I saw men and women oppressed and terrified, I have remembered that we had all a right

to life and an equal right to be *happy*. The last great claim,
however, is often weakly yielded to the strong hand of power,
and often trampled underfoot.

About this time Mr. Crittenden's brother Thomas was very
ill in Louisville, and he was summoned to his death-bed. His
family affection was very strong, and the death of this brother
was felt for years. The following letter was written at his
brother's death-bed :

(J. J. Crittenden to his wife Maria.)

LOUISVILLE, Tuesday, December 25, 1832.

MY DEAR WIFE,—Prepare yourself to hear the worst. My
brother Tom is still alive, but that is all; a few hours is all,
perhaps, that remain for him. All human aid seems to be in
vain. I never knew, till this affliction taught me, how dearly
I loved this dearest, best, and noblest of brothers.

Death has no horrors for him, and if ever a Christian proved
his faith by a triumphant death, he is doing it.

'Tis but a few hours now till the arrival of the stage from
Frankfort. If Mr. Edgar comes in it he may arrive in time,—
he is most anxiously looked for.

J. J. CRITTENDEN.

Mrs. MARIA CRITTENDEN.

CHAPTER VII.

1832-1836.

Letters—Appointed Secretary of State in Kentucky in 1834—Letters—Benton's
Resolutions as to Fortification—Letters.

(James G. Birney to J. J. Crittenden.)

DANVILLE, February 11, 1836.

DEAR SIR,—I little expected when I had the pleasure of seeing you in Frankfort that we should so soon have to lament the loss of our amiable and distinguished fellow-citizen, Judge Boyle. I lament it not only on grounds common to our countrymen generally, but because he was an interesting and pleasant companion, and we concurred in opinion on the subject of slavery, and as to the means of accomplishing the relief of our State from its suffocating pressure. Just before I went to Frankfort, I had a free conversation with him in reference to it. He was then considering favorably an invitation, which our newly-instituted society for the relief of the State from slavery had given him, to act as its presiding officer. I doubt not, had he lived, that he would not have hesitated, after hearing that you had consented to serve as one of our *Vice-Presidents*. Last Friday, our board of managers came to the decision of tendering to you the station which had been offered to our distinguished friend who has been removed from us. Our secretary, Mr. Green, told me he would write to you on the subject immediately. I know not, my dear sir, that I ought to calculate on exerting any influence over you. If I *have* any, *however* small, I will hazard its exhaustion in a cause like this, where intelligent patriotism and enlightened philanthropy have such lofty conquests to achieve and such pure rewards to reap. I trust, sir, it will not be in vain that I have added the earnestness of private solicitation to the official tender that will be made, especially when, I doubt not, I shall be warmly seconded by your excellent lady. I propose bringing the whole subject before the public in a series of letters addressed to the Hon. Charles A. Wickliffe. They will be untainted with anything like bigotry, or fanaticism, or uncharitableness towards those who may dissent from my opinions. Indeed, I propose treating the subject entirely in its political aspect. May I ask of you to

(86)

use such influence as you may have with the Frankfort editors to secure their republication?

Your friend always,
JAMES G. BIRNEY.

In 1834 Mr. Crittenden was appointed Secretary of State in and for the State of Kentucky by James T. Morehead, Lieutenant-governor, then acting as governor of the State.

In 1835 he was elected to the legislature, and returned to the Senate.

As one of my objects is to portray the character of Mr. Crittenden, pronounced even by his opponents as worthy of all admiration and imitation, I give below a letter written by him to one of his most intimate friends at this time, and showing the sentiments with which he entered upon this contest:

FRANKFORT, May 2.

DEAR BURNLEY,—The bell is now ringing to warn us that this is the Sabbath-day, and summon us to church. I must steal a few moments to write to you.

I am a candidate,—you have seen it announced. My confidence of success is *strong* and *decided*. Still, the struggle is to me most disagreeable, and it would have been satisfactory to me to devolve it on any other of my political friends. It was urged upon me, and there seemed to be no alternative but to re-engage in the contest or to see the field yielded without an effort. Pride, principle, both forbade this! If I am beaten, it shall be my consolation that I was doing what I believed to be my duty,—struggling to the uttermost for a good cause. It is but a poor expression of my feelings to say that I thank you for the kindness and friendship which mark all your conduct and sentiments towards me. There are some feelings of the heart which the tongue cannot utter, that it ought not indeed to utter.

As to the Senate of the United States, I cannot now tell you whether I shall be a candidate or not; on such a subject I would have no secrets with you; my course in this matter will depend upon circumstances. I do not seek it. But if it should be the work of my friends, if it should appear that my name can be used with a greater prospect of success than another, then I will be a candidate.

This is my view of the subject, and I cannot determine positively till after our general elections in August.

If there be any other friend who would be as acceptable as myself, and who was anxious to go to the Senate, I would not have any collision which might disunite us. I would wish to

be the foremost to sacrifice personal pretensions for the sake of
union. As I intend, however, to possess you fully not only
with a knowledge of my feelings, but of my expectations in
relation to this subject, I tell you in confidence that I think
it probable circumstances will make me a candidate. If I were
even now determined to be a candidate it would be impolitic to
avow it, for good reasons which will occur to you. It would
interfere with the wishes of others, and weaken their exertions in
the common cause, which I have much more at heart than any
selfish purpose of my own. My friends might express their wishes
and speculations, and make preparation for the probable event
of my being a candidate. Of one thing be certain, I have no
secrets with you, and as events occur which may influence my
feelings and determinations, you shall hear from me.

That we should have a majority, a decided majority, in the
next legislature, is of the *highest* and *most* decisive importance.
For God's sake, exert yourself to the utmost, and animate our
friends all around you! One spirited, united, and patriotic
effort will settle the course of Kentucky. Union is our strength
and our hope of success; I go for that; cannot therefore pledge
myself to any particular course as to the speakership. Many
will have to be consulted ; I cannot commit myself to Calhoun
or any one ; I wish to be free to do my duty, as it may appear
to me at the time.

I am your friend,

A. T. Burnley.   John J. Crittenden.*

(J. J. Crittenden to Orlando Brown.)

Washington, December 27, 1835.

Dear Orlando,—Your favor of the 18th was received last
night, and afforded me so much satisfaction that I hasten to
show my gratitude by an immediate reply. I don't value all the
politics of your letter in comparison with the domestic news
you give me. All that concerns my *home* and my friends
delights me. Distance lends an *enchantment* to it all. You
could not have chosen any two *heroes* for your story whose
achievements would have been more interesting to me than my
two little boys, John and Hick. I am glad to hear that Mason
and his wife have been dining with my wife. Washington
cannot afford me so happy a day as I *should* have enjoyed if I
could have been present with you all. Present sundry congratulations to Mason on his marriage. To such a wife as he has
been fortunate enough to get, I hope he will make a *dutiful and
obedient husband. As to politics, curse politics!* Webster's pre-

---

* Mr. Crittenden was elected to the Senate, and took his seat 4th March, 1835.

tensions are considered virtually at an end; but, as yet, he says nothing, and, as far as I can hear, his course is not ascertained. He deserves the kindest and most respectful treatment from the public on the occasion, that he may fall like a great man. Harrison's friends here dread nothing more than that White should be scared off the field, or his friends discouraged from giving him a zealous support, and perhaps relapsing into Van Burenism. To avoid this is a point of obvious policy, and I think it is neither right nor politic to exaggerate Harrison's prospects at the expense of White's. According to my best information as to the existing state of public opinion, White may reasonably calculate on receiving as many electoral votes as Harrison. Besides Virginia, and his Southern interest, he is at present stronger, and has a better chance, than Harrison for Illinois and Missouri. At this moment of some alarm with him and his friends, it is better to increase than diminish their hopes. This will open to your view the whole *pith* of the matter, and you can act on it according to your discretion. I see no alternative for you but to have a convention to nominate candidates for governor and lieutenant-governor, and *electors also.* Morehead *must* be the candidate for governor; he is *indispensable* to the present crisis, and no excuse ought to be taken from him. I agree with you that Letcher is the man for lieutenant-governor, the very man, and will give more strength than any one you can select. If it comes to a serious struggle (and that you must prepare for), you will find him more efficient than even you yourself suppose. He is essentially popular in his talents, habits, and manners, and of capacity far beyond what is generally ascribed to him in Kentucky.

Your friend,
J. J. CRITTENDEN.

ORLANDO BROWN, Esq.

On the 22d of February, 1836, Mr. Crittenden made a speech against the adoption of Mr. Benton's resolutions on the subject of national defense and the fortification bill, which had been defeated in 1835. Mr. Benton had charged the Senate with neglecting proper measures for the defense of the country. Mr. Crittenden said, "The Senate needed not his poor vindication; it was the same Senate that had maintained for years the noblest struggle for law, liberty, and the Constitution; belonged to history, whose brightest pages would be illumined with the names of those illustrious senators who had been foremost in that great struggle. In the *great reckoning* on which judgment would be pronounced upon them, the fortification bill of the last session would be an insignificant item. It appeared, however, that to vote in favor of the resolutions seemed to be the only admissible evidence of patriotism." The first distinct proposition was, that the *entire surplus* revenue should be applied, *exclusively*, to warlike preparations. As amended by Mr. Grundy, the resolutions secure *only so much* of the revenue as may *be necessary*. Mr. Benton accepts the amendment readily, as it is only a change of phraseology; Mr. Crittenden was opposed to the system; thought it unwise and improper. The money was the product of peace, and peace had claims upon it; he thought a portion of it should be returned to the people to increase their sources of national wealth; this scheme confined the whole expenditure of the revenue to the seacoast, cutting off the western and interior States from their hope of an equal distribution of the public money. Mr. Crittenden did not cherish sectional feeling; the whole of the United States was his country, but he could not forget the special interests of his section and his constituents; he did not believe in fortifications as means of defense. The sure defense of nations was the courage, intelligence, and patriotism of the people. We had had wars and rumors of wars, but we should not, for that reason, be always clad in steel, and oppress ourselves with the weight of our own armor. Mr. Benton, in alluding to our difficulties with France, had said, "We were in a *naked, miserable*, defenseless condition." This filled Mr. Crittenden with surprise. For seven years the administration had been in the hands of a President *renowned in war*, and the senator from Missouri had been one of its proudest supporters. Is it not, then, surprising to hear that the country is in a "naked, miserable, defenseless condition?" In this particular, Mr. Crittenden said, *He* must be the vindicator of the administration. The Senate was not responsible for the fate of the bill; its loss was owing to "*scruples of conscience*" on the part of members of the House, who were not willing to *act* after a certain hour on the last night of the session. Mr. C. thought it must be consolatory to its patriotic friends, who mourned so eloquently over its fate, to know that it "*died for conscience' sake.*" Neither Washington, Adams, Jefferson, nor Madison, nor any former Congress, had indulged in such scruples:

"the ways of conscience were inscrutable and past finding out;" she had made her *compunctious visitings* at the witching hour of twelve, when conscience, *long pent up* and clogged with the politics of a whole session, would most naturally break out. Mr. Benton had alluded to the probability of a war with France. Mr. Crittenden did not believe war could be made out of such slender materials; he had been anxious to know what measures were proposed by the executive, and had turned a listening ear to the senator from Tennessee, Mr. Grundy, a distinguished supporter of the administration, when he arose and announced that "he would *declare frankly what he was for.*" This promised, frank avowal was, simply, "that he was not willing things should remain *exactly as they were.*" Willing to reciprocate all good offices with Mr. Grundy (formerly an old Kentuckian), Mr. Crittenden imitated his frankness and declared, conscientiously, "*that he was not willing that things should remain exactly as they were.*" "Sir," said he, "we have seen the senator from Pennsylvania, that land of honest peace and honest industry, *rebuking* General Jackson for his '*too great moderation.*' Nothing can be added to *that picture*. The gentlemen think it is indispensable to our dignity to *compel* France to pay the sum of money which, by treaty, she owes us. I have not sensibility enough to discover that the *honor and dignity* of the country is concerned. This question affects our *interests* and not our *honor.*" Mr. Crittenden agreed with the senator as to the fact that France did owe us five millions of dollars; but, he asked, "Should we go to war *for that?* A war with *whom,*—for what? *With* France, our *first*, our ancient ally! France, whose blood flowed for us, flowed with our own, in that great struggle which gave us freedom. A war for money,—a paltry sum of money! He knew of no instance among civilized nations of war waged for such a purpose. *If* among the legitimate causes of war, it was surely the most inglorious; can afford no generous inspiration; must ever be an ignoble strife; on its barren fields the laurel cannot flourish; but little honor can be won in the sordid contest, and even victory would be almost despoiled of her triumph! But imagine that the *little purse*, the *prize* of war and carnage, is at last obtained. There it is! stained with the blood of Americans and Frenchmen, their ancient friends and allies. Could we *pocket* that blood-stained purse without emotions of pain and remorse?" Mr. Crittenden hoped and believed that we would be saved from the calamity of war with foreign nations, and would enjoy more harmony in our counsels at home.

(Mr. Crittenden to O. Brown.)

WASHINGTON, March 13, 1836.

DEAR ORLANDO,—I have yet to thank you for your letter of the 11th. If I were to rate the obligation by the pleasure it gave me, I do not know how I should ever discharge it. The description you gave of my wife and children, excited by the flattering intelligence of me, which you had furnished to them, was both painting and poetry to the heart of such a man as I am. It was a picture to bring together a smile and a tear upon a husband's and father's face. I am not willing to confess, even if it were possible to communicate, all the feelings it aroused in me.

Permit me to tell you how much I enjoy the sentiment expressed in your letter when you say, "As for myself, I do feel as if I was bound to you and yours as strongly as if there was a tie of blood between us," etc. But I must quit this subject or become altogether too sentimental.

Mangum is all you have described him to be. Through your means we found ourselves well acquainted upon our very first meeting, and have ever since been good friends. We talk often of you,—the captivation seems to be mutual. Leigh, too, is a noble fellow; I almost envy him the patriotic eminence of his present position, and never did man meet his fate with more unpretending integrity and fortitude. There is no parade in the course he has taken; not a spark of pretension or ostentation is visible. The conduct he has adopted seems to be the natural result of native truth and virtue.

"There is a daily beauty in his life" which makes these *expungers* of the Constitution, who are assailing him, look uglier than ever to my sight. I think you will sympathize in all these feelings, and I shall be proud to see in the *Commonwealth* one of those felicitous articles on the subject which I might show to Leigh. We have a temporary calm just now in our congressional proceedings. The French question has passed by, and the agitation produced by the recharter by Pennsylvania of the Bank of the United States has subsided. The discussions upon the petitions of the Abolitionists have become stale and worn out. Clay's land bill and Benton's fortification bill are, I presume, the next subjects to break the calm.

There are some here who entertain hopes of the passage of the land bill; for my own part, I anticipate nothing so good; party spirit has paralyzed Congress to too great an extent! Van Buren's election to the Presidency is, with many, a much more important object than the public good, and so, too, perhaps, is his defeat with some of his opponents. With respect to the coming controversy, I can tell you nothing more than you already know. Webster is still standing in the field, though he can hardly be considered a competitor. My confidence in him leads me to believe he will do what is right and proper. Harrison's interest in the North is manifesting itself more strongly than was expected, and every day confirms the impression that Pennsylvania will certainly go for him. The opponents of Van Buren here, from every quarter, are confident that a majority of the people are against him, and that the only chance of his success is in their divided and distracted condition. Why did not our friends in Kentucky nominate Granger when they did Harrison? I see that some of our papers in Lexington have come out for Tyler.

Upon every principle of policy, we should rather gratify Pennsylvania and the Anti-Masons of the North, by taking Granger. I do not like to turn my thoughts to your late actings and doings in Kentucky. The distance has somewhat broken the effect upon me, but still I am grieved in spirit at some events. They denote, I fear, even more than a want of union,—a bad spirit has gotten up among you; but let me say no more of things which I cannot mend.

Give my *love* to your wife; yes, my love. I do feel that I love everybody in Frankfort, and if this is so, I am sure I must love her very dearly.

Your friend,
J. J. CRITTENDEN.

ORLANDO BROWN.

(J. J. Crittenden to his wife Maria.)

SENATE CHAMBER, April 8, 1836.

MY DEAR MARIA,—I write merely for the pleasure of writing to you; it is a sort of mental association that is the best consolation for actual absence. I have nothing to write, unless I should write in the strains of a *mere lover*, and I suspect you have already had so much occasion to laugh at me for that, so I ought to be a little cautious how I proceed in that melting mood.

I am quite amused to hear of what you all *call Hick's badness*. I suspect he is more petted than whipped. Eugenia writes, " Poor Hick is whipped almost every day for *cursing*," and then adds,

" He is a most charming fellow." I suspect he is a spoiled chap, and that I shall have work enough to reform the young gentleman.

But I must attend to the business of the Senate, so farewell, my dearest Maria.

Yours,
J. J. CRITTENDEN.

Mrs. MARIA CRITTENDEN.

CHAPTER VIII.

1836-1837.

IN 1836, Mr. Webster visited the West, and came from Lexington to Frankfort to see Mr. Crittenden. He was his guest for some days at that time, and received from the yeomanry of Franklin County the usual compliment paid to distinguished visitors in that locality, "a barbecue," or, as it was called at that time, "a bergoo." This was regarded as an unusually great occasion, and extensive preparations were made to do honor to Mr. Webster. The men were rallied far and wide, and a mighty gathering was the result. The place honored by custom for this Kentucky festivity was about seven miles from Frankfort, on the farm of Mrs. Innis, the mother of Mrs. Crittenden. A romantic little stream called Benson wound about through the woods near the house, and in the dense forest along its borders the Kentucky host assembled. I cannot explain the origin of the word "bergoo;" the feast differed from a "barbecue," in that it was more primitive. Immense iron pots were kept on hand in some secluded spot, ready for such occasions, and each man was expected to bring his own tin cup and pewter spoon. "Bergoos" were always the order of the day when summer vegetables abounded; only one dish was prepared, but it was savory as the mess brought by Esau to his father, the blind patriarch. All the birds and squirrels round about were shot, prepared, and thrown indiscriminately into the large pots; then all the farms and gardens in the neighborhood were put under contribution, and young corn, tomatoes, peas, beans,—in short, every vegetable that could be found, was added. All this boiled away vigorously till the salutations of the day were over, family news told, and kindly questions asked and answered. The business of the day (which was making speeches and listening to them) concluded, then all present gathered around the steaming pots, cup and spoon in hand, to receive their portion. I don't remember that I ever tasted this famous broth, but it perfumed the woods, and I know that every one "asked for more." There was no distinction of persons on these occasions, except that the orators of the day and the visitors were first served; but a tin cup and a pewter spoon were the only implements. Mr. Webster was accompanied by his wife and daughter Julia, afterwards Mrs. Appleton, and on the great day of the feast we drove out to Mrs. Innis's. After resting at the house, we walked over to the camping-ground. Mr. Webster was received with shouts that almost rent the heavens. He was welcomed in the usual form, and called upon for a speech, which he made in his inimitable style. Mr. Crittenden, knowing *his boys of old,* feared that he also would be called upon for a speech. Before Mr. Webster concluded, he was seen quietly and stealthily withdrawing to the outskirts of the crowd, and concealing himself at last behind a tree.

One amusing feature of this occasion was seeing Mr. Webster accommodate himself to a stump. This was not the kind of platform he was accustomed to, but he would not have been equally acceptable in any other position. I suppose he had never felt his footing so insecure, but, being a quiet speaker by nature, he got through like a man and a Kentuckian. After the conclusion of Mr. Webster's speech, a great shout arose for "Crittenden! Crittenden! Crittenden!" The crowd swayed backward and forward, the merry laughter of those near his place of concealment betrayed him, and he was literally dragged out and passed over the heads of the people to a tall stump, and *put down gently.* Such a triumphant shout of victory was rarely heard on any battle-field as arose when this was accomplished. Mr. Crittenden was laughing so heartily that it was some time before he could utter a word. I shall never forget Mr. Webster's expression on that day,—amazement and amusement contended for mastery. Those who were acquainted with Mr. Crittenden have not forgotten the intensely humorous expression of his countenance when hearing or relating a good story. On this occasion his mirth was contagious. He peremptorily declared he *would not make* a speech, made a comic appeal to "*his boys*" "not to force him to hold up his little lights while greater lights were shining;" he declared that "there was not a stump within five miles that did not bear the marks of his footsteps." This *plea* seemed to touch "*the boys*,"—they behaved well, letting him off for that time, although I verily believe they would rather have heard him speak than Demosthenes or Cicero.

Before leaving the ground, many pressed forward to take Mr. Webster by the hand and to say a word on the great political questions of the day. Every man in Kentucky was a politician, and those mass-meetings were political schools for uneducated men. They listened with intense interest to public speaking, and were, many of them, natural orators. In returning to town, one of my sisters and myself occupied the same carriage with Mr. Webster. During the drive he spoke almost exclusively of Mr. Crittenden, and pronounced an eloquent eulogy upon him. Among other things he said, "Mrs. Coleman, your father is a great and good man. Great men are not difficult to find, but a great, and good man is rarely seen in this world. Mr. Crittenden is a great and good man."

In 1868 I was in Washington, and was introduced by Senator McCreery to Mr. Evarts, then Attorney-General of the United States. Mr. McCreery introduced me as the daughter of John J. Crittenden, and I received from Mr. Evarts a cordial grasp of the hand and a touching allusion to my father's public character and private worth. I told him in the course of this conversation that I was collecting materials for a life of Mr. Crittenden, and asked for his assistance. He encouraged me in my purpose, and expressed the conviction that such a book would be gladly received by the public, and promised me to write out some reminiscences, which he hoped would be useful. In this connection Mr. Evarts told me this anecdote: "At the very outset of my professional career I was associated with Mr. Crittenden as counsel in the famous trial of Monroe Edwards for forgery." (Monroe Edwards was a Kentuckian, his parents lived in Logan County, where he was born, and where Mr. Crittenden commenced the practice of law. Mr. Edwards's family were among Mr. Crittenden's most intimate friends, and Monroe had been, in boyhood, one of his special favorites. In this case, as, many years later, in the Ward trial, Mr. Crittenden came forward to exert his best abilities in the service of his old *friends*.) "Mrs. Coleman," said Mr. Evarts, "I shall never forget that trial in connection with your father. I was a young man on the threshold of my professional career, and your father's reputation was firmly and widely established as a lawyer and a statesman. His cordial manner throughout the trial is most gratefully remembered by me, and at its close he asked me to take a walk with him. During the walk he took a slight review of the trial, complimented me upon my course during its progress and the ability he was pleased to think I had manifested, and in conclusion, grasping my hand with warmth, he said, 'Allow me to congratulate and encourage you on the course of life you have adopted. I assure you that the highest honors of the profession are within your grasp, and with perseverance you may expect to attain them.' Those words from Mr. Crittenden would have gratified the pride of any young lawyer and given him new strength for the struggles of his profession. I can truly say they have been of the greatest value to me through life. When I came to Washington to take part in the defense of President Johnson, the associations of the senate-chamber recalled the memory of your father's words and renewed my gratitude for his generous encouragement of my early hopes."

(R. P. Letcher to J. J. Crittenden.)

LANCASTER, May 3, 1836.

DEAR CRITTENDEN,—I thank you for your favor of the 23d. It found me alone in the portico, taking a quiet chew of tobacco, in rather a melancholy, desponding, painful temper of mind at the prospect ahead, at home and abroad. After reading it, my spirits became animated to such a degree that I have felt cheerful ever since. Indeed, I may say that I am, at this moment, quite an amiable, agreeable, entertaining young gentleman. *Hope*, even a *faint hope*, of success is enough to encourage me in the present struggle. I can bear anything but despair growing out of division in our own ranks and the miserable selfishness of our friends. Defeat is nothing to compare with such a state of things. This desire of being *captain* or nobody, "aut Cæsar aut nihil," ruffles my *sweet temper*. I hate and abhor such an abominable principle of action. "Make me captain; if you don't, I'll be *mad*, and will do nothing in favor of my own principles." This is too bad to be thought of. It is, in fact, nothing more nor less than the ravishment of a whole party. It may be that Judge Clark can be elected governor, but I am not without apprehensions; I would not consent to run if he were *ruled off.* I knew if he *went off* in any other way than by his own voluntary consent, he would go with a dissatisfied set of friends, who would be happy to see any one beaten that took his place. I shall use every fair and strong means to elect him. I acknowledge to you I am vexed at his perverseness; not because I wanted to run myself. Our Van Buren postmaster, returned from a tour through the mountains day before yesterday, reports that Flournoy will beat Clark in that portion of the State. Unless a vigorous effort is made we shall lose the race. It would be well to call all our delegation in Congress together, and let each man determine to write six letters every twenty-four hours to his district, in relation to the election of governor. I mean *all except* Ben Hardin; I should leave him to himself. Meet in the committee-room, and let each man *pledge himself* to do his duty by writing letters forthwith. One Congress letter is worth a dozen letters from a *private*. I am sincerely gratified to hear that Webster is upon the *recovery*. The truth is I had almost brought my mind to the conclusion that his case was hopeless. I like him, but he is no such man as Clay; he is most certainly a *very great man*, and possesses many of the highest traits of character, but his ambition is a little too much mixed with *self-love*. Clay is more elevated, more disinterested, more patriotic, and he is always ready to surrender it for the possible hope of promoting his country's good. The conduct of Mr. Adams, and the verdict of the country against him, has had a good effect upon Webster. Say to Bankhead everything that a warm-hearted Kentuckian feels; drink a good glass of sherry with him *for me*, and a glass of champagne with his charming lady. I shall not forget to write to his *Majesty*, suggesting the propriety of making him a *full minister*. No doubt he will promptly obey my suggestions, as he has never refused me the first application yet. I would tell you many pretty things the public say about you, but knowing you will just do what I have done very often, throw aside a long document and never think of it again, I will reserve all that until I see you.

Truly your friend,

Hon. J. J. Crittenden.   R. P. Letcher.

(J. J. Crittenden to his son Thomas.)

Washington, Dec. 10, 1836.

My dear Son,—I received your letter of the 25th, from New Orleans. After a journey as little fatiguing as possible we arrived here safely. Your little brothers, John and Eugene, are with their grandmother. Our wide dispersion is painful to me, and would be intolerable but for the hope that it is for our common advantage, and that we shall meet again under happier circumstances. In parting with you, my dear son, I have made a great sacrifice of feeling for what I hoped might be for your good. Whether this shall be so or not depends, to a great degree, on your own exertions and good conduct. The object nearest my heart, that engages my pride and my affections, is the well-doing and reputation of my children. Of you I indulge the best and proudest hopes. I have all confidence in your principles of integrity and honor, in your manliness, firmness, and capacity. All that gives me uneasiness is the thought of your youth and inexperience. The scenes in which you are cast are full of evils and temptations. When I think how many of maturer age have fallen victims to these temptations, I cannot help asking myself, with trembling anxiety, Can my boy *resist and overcome them all?* Can his naked and inexperienced feet tread successfully the path that leads through the midst of such dangers and temptations? Has he the good sense, the virtuous resolution, the noble, manly ambition to turn away from the vices and seductions that will beset and surround him, and look only to the more distant, but *sure reward* that will crown his life with prosperity and honor? In the pride and confidence of my heart I answer these questions thus: " My son has the sense, the courage, the virtue to triumph over these difficulties ; that he *will do* so, and his father's heart be gladdened by his course of conduct." You are thrown upon the world at an early and dangerous season of life. Your constant sense of propriety must be your *guide*. Your situation demands discretion beyond that which ordinarily belongs to your age ; you must, therefore, make your conduct the subject of daily *self-examination.* · A few *principles and rules* of conduct, firmly fixed in your mind and acted upon, will insure your safety and success. Consider *truth and integrity inviolable!* Be *zealous*, be *faithful* to a *scruple*, to a hair's-breadth, in all business confided to you. Be not *forward* to take offense, or to cherish a false pride. Do not look upon your *duties* as *degrading*, but rather make the *cheerful performance* of them your *distinction* and *honor!* Be frank, open, and candid. Practice no dissimulation. Encounter any *consequences*, any *sacrifices*, sooner than utter a *falsehood* or do a dishonorable act. In this, let your pride and resolution be *fixed* as a rock. Do not frequent the *haunts* of the *idle* and *dissipated.* Be not seen at any *gaming* or *drinking* house ! Even the suspicion arising from such things will be a *stain* upon your character, and impair confidence in you. In the perplexities of business, your employers may sometimes *act* or *appear* to act unkindly. Do not take such things for offenses, but behave with *deference* and *respect*, and you will advance yourself in their good opinions. Apply your own good sense to all that I have so imperfectly written, and you will be able to adopt some valuable rules for the government of your life. I request that you will preserve this letter and read it *once a week* for the *next three months*. Mr. Erwin has promised me to be your friend, and he can be a very important one. Omit nothing in your power to obtain his good opinion. I have observed that you sometimes have the appearance of *sternness* in society. Correct this,—cheerfulness and smiles better become your age, and are, I am sure, more congenial to your natural disposition. I wish you not only to be an accomplished merchant, but an accomplished gentleman. The *manners* of such a gentleman are always *unaffected* and *natural*. *Write often.*

Your father,
J. J. CRITTENDEN.

In 1836 the whole country was suffering from pecuniary difficulties, and it was believed by Mr. Crittenden and his political friends that this embarrassment in the general circulation of the country was the consequence of the *Treasury Circular*. Under this order all the specie was collected and carried into the vaults of the deposit banks. Mr. Crittenden thought the great commercial cities, where money was wanted, were its natural depositaries. He contended that when specie was forced by treasury *tactics* in a direction contrary to the natural course of business, it was in exile. Men might be deluded on the subject, and while the *mystification* lasted, the "*Treasury order*" might be held before the eyes of men as a splendid financial arrangement. Like the natural rainbow, it owed its very existence to the *mist* in which it had its being. The moment the atmosphere is clear, its bright colors vanish from view. The senator from Missouri charged that the *distribution bill had* done all the mischief. Mr. Crittenden bore cheerfully his share of the rebuke; he was proud of having been instrumental in getting so beneficial a bill passed. As to the honorable senator's bill, relative to the expediency of making gold and silver *only a tender* in payment for the public lands, on motion of Mr. Ewing, it had been laid upon the table. In that inglorious repose it remained; but no sooner had the Senate adjourned than the measure was brought forward and furnished materials for the "Treasury order." Legislative authority was supplied by executive authority. Mr. Crittenden wished to know if a few individuals were to determine such questions of policy involving the interests of the country far and wide. He thought they were questions for Congress. Mr. C. objected to *what* was done, and to the *manner* of doing it. The order should be rescinded, it encroached upon the power of the Senate, increased the power of the executive. There should be no discriminations made between purchasers of public lands in regard to payments, and no discriminations between debtors for public lands and all other public debtors. "Where is the right to demand payment in the terms of the 'Treasury order' found? No such right exists. Even if it be conceded that *Congress* has the right to make such, discriminations, has the executive such power? The order is illegal and beyond the power of the President. I thought at first," said he, "that there would be no great difficulty in transporting specie to the West from the great cities of the North, by means of *railroads*. I understand now, there is a much better scheme in operation. Suppose a man in the city of Washington intended to go West to purchase land; he would take a draft to the Washington Bank and present it, and would be asked what kind of money he wanted? '*I want specie.*' Then a little keg is taken out and *wheeled* from the bank to the Treasury. Of this fact I have been informed by a gentleman on whom I rely implicitly. Well, this same *little keg* has been so frequently *backwards and forwards* on the same errand that it has become ridiculous to the people in the Treasury Department. It had been rolled *to and fro* so often for a distance of only sixty yards, that upon calculation it had traveled eleven hundred and odd miles. The officers of the country have undertaken, like common porters, to transport money across the country. Pecuniary difficulties do now exist to an alarming degree. The honorable senator spoke lightly of a *panic*. A little starveling *panic* had the honor of dying by the hand of the senator, and is this all the comfort that a distressed community is to receive? The honorable gentleman loves this 'Treasury order,' and the pressure produced by it is to be called *a panic*. This term *panic* has been found useful when argument was wanting, and by this sort of senatorial cry of *panic* the country must be pacified. Does your statesmanship go no further than this? A little *panic* gotten up by the certifiers of General Jackson's enemies. The gentleman thinks there is a party in this country, whose origin he traces up with the skill of a political genealogist to the days of Alexander Hamilton, who *hate gold and silver.* I assure the gentleman I am am not one of the *haters of gold and silver.* These rascal counters I have a great affection for. The haters of gold and silver are not to be found among politicians. Those who wished the bank rechartered were the friends of gold and silver. Congress is not bound to think the order right, because the President thought it right." Mr. Crittenden could see no occasion for adopting the language of the senator from Missouri, indicating gratitude and *thanks* to the executive for causing this "Treasury order" to be issued; he would respect the executive in proportion to his fidelity and wisdom in the discharge of his duty. There is no necessity for treating him as a demigod. In 1838 Mr. Crittenden spoke against the new Treasury notes; he considered this only a new form of national debt. The people were deceived, while the government moved softly on, *fed fat* by the facility with which it supplied itself with means. He thought if it took ten millions of extraordinary supplies every six or eight months to keep the administration on its legs, the sooner they were recorded on the bills of mortality the better for the people. The cry of this magnificent administration was still "*Money! money!*" but for his part he would say, "Take physic pomp." He would not vote a dollar for the cry of *exigency*; he must have *light*, so as to excuse himself to his constituents.

(Hon. J. J. Crittenden to his son Robert.)

Senate-Chamber, January 3, 1837.

Dear Bob,—I am so much pleased with the number of your letters, and so anxious to encourage in you a disposition to write, that I shall not fail to do my part in the correspondence. No exercise of the mind seems to me better calculated to form the invaluable habit of accurate *thinking* and of *easy* and *proper expression* than the practice of reducing our thoughts to writing, and letter-writing is the most familiar and easy mode of doing this. But yet how few there are who ever attain to excellence in this most useful and important art! There is scarcely anything more indispensable to success in life. An educated man may be dressed in rags, his outward appearance may not indicate his character; but let him put his pen to paper, and his merits are instantly disclosed. Nothing is more sure to condemn a pretender than an ill-expressed, ill-spelt piece of writing. In the judgment of a man of taste such a production would condemn the author irretrievably. Let it be your ambition to learn early, and strive by steady practice to improve your style and manner of writing. Though certainly less in importance, even the *handwriting*, the mechanical part, is worthy of consideration,—sufficiently so, at least, to deserve your earnest attention. When I say to you that I know you have high capacity, I do not say it to flatter, but to make you sensible of obligations to employ and improve it. My hopes of you are high and proud, and no small portion of my future happiness or unhappiness depends on you,—on your fulfillment or disappointment of those hopes. I trust the recollection of all this will be cherished by you and stimulate you to every honorable exertion in pursuit of honorable distinction. Do not be satisfied with *mediocrity* either in your exertions or successes. Cherish also feelings of honor and kindness, and principles of truth and integrity. *Suffer anything* rather than utter a falsehood or do a dishonorable act. Cultivate and guard a sense of honor, and struggle, my boy, my dear boy, to be all that you know I wish you to be. Your mother, I think, wrote to you a few days since, and sent you some *newspapers*. I hope, however, that you will not give up much of your time to newspapers. You asked my permission some time since to give up the study of Greek. I am very unwilling, my son, that you should do this. It is a most beautiful language, and easy to be acquired after the first difficulties are overcome. In twelve months, and devoting only a part of each day to it, I had learned it so well that I read for a single lesson an entire book of Homer. I was then older than you are and better prepared for the study; but go on, you will find it easier than Latin, and will rejoice that you have learned it,—go to it with cheerfulness and spirit, determined to master it. I send you a five-dollar note, as you complain of being in want of *cash*. Your wants cannot be very extensive; probably this sum may do, if not, write again.

Your affectionate father,
J. J. CRITTENDEN.

ROBERT H. CRITTENDEN.

(Henry Clay to R. P. Letcher.)

WASHINGTON, January 17, 1837.

DEAR LETCHER,—I yesterday addressed a letter to the General Assembly, accepting the appointment which it has recently conferred upon me. I need not say to you, *who know me*, with what unaffected sincerity I desire to retire, that this decision has cost me the most painful sacrifices of feeling, and I shall hail with the greatest pleasure the occurrence of *circumstances* which will admit of my resignation with satisfaction to myself and without dishonor to myself. The Senate is no longer a place for a decent man. Yesterday Benton's *Expunging Resolutions* passed, 24 to 19; and the disgraceful work of drawing *black lines* around the Resolve of 1834 was executed at *nine o'clock at night*. The darkness of the *deed* and of *the* hour was well suited to each other.

You will observe that a bill for the relief of yourself and your friend Moore has passed the House. The latter part of it will be a *bitter pill*, which I do not know that I can swallow.

Your friend,

R. P. LETCHER.   HENRY CLAY.

(J. J. Crittenden to A. T. Burnley.)

WASHINGTON, March 8, 1837.

DEAR BURNLEY,—I have at last the pleasure of announcing to you the recognition of the independence of Texas by this government. Yesterday the Senate confirmed the nomination of M. La Branche, of New Orleans, as our representative to the government of Texas. The destiny of Texas may now be considered as settled, so far as relates to her national independence ; and I trust that independence will be fruitful of all the blessings of good government to her people. In the midst of this jubilee for the birth of a new nation, I cannot forget to rejoice a little at the brightened prospects of my friends, whose private interests have been connected with the fortunes of Texas. I wish for you an *estate* of a *million only*. That will be enough for a plain republican, and I hope you will be satisfied with it. General Jackson left the District yesterday on his way to the Hermitage. As it was said of Richard's *natural life*, so it may be said of Jackson's political life, that " nothing in his life became him like the leaving it." The Senate is yet in session. I *shall* leave here to-morrow morning. After the glorious news from Texas you will have no *taste* for anything I could write. I am in all haste and confusion, in perplexity and preparation, for my departure. For God's sake, be an adviser for George. Get acquainted with my old friend Archer, and make George known to him ; he is a noble fellow and true friend.

Your friend,

A. T. BURNLEY.   J. J. CRITTENDEN.

CHAPTER IX

Admission of Michigan—Purchasing Madison Papers—Letters.

IN 1837 Mr. Crittenden advocated the immediate admission of Michigan, and opposed the adoption of the preamble attached to the bill, because it did not tell the whole truth. He also spoke eloquently in favor of purchasing the *Madison papers*, stating his conviction that nowhere could more light be found as to the just interpretation of the powers of the Constitution. He declared that if the remains of Mr. Madison were known to exist, in the remotest corner of the world, he would vote for an expedition to bring back *dust so sacred* to this country; as to the copyright, so precious did he hold the manuscript that, if he possessed it, he would not sell it for thirty thousand dollars.

Mr. Crittenden was always in favor of the distribution bill; he did not advocate the collection of revenue for the purpose of distribution, but if a surplus of revenue occurred legitimately, he contended that it should *not* be thrown into the deposit banks, to excite the cupidity of those corporations, *but back* into the hands of the people; it should not be kept on hand to meet the *fancies* or *lusts* of those in power. He believed that virtue was the foundation of republican government, and that a lavish expenditure of public money had a direct tendency to undermine public virtue.

The executive had told the Senate that a surplus furnished means for speculation; and so strong had been *his* conviction of the evil, that, with a view to prevent it, he had assumed the responsibility of the "Treasury order." Mr. Crittenden remembered well when the President commenced his attack on the United States Bank. He had held out to the nation the golden prospect of a specie circulation. This was the cheap purchase of anticipated glory, and rang from Maine to Georgia; but when the promised time came, the objections were many and insurmountable. The argument used was, that this money would *corrupt* the people, and it must therefore be left in the hands of the *pure* and incorruptible men who now had the management of it. With regard to the fourth installment of the deposit bill, Mr. Crittenden contended that it must be paid, that the faith pledged by an act of Congress should not be so lightly broken. The government could get no available funds by means of this bill; so great was its tenacity for a metallic currency that it would not even acknowledge the money of the country. The States had entered into contracts, and incurred expenses, on the expectation of receiving this money. The States will gladly receive these funds which the government rejects; the people have full confidence in the banks and would take their paper. Mr. C. declared that the money *belonged* to the people, from whom the government had collected it. Notwithstanding the great distress of the people, and the lessons in economy read to them by the President, the only object of the administration seems to be to fill the Treasury.

In the early part of this year, Mr. Crittenden opposed the bill for the increase of the army. I believe the bill proposed to fix the minimum of the army at 12,500. The pretext for this was the danger of sudden irruptions of the Indians on the frontier. Mr. Crittenden said it was vain to affect a terror of this down-fallen race, trampled in the dust, broken in spirit, borne down by oppression and injustice; they were a poor, degraded race, living on the charity of the government. He opposed all increase of the army, or of the fortifications, considering them a useless burden on the nation. The bill formed part of a mischievous system of policy founded on principles repugnant to the genius of our country.

(J. J. Crittenden to Leslie Coombs.)

SENATE, March 20th, 1838.

MY DEAR SIR,—I received your letter relating to the claim of our friend Allen. The excitement which was created here by the *duel* was, for a time, great. The affair was to be blended with politics, and all the *little politicians* were set to work accordingly. The case was suited to their capacity, and, for a time, their success was great, and the excitement high. But a reaction is now, I am told, taking place with almost equal rapidity. A vile spirit of political persecution is seizing on the occasion to injure or destroy Graves, and for other party advantages. We believe that they will be disappointed in this, and that they can derive no advantage from it when the public has been made acquainted with the whole matter. I shall not now attempt to give you any history of the affair. Graves acted from a sense of honor. If he went a step too far, it was from extreme sensibility which he felt as a Kentucky representative. He worked to *avoid* every possibility of reproach upon his honor and his gallantry at the hazard of every peril. You know how a Kentuckian feels when at a distance from home. The honor of *his State* is in *his hands,*—so *he* thinks and feels,—and the sentiment, though it may sometimes err, is worthy of encouragement. You will have learned all the circumstances before this reaches you, and will, I hope, be prepared to think favorably of Graves's case. Depend on it, he is a pure-minded, noble-hearted fellow, and as brave as Julius Cæsar. He ought to have *your sympathies.* I have no room for comment. The Kentucky blood here is all *warm* toward Graves. From the administration presses the vilest abuse is poured out on *him,* and on *Wise* particularly. We *hoped* to hear a somewhat different note from our Kentucky papers, but, really, their style has been almost as damning, by its faint, puny, stinted sort of defense. I appeal to you for Graves. Look to this subject, and give the proper *tone* to his vindication in our papers in your town, if it meets the approbation of your judgment.

Your friend,

Leslie L. Coombs.   John J. Crittenden.

In 1838 Mr. Calhoun's resolutions, authorizing anti-slavery documents to be taken from the Southern mails, were under discussion. Mr. Crittenden denounced them as vague abstractions, calculated to produce agitation, fine-spun theories, upon which no two men could agree. The mover of the resolutions was continually uttering the *trite cry* of danger to the *Union,* and declaring that, if he is not followed in this movement, the Union will be destroyed. Mr. C. thought the surest way to break up the Union would be to follow that gentleman in his violent course. Such language might be only a polite method of carrying, by wild alarm, every trembling vote in his train. "Has the South no friends but the gentleman and *his little party?* Is no other banner displayed, under which the friends of the South can range themselves, but the tattered, shattered flag of this little States Rights party?" Mr. Crittenden thought himself a States Rights man, but he could not follow Mr. Calhoun in his vagaries ; could not go along with him in his *mental terrors.* Mr. Crittenden did not think the language of the resolutions decorous. The sovereign States are the sovereign elements of this Union. He thought a State had a right to petition.

In 1838 the General Assembly of Connecticut instructed their representatives, Mr. Miles and Mr. Smith, to vote against the sub-treasury bill. These representatives denounced the proceedings of their legislature as dishonorable. Mr. Crittenden declared that he did not profess to be under the obligation of unlimited and passive obedience; *but* he protested against that sort of language held by the senator against his State ; he was sorry to see the spirit with which gentlemen submitted to their political *retirement.* In fact, he thought they had gone beyond their depths in a sea of glory. When they had conned their lesson in the school of adversity, they might, *perhaps*, be brought to their senses, and be made useful members of society in their proper places.

In 1838 Mr. Crittenden introduced a bill to prevent the interference of Federal officers in elections. Some time after he expressed a hope that an early period might be allowed him for its discussion. He desired to bring to the notice of the Senate the sophistries by which this *greatest vice* in our system was defended.

There was a great outcry against this bill of Mr. Crittenden. It was called the *gag-law.* In 1840 a great Southwestern convention was held in Nashville, which Mr. Crittenden attended, and at which he made a speech, which was said to be one of his most masterly efforts. The legislature of Tennessee instructed her representatives to vote against this bill; and Hugh Dawson White, senator from Tennessee, felt that he could not conscientiously obey these instructions, and resigned. The allusion which Mr. C. made in his speech at the convention to that scene in the Senate, and Mr. White's death, which soon followed, is most touching.

(J. J. Crittenden to his wife Maria K. Crittenden.)

SENATE, February 28, 1839.

MY DEAREST WIFE,—On Sunday next, three days from this time, I shall leave here on my return to you. Sunday week at furthest, I hope to be with you. I count the days now with as much impatience as I did months at the beginning of the session. My heart almost leaps forward to meet and embrace you.

My highest wish is to find you full of health and happiness, and arrayed in all those smiles which you know I have so long admired. I was engaged almost all day long yesterday in the Senate, and I feel a little worsted by it to-day. Judge Underwood was married last night to Miss Cox, of Georgetown. The Kentucky delegation were at the wedding. Farewell, my dearest wife; kiss our children for me.

J. J. CRITTENDEN.

Mrs. MARIA K. CRITTENDEN.

(J. J. Crittenden to A. T. Burnley.)

April 22, 1839.

DEAR BURNLEY,—I inclose you letters to Webster and Sargeant. With your skill and address, I think you may engage those gentlemen in your cause. There is something stirring to generous minds in the idea of patronizing and aiding *young nations*, and of having these things remembered. Your *gentle suggestion* of the grateful sentiments with which Texas would remember *such* assistance would not be without *some effect*. But it is not for me to make *such suggestions* to an *old diplomatist*.

I shall not see you again, I suppose, till your return from Europe.

Farewell, then, and "may all good fortune attend you" by sea and land, and bring you back to your home and friends, *speedily*, in health, and crowned with success and wealth.

Your friend,

To A. T. BURNLEY.   J. J. CRITTENDEN.

(Daniel Webster to J. J. Crittenden.)

LONDON, July 31, 1839.

MY DEAR SIR,—I received yesterday your letter by Mr. Burnley, whom I was glad to see, and to whom it will give me pleasure to render any service in my power. When I parted with you, I hardly supposed I should ever write to you from London. We have been here now nearly two months, and have been occupied with seeing and hearing. Political excitement, and the state of parties here, made it rather an interesting period. I have attended the debates a good deal, especially on important occasions. Some of their ablest men are far from being fluent speakers. In fact, they hold in no high repute the mere faculty of ready speaking, at least not so high as it is held in other places. They are universally men of business; they have not *six-and-twenty* other legislative bodies to take part of the law-making of the country off their hands; and where there is so much to be *done*, it is indispensable that less should be *said*. Their debates, therefore, are often little more than conversations across the table, and they usually abide by the good rule of carrying the measure under consideration *one step*, whenever it is taken up, without adjourning the debate. This rule, of course, gives way on questions of great interest. I see no prospect of any immediate change of administration. The minority acknowledges itself to be weak in the number of its supporters in Parliament; but their opponents, if they should come into power, would hardly be stronger, without a dissolution and a new election. It is thought that, upon the whole, the conservative interest is gaining ground in the country, especially in England. Still, the leaders of the party feel very little inclined, I think, to be eager for the possession of power. Office here is now *no sinecure*. Business matters have been in a bad state, and money remains quite scarce; but *cotton* has risen a little, and some think the *worst* is over. I expect to hear bad news from the United States. I fear greatly for many of the banks. Nothing can be done with the securities of our States, nor can anything be done with them on the Continent, though money is plenty in *France* and *Holland*. My dear friend, I fear it will be very many years before American credit shall be restored to the state it was in at the time the late administration began its experiments on the country.

My wife and daughter are, of course, much pleased with what is to be seen in London, and Julia was greatly grieved to hear that Cornelia was so near coming the voyage hither and afterwards *gave it up*. The weather is hot; if no change shall come soon, the wheat crop will be in danger.

I am, dear sir, with true regard,

Your friend and obedient servant,

DANIEL WEBSTER.

Mr. CRITTENDEN.

(General W. H. Harrison to J. J. Crittenden.)

NORTH BEND, November 7, 1839.

MY DEAR SIR,—My intimate friend (for forty-four years) Judge Burnet, of Cincinnati, was appointed with Judge Pease by our State Convention as delegates (at large) last winter. Pease died some weeks ago. I saw Burnet yesterday; he is in good health, and is preparing to attend at Harrisburg on the 4th proximo. The delegate from this district will be chosen on the day after to-morrow. None but an intimate and zealous friend of mine will receive the appointment. Several are mentioned, but I think Colonel N. G. Pendleton will be chosen. Both B. and P. have seen your letter of the 25th, from Philadelphia, as have two other friends who have been spoken of as the district delegate. Burnet (and whichever of my other friends may go with him) will endeavor to see you and consult with you as they go to Harrisburg. They will explain to you my objections to the use you suggest of certain letters in my possession. The policy pointed out by the present state of the contest appears to me to be that of conciliation; for I think that the friends of Clay, in the Convention, will be convinced that he cannot obtain the votes of either Illinois, Indiana, or Ohio, and that I can get them all. There never was a time when I could not beat V. B. in either of the two last, and I assure you that I am (in the latter particularly) daily gaining strength. There are many, very many heretofore warm partisans of the administration who have declared their determination to vote for me if I should be the candidate. Some find an apology in the principle of " rotation in office," and that they cannot see any difference in my pretensions and those of Jackson. Others begin to see something wrong in the conduct of affairs, and are willing to give their votes to another candidate than the incumbent, provided " he has always been on the side of the people." This they believe of me, but obstinately persist in refusing to accord to Mr. Clay in despite of facts the most undeniable.

Some of my friends are desirous that I should place, in some shape or other, with a view to its being laid before the people, my views of the " present desperate state of the country, and my opinions as to the necessity of a thorough reform." But I do not agree with them as to the necessity or even the propriety of such a course.

It appears to me that no one should be supported for the Presidency of the United States who cannot give a better guarantee for the correctness and fidelity of his conduct than that of opinions given and pledges made during the pendency of the contest which was to decide on his pretensions. How many instances can be adduced of the fulfillment of engagements made under such circumstances when there was strong temptation to violate them! What, then, it may be asked, is the security of a free people in conferring power upon those who are to administer their affairs? I answer that an effectual remedy is only to be found by limiting the powers granted to a measure which shall be only equal to the proper discharge of the duties required to be performed, and even those for as short a period as possible. I am satisfied that this general principle does not meet the exigency now to be provided for, because the powers annexed to the office of President are greater than are necessary for the chief magistrate of a republic to possess, and the reduction of them to the proper standard not immediately in the power of the people. Indeed, the reduction of the unnecessary and dangerous powers depends upon the selection of the President, as the prerogatives conferred upon him by the Constitution, or claimed to have been conferred, are such as totally to preclude any hope of reform but with his consent. The question, then, recurs, What guarantee, under such circumstances, can be given to the people that their confidence will not be betrayed, and that the measures so necessary not only for their prosperity, but for the preservation of the republican principles of the government, will not be thwarted by the candidate whom they may select? The answer seems to me to be obvious. Since it appears from the records of history, confirmed indeed by our own experience, that pledges given by candidates for high trusts are not to be relied upon, the people must look for security to a strict scrutiny of the character of those who are presented for their choice. Have they been before intrusted with power? In what manner was it exercised? Was it used with a single eye to the advantage of those for whose benefit it was given? Was there any manifestation of a desire to increase it beyond the limits which the common-sense meaning of the grant which conferred it would authorize? Any selfishness discoverable amidst the general display of magnanimity and devotion to the public good? There is one candidate for whom I would readily vouch for his passing through such an ordeal without the slightest imputation upon his honor or patriotism. I allude to Henry Clay. During a large portion of his public life I was in his confidence, and I am perfectly sure that the interest and happiness of his country were the objects to which his great talents were devoted. General Scott I only know as an honorable man, a gallant and able officer, and a sterling patriot. Of his political opinions I know nothing.

As I am myself the only other candidate of the opposition, I must leave it to the people to determine the character of my conduct whilst I was in their service. For many years I filled offices of no inconsiderable importance, and the powers with which I was often clothed great almost beyond example in our country, and for that reason greatly enhancing the obligation to a faithful discharge of the duties they imposed. To the crime against the people a contrary course of conduct would have superadded that of bringing disgrace upon the administrations of Jefferson and Madison,—those pure patriots by whom I was patronized and trusted. If, under circumstances such as these, I could in a single instance have departed from that course of conduct which marks an upright and faithful public servant, I am unworthy of the further confidence of my fellow-citizens. The deep stake they have at issue in the election of a President for the next term, the important consequences which are to flow, for good or for evil, from the way in which the contest may be decided, create an obligation upon the part of the people greater than at any former period strictly to scrutinize the conduct of those submitted to their choice, when in the exercise of power heretofore conferred. To bring them to the test of the Scripture parable, whether having been "faithful over a few things" they may be safely trusted "to rule over many things."

It is in no spirit of arrogance that I challenge such an investigation in relation to myself. I cannot hope that in the discharge of the various and complicated duties which have been committed to me (and which, in the opinion of the patriotic Shelby, were at one period "greater than he had ever known imposed upon one individual") that it would not be found that I have committed errors. I am too conscious of my own imperfections to entertain any such idea. My confidence rests solely upon my intentions to do right, and to carry out in practice those democratic republican principles, in the theory of which I had from early youth been trained. I trust that an investigation would clearly show that, instead of endeavoring to enlarge the great powers which as governor of Indiana I possessed, I sedulously sought for opportunities to place them in the hands of the people.

I have said above that I considered pledges given by a candidate for the Presidency as to what he would or would not do, unnecessary and improper. I have endeavored to show that they were "unnecessary;" and I think, by reference to the opinions I have given in my letters to Mr. Sherrard Williams and Mr. H. Denny in relation to the exercise of the veto power by the President, that it would be highly improper in one who limits the President's power as I have done, to pledge himself to any particular course. Give any other construction to the Constitution than that which I have given in those letters, and it seems to me that the whole character of the government would be changed, and that the President, by the union of the direct and indirect means which I have pointed out, would become as effectually the legislator of the country as is the autocrat of the Russias. The veto power was evidently given to guard the Constitution and to prevent the effects of a too hasty legislation. I conceive, that even in cases of doubtful construction of the Constitution, the opinions of the President must yield to the deliberately expressed wishes of the American people. But, again, let the precedent already set become established, and the Presidency every fourth year will be at auction, as was the Roman empire upon the death of Pertinax. The leaders of the different interests and parties will be the bidders, and the high prize will be knocked off to the highest offer, *i.e.* to the party that can bring most strength to the aspirant, although the interests and perhaps the constitutional rights of the weaker party may be sacrificed by the discharge of the debt. What a field for intrigue will be here opened,—what a school for giving the last polish to political hypocrites! Further, if the precedent of pledges is once established, it would render abortive the now so generally favored opinion of confining the presidential service to a single term. Will the man who pledges himself to support the efforts of a party in the accomplishment of any particular object hesitate to pledge himself also to aid with his influence the succession of his allies to the seat of power, and thus perpetuate the injustice by which his own elevation was effected?

It will not, I hope, be considered by what I have said above that I am opposed to every effort being made by the people perfectly to understand the political opinions of a candidate for the Presidency, as far as it relates to the principles of the Constitution and the fundamental principles upon which it is founded. No one should be supported for the Presidency of whose sentiments in relation to them there hangs the slightest shadow of doubt, of whom it was not believed that having received the highest evidence of favor and confidence which his fellow-citizens could bestow, that it would be the dearest wish of his heart, the constant object of his thoughts, and that upon which all his official influence would be devoted to restore the government to the purity in which it came from the hands of Jefferson, Madison, and Monroe.

In the letters to Mr. Williams and Mr. Denny above referred to, I have endeavored to give my opinion of the principles of our government in a manner not to be misunderstood. But I refuse to pledge myself in advance, as to the application of these principles to particular cases or to the views of any particular party; because by so doing I should usurp upon the privileges of the legislative branch of the government, of which the President, notwithstanding his veto power, constitutes no part. And because, from my construction of the Constitution, a President of the United States is chosen, not for the purpose of carrying into effect his own political views, but those of the people of the United States declared by themselves or their more immediate representatives.

I am, dear sir, yours truly,

W. H. HARRISON.

(J. J. Crittenden to his wife Maria.)

WASHINGTON, January 2, 1840.

MY DEAREST MARIA,—A happy New Year to you! and all
the blessings *due* to the tenderest and best of wives! Oh, what
a feast of the heart it would have been could I have transported
myself suddenly home and met the joys of the season with my
wife and children in my arms and on my knees! It is some
enjoyment to think of this. And now again I ask you when
will the weather permit you to start for Washington? This is
the most interesting point for me. I was at the President's
yesterday, and at night at the theatre for the first time. There
was as usual a great assemblage of all sorts of people and all
sorts of dress at the President's. I met there with Mrs. Pope,
of Louisville (formerly Miss Preston), and acted as her gallant
during the evening. She is clever, and I shall like her; her being
a Kentuckian is enough to secure all my predilections. I went
to the theatre to see Vandenhoff and his *more celebrated daughter*,
particularly the latter, of whose beauty and talent I had heard
so much; and I think she deserves it all. She is unquestionably
the finest actress I ever saw. Without offense to your *Pres-
byterianism*, I wish you could have enjoyed it all.

I have not heard from you for several weeks, and begin to
be out of temper with the *postmasters.*

Farewell, my dearest wife. My love to all.

J. J. CRITTENDEN.

(J. J. Crittenden to his wife Maria.)

SENATE, January 8, 1840.

MY DEAREST WIFE,—I have not a word to write, and yet I
must write to you. It is a sort of aliment that my nature seems
to require, and as without any cause that I am conscious of, I
feel rather gloomy and despondent, I naturally turn to you for
relief. I should indeed feel that "the world was a waste," and
bore neither fruit nor flowers for me without you. Get well
and come on to me as soon as possible, but do not expose yourself too much to the inclemency of the weather.

Kiss our little boys for me, and believe that I love you with
all my heart.

J. J. CRITTENDEN.

(R. P. Letcher to J. J. Crittenden.)

FRANKFORT, April 2, 1840.

DEAR CRITTENDEN,—My political speculations are not worth
a copper cent! I have never believed that Seward would be
the candidate of the Black party, or that Douglas would be
the choice of the Democrats; but I confess your letter almost

convinced me that my views were erroneous. If, as you suppose, it is distinctly understood, upon the meeting of the Charleston Convention, that Seward will be selected at Chicago, then
I think Douglas will be the nominee, upon the calculation that
he will be able to carry Illinois and Indiana. I have had a talk
with Guthrie; he was confident of obtaining the nomination at
Charleston. I told him, *frankly*, he had not the ghost of a
chance. I believe *now* he is of my opinion. The friends of
Breckenridge *here* and at Lexington seem to be confident that
he will be the lucky man. *I* don't believe *that*. We hear
Buchanan has taken him up; I doubt if he will *be true* to
him. I know he hates him, not perhaps as much as he hates
Douglas. I have read B.'s plea in abatement, protesting against
an inquiry into his official conduct. The plea is, I think, well
drawn and adroit, but the points of objection appear to me indefensible. You are right to have nothing to do with a nomination. Let Hunt or Everett, or somebody, take the place. Tom
Clay says if his presence is necessary at the Baltimore Convention to vindicate you, he will go on at once. Coombs begged
himself in as a delegate to the exclusion of Tom. I see no
fun whatever. Go to Burnley's and talk to him, then to the
bank, then back to Burnley's, then home, read, lay down, get
up, and do the same thing, take medicine, and have myself
rubbed like a race-horse. Come home! The *queen* is thinking
of what she will have for breakfast the day you get home. One
thing I know, there will be a quart of rich cream, and I sha'n't
get a drop of it. I am glad Mrs. Crittenden does not *go out* in
Washington; she will be better prepared for a "*poor man's
breakfast.*"

Your sincere friend,

J. J. CRITTENDEN.　　　　　　　　　　　　R. P. LETCHER.

(J. J. Crittenden to Orlando Brown.)

SENATE, April 30, 1840.

DEAR ORLANDO,—Our intelligence from Virginia enables me
now, as all here think, to say to you that the Whigs or Harrison men have carried that State by the election of a majority
of the legislature and with a majority of the popular vote. The
first fruits of this will be two senators from that State and then
its electoral vote for Harrison. This latter consequence, however, is our inference. The administration men say there will
be a *reaction* in Virginia, and that they will carry the State then
by a large majority. And it is upon such dreams and visions
they feed their sickly hopes. Nothing can exceed the confidence of the friends of Harrison. That confidence generates
and sustains a corresponding zeal, and as far as there can be

any certainty in respect to future political events, it seems to me that his election is *certain*, and by a very great majority. The nation is *now* for him. The current of events is in his favor, and the same great causes that have produced that current will continue to give it increased rapidity and force. The abuse lavished on Harrison is like oil thrown on the fire, and will endanger or consume the incendiary only. The popular feeling breaks forth in favor of Harrison where it was least expected, and makes glad places that were considered as "waste." Georgia, notwithstanding all efforts to the contrary, has, of a sudden and as by some general and spontaneous impulse, raised a mighty shout for him, and seems like all the other States in her zealous support of him. I speak from information which I consider the very best and most indubitable when I say to you that I believe Georgia is just as certain for Harrison as any State in the Union. Though the leaders of the administration party here affect the language of confidence, it is evident that their ranks are wavering with fear and alarm, and that they can scarcely withstand the tone of courage and confidence that constantly resounds from the host of their adversaries.

They are, in effect, already dismayed and beaten. And if the friends of Harrison can only resist the efforts that will be made to divert and deaden public sentiment, and will only preserve their present patriotic spirit, their opponents will not only be beaten, but utterly routed,—" horse, foot, and dragoons."

The presidential question absorbs everything else, and but little is doing, or will be done, in Congress at the present session, though the session will, in all probability, be a long one.

In the great struggle for political deliverance that is now in progress, I hope that old Kentucky will not be behind the foremost. Her place is in the front, and in that *post* of patriotism and honor I had rather see her trodden down than make one disgraceful step from it.

Who is our candidate for our county? You must not surrender Franklin at this crisis. We must have a candidate, and one that can be elected.

While I write you, the first number of the *Campaign* is laid on my table. I hail it, and that I may pay my respects to the stranger, must conclude my letter. I don't understand that you have yet erected at Frankfort a "log cabin." This ought to be attended to; it is all the rage on this side the mountains, and the common impression is that neither Grecian nor Roman architecture ever constructed anything superior to the " Log Cabin." My best respects to your wife, and kindest remembrance to all our townsmen and friends. Write to me.

Your friend,

O. Brown, Esq.   J. J. Crittenden.

CHAPTER X.

1840.

THE great Southwestern Convention met on the 17th of August, 1840, at Nashville, and, after adopting certain resolutions, it was addressed by Mr. Crittenden. I am persuaded that no mortal man ever made a greater impression upon a popular assembly. Never before did I see such a multitudinous audience tremble under the power of eloquence, never were the deep fountains of my emotions so stirred. Peal after peal followed, blow after blow fell with merciless power, sarcasm after sarcasm, and coruscations of wit delighted the vast assembly. Mr. Crittenden's eye flashed, now with scorn, now with other emotions. He has left behind him a name which time only can obscure.

I feel it would be murder in the first degree to attempt a description of this masterly display of oratory. No pen can truly write out that speech, no tongue can truly describe it. Great as is the reputation of its author as a statesman and an orator, his warmest admirers declare that they never heard him on any occasion make a better speech, more eloquent, more appropriate. I heard conspicuous Van Buren men proclaim that it was the greatest speech they had ever listened to.

The style and manner of the distinguished statesman cannot be spread upon paper: an outline only of the principal points he dwelt upon will be attempted.

Mr. Crittenden began by expressing a wish that he could feel himself worthy to address such an audience, feel himself able to entertain so vast a multitude on so great an occasion:

Fellow-Citizens,—We can all do something for a great cause. Let no man say he can do nothing, but rather let him gird on his armor, take one step forward, and he will find himself engaged in the struggle of the people against power and oppression. Let him look at the great and critical measures which are involved in this contest. Let him reflect upon the sad, the fatal consequences which will be visited upon the people if the executive should triumph; let him calmly survey this overshadowing power which the executive is contending for; let him reflect that the great issue is liberty against oppression, the people against the office holders,—then let him prepare for the contest and say, he *can* and *will* do something in the conflict.

Fellow-citizens, every man knows that the office holder feels bound to electioneer for the President. In order to hold his place he must give up his independence as a freeman, submit to the requirements of his master the executive,—he knows that this is one of the cardinal principles of Van Buren democracy. As my illustrious colleague truly observed yesterday, all the qualifications an applicant may possess will avail him nothing. The questions put by, or in behalf of, Martin Van Buren are not, Is he honest? Is he capable? Will he support the Constitution? Oh, no, fellow-citizens, these old-fashioned questions, recognized by Jefferson's democracy, have been *superseded* by another catechism which was somewhat after this fashion: What has he done for our party? Who has he bullied at the polls? Has he used means to mislead the people and entice them to our support? Have the people rejected him? Let him establish these claims, and his reward is sure. All who are willing to come under this Russian serfdom and to give up the breath of freemen are qualified for office under Martin Van Buren. All applicants who have been thus meanly willing to submit to such terms have been rewarded with office.

But do such officers answer the purpose of the people, to whom indeed all the offices belong? Are their best interests faithfully watched and guarded by such servants? Is the money of the people faithfully guarded? No, fellow-citizens, no! out of sixty-seven land officers, sixty-three have proved to be defaulters. What do the people think of this? What is its moral tendency? What the moral effects of such a state of things? Who does not see that it is Mr. Van Buren's object so to vitiate, to corrupt the public mind that he may appoint the most desperate and despicable politicians to office, who will stop at nothing in assisting him in the accomplishment of his grand scheme of subjecting this great people to his arbitrary rule for another term? I do not believe Mr. Van Buren possesses either the head or the heart to be the President of this proud and independent nation. He was nurtured in the Albany

Regency school of politics; he has not the capacity or sensibility to act or feel like a Western politician. Van Buren is a *free-trader* in politics, buying where he can purchase cheapest, and selling where he can command the highest price,—he was *for the war*, and he was *against the war*. Should the Federalist say to him, " Mr. Van Buren, we can support no man who advocated the last war, which ruined our commerce and brought our country so deeply in debt," how readily would he reply, Gentlemen, who took more decided ground against that *war* than I did? Madison I opposed, and gave my hearty support to Clinton, your own favorite candidate. On the other hand, should the Republicans approach him, and say, " We can support no man who did not advocate the last war," how promptly he would assure them that he did support it, and point to his reports and speeches in its favor made after Madison's re-election, after the war had become popular. Now, take the subject of abolition. Should leading Abolitionists tell Mr. Van Buren that they would like to vote and use their influence for him if they could only have some evidences that he would help to carry out their principles, who could furnish them with stronger and more enduring proofs than Mr. Van Buren of his firm attachment to their cause? How gravely, with what sincerity, he would point to his vote instructing the New York senators upon the Missouri question; his vote in the New York Convention in favor of extending the right of suffrage to negroes; to his vote in Congress to restrict slavery in Florida; to his declaration, for the public, that Congress has the constitutional power to abolish slavery any day in the District of Columbia, and to his recent rescript, that he saw nothing of the admission of negro testimony in court against a gallant officer of the navy that called for his interference!

On the other hand, should the Anti-Abolitionists say to him, " Mr. Van Buren, what guarantee will you give us that if we vote for you, you will not favor the scheme of these infamous fanatics?" how quickly would he refer them to his repeated declarations that he would apply the veto to any bill having for its object the abolition of slavery in the District of Columbia! Upon the subject of internal improvements he is as well prepared. To one party he points to his vote to establish toll-gates upon the Great Cumberland Road,—such was his *love*, his *zeal*, for internal improvements! He calls attention also to his approval of numerous other bills making great appropriations for works of that nature.

To the opposing party, he will avow that he is against internal improvements by the general government, and point with exultation to the complaints of the friends of the great national road, that he asked for no appropriations for it in his last table of estimates and expenditures.

On the subject of Federalism he pursues the same policy. To the Federalists, he can turn to his evident support of Rufus King, their great champion, and exhibit the book he wrote in his favor. To the Republicans, he can point to his support of Daniel D. Tompkins. Now, am I not justified in calling Mr. Van Buren a free-trader in politics? What has he ever done to advance the true interests of his country, or promote its prosperity? There can be but one answer,—he has done nothing! If old Plutarch were to burst from his tomb and be called upon to record the services he has rendered to his country, what a dread blank the old historian would be compelled to present to the world! What reasons have the people to advance such a man to the highest office in their gift? Repeat his name to his countrymen: does it fill the heart with grateful emotion? No! but at the name of Washington, or even Jackson, and of Harrison men's souls are moved; but sound the name of Van Buren and the hearts of men are as cold as a tombstone, or even as cold as Van Buren himself. His administration has been, thus far, a series of unprovoked wrongs and violated pledges.

Look at the ruined currency, the depreciated paper now floating over the country, the only currency almost in circulation. For his country, Mr. Van Buren has done nothing; for the office holders he has done much! He has given them a currency far above that of the people, and he had reduced the wages of the laborer to enhance the salaries of the office holders. When I see office holders busying themselves in elections, I think of the declaration of my friend Grundy, who said, "They were voting for their bread." They are the Prætorian bands of the executive; they come all "drilled, armed, and paid into the contest," while the people, whom they oppose, are only armed with the republican principles instilled in their minds by their fathers.

Here the great orator drew a striking parallel between the President's army of office holders and the Prætorian bands of Rome, and mirrored forth the fatal consequences that would inevitably ensue if our people did not fully rouse themselves and put the usurper down. He spoke of England's democracy; how much it had at one time accomplished by resolving to submit no longer to the arrogance and insufferable dictation of the throne. He took a glance at our own country, when Jefferson was elected Vice-President, and told what the great Republican promised if the people elected him President,—that he would effectually put a stop to the interference of office holders in elections. This evil, even at that early day, was beginning to alarm the Republicans of the country.

Jefferson was elected, and fulfilled his promise. Harrison now gives a similar pledge, which he will surely fulfill. Seeing that no check in that direction was to be expected from the present President, Mr. Van Buren, he had introduced a bill, a year or two ago, into the Senate, to bring about again what Mr. Jefferson effected, but which Mr. Van Buren opposed, and, indeed, he was constantly seeking to aggravate the offense complained of. His bill was designed to secure the freedom of elections against the interference and dictations of office holders. It left them free to vote as they pleased, and made them independent of the executive. Under this bill they were not compelled, in order to retain their places, to electioneer for the President. They were filling the people's offices, and ought not to be required by the executive to neglect their legitimate duties in order to electioneer for him. In selecting a judge of a court the main object ought surely to be to obtain one who will faithfully discharge the duties of his station, biased by none, uncontrolled by any superior. This bill had been most grossly misrepresented. It had been called a *"gag-law"* by those who were really attempting to gag all office holders, closing their lips, not allowing them to say one word against the powers that be, however corrupt and dishonest they might have found them. Instead of gagging them, the bill would relieve them from that state of surveillance and make them independent; restoring to them the liberty to vote for whom they pleased. Mr. Crittenden said, "this was the object he had in view in introducing his bill." He referred to Benton's bill to restrict executive patronage, introduced in 1826, and stated some of its arguments and predictions. Those predictions had been verified. The President says to his office holders, "Electioneer for me and secure my re-election, and I will keep you in office." Benton's prediction has been fully realized. This worst species of venality and corruption has come upon us. His bill was intended to put a stop to it. He loved freedom of speech, partly, perhaps, because he used it so freely. When his bill came before the Senate for action, and Benton opposed it, he referred him to his own bill and predictions of 1826. When Mr. Buchanan opposed it, he referred him to what he had said on a former occasion against the interference of office holders in elections. He read to the Pennsylvania senator, who was taking notes to reply, his own words. The senator dropped his pen and stood aghast. Three days after he got himself prepared with a defense which he pronounced before the Senate. But this was not enough, though Mr. Buchanan was an old Federalist and was presumed to be well acquainted with the best method of defending Federal and opposing Jeffersonian Republican doctrines. Mr. Hall, of New Jersey, another old Federalist, stepped forward to the rescue and framed a report, which not only countenanced the office holders in all their indecent interference in elections, but absolutely enjoined it upon them as one of their duties. This report was adopted by the administration, and thirty thousand copies were ordered to be printed and circulated. He said he thought the number should be a hundred thousand, so that every office holder could have a copy of his orders. "For himself," Mr. Crittenden said, "his motives were pure in offering that bill." He was proud of it, and no name its revilers could give it would make him ashamed of it. He knew to what use the bill had been turned by demagogues in Tennessee to effect the object which was accomplished last year; he knew it had been used against the senators of this State (Tennessee) who voted with him for its passage. They, like himself, voted for it, wishing to effect what Jefferson had the " honesty to order done" without the aid of legislation, and it gave him pleasure to have it in his power to proclaim that, had his colleague, Mr. Clay, been present when the vote was taken, he, too, would have given it his support. By means of that bill the Senate had been deprived of the services of the State of Tennessee, and the whole country had been deprived of the valuable services of his distinguished friend, Mr. Forster, now presiding over the deliberations of this Convention. But justice will be done him, and that, too, at no remote day.

Fellow-Citizens, said Mr. Crittenden, I wish that I could stop here. I wish I could say that no other statesman but my honorable and esteemed friend Forster had been sacrificed by means of that bill, and the manner in which it was grossly per-verted and misrepresented. Some of your banners floating over us this day tell me, tell us all, of his departed colleague, Hugh Lawson White. It was my good fortune to know that venerable patriot well, to possess his full confidence. He was a good, honest, upright, and sincere man,—as sternly honest as Cato, as scrupulously just as Aristides! Full well do I remember that most solemn and imposing scene in the senate-chamber, on the Instructing Resolutions, when he took his leave, forever, of that body, of which he had been a bright ornament for many, many years. Hugh Lawson White stood erect, with his old gray locks floating over his shoulders, and calmly, but sternly, performed his duty. All was hushed and still as death; it was a scene which filled the beholder with awe and veneration. When on the point of leaving Washington to return home, I strove to detain him. I sought him for that purpose, and found him, not in his carriage, but on *his horse*. I warned him that the winter was rude and cold, the winds bleak, the snows deep and treacherous. I implored him not to depart at such an inclement season. His reply—so simple, so characteristic—I shall never, never forget: " Tennessee recalls me; I must go." No human power would have swayed him; he loved and honored his State, and when she spoke he was ever ready to obey. He did return at her call, and now lies buried beneath the green sod in her eastern mountains. He died a martyr to that bill which the partisans of the administration so loudly and vehemently condemned. Well, let them denounce it,—Jefferson proclaimed it, Harrison proclaims it, Clay is for it, and White died a martyr to it.

Mr. Crittenden said that the terms he applied to Mr. Van Buren and his leading partisans he did not apply to the great body of the party, that from one cause or other suffers itself to be led by them:

Mr. Van Buren calls himself a Democrat. I, said Mr. Crittenden, call myself a Democrat. He maintains that it is just and right to possess and wield the power he claims; I avow it is unjust and wrong. He pretends that his measures are Republican; I contend that they are ultra Federal. He usurps the name of Republican; by this he hopes to carry out his ultra Federal doctrines, and get his office holders to deceive the people into the belief that he is a Republican, a pure Democrat. Martin Van Buren a pure Democrat! Great God, what a pedigree for Democrats to refer to hereafter! By creeping about on his hands and knees he has got the start of the Democracy. Are my hearers willing to confide in such a man—

in such a President? He wished "to extenuate nothing, to set down naught in malice." If he had not painted Mr. Van Buren's character fairly, he wished his hearers to add what they could in his favor, and then, for the sake of comparison, place him by the side of Harrison; then choose, shall it be this cologned and whiskered Democrat, or the plain, clear-headed, substantial old resident of the West? General Harrison is an honest man; the testimony of the numerous old soldiers guaranteed this; he knew himself something of Harrison in the field, but the testimony of others proved enough. Mr. Crittenden referred to the many offices Harrison had filled, by means of which he could have enriched himself, lived in a costly mansion, and, like Van Buren, drank wines from the south side of Madeira. General Harrison was content to perform his public duties faithfully, then retire to his farm, and live by its cultivation, dwelling in his plain, old-fashioned house. Will you have such a man for your President? Now, I will tell you what old Van Buren and his advisers at Washington are probably thinking: "Oh, well," say they, "these little transient excitements, conventions, etc. of the Whigs are foolish affairs; they will die out by-and-by, and all will go smoothly for us."

Their long enjoyment of public office and continued plunder of public money makes them hopeful.

They say to us, "Oh, you have begun too soon, you'll get tired before November." Thus power was flattering itself; but he could tell the spoiler that the zeal and enthusiasm now in action throughout this broad land will not subside till the Goths are driven from Rome and honest men put in their places. The deep-seated feeling which we now see is not ephemeral. A spark of the glorious old Revolution is blazing! it is not dying out! It burned seven years in darkness and storm, and it will burn on now, and blaze higher and hotter, until freedom shall again trample upon oppression.

The spirit of liberty was aroused everywhere throughout this vast country; he had seen it up in the North. The aurora borealis was nothing to it. He had seen the people with uplifted hands pledging themselves not to lay down their arms till the nation is restored to her just rights.

Mr. C. reminded his hearers of Commodore Hull's address to his men on board the Constitution, just before going into action with the Guerriere. After picturing to them the consequences of defeat, he said:

"*You can conquer* if you will. Will you do it?" I tell you, in the language of the great Hull, You can conquer if you will. Will you do it? Do not let the predictions of the President and his office holders prove true.

Mr. C. portrayed with thrilling effect the consequences of defeat, and declared that it would be better that we should fall before some Cæsar or Napoleon, "with our backs to the field and our feet to the foe," gazing up to heaven from a death-bed of glory, than to be conquered by venality and corruption. He referred to the sister States of Tennessee and Kentucky, said they were alike in soil, climate, and pursuits, and about equal in population. He wished to see, and believed he would see, them side by side, hand in hand, in this great struggle for liberty. He knew the fire was up in the mountains; it will burn yet brighter. He had heard that to the North the flame of liberty was blazing; he had himself seen there flags flaunting the heavens as high as a bird can soar.

Old Virginia—God bless her!—the mother of States, was up and doing. As for New York, she is determined to call home her son. Martin has been out too long already; she knows him for a wayward boy, and is anxious to have him back.

He assured his audience that the enthusiasm they were now witnessing was but a small part of that which was pouring down the Alleghany, the Ohio, the Mississippi. These great streams are vocal this moment with the shouts of freemen, the gladsome songs of children!

The people, like Noah's Ark, have been out for a long time in the dark and troubled waters. Noah saw a sign of relief in the myrtle which the dove bore back to the ark. Have we not also a glorious augury of success in the bright eyes which now look with smiling approbation upon our proceedings? Everywhere the grace and beauty of the land have blessed our assemblies with their presence,—God bless them! In their footsteps I am willing to follow. The women of America always have favored, and always will favor, every great and good cause.

I feel confident of the triumphant success of the Whig cause, but I would not exult over a prostrate foe. I would have the Whigs magnanimous in their triumph, giving no needless offense to the enemy.

The victory achieved, General Harrison will rule like a loving father over all this great people.

(Archbishop Spalding to Mrs. Coleman.)

BALTIMORE, December 26, 1870.

MY DEAR MRS. COLEMAN,—As I am not a civilian, *but* a clergyman, I feel some reluctance in complying with your request to write out the substance of what I related at the elegant breakfast of our mutual friend, Dr. Samuel D. Gross, in Philadelphia, on the 9th of August, in regard to your venerable father, John J. Crittenden. I recalled that reminiscence as a Kentuckian, whose State pride was all aglow when remembering an incident among the popular forensic efforts of one of Kentucky's most eloquent sons. The facts, briefly referred to on that occasion, were, in substance, as follows :—Finding myself accidentally in Nashville, in August, 1840, whither I went for purposes of recreation, I was induced by my friends to attend the great Southwestern Whig Convention. Mr. Crittenden was to be the chief orator of the day,—Mr. Clay having spoken the day before. I went, *not* as a politician, for I took no interest in politics, but as a Kentuckian, anxious to hear a brother Kentuckian speak, and I was well repaid. Though thirty years have elapsed, I have not forgotten the deep impression produced upon my mind by one of the most brilliant and impassioned bursts of oratory it has ever been my privilege to listen to, either in Europe or America. The whole scene is before me now, *fresh* and *vivid* as on that morning when I stood enraptured by your father's eloquence. I still hear his silvery voice; I still hear the acclamations of thirty thousand people, whose very souls he commanded and bore along with him throughout his masterly oration. Mr. Crittenden had taken a low stand upon the platform, and I still hear the cry, " Higher, higher, Mr. Crittenden ! Go up ; we wish to see your *whole stature !*" And as he ascended higher upon the stand, so he rose higher and higher in eloquence. He took up every cry of that vast audience (as, when he was about to close, they threw to him first one and then another of the great political questions of the day) and rang the changes upon it, becoming more and more grand in eloquence at every step of his physical and moral elevation, showing that he and his audience were *one.* I particularly remember his comparing the outcry of the people for a political change to an avalanche rushing down from the summit of the Alleghanies to the East and to the West, and bearing all before it. This brilliant figure was carried out till the immense multitude made the welkin ring with their applauding shouts. Seldom have I witnessed such a success. I well remember, also, the acclamations with which Mr. Clay and himself were greeted by the multitude on their departure from Nashville. Mr. Clay spoke *first,* from the guard of the steamer, with his usual grace and eloquence; then the cry was, "Crittenden, Crittenden!" Your father stepped forward, and in his most happy manner he said (smiling and bowing to Mr. Clay), "I suppose this flattering greeting is chiefly owing to the *good company* in which I have the privilege to be found?" "*Not at all!*" shouted the multitude. "Not at all; it is for yourself! Come again,—come alone next time, and we will prove it to you!"

This, my dear Mrs. Coleman, is the substance of what I related at Dr. Gross's of the great Southwestern Convention.

Faithfully yours,
M. J. SPALDING,
Archbishop Baltimore.

(Complimentary Resolutions as to the Trial in Baltimore of R. J. Breckenridge.)

At a meeting of the Board of Trustees of the Second Presbyterian Church of Baltimore,—the first that has taken place since the trial of their highly-respected pastor, the Rev. Dr. Breckenridge, for an alleged libel on a certain James,—it was considered to be both proper and necessary on the part of this Board to express their opinions and feelings in regard to that matter. Accordingly, several resolutions were moved, seconded, and unanimously adopted; one of which is as follows:

Resolved, That the most sincere and hearty thanks of this Board and of the whole congregation are justly due to the Hon. J. J. Crittenden, of the United States Senate, who so promptly left his seat in that honorable body at the call of friendship, to interpose the ægis of his talents and his fame, in order to cover the head "of one whom he had known from his earliest boyhood, and known him to be every way worthy of his best exertions."

And nobly did he sustain the high reputation which preceded him here by his masterly and powerful arguments, and by his chaste and manly eloquence. His speeches will long be remembered by the citizens of Baltimore as fine specimens of oratory, and they most cordially unite with their fellow-citizens of the West in assigning to Mr. Crittenden a distinguished rank among the most profound lawyers and the best public speakers in America.

This Board considers it to be the glory of the legal profession, that in the worst of times the cause of truth, justice, and innocence never wanted able and disinterested advocates,— a position so illustriously exemplified on the present occasion, and to which the present triumph may justly be ascribed.

BALTIMORE, April 2, 1840.

VOL. I.—9

(J. J. Crittenden to Mrs. Lucy Thornton.)

November 12, 1840.

MY DEAR SISTER,—I cannot tell you how much I was gratified by the receipt of your letter; you atone so handsomely by your flattering excuses for your delay in writing that I *not only pardon it*, but am tempted to wish for a little more of your neglect to be atoned for in like manner. I had the happiness of meeting with your friend, Judge Hopkins, at the great Convention at Nashville, and of making the acquaintance of many other interesting and agreeable gentlemen of your State. How is it that with so many very clever people your State should be so Locofocoish? Since your election in the summer, I have not allowed myself to expect anything from Alabama in the great presidential contest. I shall give her the more credit if she shows herself superior to Van Burenism, with its patronage and spoils. With or without you, we shall elect Harrison. Whatever course your State may take, I suppose we must admit you to a share in our *victory*, as you talk *so patriotically* on our side. We shall, therefore, be glad to see you in Washington as soon as we are *fairly in possession* of the *White House* and the Capitol, which, without a special Providence to the contrary, we humbly think will happen on the 4th day of March. If I could say it without flattering you too much, I should say you have cause to be proud of your children. I make an exception of your little Bess, who ought to have been a boy, though I suppose that is not her fault, and she ought not to be blamed for it. Are you not *proud of old Kentucky*, your native State? Her majority for Harrison will be twenty-five thousand. Let any State *beat that* if she can! Kindest regards to Mr. Thornton.

Your affectionate brother,

J. J. CRITTENDEN.

Mrs. LUCY THORNTON.

(Thomas Corwin to J. J. Crittenden.)

LEBANON, November 20, 1840.

DEAR SIR,—I received a week ago your kindly letter of congratulations, and have just now bethought me that I must say a word or two by way of reply. I feel uneasy about the future, and scarcely know why. I perceive, in various quarters, newspaper instructions as to the principle on which the President should construct his cabinet, and *this* from some of the most respectable of our prints. Among other things, it is strongly insisted on that no member of the cabinet shall be taken from either branch of Congress. I do not object to this *principle*, but it seems to me to be carried further than has yet been contemplated by anybody. If this is to be the rule, will it not limit the range of choice, as matters now stand, to a most inconvenient point? I should be glad to know whether you would accept a cabinet appointment; and, if so, *what* place you would prefer. I could give you a satisfactory reason for this. I do not suppose that Mr. Clay would take *anything* General Harrison could give him. I feel anxious that some I know should be near the President, for the reason that I should carry about with me an assurance that there was one honest man to give counsel when needed. I dare say you will think all this *arrogant*. Well, be it so; but you ought to remember that I have made more than *one hundred* regular *orations* to the people this summer; that I have, *first* and *last*, addressed at least seven hundred thousand people, men, women, and children, dogs, negroes, and Democrats, inclusive; that I have made promises of great *amendments* in the administration of public affairs, and I do not wish to be made out liar, fool, or both, by the history of the first six months of the *new era*. I have the utmost confidence in *Old Tip*, but I know also that his cabinet advisers will and ought to have great weight with him. Pray let me hear from you in *confidence, if you so wish it.*

Yours truly,
Thomas Corwin.

Hon. J. J. Crittenden.

(R. P. Letcher to J. J. Crittenden.)

Frankfort, November 30, 1840.

Dear Crittenden,—General Harrison is to return here to-morrow evening, and to dine at the *Palace* with the electors. The arrangement was that he was to dine with Peter Dudley with the electors, and I was one of the invited. It seems he has changed the *venue* without notice. It's all right! I understand he had a hard time in Lexington. I hear the strongest movement has been made upon him to appoint C. W. Postmaster-General, and the young D. private secretary. I don't believe it! When here he made two or three attempts to *chat* with me, but was interrupted. I think *then* he talked in the right strain; how he feels now can't say. Apprehending he might be fed too highly during his sojourn in Lexington, and possibly need a physician, I told Dr. Dudley *how to treat his case*. The doctor is a man of science, and if there is any difficulty in the treatment of the case, he will apprise me. I am a good doctor, of long experience in all diseases of the brain as well as of the stomach. I am overloaded with petitions; at least four have been *poked* under my nose since I commenced writing. What a charming thing this government business is! I know you want to be my successor, and, if you behave yourself well, *I will appoint you.* The office ought to be held by a good Christian man of meekness, patience, and humility. We have had all sorts of venison dinners and suppers since you left us. There has been more eating done in Frankfort during the last ten days than you *ever heard of.* Electors are pouring in upon us from all quarters. A few words of instruction, by way of practical improvement: *Take strong hold,—don't be too modest.* I know what I say.

Your friend,
R. P. LETCHER.

Hon. J. J. CRITTENDEN.

(R. P. Letcher to J. J. Crittenden.)

December 14, 1840.

DEAR CRITTENDEN,—As I told you, your election to the Senate will take place on Wednesday. It may be that some gentlemen will press you hard to say whether you will hold the station or resign it before the legislature adjourns. Some wish, no doubt, to have an election this session. Should you go into the cabinet, I do not wish to be under the necessity of appointing your successor; but still, let me tell you, take your time,—view the ground, and *don't be hastened.* If, after mature reflection, you can see your way clear, I would be pleased that the legislature should know the fact and make an election, *but* understand well what you are about. The old D. is butting himself against some resolutions, offered by Pirtle, in favor of a national bank. He has been speaking an hour or two. When will wonders cease? He will be tired of his honors before this session closes. I understand he says, "That Harrison's cabinet will be a *Clay fixing, out and out,* and that it will all *go down.* Crittenden is to go as Attorney-General (Clay's work), and he can't hold out twelve months," etc., and some other little compliments he paid you, which it would make you too proud to repeat. Since the young D. returned from his *scout* after Harrison, the old fellow is in a bad humor. There are many very uneasy souls here lest W. should get some place. You have no idea of the feeling of hostility created by the conjecture that he was to be provided for. I *entertain* no personal feeling against him myself, but what I tell you is *so.*

Truly your friend,
R. P. LETCHER.

CHAPTER XI.

1840–1841.

IT is generally known, that on the evening of the 18th of April, 1775, the British army left Boston to proceed to Concord, where the colonial stores were collected, and to seize them. This was the commencement of the war. The morning of the 19th this intelligence had been communicated to a considerable distance by the use of torches, tar barrels, and other signals; and before noon Isaac Davis, a young man of eighteen or nineteen years of age, captain of a militia company, was on his way to protect the colonial stores. Isaac Davis was the husband of Hannah Leighton. Before the British troops could arrive at Concord they sent forward a party to take possession of two bridges on the Concord River, which were situated three or four miles apart; and this was known at an early hour for many miles around. Isaac Davis with his company were soon under arms and on their march. They arrived at Concord by a road that led to the lower of these bridges, and there on the right and on the left were seen other collections of Massachusetts troops, but there was no organization amongst them. Davis, however, kept on his course; before he reached the bridge admonitory shouts were given to the militia not to approach; this was disregarded; the British fired, and several men fell; Davis pressed forward, and as he neared the bridge the British fired, and he fell. In the contest that ensued, the British were driven back to Boston. Davis's widow married a man by the name of Leighton; she was ninety years of age, was penniless, and asked relief from the government.

Mr. Calhoun said he considered the pension-list no more than a great system of charity, and that the pension to men for six months' service was an imposition; to call it a pension was a fraud on the public; it was under the name of charity, but its true name was plunder.

Mr. Crittenden said: I have been under the impression that this bill had passed through both houses of Congress at the last session. Am sorry to find I was mistaken. It is vain to say that this case is like every other case, vain to tell me that this can be tortured into a precedent which could be abused. This case stands by itself, morally, socially, indeed, in every point of view.

It is an application in favor of the widow of the first man that fell in the Revolution, when there was no regularly organized government. That man, stirred by his own patriotism, without a country, I may almost say, went forward to *make*, and then to *defend*, that country. Shall I, then, be told that this case would not be distinguished, both in the hearts and reasons of men, from the case of others under an organized government? Such a statement cannot reach my understanding or my feelings. I hope the bill will pass, and that this nation will no longer remain under the reproach of refusing a piece of bread to maintain this poor widow of a Revolutionary officer who received his death-wound under such circumstances. I shall call for the ayes and noes that I may record my vote; and if these are abuses, let those who commit them take the responsibility.

(R. P. Letcher to J. J. Crittenden.)

Frankfort, January 1, 1841.

Dear Crittenden,—One word: I have just received and read your letter to a few good friends who happened in my office. Your warm expressions of gratitude to your State for the kind manner of again electing you to the Senate made the *tears* run down their cheeks. I could hardly read it in an audible voice. I have heard no one of any sense say you ought to resign before you actually accept some other office. Do nothing from motives of *delicacy*. I am persuaded you ought to run no risk whatever. Suppose General Harrison should die before the 4th of March, what might be your condition then? Suppose your associates in cabinet should be anything but agreeable to you, how would the matter stand? There is some hazard in resigning, and none by holding on. A *safe* course in *this* life is the better course. I again repeat, do nothing to relieve me *from embarrassment* (in case of a called session), to fill the vacancy. I am ready to *act*, or *not to act*, as occasion may require, and care nothing about responsibility, or as little as I ought. All well. Went last night to a party at Judge Brown's. To-day, have a *small* dining-party of *thirty* myself.

Your friend,

Hon. J. J. CRITTENDEN.   R. P. LETCHER.

On the 5th of January, 1841, Mr. Crittenden proposed an amendment to the pre-emption laws; he thought that before granting to foreigners any of the privileges provided by the bill, they should record evidence of their intentions to become naturalized. The advocates for the bill had urged its passage upon the ground that the foreigner exposed himself as a bulwark to guard our frontier. Mr. Crittenden declared the American people were not yet reduced so low as to offer mercenary rewards to strangers to bribe them to expose their bosoms as a rampart against a foe. Not "against a world in arms" would *he* seek such protection, much less against a horde of naked savages. He contended that the soil of the United States belonged to the citizens of the United States. He was the son of a pre-emptioner, was born on a pre-emption, and was ready and willing to give a pre-emption right of three hundred and twenty acres to every real *bona fide* settler who was not worth over one thousand dollars. As to a distribution of the proceeds of the common estate in the public lands, Mr. Crittenden always contended that the people had that right, that it had not been denied, and could not be disproved. In a speech made by Mr. Crittenden on pre-emption and distribution, he alluded to Mr. Benton's having stated that the presidential election of General Harrison was brought about by bankers and stockbrokers in England. Mr. C. declared that the result of the late election was not the effect of British gold, but the *sense* of the American people as to the management of their public affairs. The expression of opinion came from the *old genuine Republican stock;* it was a *spark* from the old Revolutionary flint, and had blown the gentleman "*sky high.*" He hoped they would not, *now* that they had reached the ground and were rubbing their bruised and broken shins, try to disguise the truth to themselves. The people were coming on the fourth of March, and bringing the man of the *Log Cabin* with them. The Van Burenites were puzzling their heads to account for it, but we will work out the sum for them. The honorable gentleman from Missouri seemed to think that if the States once lapped blood during this process of distribution it would eventually become their common food, and the general government would be stripped of its revenue. The general government was the offspring of the States, and the States were not vampires; they would not feed upon the strength and empty the veins of their child.

The following letters, received and written by Mr. Crittenden, explain fully the circumstances connected with his re-election to the Senate, and his immediate resignation, to take a place in General Harrison's cabinet.

General Harrison was elected President, and took the oath of office 4th of March, 1841. The President called an extra session of Congress, to meet the 31st of May, but did not live to see it meet; he died on the 4th of April, 1841.

(John Bell to Governor Letcher.)

WASHINGTON, January 13, 1841.

DEAR GOVERNOR LETCHER,—I presume White keeps you advised of all the *on dits* of the day here,—of the *under-current* plots and *counter-plots*, etc.,—so I shall say nothing of them. Of myself I will say, that I believe for the whole time since the opening of Congress the *rank* and *file* of our party here have been strongly in favor of my going into the cabinet. With not a few the feeling has been a positive one, not of mere acquiescence. Still, the great leaders evidently hang back.

Both Clay and Webster would be glad to have some more active or unscrupulous partisan (I know not which) than either of them think I could be made. Webster thinks I am, or will be, a decided partisan of Clay, and the latter thinks I would not go far enough, or be bold enough in his service. This is the gospel truth of the matter.

It is either so or General Harrison himself has objections, for I have learned that he, or his friends about him, have been long since well advised of the course of sentiment in regard to me. Yet the War Department is still held up for the further development of public sentiment. I am growing pretty sick already of this thing of *office* in my own case, and the increasing tide of application from new quarters that daily beats against my ears gives me spasms. In truth, I begin to fear that we are, at last, or rather that our leading politicians in the several States are, chiefly swayed by the thirst for power and plunder. Would you think that Senator Talmadge is willing to descend from the Senate to the New York custom-house? This is yet a secret, but it is true! God help us all and keep us, I pray. I fear to speak of the list of congressional applicants.

You gave me from the 25th December to the 4th March,—two months' time on the draft! Great stretch of liberality! Don't you think so? Much I got by the liquidation. Do you suppose the 4th March is to put me in funds? Be ashamed!

Yours truly,
JOHN BELL.

P.S.—It has been a great mistake in General Harrison not to come on sooner. We have great questions of policy to settle upon before we separate on 4th March. He will be too late to have anything well considered before we have to break up.

(R. P. Letcher to J. J. Crittenden.)

Tuesday Morning.

DEAR CRITTENDEN,—I have been too constantly occupied day and night to write to you. This, however, is the less to be re- · gretted, as the intelligence which you have received from a hundred different persons of your election to the Senate, *is*, or ought to be, sufficient to fill you with joy for the next six years. The plain fact is, taking into consideration the whole manner and matter of this election, it must be set down as the greatest triumph of your life. To beat a candidate for President and Vice-President,—all at the same time, by such a majority,—after so much boasting and parading, and threatenings to carry so many of his own party, is just about the severest operation I ever saw. I am told the *old cock* is very much dissatisfied with having been *run*, though there is no doubt he fully consented to the arrangement. This election has created quite a heart-burning with the whole squad of *Locos*. The impression is gaining ground that the affair was arranged to kill the Colonel for the benefit of the little Dutchman. He was brought to the stake and burnt for the honor and glory of Van Buren, so say many of his friends. The truth is, he is *dead* and damned for-ever. I believe they have recommended him to be brought before the great Convention, and to submit patiently to what is then and there done to him. All a farce! Nine out of ten of the Democratic party are for Van Buren. There will be a hell of a quarrel before long in *"these diggings."* I had a fine saddle of venison sent to me *last night*, which is to be eaten to-morrow night. My wife wishes you could be present upon the occasion.

Most truly your friend,

Hon. J. J. CRITTENDEN.   R. P. LETCHER.

(J. J. Crittenden to R. P. Letcher.)

SENATE, January 11, 1841.

DEAR LETCHER,—Though I feel all the pangs "that flesh is heir to" at the idea of even the least apparent separation of myself from good and noble *old Kentucky*, I suppose the probability is that I shall, for a time, quit her immediate service to take the office of Attorney-General. I say probability, because the state of the case remains essentially as it was, subject to all the circumstances and contingencies that may change the views of General Harrison, or may influence my own judgment when the time comes for effective decision. As an honest man and politician, I ought to know who are to compose the cabinet, and some other things, before I commit myself as a member of any administration. And these matters I must, to a reasonable degree, ascertain before I act. I shall, I think, be enabled to *act* as I ought soon after General Harrison reaches here, and in time to enable my successor to be here on the 4th of March. It may be of importance that Kentucky be fully represented on that day. It is a matter of regret to me that, if I should resign, my resignation should not be made to the legislature, and that it may devolve on you the *responsibility* of making an appointment. But it may be that I cannot help it : and, indeed, the probability is that I cannot avoid such a result. Since I began this letter I have become party to a hot debate that is now going on in the Senate. Farewell.

Your friend,
J. J. CRITTENDEN.

(J. J. Crittenden to Orlando Brown.)

WASHINGTON, January 17, 1841.

DEAR ORLANDO,—I have just received your letter of the 8th instant, and before this I trust you have received a long letter that I wrote you some time ago. I do not remember how long ago it has been, but I should say long enough for you to have received it before the date of your last. It may be that you have lost it altogether in the great mail robbery that took place some weeks ago between this and Wheeling. I am not accountable for that, and you will, therefore, so far as I am concerned, please to retract proportionably from the scolding you have directed against me ; and my present diligence in answering will surely protect me for awhile longer.

I learn from my wife that both you and she are somewhat indignant at the frequency of my letters to Letcher. Isn't he a governor ? and has he not at this time the management of two governments (the general government and government of Kentucky) on his patriotic hands ? and does not all this require a very active correspondence? Ah! when you become a governor, you will then know the difference between governors and common folks. In one word, I am for you as governor of Iowa; and I shall not, as lazy lawyers often do, *submit* the case; I shall *argue* that case; I shall try and give Chambers some other directions. We are old friends, and I can do as much with him as almost anybody else can. We now expect General Harrison here about the first of next month. In the mean time there seems to be a great pause in the affairs of men, as if every one was holding his breath. He will bring along with him such a storm as old Æolus could hardly raise. In anticipation that the houses of the city cannot accommodate all that will be here, the Baltimoreans are now engaged in erecting, near where I am, a log cabin, about one hundred feet long, for their reception. I believe we have done all the cabinet-making that we can do here before Old Tip's arrival. It seems settled here that Webster, Ewing, and myself are to have places offered to us; and as to the other cabinet appointments, nothing is known here, nor is there any very settled or definite opinion or preference among our politicians.

Very little business, I think, will be done by the present Congress. We can't do what we would, and the Van Buren men, who are mustering for opposition, will leave us as many difficulties and embarrassments as they can. We apprehend that they intend to leave us in debt and without money. How does Letcher bear the afflictions that Mr. Wickliffe has made him *heir* to? To me he pretends to laugh over them like a philosopher. And how is D. succeeding in his new career? He must seem a strange figure to those that have observed him in past times and past scenes. He appears to be *advancing* backward about as rapidly as he ever went forward. He must find a wonderful confusion of tracks on his path. Remember me to our friends. Thank God, they are so many that I cannot conveniently name them all. But you and they will know who I mean. Tell Mason he is a lazy fellow, and to his wife and your own present my most respectful compliments.

Your friend,

Orlando Brown, Esq.   J. J. Crittenden.

(Letter from J. J. Crittenden.)

January 25, 1841.

Dear Letcher,—Yesterday brought me your letter of the 16th inst. I feel for Coombs all the esteem and sympathy that you or any of his best friends can entertain, and I stand ready to endeavor to do whatever can and ought to be done in his behalf. I shall bear his case carefully in my memory. But

what can I do?   I begin already to perceive that even he who
has power to dispose of all the offices, is only made to feel more
sensibly the poverty of his means to satisfy the just claims of
his friends.   Although, as yet, it does not seem to me that any
extraordinary *avidity* for office has been disclosed, yet I must
confess that the number of *claimants* far surpasses my expectation.   With this mass of claimants, I hope that no one will confound our friend Coombs; but still, they create obstructions and
embarrassments in making proper selections.

All I ask of my friends is not to *overrate me* or *my means*,
and to be sure I shall never be found wanting in any proper
case, when the interest of a friend is at stake.

I am quite amused at Hick's becoming one of your visitors
and companions.   You must remember that if, as is very likely,
he should become troublesome to you, it will be your own fault;
and you may remember, too, that you will not find it so easy
to dismiss him from office.

Inter nos—I had hoped that Harrison's arrival here might
enable me with propriety to determine on my own course, and
to resign, if it became necessary, in time for my successor to be
here by the 4th of March.   But I doubt now whether it will be
either in my power, or proper for me, to send you my resignation till after the 4th of March.   This has been a subject of
anxious reflection to me.

The general opinion—the almost unanimous opinion—here is
that an extra session of Congress is *necessary* and expedient,
and that it ought to be held as soon as the elections will permit
it.   I was sorry to hear, therefore, that some of our friends in
our legislature were in favor of appointing some day, as late as
the latter part of May, for our elections ; it should, I think, be
at least as early as the first Monday in May.

I heard that *Old Master* had a sore foot, and, from the scolding letter I received from him the other day, I *guess* he has a
very sore foot.   You should call and see him.   I gather from
my wife's letters that both he and she are made a little jealous
of my frequent correspondence with you.   And if you wish to
suppress a little rebellion, I would advise you to have a little
care in the direction to which I have pointed you.

Your friend,

To R. P. LETCHER,   J. J. CRITTENDEN.
          Governor.

(J. J. Crittenden to R. P. Letcher.)

WASHINGTON, January 30, 1841.

DEAR LETCHER,—I feel myself overcharged with dullness to-
night, and I must endeavor to relieve myself by pouring out

some of my stupidity upon you. I know no gentleman who can better bear it, or whose cheerful, active spirits, can sooner overcome such visitations. We know nothing yet of "old Tip's" approach, but our information leads us to suppose that he started from Cincinnati on the 26th inst., and will be here in about a week. I hear a rumor within the last hour that our State Senate had laid upon the table the bill providing for an earlier election of our members of Congress in the event of an extra session of Congress. I cannot credit such a rumor. Considerations of the highest necessity, as well as expediency, seem to me to require that the President elect should convene Congress at the earliest practicable period; this is the general opinion. I was present, a few evenings since, at a dinner, where almost every Whig senator was assembled. The necessity and propriety of a called session of Congress was made the subject of general conversation, and it appeared that there was an *entire concurrence* in the measure, and an *almost unanimous opinion* that it was proper and would be found to be *absolutely necessary.*

My belief is that the party now in power, while professing to deprecate a called session, are resolved to leave the coming administration in such a situation that it must be swamped or resort to that measure. Under such circumstances, it seems to me that the friends of Harrison ought to give him every encouragement and facility to convene Congress, and do whatever else the propriety or necessity of the case may require. And in the adverse circumstances in which his opponents will be sure to place the commencement of his administration, it would be most discouraging indeed if his supporters, if Kentucky, should refuse to afford her assistance in the only mode of remedy or defense that may be left him. I do not believe that the party in power intend to make, or will make, any adequate pecuniary provision for the support of the government. They have spent everything. Have delayed and postponed many payments that they ought to have made; and while they will leave to Harrison's administration many of their debts, they will leave the Treasury without a dollar.

Harrison, in my opinion, can succeed only by an energetic administration. He must *go on* and he *must act.* The people expect it, and are entitled to expect it. The fears that some entertain of an extra session are visionary. The real danger is in inaction, and falling behind, and disappointing the high hopes and feelings of the people. This is my judgment of the matter, and I go for serving the people and *not* for attempting to rule them.

I dare say, by this time, you are ready to cry "Enough," and, according to Kentucky law, that ought to put an end to all further infliction, and so I conclude.

Your friend,

Robert P. Letcher,   J. J. Crittenden.
     Governor.

(R. P. Letcher to J. J. Crittenden.)

FRANKFORT, February 1, 1841.

DEAR CRITTENDEN,—Don't forget, for the sake of the Lord, that *best of all good fellows*, Judge Eve; he is overwhelmed with the weight of debt, but sustains himself with dignity, modesty, and cheerfulness. He declares he would almost as soon be *hung* as trouble his friends to ask for office for him. I will write to Webster and General Harrison in his behalf, and refer Webster to *you* for his character and claims. I have been too busy to write, but no doubt others have informed you of the little, mean, culpable manœuvring in this quarter, by a few restless spirits. Keep cool! take pattern by *me;* I am always *cool;* don't believe Old Master,* he has "*a sore foot*," and does no man justice while he is confined to his room. There he sits smoking and damning everything *but Iowa.* He hopped up here yesterday, and told me he had drawn the most vivid picture *of me*, in a letter to you, that was ever seen. "Ah," said he, "I never wrote as pretty a thing." Did it contain a word of truth? I inquired. "No," said he, "not a word; but that don't mar its beauty." Here he is *now;* has just hopped in out of breath. "Listen to this short article," said he; an answer to a letter in the *Observer*, attacking you, and *gently touching me.* "Will that do?" said Orlando. H. says if our young friend is appointed private secretary with the privilege of opening all the letters and writing to the newspaper editors, Crittenden ought to take office in no such concern. So say I, replies Old Master.

Your friend,
R. P. Letcher.

J. J. Crittenden.

(R. P. Letcher to J. J. Crittenden.)

February 2, 1841.

DEAR CRITTENDEN,—I did my best to keep your enemy, and all his tribe, off of you, but all to no purpose. You will see his last *love letter* in the *Reporter*, to which I alluded in my hasty letter of yesterday. He wrote that letter himself, in my opinion. Dr. Watson is much excited upon the subject; has received a letter from Lexington, telling him that villainous article ought

---

* Orlando Brown.

to be noticed. The truth is, the old gentleman wishes a change of *venue*, and you may look out for some of his heaviest blows. He is tired of abusing me, and, I was told the other day, he undertook, with a bad grace, to praise me in the Senate. Upon hearing this fact I requested one of the senators to *call him to order* if he ever *dared* to utter similar language during his natural life. Laying aside all jokes, and in sober earnest, he and his set have been lavish of their abuse upon you, but in fact I pay little heed to such poor stuff. I know this much, however, many of your friends, both in and out of the House, give him the very *devil* upon all occasions, and his coadjutors are not spared. Since God, in his infinite wisdom, created the heavens and the earth, such another set of untiring intriguers never existed as are now walking abroad. Mark me: I am not in a passion by any means, and have no "sore foot," but I speak my deliberate opinion of the matter. Hick has been here to-day; he gives notice of his appearance by a loud laugh. "Banish him!" No! he sha'n't be removed from office. I would rather see him than any ten members of the legislature. Oh, yes, Mrs. Crittenden and Orlando were getting quite jealous; I often pretended to get letters when none came, and would send word that if they wanted to hear from you *every day*, they had only to send up to the office of the Secretary of State. Orlando was merry over your letter. "Oh," said he, "if you have two governments under your charge, the thing is explained." Here comes five or six members! How happy I am to see them with their petitions!

Yours,
R. P. LETCHER.

(J. J. Crittenden to R. P. Letcher.)

SENATE, February 9, 1841.

MY DEAR LETCHER,—Yesterday and to-day I received your letters of the 1st and 2d inst. Let my wife and Orlando say what they will, and be as jealous as they please, you are an excellent correspondent and entitled to the highest consideration. The D. cannot harm me, if he would. All that surprises me is that he should have any disposition to injure or attack me. I am not conscious that I ever gave him cause. On the contrary, I have served him and his. Whatever of malice he has to me must be unmixed and primitive, and the sole product of his own heart. I say to myself "that he cannot hurt me unless I afford him much better cause for attack than he now has." I would have you to know that I am more of a philosopher than to be much disturbed or perplexed by such attacks. From the apprehensions you express for me, I cannot help inferring that you have suffered a good deal from the patriotic and *philosophical* animadversions of the senator and his organ at Lexington. Orlando's account of your mingled smiles and contortions, your inward grief and outward cheerfulness, under the operation, cannot be altogether fictitious. For myself, I am a cool, unimpassioned man, looking on in calm humility at all such personalities. I wish I could impart some of this moral fortitude to my suffering friends.

I do confess that, from all I have heard, I do occasionally feel some natural resentments against him and his would-be party. "I do not lack gall to make oppression bitter." The Scripture teacheth us to love our enemies, but it does not go so far as to require us to love perfidious friends. I take my stand on that ground, and it will puzzle any one to dispute its orthodoxy; I conclude that I am not bound to love the old gentleman. You, too, will be justified in going that far, but I admonish you not to pass that Christian limit. The gentleman is, doubtless, a purely patriotic old man, and member of the church, and what may appear to vulgar eyes to be selfishness or malice must, in him, be regarded as mysteries of patriotism and piety. I trust that this conclusion will suffice to convince you of the good state of my feelings. I have addressed to you, under cover to my friend C. S. Morehead, two letters, the *one* or the *other* to be delivered, as the legislature *may* or *may not* happen to be in session. The reasons for this are explained in my letter to Morehead. Before this reaches you that communication will, I hope, be received. The circumstances had occurred and the period arrived, which I have constantly looked forward to as the only state of case in which I could *properly act.* I feel it a *duty to act* and *to act promptly.* Be assured I have not only *not* been hastened, but entirely unmoved by any of the exhibitions of impatience which appeared in certain *quarters.* You are not to regard this, by any means, as even a *constructive* resignation. My purpose on that subject will be made known to you by my letter, which you will receive through Morehead. Old Tip arrived here to-day amidst a storm of snow and of people. He is in the hands of the city authorities here. I have not yet waited on him, but am to see him by appointment this evening. Write to "Old Tip" a strong letter in favor of *Old Master* and inclose it to me, so that I have it by the fourth of March. Farewell.

Your friend,
J. J. CRITTENDEN.

R. P. LETCHER,
    Governor.

(R. P. Letcher to J. J. Crittenden.)

FRANKFORT, February 9, 1841.

DEAR CRITTENDEN,—Promises, you know, must be complied with. Keep cool; a *warm, decided, whole-enduring*, everlasting friend of yours and of the Whig cause, has a call to go to Missouri and aid them in their political struggles against *Benton & Co.* I believe he is inclined to obey if he can be made register or receiver in the Platte County. You know him,—he was once lieutenant-governor of Missouri, and deservedly popular. I like him, and he will make a faithful officer in any station. Mr. Clay must not consider himself *slighted* if I do not write him a similar letter upon this occasion. I hope you will explain to him that I mean *no offense;* he is just as welcome to throw in a word for my friend as if he had been specially solicited. I received your letter of the 30th this morning. I hope you will often get into a similar mood and inflict similar letters upon me to relieve yourself. Some of the *chaps* who wished to administer upon you before the breath left your body have been, I learn, a little cunning,—have written letters to members of Congress pretending that everybody here thought you ought to resign before you accept another appointment; these letters were to be read to you, and to produce the *desired effect.* I heard of *that game* the other day. Don't give yourself a moment's uneasiness. I heard, this morning, the old ——— swore if they did not take care he *would resign* his seat. How unfortunate that would be to the country, and how *cruel to me!* Do you cry " Enough?" Then get up like a man, give me a list of the cabinet, I want to see *how* it looks. I wish I had the making of the *critters.* Don't Bell look scared? Wise is a case. *Clayton,* I have heard nothing of him this winter; he is the best fellow in the world. I want to see his name on the list. Don't speak of Thad. Stevens; rumor says he is to be one, but if the old gentleman talks over the matter, *Thad. can't succeed.* Take care of *our little darling*, the young ———.

R. P. LETCHER.

(R. P. Letcher to J. J. Crittenden.)

FRANKFORT, February 19, 1841.

DEAR CRITTENDEN,—The legislature has adjourned, and the village looks gloomy. I feel as if it was a funeral occasion. They made a senator this morning,—Governor Morehead is the man. This was unexpected to me. From all I have heard during the progress of the *run*, the result was produced by a violent and heated state of feeling between the friends of Buchner and Calhoun. The result is by no means dissatisfactory to me. Considering the governor's condition, to say nothing of his amiability and true devotion to the Whig cause, no one will, I think, regret his success. I am gloomy this morning, indeed I may say *sad*. You have not forgotten how a boy feels when his associates all separate from him the last day of the school? This is *now* my case. I shall write a letter for Old Master to old *Tip*. Now, look here! Woman with a crying child has just come in to get her husband out of the Lexington jail. This is too bad! It is a case which would call into requisition all *your* Christian virtues.

Your friend,

JOHN J. CRITTENDEN. R. P. LETCHER.

(Letter from J. J. Crittenden.)
February 20, 1841.

MY DEAR LETCHER,—We have not yet heard of your reception of my *official* communication to you. It will produce, of course, a considerable excitement in the legislature, and among the competitors for the succession. It is quite probable, I think, that though my course may disprove the charge of conspiracy between us, that is, of withholding my resignation till adjournment of the legislature, it may give rise to another, and that is, that, upon some collusion between us, the thing has been so timed as to take some candidate (our friend C. for instance) by surprise. I must cut your acquaintance, it subjects me to so many suspicions; all the charges against me, I find, are founded on the presumptions arising out of my intimacy and connection with you. You are the great contriver and politician that has seduced my innocency. Our amiable friend, Mr. W., must have taken this view of the matter. I am sure that of me, taken alone and in the abstract, he entertains the kindest and highest opinion. You have, in some way, sadly deranged his notions as to persons and things. His proposed amendment to elect members of Congress to serve till the first Monday in August is a fine specimen of constitutional learning and legislation. He is a capital old fellow, and I don't know what you would do without him if Providence should remove him from your councils. You would be left in *darkness*. I trust in Heaven that the legislature will not separate him, or any of his adjuncts, from you, by sending him or them to my place in the Senate. You will perceive by this I still retain a friendly regard for you, notwithstanding the various charges and attacks that your acquaintance has exposed me to; and in despite of all the past, I must still subscribe myself,

Your friend,
J. J. CRITTENDEN.

P. S.—Old Tip is absent in Virginia. The cabinet he has

designated meets with general approbation here. At the instant there was some little sensation produced by some of the appointments (Granger and Badger), but this has subsided, or is subsiding, and, so far, we shall have a fair start. General Harrison, so far as I know, has not here announced any resolution as to the measure of a called session; but my own impression is confident there will be one. You need not fear that the little clique who are opposed to you at home will have any undue influence or favor here.

J. J. CRITTENDEN.

(J. J. Crittenden to his daughter, Mrs. A. M. Coleman.)

SENATE, March 2, 1841.

MY DEAR DAUGHTER,—It is impossible for me to convey to you any just idea of the incessant occupation of my time. Between the court, the cabinet, the Senate, many friends, and a host of office seekers, I can hardly say that my life is my own, much less one moment of time. It seems to me that if I had the sole disposal of all the *offices* and *honors* of the government, I could not be more hunted after, and *hunted down*, than I am. I am hardly sure of keeping my senses, and yet I reproach myself for not writing to you in despite of all obstacles. Your letter of the 23d of February, just received, has brought back upon me an increased amount of self-reproach. You know, however, that my silence cannot proceed from any want of affection for you. You know that I love you dearly and with all my heart. You know now how the cabinet is to be constituted. My position in it is exactly that of my own *choice*,—the only one I *would accept*. I could have selected another if I pleased. General Harrison's offers to me were very kind and flattering. I was really imposed upon by *Bob's joke*; I could not be angry about it, and I can *now* laugh at it; but I feared that you were all about to make some concerted *attack* on General Harrison in my behalf, and that would have grieved me. It was unnecessary, and I would have no solicitation for me. I am impatient to be at home. My new duties will soon call me back, and here I must *fix* my residence.

Kiss the children for me.

Your father,
J. J. CRITTENDEN.

Mrs. A. M. COLEMAN.

(R. P. Letcher to J. J. Crittenden.)

FRANKFORT, March 4, 1841.

DEAR CRITTENDEN,—You have cut my acquaintance by way of soothing D., and what have you gained by it either in this

State or the United States? I see that, just at that time, you drew upon yourself a burst of indignation from the galleries, and a mighty rebellion would have been the consequence but for the generous and humane interposition of your friend, Tom Benton, who had the goodness to cry out with a loud voice, " Take away the blackguards! out with the blackguards!" I have read it in the papers this moment, and very good reading it is. "Old Master" says the riot was occasioned by Preston's bestowing a high compliment upon you, which created the disturbance in the galleries; but *he* don't know everything.

However, Benton saved you, and I feel just the same kind gratitude to him for his timely interposition in your behalf, that I felt to the old D. for his special attention and benevolence towards me. "Out with the blackguards!" said Benton. "Save the ladies!" said Clay. Sensible to the last, never unmindful of the ladies in any emergency. It is well for Benton that his order was not strictly executed. However, you owe him a debt of gratitude, that's certain, and I hope you will always acknowledge the obligation, though you may not live long enough to discharge it. *He* must have the offer of a big dinner when he comes through this State. Kentucky will never fail to treat the benefactor and protector of one of her distinguished senators with becoming and marked respect. This is the 4th of March. What a great day this is in the city! Yesterday was a great day also to the nation!—the last day of Van Buren's reign! The Lord be praised for all his mercies! Van Buren went out of office yesterday, and so did two fellows go out of the penitentiary. I turned them out; they had but *five days left* to hold their places, and I thought it was but just and right to emancipate them at the same time Van Buren was emancipated. When will you be at home? How does Bell *look* and *act*, and *walk* and *talk?* I should like to see him very much indeed. Secretary of War I think he is. Well, that's a very good place; I hope it will be well filled.

I must tell you, this is rather the dullest place since the legislature adjourned that the Lord ever made in his six days' work. I should die of ennui, if I had not the pleasure of being annoyed by everybody and everything. Come home and stay here six weeks, receive my instructions, and, if necessary, aid me in making out directions for the governor of Iowa.

I would not be at all surprised if, instead of two governments, I shall have the care of *three* at the same time,

Your sincere friend,
R. P. LETCHER.

CHAPTER XII.

1841.

ON the fifth of March Mr. Crittenden was appointed Attorney-General by General Harrison. The trial of McLeod for the burning of the steamboat Caroline was expected to take place in New York about that time.

The British government had avowed the transaction as done under their authority, and demanded the release of the prisoner. At the urgent solicitation of the President, Mr. Crittenden consented to go to Albany and look into the matter, though he considered the undertaking as altogether distinct from his official duty as Attorney-General. The following letters and papers were found among Mr. Crittenden's papers, and possess, I think, a general interest as relating to this important matter:

(J. J. Crittenden to Robert P. Letcher.)

March 14, 1841, 11 o'clock at night.

DEAR LETCHER,—See what sacrifices I make of time and sleep to my correspondence with you! God knows how you manage two governments and yet live. For my part, with only a small portion of one resting on my shoulders, I can scarcely find time to say my prayers. I am in arrears to you several letters, and I acknowledge the debt. I have the best of all excuses: it has not been in my power to pay up punctually. To-morrow I start for the remotest part of Western New York to attend the trial of McLeod, indicted for murder and burning the steamboat Caroline. You understand the case: the British government avows the transaction as done under its authority, and demand the release of the prisoner; it has thus become a national affair of delicacy and importance, and it is the Presi-

(149)

dent's pleasure that I should attend the trial. This has disappointed me sadly, in deferring my return home. You, too, must be grieved and make yourself very unhappy on this occasion. That will be some consolation to me. I may be absent two weeks on this trip, but I *shall* then return home if I have to run away from office, President and all! We are laboring along and endeavoring to keep the peace among the office seekers; but nothing less than a miracle could so multiply our offices and patronage as to enable us to feed the hungry crowd that are pressed upon us.

I have one sad thing to communicate. It has grieved me sorely. I have been laying my trains and flattering myself that I was making progress towards the accomplishment of our object in making Orlando governor of Iowa. Chambers was to be located here. I was pleased to think *that* was fixed. To my surprise, in the last few days, I have understood that Chambers has changed his mind, and is to go to Iowa as governor, and the indications now are that such will be the result. This is going a little ahead of what is generally known, and you must treat it as confidential; but disagreeable as it is, you must let Orlando know. I like Chambers, and cannot blame him, but he has disappointed me in two respects,—by not staying here himself, and interfering with my hopes for Orlando. Now I must go to bed. Farewell.

Your friend,

ROBERT P. LETCHER. J. J. CRITTENDEN.

(Paper relating to McLeod found among Mr. Crittenden's Letters.)

My visit to New York in March, 1841, and all my agency in regard to the case of McLeod, was undertaken at the instance of the President, General Harrison. It was inconvenient to me,—my wishes and my interest required my return to Kentucky. I proposed the selection of some other person; but it was insisted on that I should go, and I submitted. It was an undertaking altogether distinct from my official duty as Attorney-General. The object of my visit and the duties enjoined on me appear from the letter of instructions addressed to me by Mr. Webster, the Secretary of State, and drawn up by the direction of the President. I had before received in substance the same instructions orally from the President himself, and it was to his authority and not that of the Secretary that I considered myself subordinate. At Albany I met Governor Seward, exhibited my letter of instructions, and delivered to him the papers therein alluded to as intended for him. We conversed a good deal at large on the subject of my instructions. They were before the governor, and I desired to know what his views were in respect to the case of McLeod. He was unwilling to direct a *nol. pros.*, and perhaps added that he had no such power; but he stated his entire confidence that McLeod was not guilty, and that the proof was clear that he was not engaged in the expedition against the Caroline, and was absent in Canada when the murder charged against him was committed, and on this ground he must be acquitted whenever tried; and furthermore he stated that if convicted he could and would pardon him, and so avert the threatened war; that the President might rely on his pursuing this course. He professed his earnest wish to act in harmony with the Federal government, but was unwilling, as before stated, to direct a *nol. pros.*, and thought the preferable and best course was to await the acquittal of McLeod by a jury, a result which he considered certain, and that such an acquittal, or proof of his innocence, would be more satisfactory to the community and tend to allay the great popular excitement then prevailing.

Wishing to know, as far as I could, what would be the course of Governor Seward in any contingency, a question was suggested as to the pardoning of McLeod before the trial. The governor was averse to this; it would be unsatisfactory to the community, and still said he could and would pardon him if convicted, and thereby prevent the anticipated hostility. We did, after the examination of Mr. Fox's letter and consultation on the subject, agree in the conclusion that, though his demand was for the *release* of McLeod, then in prison, there was no ground to apprehend that hostilities would be attempted unless or until McLeod should be sentenced and punished. The governor knew that the chief object of my agency in attending the trial was to see that the case was properly placed on the record in the event of a conviction, so as to enable the Supreme Court to exercise its revisory jurisdiction, if it had any. Though I do not know that the governor made any objection to any lawful proceeding having such revision in view, I think he manifested, *if* he did not express, some objection to the Federal government taking any part in the prosecution against McLeod, and perhaps mentioned it as an objection to the appointment of Mr. Spencer as District Attorney for the United States that he had him employed as counsel for McLeod.

(To Mr. Webster.)

I have the honor to make known to you for the information of the President of the United States that, in obedience to his instructions received through you, I set out from this place to attend the trial of Alexander McLeod, which was expected to take place at Lockport, in the State of New York, on the day

of   March last.   I had proceeded on my way as far as Albany,
where I received certain intelligence that the trial would not
take place at the time appointed, and that the case would necessarily be continued in consequence of some irregularity or defect in the legal preparations for the trial.   It was also said that
the prisoner had given notice of his intention to ask for a continuance and a commission to take depositions, etc.   Under
these circumstances, it was unnecessary for me to proceed further, and, after resting a few days at Albany, I returned to this
city.

At Albany the case of McLeod seemed to be a subject of
interest and general conversation, and with the distinguished
governor of that State and his enlightened secretary I frequently
conversed on the same subject; and, disappointed as I was, I
think I may assure the President that there has been great exaggeration in the rumors that have reached him of the violence
of popular feeling and excitement against McLeod.

At Albany I had the honor of several interviews with Governor Seward, in which I made known to him that the case of
McLeod had acquired a character of some national importance
and delicacy, in consequence of the recent formal avowals of
the British government, and demand for his release; that it was
only in this national aspect of the case that the President had
any care or concern about it, and that he was only desirous to
be fully informed of the truth of the case, and that it might be
dealt with and disposed of upon a full view of all the facts, in
a manner conformable to the justice of our laws and the character of our country; that he entertained the highest opinion
of, and confidence in, both the wisdom and justice of the courts
of New York, and, not doubting but that they would dispose
of the case properly, he wished that it might be so conducted
that all the facts of the case, and questions of law arising out
of them, might be on the record, so as to be subject to any
revision that the courts of the United States might have a right
to exercise and to stand as a perpetual and authentic memorial
of facts,—of a case which had become the subject of complaint
by the British government, and might become the occasion of
still more interesting negotiation and controversy between that
government and the government of the United States; that it
was for these objects, and not for the purpose of any *interference*
in the case, that it had pleased the President to direct me to
attend the trial.   It would thus appear that he had not been
inattentive to a matter which, in possible contingencies, might
affect his duties as chief magistrate.

Governor Seward expressed himself anxious to act in harmony
and concert with the general government; but I need not attempt

to give you his views as he has himself communicated them in letters to you. From conversations I had at Albany with many intelligent gentlemen, well acquainted with Western New York, and some of them residing in that part of the State, I am sure the account of excitement has been greatly exaggerated.

As to the object of my intended visit to Lockport, it may be proper, perhaps, for me briefly to state the information I obtained from all those sources that were accessible to me at Albany. There can be no doubt that the invasion of our territory, the destruction of the Caroline, and the killing of one or more of the unresisting people that were sleeping on board that vessel on the night of her destruction, are regarded by the people of Western New York as a great outrage and insult, and that a deep sense of the injury still prevails in that community, although the excitement of the moment has generally passed away. It was in this temper of the public mind that McLeod, voluntarily coming into New York, and in the very neighborhood of the place where the outrage was committed, proclaimed and boasted publicly in a hotel of his participation in that outrage. By this offensive conduct the resentments of the people were excited; he was arrested, an indictment was regularly found against him for the murder of which he boasted, and he has ever since remained in custody for his trial on that indictment. Public sentiment demands that the law should have its due course, and that if entitled to it on any ground of national or municipal law, he should receive his discharge from the legal tribunals in the regular course of jurisdiction. Any executive interference to prevent or arrest the judicial examination and decision of the case would be regarded with great jealousy and disapprobation. If this case is left to the judiciary, and he is acquitted or discharged upon a hearing by their courts, they would be satisfied. They have no disposition to make him a victim to their vengeance or to see any injustice done him; but now that his case is regularly in the hands of the law, they think it due to public sentiment and to the administration of public justice that it should be disposed of by their courts in due course of law; they desire that his defense, whatever it may be, may be fully heard and justly decided upon,— and the universal opinion seemed to be, that if he were otherwise guilty, the recent avowal, by the British government, of the transaction in respect to which he stands accused, will be received and adjudged a good and sufficient defense. From the professional and public opinion that I heard everywhere expressed in New York, I entertain not the least doubt that whenever his case shall be heard by the proper tribunals of New York, he will be acquitted or discharged, if it shall be made to appear that the acts for which he is charged were done under the sanction or orders of his government; *that* can only be made to appear to the legal tribunals by some regular course of judicial procedure. It may be well known to the executive, but neither the executive of this country or a king of England, acting upon their knowledge, can enter a court of law and dictate or interrupt the course of its proceedings. The king may cause a *nolle prosequi* to be entered in a criminal prosecution, or pardon a condemned man.

(William H. Seward to Hon. J. J. Crittenden.)

ALBANY, May 31, 1841.

MY DEAR SIR,—I welcome the news of your return to Washington. If it is regarded as worthy of your consideration, you will learn that during your absence a correspondence, not more unpleasant than unprofitable, has taken place between the President and myself concerning the affair of Alexander McLeod. Your memory will retain the views presented to you, when here, concerning the disposition of that subject deemed proper by me, and the fact that it was requested that if those views were not approved at Washington, a further consultation might be had with me before definite action was adopted. You will, I trust, remember that I distinctly advised against any extraordinary proceedings being taken, or with the consent of the government *permitted*, to secure the prisoner's release without a trial before a jury, and that I, with all my counselors, especially advised against the appointment of his retained counsel as district attorney, especially on the ground of its *incongruity* and of the injurious and unseemly effect it would present. From that time no communication, formal or otherwise, was received here until very recently, and in the mean time the course of the government was left to be learned from rumor, until the subject of a supposed collusion between the government at Washington and that of this State, to effect the prisoner's discharge without a trial, became a point of legislative inquiry and a *charge* of the opposition press. While satisfying the legislature and the public on that subject, I, in good faith, addressed a brief letter to the President concerning Mr. Spencer's appearance as counsel, to which I received a kind reply. From that reply I was induced to believe that the subject was viewed as having less importance at Washington than, considering *its bearings* upon so delicate a question, I thought it really had, and that, at all events, my acquiescence in the course adopted would not be proper and safe. I therefore addressed a second letter to the President, in the same kind and confiding spirit as the former. An answer from the President, in any general form, overruling my opinions (although I should not have been convinced by it) would have ended the correspondence, and, leaving both parties to their proper *responsibilities*, would have avoided all unkindness. The President, however, replied at length in a spirit that seemed to me unkind, and in a manner which required the firmest adherence to my positions and the most vigorous defense of them I could make. I replied accordingly, and his rejoinder is before me, in which (as I cheerfully admit was to be expected) he preserves the same disposition and tone as before. My further reply will go with this letter.

Although I feel that I am injured in this matter in the house of my friends, I care nothing for *that*, but I regret that I am misunderstood. I cannot but believe that the confusion into which things necessarily fell for a time at Washington was the consequence of the death of General Harrison, and your absence from Washington in a season when your explanations would have been useful, has contributed to this result. My object in addressing you is to call your attention to the subject, in order that you may now do whatever shall seem to you to be useful. I do not ask your *interposition*. I have no personal reason for desiring it. I do not ask you even to acknowledge this communication. I should deem it improper for you, as a member of the cabinet, to write me on the subject, except in support of the President, but I think it well, in this informal way, to suggest that the *talent* and *wit* of a Whig administration might be more profitably employed in some other manner than in an unavailing effort to drive me from a course which, in my poor judgment, is required not less by patriotism and the honor of this State than by devotion to the administration itself,—that enough has already been written by the President upon an exciting subject (in regard to which I must take leave to think the feelings of the people must be better understood *here* than at Washington) to do incalculable evil if it should ever meet the public eye. I think that during your visit here you acquired information enough to know what President Tyler cannot know, that in all that has passed I have been firm, frank, and consistent. The course pursued in regard to the same question at Washington has not been so. If you think it well to acquaint the President with what you know concerning the matter I shall be personally obliged; but I desire that it may be understood it is done only as a thing of public importance, and by no means in such a manner as to induce an opinion that I would either solicit notice of a personal grief or carry it into the general account.

With very sincere respect and esteem,
your friend and obedient servant,
WILLIAM H. SEWARD.

Hon. J. J. CRITTENDEN.

(J. J. Crittenden to his son Robert.)

June 7, 1841.

My dear Robert,—Your letter has just reached me, and I am now taking the remnant of a most laborious day to answer it. You requested me to send you ten dollars to defray the expenses of your trip to Harrodsburg on occasion of the celebration of the settlement of Kentucky. I inclose it to you, and am pleased to find you interesting yourself in the early history of your own State. If the fact was not so common, it would appear strange that there should be so many persons well acquainted with Rollin's Ancient History who know little or nothing of their own country. You are reading the life of Alexander Hamilton, and I am not surprised that you should feel great admiration for him : he was undoubtedly a man of the rarest and greatest mental *endowments;* but you should be a little careful of adopting your opinions of Mr. Jefferson from his biography. You must know that Alexander Hamilton and Mr. Jefferson were the great rival and popular political antagonists of their day, and no doubt *felt* and communicated to all within the range of their influence, unfavorable opinions and prejudices in respect to each other. Mr. Jefferson was a man of great genius and learning, and devoted to the cause of human liberty and the principles of free government. There are some things in history, some *specks* in the character of Mr. Jefferson, we must regret ; but these imperfections may be overlooked and pardoned, to some extent, in consideration of the great passages of his life, and the many illustrious exertions of his genius in the cause of his country. It does you credit, and shows *taste* and *judgment,* that you have read Chevalier's U. S. with so much satisfaction. It is an able political and philosophical work. It is singular that Chevalier and De Tocqueville should be the two most profound observers and commentators upon our country and its institutions. I am gratified at your taste for history, but take care not to withdraw from your collegiate studies. I wish you to *graduate* with as much reputation as possible. I believe you can obtain the *first honor* if you make *the effort.*

Your father,

J. J. Crittenden.

R. Henry Crittenden.

(Henry Clay to E. M. Letcher.)

Washington, June 11, 1841.

My dear Sir,—White was elected Speaker. He does not come up quite yet to my hopes, but I trust he will improve. I took no part in his election. We are in a crisis as a party. There is reason to fear that Tyler will throw himself upon Calhoun,

Duff Green, etc., and detach himself from the great body of the Whig party. A few days will disclose. If he should take that course, it will be on the bank. It is understood that he wants a bank located in the District, having no power to *branch* without the consent of the State where the branch is located. What a bank would that be! The complexion of the Senate is even better than I anticipated, and although Mr. Adams has created some disturbance in the House, there is a fine spirit generally prevailing there.

Your faithful friend,

Mr. E. M. LETCHER. H. CLAY.

This opinion, given by Mr. Crittenden during his term of Attorney-General, under General Harrison, is the only one which will be published:

In respect to your second question, it appears to me unnecessary to go into the general question of interest, or the liability or obligation of a government to pay it. In this instance the single inquiry is, not whether interest ought, in justice, or any principle of analogy, to be allowed, but whether the judge has been invested with any authority to award it; and this depends on the proper construction of the act of Congress of the 26th of June, 1834,—his sole and whole authority is derived from that act. It is the standard by which his jurisdiction must be measured and limited. By the terms of this act he is authorized to receive and examine, and adjudge, in all cases of claims for *losses* occasioned by the troops in the service of the United States in 1812 and 1813. Interest on the amount of such *losses* is certainly a thing very distinguishable and different from the *losses* themselves. It may be that justice would have required, in this case, the allowance of interest as well as of the principal that was lost; but Congress alone was competent to decide the extent of its obligation, and to give or withhold authority for the allowance of the principal,—that is, the value of the property lost, with or without interest. The whole subject was before them for consideration and legislation, and the question of interest was as important in amount as the principal. They did legislate, and provided for the liquidation and payment of claims for *losses*, but made no provision for any claims of interest. The inference, to my mind, is irresistible that they did not intend to authorize the allowance of interest.

It is confidently believed, that in all the numerous acts of Congress for the liquidation and settlement of claims against the government, there is no instance in which interest has ever been allowed, except only when these acts have expressly directed

and authorized its allowance. I feel myself constrained, therefore, to entertain the opinion that, so far as relates to the allowance of interest, the decision of the judge is unwarranted and
erroneous.

Very respectfully yours,

Hon. Thomas Ewing,   J. J. Crittenden.
   Secretary of State.

CHAPTER XIII.

1841–1842.

Letters from Clay, R. Johnson, R. P. Letcher—Crittenden's Letter of Resignation of his Place in the Cabinet of J. Tyler—Letter of G. E. Badger—Letters of Crittenden to Letcher.

(J. J. Crittenden to Henry Clay.)

WASHINGTON, August 16.

MY DEAR SIR,—It is understood that the President concedes the power of establishing agencies or branches, with authority to deal in the purchase and sale of bills of exchange, and to do all other usual banking business *except* to discount promissory notes or obligations; that with the assent of a State branches *may* be established, with authority to discount *notes* and to do all other usual bank business. Upon this basis it does seem to me that a bank may be constructed with a larger recognition of Federal authority and of more efficiency than the one which the President has refused to sanction. It should be done by conferring on the bank and its branches *all* the usual banking powers, and then, by restrictions and exceptions limiting them to the basis before stated; there is less danger of embarrassment and error in this form of legislation than in the attempt to limit the powers· of the institution by specific description and enumeration of them. I pray you to consider this well, with all the great consequences which attend it, and do whatever your known liberal spirit of *compromise* and your *patriotism* may direct. Mr. Clay can lose nothing by a course of conciliation; his opinions are known to all, and to whatever extent he may forbear to act or insist upon them, it will be regarded only as another and further sacrifice made to his country. Do not believe that the least *selfishness* influences me in anything I have suggested.

P. S.—Consider if it would not be better to drop everything about the *assent of States*, and making the banking power a mere emanation of congressional authority, exclude it from the discounting of promissory notes. The moneyed transactions of men will be put into the shape of bills of exchange, and the bank thus formed may be easily amended by future legislation, if the power of discounting *notes* should be found useful or

(159)

desirable. The political effect of settling this matter now and by *your means* will be great.

J. J. CRITTENDEN.

(Reverdy Johnson to J. J. Crittenden.)

BALTIMORE, August 30, 1841.

MY DEAR SIR,—I have just heard, from a source which I know may be relied upon, that Mr. Alexander Hamilton, of New York, who, it is understood, has been for several weeks in Washington and almost an inmate of the President's house, came over *last* evening from Washington to have an interview with Mr. Maher, of this city, and Judge Upshur, of Virginia, who has been in this place several days. Not being acquainted with either of the gentlemen, he obtained this morning an introduction to them. Mr. M. at once introduced the President's course in regard to the bank bill, and heard only the most decided opinions against it from him, which seemed to surprise him, and in a few moments, without more being said of a political character, the interview terminated. He then went to see Upshur, and was with him *in private* for several hours. Now, sir, *our impression is* (that is, the impression of the few to whom these facts are known) *that he has been sent up to sound these gentlemen in regard to a new cabinet,* and Mr. M., in respect to the department *you hold;* so thinking, I deem it due to you—to the friendship existing between us—that I lose no time in making this fact known to you for your consideration. It is exceedingly improbable that the visit of Hamilton could have any other purpose, and, if half the reports we hear from Washington are true, it is almost certain that the object I suggest is true. If you think it proper, you are at liberty to show this to any member of the cabinet you please. Assuming my conjecture to be right, I forbear to speak of the movement, because I cannot do it without using terms of the President that should not be applied to him except in the last emergency.

Sincerely your friend,

J. J. CRITTENDEN.   REVERDY JOHNSON.

(R. P. Letcher to J. J. Crittenden.)

FRANKFORT, September 3, 1841.

DEAR CRITTENDEN,—I have just read your letter of the 26th with the liveliest interest. All your trials, difficulties, and vexations were fully understood by your friends in Kentucky as accurately as I now understand them after reading your interesting communication. No friend blamed you for not writing. Your silence told everything. We talked matters over and expressed our sympathies and our heartfelt regrets that official connection, obligations, and prudence necessarily limited your freedom of speech and action. No one, so far as I know, has intimated that you ought to have resigned upon the coming in of the veto. Some of your friends believed you would do so; others feared that in a moment of indignation and disappointment you might do so; but those who knew you best thought you would take no hasty action, but be governed by circumstances which should or might control a majority of the cabinet in their movements. I rather think that, under the influence of that opinion, I wrote you some five or six weeks since *to keep wide awake and be cool.* The *veto* did not surprise me. I was fully apprised of the Captain's intention for some considerable time before. I had rather indulged in the hope that his heart might fail him before the time for final action. Duff Green told me the President told him he would veto the bill. The Van Buren party, in this quarter, announced that the *veto* would come weeks before it reached us.

After I saw he had some four or five Virginia schoolmasters around him, I confess I lost all hope. Ah, that was too bad!—our chief cook, in whom we placed all confidence, to poison óur favorite dish! Yes, I believe most confidently he has the arsenic ready for the second dish, and will certainly dash it in if Wise and Rives and Mallory tell him. Just let those fellows say "*Go* it, my Captain Tyler, old Virginia is at your back; Clay is trying to head you; don't be frightened by one of Clay's mobs. If you do, Virginia will disown you; Virginia will be everlastingly disgraced in your person if you yield. Jackson carried everything before him by his *firmness*, and so can you. *You* are the most popular man in America; *you* elected Harrison, and can elect yourself again easily. If you give way, you are a lost, ruined, disgraced, discarded creature, and Clay will be the next President!" Then let Calhoun make him a secret visit, and the poison goes in to a dead and moral certainty. The motives by which the Captain is influenced are as distinctly known throughout all the land as his illustrious name is. All parties speak of it openly, mixed up with abuse, scorn, and ridicule. Should the cabinet be placed in such a situation by the President as to force them to resign, *he* will have no party. He may have five or six miserable, vain, foolish abstractionists, three nullifiers, and one Anti-Mason,—not enough for a decent funeral procession. The Whigs, before they adjourn, in the event of a dissolution of the cabinet, ought to hold a meeting and solemnly devote him, transfer and assign him over to the "Locofocos." They ought, furthermore, by resolution, to declare "that no honest Whig should hold office under such a faithless public servant." Then let the Captain "paddle his own canoe," assisted by his Virginia friends. If once he gets ashore, I will give him a certificate of honesty, probity, and good demeanor,—qualities which he never had and never can have except upon paper. I am rejoiced in my soul that Webster will conduct himself like a man in this business. To tell you the plain truth, I honestly distrusted him. I feared he would disgrace himself by giving up his principles rather than his place. I thought he was upon the edge of a precipice, just ready to fall into an abyss, not knowing how far down he had to go. Now, I am relieved in my feelings, and am highly gratified. I feel as joyful over him as a good, old, faithful member of a church would feel over a brother who had wandered off from the true faith in pursuit of idols and had just returned to the fold, full of prayer and devotion, ready and willing and able to persevere to the end in the good cause. The Whigs are more firmly united now than before ; rely upon this. *The vetoes* are a good cement to hold them together.

I received your letter this evening just after I had finished the labors of the day, and this accounts for my long letter. Should the cabinet dissolve just after you finish reading it, you will be ready to come to Kentucky, where all will be rejoiced to see you, and none more so than your friend,

R. P. LETCHER.

(Governor Letcher to J. J. Crittenden.)

Sunday Morning, September 5, 1841.

DEAR CRITTENDEN,—We got no mail from Washington to-day nor yesterday. Our anxiety to hear how matters now stand in the city has, I assure you, become too intense to be altogether agreeable. My own fears, I confess, as to a favorable issue are much greater and stronger than my hopes. I have talked over matters with a very few select friends, again and again speculating upon this, that, and the other thing, so repeatedly that really I have lost all sort of interest in my own conversation; still, I allow myself to be harassed, fretted, vexed, excited by reflection to such a pitch, that, by way of a sort of occupation to keep myself as *cool* as possible, and to avoid all intercourse to shun the everlasting question, What is the news ? do, for God's sake, tell us the news from Washington? I have shut myself up in the office (Sunday as it is) and find myself writing, for what purpose or for what object the Lord only knows. Why don't you go to church, say you, and take the benefit of the clergy ? Why, it would be a great sin in me to go to church with my state of feelings at this moment. I should be cursing and d——g at all the Virginia politicians (with a few exceptions), the schoolmasters, and "Tyler too," during the whole of the service.   I could not hear with any patience the Apostle Paul preach just at this time.   If I had all power in my hands for one month I wonder if I should not be the mildest ruler that ever lived! I should not ask Lynch for any of his assistance. I would be calm, and cool, and prudent, though not *wise* by any means; but as sure as the sun shines I should afford materials enough for some historian to write a mighty big book, in which there would be a great deal of good reading too.

In the first place, I would have the law of treason better understood, more practically defined, and more clearly illustrated, so that the weakest man in society could comprehend it, and "Tyler too" should be able to see and to feel its force.   Impeachments! why, there should be no such foolish word in all my vocabulary.   As a man gets older he gets more sensible,— I know I do.   He sees things in a clearer light.   I feel quite sure Botts does.   I have just read his *love letter* to his constituents, and I would not be at all afraid to trust him with all *necessary powers* for, and during, a short reign.   I don't know Botts personally, but I like him; he is an honest man, a bold man, and a sensible man.   I wonder, if Tyler should make another electioneering tour to the great West, if Botts will bear him company! I should say they would be exceedingly agreeable to each other, just at this time, as traveling companions.

But enough of all this.   If you are under the necessity, both as a patriot and as a gentleman, to quit the miserable concern, come home quickly.   There is but one Kentucky.   Keep up your spirits; be of good cheer and of good temper; above all things, come back to my *government,* and my *people* will take care of you and will take a pleasure in it.

John Russell told me, some days ago, when I wrote to you, he wished to say if you returned to Kentucky you must send to his mill all the time.   He says he will *whip* any man who denies his right to furnish you with corn-meal, and flour, and pork, and whip *you* if you don't take it, or if you make a wry face at it.

Having written thus far, I feel much better, I thank you. One idea: if you return to Kentucky and feel like practicing law, take my everlasting worker Harlan, for your partner, and he will be pleased, I have no doubt, to join you.   Such another partner could not be had in any country.

Still, I have a little sort of a hope that Tyler's advisers will admonish him to yield, and that all may yet be well.   I am going to join a hunting-party, Wednesday,—Charley Morris and the Bacons,—about three miles from town.   I shall make the experiment whether the chase is not more agreeable and amusing than reading petitions and cursing our rulers.

Now, if you halloo *Enough!* I will let you off. Enough! you say, then I am done.

Your friend,
LETCHER.

P.S.—Give Webster, when you come away, one good, affectionate shake of the hand for me, and say every kind thing to him you please.

(R. P. Letcher to J. J. Crittenden.)

September 8, 1841.

DEAR CRITTENDEN,—What's a man to do when he sees nothing, hears nothing, knows nothing, and wants to *see, hear,* and *know* everything? Such is my condition at present. We get nothing from Washington, except the passage of the land bill, which may be vetoed, and if so, we shall run distracted without a doubt. I wrote you yesterday, and I write again to-day, just for the want of occupation. What adds to my vexation is, that I had the misfortune, returning from dinner, to meet old W., or rather as I stepped into the judge's room, there he was, talking loudly against a United States bank. My presence brought him to a conclusion, and, when he recovered, he did me the favor to walk out. I am told he is much tickled with the idea that "brother C." is to be one of the cabinet. Should there be a new cabinet Calhoun will have a finger in the pie, and one of the dynasty comes in to dead certainty. I saw by a paper of the 2d that Archer was to make a speech in favor of the bank bill. I am rejoiced! I like Archer much, and should be highly gratified for him to do his country some service, and add to his own reputation. The bill will pass with Archer's vote, and who knows but Tyler may have *a dream, or see sights,* which will bring him to a knowledge of the truth? If he don't see sights now, he will after awhile. I expect to hear of his talking and crying in his sleep before long; he has raised the devil in this country. I received a letter this morning from a man in Russell County, asking me if I thought it would be an unpardonable sin to go to the city and kill him; the fellow wrote as if he thought he had a call to put him to death. Another writes me, to call the legislature together for the purpose of passing a Commonwealth's bank, and damning John Tyler. I don't know whether you will be a private gentleman or a public one when you get this. If you have left the city, I hope you have authorized John Tyler to open this letter.

Truly yours,
R. P. LETCHER.

Hon. J. J. CRITTENDEN.

(J. J. Crittenden to the President.)

WASHINGTON, September 11, 1841.

SIR,—Circumstances have occurred in the course of your administration, and chiefly in the exercise by you of the veto power, which constrain me to believe that my longer continuance in office, as a member of your cabinet, will be neither agreeable to you, useful to the country, nor honorable to myself.

Do me the justice, Mr. President, to believe that this conclusion has been adopted neither capriciously nor in any spirit of party feeling or personal hostility, but from a sense of duty, which, mistaken though it may be, is yet so sincerely entertained that I cheerfully sacrifice to it the advantages and distinctions of office.

Be pleased, therefore, to accept this as my resignation of the office of Attorney-General of the United States.

Very respectfully yours, etc.,

J. J. CRITTENDEN.

The PRESIDENT.

The following March Mr. Crittenden was elected to the Senate to fill Mr. Clay's unexpired term, and was re-elected for a full term.

(J. J. Crittenden to R. P. Letcher.)

WASHINGTON, September 11, 1841.

DEAR LETCHER,—I have just received and read your long and interesting letter of the 3d instant. You say towards the conclusion of it, "Should the cabinet dissolve just after you finish reading this," etc. Now, for so long a shot this is absolutely the best on record; it was exactly to the centre. The cabinet was in the process of dissolution. The resignations of Ewing, Bell, Badger, and myself were on the way to the President's when your letter was brought in and thrown on my table. I fear you will have to detract somewhat from your *eulogiums* on Webster; he has declined to join in our resignations, and will continue in office, finally, as I *calculate*, to be turned out. Granger, too, will continue in office, and perhaps be reserved for the same fate. I do not know who will supply the places of the resigned. I am not even fully apprised of the speculations of the day. Baillie Peyton is here and greatly pressed to take a cabinet place. I have talked with him; he is resolved *not* to accept, but may *be overcome*. I have just heard General Clinch spoken of for Secretary of War. I am satisfied he will accept. Judge Upshur, of Virginia, is spoken of, and will, I suppose, accept. The President will have hard work to make up a cabinet which will please the Senate. As the time is but short, he will probably have to resort to the alternative of nominating unexceptionable individuals at a distance; if they do not accept, he gains time and may supply the vacancies in the absence of the Senate. There is great firmness and great excitement among the Whigs in Congress, and a more resolute union among them, except, perhaps, as to a portion of the Northern Whigs, who are held in a sort of neutrality and suspense by the course of Mr. Webster. The Whig members from the great West are, to a man, united, fierce, and denunciatory towards Mr. Tyler. From what I have heard, they will publish an address to the people of the United States, recommending a course of action to the Whigs of the Union, denouncing the course of Mr. Tyler as a betrayal and abandonment of the Whigs, and proclaiming that they will no longer consider themselves responsible for the conduct of the Executive Department, etc. A nobler set of fellows than the Whig members of the present Congress never represented any people, and the energy, union, and firmness which has marked their conduct is worthy of all praise. The difficulties, trials, and mortifications to which they have been subjected were very great; yet, so far, they have been equal to it all, and but few have been faithless or slow of heart.

Since I closed the last sentence, I have heard that the new nominations for the cabinet have been made,—Walter Forward, Secretary of Treasury; Judge McLean, Secretary of War; Judge Upshur, Secretary of Navy; and Mr. Legare, of South Carolina, Attorney-General. What the Senate will do with them I am not informed. The great difficulty will be with Upshur.

Do not prepare any of your sympathies for me. I am proud and happy, and as for all the losses and inconveniences that may come on me from the loss of my office, I shall bear them manfully, strengthened to do so by the consciousness that I have acted as honor and duty to the country required. Between the first and tenth of the next month I shall take a drink with you in your own house. Keep your bottles set out and full, and if your liquor be good and your entertainment the same, I will then give you all the particulars about the great affairs at Washington. Farewell.

Your friend,

R. P. Letcher,　　　　　　　　　J. J. Crittenden.
　　Governor.

(J. J. Crittenden to R. P. Letcher.)

Washington, September 13, 1841.

Dear Letcher,—I wrote to you the day before yesterday, and I promise that this shall be a short letter, provoked chiefly by your letter of the 5th instant, received this morning. Since

I last wrote you, Granger has resigned, so that Mr. Tyler has been deprived of the whole of his most enlightened and patriotic cabinet, *except Mr. Webster.* He holds on, and looks like grim death ! What say you ? shall I give him all the affectionate gratulations and messages you sent in your last letter ? or what disposition shall I make of them ?

He has, at least, faltered on the way ; I still hope that that is the most of it, and that, though he has faltered, it will be but for a moment, and that he will redeem himself by an abandonment of Mr. Tyler. His time for repentance is very short ; the thoughts and feelings of men are moving on too rapidly to afford him much delay.

He may yet, by energy and decision, rescue himself ; his delegation are uneasy at his situation, and if they advise him manfully it may save him.

The Whig members of Congress are about to publish an address ; it is said to be a very good one ; you will get it almost as soon as this letter, and that, together with Ewing's letter in the *Intelligencer* of this morning, will give you a full view of the state of affairs here.

Your friend,
J. J. CRITTENDEN.

You do not think more highly of Harlan than I do, and when I get back to Kentucky, if he should think a partnership would not be disadvantageous to him, I dare say it would be quite to my liking. On my return we will talk more of this.

J. J. CRITTENDEN.

(George E. Badger to J. J. Crittenden.)

RALEIGH, February 4, 1842.

MY DEAR SIR,—I learn from the papers that you are in Washington. What on earth are you lurking about there for ? Do you expect any favors from the White House ? or are you endeavoring to get Legare to appoint you his clerk ? Are you prepared to become a Tyler-man in politics ? and do you, in poetry, prefer the Poet's Lament to Milton, or *Ahasuerus* to Paradise Lost ? This latter question you ought to be prepared to answer before you indulge any hopes of advancement. Pray give an account of yourself. Do you ever visit President Square ? If you do, you can think of a late Secretary of the Navy. Do you remember a certain carpet which will owe its preservation from moths for half a century to your diligent sprinkling thereon of what *we boys* used to call "*Amber?*" Do you remember a certain lady of a certain Secretary of the Navy, who exhibited the greatest singularity of taste in saying that a certain Attorney-General was a *good-looking man ?* I know you have been longing to write to me, but have been withheld by the fear of the seeming presumption of an *ex*-Attorney-General addressing an *ex*-Secretary, and I write as a proof of my favor, and an evidence of my condescension to put you at ease. What is to hinder you from getting in the cars and paying me a visit? I can give you a good bed, a good dinner, good wine, and a hearty welcome. I suppose Ewing is endeavoring to get an appointment. His *corn-planting* letter of resignation ought to get him a clerkship, particularly if he has read Ahasuerus, and committed half as much of it to memory as he once recited to me from Dante's Inferno. Wishing you success in all your efforts to obtain executive advancement,

I am very truly your friend,
GEORGE E. BADGER.

(Letter from J. J. Crittenden to R. P. Letcher.)

February 8, 1842.

MY DEAR LETCHER,—I have just finished a sort of business or semi-official letter to you, and now I wish to write you entirely on private and personal account.

You are, I know from past experience, a sagacious gentleman, and good at far-seeing and guessing; but still, I think you can hardly have an adequate notion of the state of things here. Utterly condemned as the administration has long been, and it is still growing in scorn and contempt, and there is really danger of its sinking into such impotence and odium as to paralyze the whole government,—and yet Mr. Tyler, in this condemned and desolate condition, steeped to the lips in shame, is still, if the universal reports that I hear be true, inflated with ideas of his *great popularity*,—second to none but Washington, —thinking of nothing so much as his re-election,—holding Whigs and Locofocos equally as his opponents, and reserving his favors and offices for *Tyler-men.* From all I can collect, such is about the condition of your President. Of his ministry I know but little. Webster looks gloomy and sad. In Congress they seem to have but little influence. The little corps of Tyler-men do not seem to thrive well, and even they do not always conform to administration measures. In the midst of such disasters, discipline may naturally lose its force.

Notwithstanding the necessity of the case, and that even members of Congress were without their pay, the treasury-note bill for five millions of dollars was forced through Congress by a nominal majority of one in each branch, and that majority obtained only by the silence or voluntary withdrawal of members whose votes, if given at all, would have changed the majority and defeated the bill. There was, in fact, a majority against it in both houses of Congress, and yet, without that supply, there was not a dollar in the treasury to pay either army or navy. In one month I suppose it to be inevitable that Mr. Tyler must come before Congress for another supply of treasury notes, and I doubt whether any exigency will induce them to grant it. Such is the state of affairs, and from their sad condition I must infer that you have withdrawn that salutary participation which you were formerly pleased to exercise in the administration of this government. Clay, I think, would now acknowledge our wisdom in advising against his coming to this session of Congress. You have saved him from a most critical and delicate position by the failure to pass the legislature resolutions against the bankrupt law. He will soon resign, and in time for the General Assembly to elect his successor, and that event will occur with some circumstances rather disagreeable to me, in respect to my being a candidate. I was, year after year, a somewhat prominent advocate of that law; but yet it is one of those measures in respect to which I should have conformed to the wishes of my constituents had I remained in the Senate. To declare that sentiment on the eve of an election might expose me to the suspicion of sacrificing a former opinion, not to a high sense of duty, but to the ambition of obtaining a seat in the Senate.

And now, sir, I wish to take a little hand in your administration. Imprimis, being informed that Bishop Smith is not to be reappointed to the office he now holds, or lately held, of superintendent (I believe that is the title) of common schools, I do very cordially recommend Mr. Sayer, of our town, to that office. I think he will devote himself to it zealously and usefully; he has education and talents and manners; and lastly, my wife writes me, quite imploringly, to entreat you to give to Atticus Bibb the office of Commonwealth's Attorney, for the district in which he lives.

He is said to be a noble-hearted and talented fellow, and his late reform may entitle him to kind consideration. I hope that you may be able to reconcile it to your sense of duty to give him the office.

Remember me kindly to our friend, the Lieutenant-Governor, and to all our other friends in and out of the legislature, and, as the Chinese said to Mr. Van Buren, "May you live long to be a *security* to your people."

Your friend,
J. J. CRITTENDEN.

R. P. LETCHER,
    Governor of Ky.

(J. J. Crittenden to R. P. Letcher.)

WASHINGTON, December 9, 1842.

MY DEAR SIR,—After a most toilsome and most dangerous journey I reached here on the second day of the session, being the eleventh day after I left home.

The Whigs from all quarters seem to me, as far as I can see, to bear their defeats with fortitude and spirit, and to look to the future with all the confidence that could be expected. It appears to be the general impression of those that I have talked with here, that, for want of a present motive and immediate object, the Whig party has not been and cannot be roused to a full exertion of its strength till the next presidential election. This is at least a consolatory view, and I am willing to confide in it as the true explanation and state of the case. But this fluctuating zeal, that requires so much to get it up and so little to put it down, is not the most reliable. Under present circumstances, Clay's truest friends here seem inclined in favor of a national convention. They do not doubt his nomination by such a convention, and think it will have the effect of reassuring the party and combining all the little fragmentary parts that might otherwise be disposed to fly off in the hour of need. I incline to this course myself, and regard it as a measure to fortify, and not really to bring in question, the pretensions of Mr. Clay.

I send you with this a copy of the President's message, that the people might not be delayed in the enjoyment of this precious document. Expresses were prepared to convey it with the rapidity of steam throughout the land at the moment of its delivery to Congress, and upon some false rumor that a quorum of the Senate was present on Tuesday last, off went the message in all directions one day before there was any Congress assembled to receive it. This little accident produced so much ridicule as to disturb that grave consideration with which such a revelation from John Tyler might otherwise have been received.

Since my arrival here I have been surprised to learn, from inquiries made of me, how extensively the hopes and apprehensions of my defeat in our senatorial election had gone abroad. A Loco member of Congress, from Arkansas, told another member, a Whig, who scorned the idea of my being beaten, that he was well informed about it, and thought I would be defeated, and I suppose that the Tyler party fully expect it. All this furnishes grounds to apprehend that greater effort and preparation have been used for the purpose than we anticipated.

Owsley heard, as he passed through Lancaster, that your nephew, George McKee, would vote for Hardin in preference to all others. And Phelps, of Covington, informed me that the member from Kenton, a Mr. Bennett, I think, was very indifferent for whom he voted. He was elected as a Whig, but his county, I believe, is Locofoco. This was told me as I came up the Ohio. And Phelps also gave me to understand that he had defeated an attempt that had been got up by the Locos to instruct him to vote against me. I give you these particulars that they may be remedied in equity, if any such remedy there be. My old acquaintance and friendship with his father and relatives would make McKee's opposition quite mortifying to me. I know that the mere fact of your relationship puts it out of your power to do anything in the matter. I hope, however, it will turn out that Owsley's information was incorrect.

You will see that in both houses of Congress propositions have been made for the repeal of the bankrupt law. I thought from the first that a temporary bankrupt law was better suited to this country than a permanent system, and was in favor of limiting it to two years. It was one of a series of measures urgently sought for by the Whigs of New York, Louisiana, etc., and rather conceded to them than desired by those of the Kentucky Whigs who supported it. It has to a great extent accomplished its object, and, though there may have been abuses, it has relieved from imprisonment (for in many of the States that remedy is continued) and a hopeless mass of debt many an honest man whose fortunes had been wrecked in the disastrous times through which we have passed. Under all the circumstances, and especially in deference to the opinions of my constituents, who, I believe, are opposed to the continuance of the law, I have made up my mind, I think, to vote for its repeal.

Your friend,
J. J. CRITTENDEN.

To R. P. LETCHER,
   Governor.

P.S.—Aren't you glad my paper has given out?

(R. P. Letcher to J. J. Crittenden.)

February 25, 1842.

DEAR CRITTENDEN,—The election for senator will come off this afternoon at three o'clock. I doubt whether there will be any opposition; none unless it should be *old Duke,*—your *friend* and my *enemy.* I don't believe, however, he will run. Colonel Johnson has just left me again, after *renewing his bond of fidelity.* We are getting very thick, I can tell you. If I had time I would make you laugh heartily about many matters connected with this election. Oh, the duplicity of this world!

Your friend,
LETCHER.

Hon. J. J. CRITTENDEN.

(R. P. Letcher to J. J. Crittenden.)

February 24, 1842.

DEAR CRITTENDEN,—I have only a moment to say a word or two. Mr. Clay's resignation was filed yesterday, and I am told that in one moment afterwards a few *demons* set about the *work of mischief*. They are endeavoring to bring out all sorts of opposition, trying everybody and anybody. Underwood, they think, would embody the greatest force, because of his Green River residence; but *that point has been guarded*. His friends won't allow the *trick* to be played, *that is settled;* and if Underwood was here he would settle it in the same way. Charley Morehead is talked of, but, in my opinion, he won't make the attempt. Ben Hardin is here; I presume he will be the opposition,—hope he will make a poor show. The old Monarch is also here, but I don't believe he came on that business. The D. is heading the party in opposition to you. I am told that a caucus was held last night; don't think there is the slightest danger of the result. Colonel Richard Johnson is now with me; he will act the gentleman, and go for you "*through thick* and *thin.*" Had a long talk with him since I commenced this letter. He will carry with him as many friends as he can, and really I must tell you that you are not to forget his honorable feelings and fair dealing. I know you like him, and you ought to like him.

Yours,

Hon. J. J. CRITTENDEN.   R. P. LETCHER.

(R. P. Letcher to J. J. Crittenden.)

FRANKFORT, February 26, 1842.

DEAR CRITTENDEN,—O. K., as you will, no doubt, hear from various quarters. The affair went off handsomely, quietly, flatteringly. Old man Golhom aided like a gentleman after he took time to cool. *He nominated you.* Colonel Dick Johnson called upon me last night, and swore " he had never exerted himself so much in all his life to keep down (as he said) a damned factious opposition of damned rascally Whigs, as well as Democrats." He did behave well, indeed, and *no mistake.*

Yours truly,

Hon. J. J. CRITTENDEN.   R. P. LETCHER.

(R. P. Letcher to J. J. Crittenden.)

FRANKFORT, April 9, 1842.

DEAR CRITTENDEN,—Clay's valedictory is exceedingly fine and appropriate; I admire it much. This village is crowded with bankrupts and lawyers. The D. and young D. are among the distinguished visitors. I know you will take pleasure in hearing that these two noble fellows are in good health. I had the honor to see them this morning, *face to face*, at the State-House gate. They looked interesting, but I had only a moment's satisfaction in beholding them. They appeared anxious, I thought, to deprive me of that pleasure. *When* will Congress adjourn? *When* will you be at home? What will Congress do? How does Captain Tyler stand? *How* do his promising boys behave? *How* does Webster stand the *racket?* Has he proved himself *clear* of all fornications by affidavits or otherwise, and will he remain in his present situation long, or will he be pushed out? I think he will be thrown overboard before very long.

Your friend,

Hon. J. J. CRITTENDEN.   R. P. LETCHER.

CHAPTER XIV.

1842.

THE following eloquent and touching appeal to the senator
from Arkansas, will strike all who knew Mr. Crittenden
as eminently characteristic of him:

Mr. Crittenden.—Mr. President, in reference to the charge
made against the Whig party by the senator from Arkansas,
that they were a debt, loan, and tax party, I can only observe,
that I had hoped a pause would be allowed, in the present condition of the government and the country, for breathing-time,
for patriotism to come into action. I have, however, heard, in
the last few days, two speeches from a gentleman known to me,
and esteemed by every one in all the relations of life, in which
he charges his friends with unworthy objects and intentions. I
have heard this charge uttered with deep regret. The calamities which menace the country require the co-operation of wise
counsels and unimpassioned deliberation. What tendency can
crimination and recrimination have to reach just conclusions?
What light can they shed upon public counsels? The fierce
fire of party is one that burns, but sheds no light. I am sure
it is impossible that in a heart so generous and so just as that
possessed by the senator from Arkansas, there should exist a
belief that the object of the Whig party was to bring down destruction on the country, or to involve him and his posterity in
the calamities that he depicts. It seems to me we might debate
on the affairs of government without so much asperity. I am
willing to bear all my responsibility; but it is known to every
gentleman in this body that the Whig party have not the control of the government, and in all fairness an undue share of
responsibility should not be thrown upon them. There is no man
more willing to retrench and reform than myself, and I believe
this to be the case with my friends. We are willing to take
counsel with these gentlemen themselves, and I implore them
not to suppose that we wish to fill the hands of the government
with money to squander in extravagance. How can the senator

from Arkansas, after casting an imputation on the Whig party of opposing and abusing the President, suppose that they were anxious to place in his hands the means of wasteful expenditures? I will vote for this bill, but I will do so with profound reluctance; I vote for it under a sense of obligation, which impels me to act from public duty. It seems to me that the allusions made by the senator from Arkansas, to the relations of the Whig party with the President of the United States, were unkind and ungenerous; but I will not be drawn into any debate on this point; I will choose the time and occasion to revert to such matters, if it should be ever necessary to do so. I had hoped the time had come—a marvelous time—when the two great contending parties might meet on one common platform and reason together.

On the 24th of May, 1842, there was a debate on the apportionment bill, and Mr. Crittenden argued for the smallest ratio of congressional representation. In relation to the other amendment proposed, that of not requiring States to be *districted* for the election of representatives, Mr. Crittenden did not approve of the modification; he did not wish it to be left *optional* with the States to take the district system or the general ticket system; he was conscientiously opposed to the latter and in favor of the former; he believed that the only fair mode of obtaining a just representation was by the local district system; he thought the general ticket system nothing but a return to the old continental Federal system. Give the States of New York, Pennsylvania, and Ohio that general ticket system, and these three States, he was confident, could control the other *twenty-three* with imperial power; he believed there was not now a single State which elected their presidential electors by district, and in that there was a bright example burning with evidence of what might be expected in relation to elections for members of Congress. He was not willing to convert our republican system into an oligarchy. The senator from New York, Mr. Wright, tells us that if we pass the law for districting the States, New York will not obey. This sort of defiance should not be brandished in the face of the country to weaken our great bonds of union. He trusted this sentiment, though forcibly spoken, was uttered without deliberation.

(James Buchanan to R. P. Letcher.)

WASHINGTON, April 17, 1842.

MY DEAR SIR,—I have done all I could do for Kentucky and her highly esteemed governor. I believe the course I have pursued has been satisfactory to his magnificent ambassador, General Leslie Coombs, and to *Mr. Crittenden.* By-the-by, this same ambassador is a man among a thousand; I like him very much, and yet I have never seen any specimen of human nature with which *he* could be compared. I think he possesses a clear head and a warm heart, and yet he talks too much for a diplomatist, unless he acts upon the principle of Talleyrand, that the use of speech was given to man to conceal his ideas. He is an agreeable study, however, and I should be pleased to have another chance at him. I think the Whig party, just now, is in a sick and lowly condition, and the sooner you get out of it the better. The grand *Sir Hal* is worth the whole concern, and they will, in the end, be false to him. Some of them are beginning to look over their left shoulder already. With how much more dignity he would close his political career by retiring to Ashland, and keeping out of the presidential struggle! The just fame which he has acquired ought to satisfy any man's ambition. So far as I am personally concerned, I am sincerely sorry he has left the Senate; he was an *ugly customer*, it is true, but there was a pleasure in contending against such a man, and one sustained no disgrace in being vanquished by him. I like Crittenden very much, and he is a very able and adroit partisan debater. I know nothing of the four-horse team to which you allude; I think they do not desire to hitch on with them the *hero* of the Thames. The late minister to England, or the late governor of Tennessee, will, most probably, be Van's *Vice*, should he be nominated. But you will learn all about it from his own lips, as I presume you will be of the party at Ashland to welcome the ex-President and his *Neptune*. Tyler and his cabinet are a poor concern; they live upon expedients from day to day, and have no settled principles by which to guide their conduct. The *Toadies* flatter him with the belief that whilst the politicians are deadly hostile to him, from jealousy of his rising fortunes, the people are everywhere rising *en masse* and coming to his rescue. Such is the tone of the Madisonians, and if you desire to obtain an office from him I advise you to pursue that course. Unless I am greatly mistaken in the signs of the times, an attempt will soon be made to *head Mr. Clay* on the subject of a national bank. It would seem that Tyler is now willing to approve the bill of Ewing, and Mr. Clay is to be attacked for having defeated the establishment of a bank from jealousy of Tyler,—Heaven save *the mark!* His constitutional scruples would be satisfied with the *provision*, that no branch should be established in any State without the consent of the legislature, though an agency to transact the business of the treasury would not require such permission. Tyler and Webster, then, are to become the *chiefs* of the great Whig National Bank party, and Clay is to be denounced for having *prevented* the adoption of his own favorite measure. So we go! This seems to be the present track, but how they may continue it is *mighty uncertain*. For myself, I am a looker-on here in Vienna. I have been long enough here to understand the game, though I never *play myself*. The movements in Pennsylvania have been voluntary, so far as I am concerned. The attempt of Colonel Johnson's friends there has been a greater failure than I anticipated. We shall not divide upon our presidential candidate. We have a way of chopping off the *heads* of those, without ceremony, who will not submit to the *decisions* of the party in the National Convention assembled.

With sentiments of grateful kindness,

I remain your friend,

JAMES BUCHANAN.

(J. J. Crittenden to Governor Letcher.)

WASHINGTON, May 1, 1842.

DEAR LETCHER,—My wife's arrival and my change of location, etc. have interrupted my correspondence for a time.

Clay's leaving Congress was something like the soul's quitting the body. His departure has had (at least I feel it so) an enervating effect. We shall gradually recover from it. Captain Tyler will serve as a *blister-plaster* to stimulate and excite us, and that, perhaps, is the very best use that he is susceptible of.

Tyler has produced the strangest sort of distraction and inaction that was ever seen. He sits in the midst of it, mighty busy and bustling,—the Tom Thumb of the scene,—thinking himself the admiration of the world and the favorite child of Providence. Take it altogether, it is the most severe burlesque on all human ambition and government that was ever witnessed. I know, however, that I can add nothing to your conception of the full merits of the scene. You have a quick taste for the perception of such rare exhibitions, and to your imagination I leave them. We understand here (and certainly the *Madisonian* gives signs of wrath) that the President is very angry with the poor Senate for its rudeness in rejecting some of his nominations, and especially that of Mr. Tyson, and threatens to turn out of office all "Clay Whigs and ultra Democrats," and to appoint none but "moderate men," *alias* Tyler-men.

The President and his men have been blustering about that matter, and I do believe that it has of late been seriously thought of, if not determined on, in his councils. But they will not dare to execute such a purpose. We cannot restrain him from turning men out of office, but the Senate can, and will, control him, as they ought, in respect to his appointments. There is not in the Senate a *single member* who calls himself, or is willing to be called, a Tyler-man. There are some of *both* sides of the chamber that are more or less infected, but this rather contributes to unite all the others, and to insure a majority against improper or unworthy appointments.

Benton acts and speaks openly and manfully, and says he will have no wh—g with this administration. On the contrary, Calhoun is supposed to be contracting a little more kindness for it. I understand that he is not unfrequently of their parties and councils, and things are supposed by some to be tending to a closer union between him and the administration. This is mere surmise, but it seems to me not at all improbable from the character and condition of the parties. They both want help badly, and each, perhaps, counts on using or cheating the other in the end. It is a pity such congenial parties should be kept asunder, and I wish, with all my heart, for a consummation of their union. If the administration will flatter Mr. Calhoun's ambition for the Presidency, he may carry over his followers to their support, and give them something of a basis for an "Administration Party." The very first movement, however, towards such an end would be the signal of alarm and hostility on the part of Benton, Buchanan, etc. But what is to issue out of the strange and unsettled state of things that now exists no one can foretell, and all seem to be standing still and looking and waiting for events. So far as I can learn, Clay's retirement has had the happiest effect upon the public feeling and opinion in respect to him, and all the indications seem to be that, without the aid of any convention, he will be the candidate of the universal Whig party. I think we have every prospect of unanimity on our side, and that there is on the other side almost a certainty of division and discord.

I hope that Kentucky will give Clay a triumphant reception on his return home. If ever man did, he deserves it, and Kentucky will be as much honored in giving as he in receiving. Its effect abroad will be good, and will give a tone to that public feeling which, I hope, will be everywhere awakened.

I am weary of Washington, yet see no prospect of getting away from here sooner than the middle of July.

The prevailing impression here seems to be that Lord Ashburton will settle all difficulties with us. He appears to me to be a clever old gentleman, and that, you know, is saying a great deal for a lord. Webster must hope to heal his character a little by making peace, and I think, therefore, that we may expect it.

I have no intercourse with Tyler and his secretaries. I do not seek them, and they seem to avoid me. I can hardly imagine how you get along without me. I hope that you suffer greatly from my absence. I should like to spend the balance of this evening with you, "Old Master," Mason, etc. Coombs must be doing a good business in Philadelphia, and I hope will be able to bring the Schuylkill Bank to terms. My best respects to Mrs. Letcher.

Your friend,
J. J. CRITTENDEN.

(R. P. Letcher to J. J. Crittenden.)

FRANKFORT, May 30, 1842.

DEAR CRITTENDEN,—Van Buren arrived and departed very soon after I wrote you last; he reached here in the evening and left next morning. *Don't mention* it, for the honor of our city, but such another reception never occurred in any *age* or *country*. He was received on *top of the Hill* by some *thirty Locos*, and the *procession* formed immediately with all the pomp and parade you can imagine. *Four* rickety buggies, sixteen horsemen,— *poor* horses and shabby riders *at that*,—a stage with *three* passengers inside and twenty little boys outside, an open barouche in front with the musicians (exclusive of negroes and boys), constituted the procession. I don't know *where* the little fellow was placed, whether in the middle or behind. Jeptha Dudley and the honorable gentleman were somewhere in the same vehicle. They marched through the city, down by Phil Swigert's, and up by your house, and up to the front of the Capitol. And where was Phil Swigert? I can't tell you. Phil was one of the committee to receive Mr. V. B. from Colonel Johnson and his friends, and give him a *grand entry into town*. Well, poor Phil, when he saw the sight on top of the Hill, and heard the *little* rascals cry out, "Stand back, gentlemen, *don't crowd*," broke down the Hill and got into the railroad *cut*, and has not been seen since. Well, when *the show* arrived in front of the Capitol, there was quite a good-looking crowd assembled. Hewitt *spoke at him*. I heard *not a word of it*. Van Buren spoke a word or two, in a sort of confidential whisper, when two or three fellows called out, "*A little louder, Mister!* we want to hear you." "The speech is over, anyhow," cried another fellow. Taking it altogether, this was the most complete burlesque on all public receptions that could be devised by the art of mortal man. I was vexed and a little mortified, but my mortification went off in a roar of *laughter* all by myself.

Your sincere friend,
R. P. LETCHER.

(Henry Clay to J. J. Crittenden.)

ASHLAND, June 3, 1842.

MY DEAR SIR,—I received your favor of the 27th with its inclosure. I was glad to perceive that you had taken ground in favor of a numerous House of Representatives. I have long entertained that opinion, and I believe the larger house will have always a greater effect in checking executive power, as well as being a better representative of the people. I am very sorry that you think so little good is to come out of Captain Tyler. I hoped that my absence from Washington might have contributed to his improvement; if it has had no such effect, he must be incorrigible. Is it true that he has threatened, and means to turn out the Collector of Philadelphia, because he would not dismiss some forty Whigs from office? There is a very great embarrassment and distress prevailing in Kentucky, much more than I imagined before I came home. Every description of property without exception is greatly depressed and still declining in value, and what aggravates the distress,—no one can see *when* or *how* it is to terminate. Most of our hempen manufacturers are ruined, or menaced with ruin. This is owing to the introduction of India and other foreign stuffs used in bagging. Our people say that they cannot do with a less protection than five cents the square yard upon bagging. When the tariff gets to the Senate (will it ever get there?) you and *your colleague* are expected to take care of this single Kentucky manufacture. I am glad that our friends in Congress bear up so cheerfully under recent adverse results in State elections. Seeing, however, that the Captain claims the victory (whether it be won by Democrats or Whigs, with rather more pleasure when achieved by the former), I hope that our friends will recover from their apathy and disgust and treat him to some Whig victories. Will you not concur in the Senate in the reduction, made by the House, of the enormous appropriations asked by the Departments of War and Navy? It seems to me that the state of the country, the state of the treasury, and the interest of the Whig party, all unite in favor of that reduction. The senseless cry of the *defenses of the country*, the augmentation of the navy, etc., ought to be wholly disregarded. Had the estimates been double what they are, and a proposition made to bring them down to their present amount, this same cry would have been raised. Mr. Van Buren spent four or five days with me, accompanied by Mr. Paulding; we had a great deal of agreeable conversation, but not much of politics. Both the gentlemen appeared to be pleased with their visit. The public reception was quite imposing in Lexington,—much better than Van Buren has probably received anywhere during his journey.

Present my warm regards to Mrs. Crittenden and your messmates, General Green and lady.

Faithfully your friend,

Hon. J. J. CRITTENDEN. H. CLAY.

(R. P. Letcher to J. J. Crittenden.)

FRANKFORT, June 3, 1842.

DEAR CRITTENDEN,—I cannot imagine what you will all do in the city to keep yourselves out of a state of torpidity since the war in Rhode Island is ended, and the Stanley and Wise affair is compromised *honorably to both parties*. I have not seen the terms of adjustment, but it is enough to hear the affair was arranged to the mutual satisfaction of each party concerned in the handsomest manner possible. *Killed none, wounded none, scared none*, and *honor* divided. Well, I am really glad there was nobody hurt, and that there was no fight; but just between ourselves, I don't exactly see how that *lick* was withdrawn. I guess it was all right and proper; but, for want of accurate knowledge, I cannot quite see into the thing. Hereafter I hope each will entertain towards the other all proper respect.

The judges of the Court of Appeals adjourn to-morrow, and I shall be left very much alone. Hodges has gone to Washington to get an office. Phil Swigert has eloped since the Van Buren reception, and may possibly never return. Judge Brown is sick in bed, but will be well enough to take a little of my old brandy to-day with the judges,—none of whom, I am sorry to tell you, have joined the temperance cause. Old Master is entirely *incog.;* nobody even sees him. Cates is very gloomy and snappish, and is exceedingly disagreeable; he has lost all his bets upon every race that has been run. Jake Swigert has retired into private life. Edmund Taylor is agreeable at all times except when Cates is about, and then he takes the *pouts*. Colonel Dick Johnson was here a few days ago; he seems to understand very well that Mr. Van Buren is *stacking the cards;* but he will have to stand it. Dick is much the best fellow of the two; but he will be bamboozled as sure as a gun. He intimated to me he would prefer Clay next to himself to any man in the Union. You never saw a more restless, dissatisfied man in your life than Dick is.

The Clay barbecue is all the talk now. I wrote to Governor Morehead this morning about one hundred and ninety-five stand of arms due the State of Kentucky from the United States. You once introduced a bill about them; look into the affair. The claim is perfectly just. I wrote to Morehead last winter or fall upon the subject; but he may have forgotten the business altogether.

Your friend,
R. P. LETCHER.

(R. P. Letcher to J. J. Crittenden.)

FRANKFORT, June 7, 1842.

DEAR CRITTENDEN,—I write to-day merely to keep up a sort of running fire. Since Van Buren's departure I have not *seen* or *heard* of Clay. I presume he is engaged in loading his *big gun*, to make a great report Thursday next. The *old horse* is upon *rising ground*, I think, and if he should meet with no accident, will run a great race. Keep a good lookout in your part of the track and see that there are no obstructions thrown in his way; he "can win the race if he is kept well, turned well, and rode well." Phil S. has once more made his appearance in public; he laughed at himself till the tears ran down his cheeks. What has become of John Russell? Is he helping Hodges to get an office? The Relief party are not so *rampantaut* as they were in the spring; such another pressure was never known in this State. I had a hearty laugh with Van Buren. He asked me how I stood the campaign for governor, how I liked crowds, etc. I replied, "Well, I delight in crowds." "But," said he, "did you not get tired of speaking, and how long did you speak?" "Generally about four hours," said I, "in the daytime, and then a small *check* of about two hours *at night*." "Is it possible?" said Van. "But I suppose you must have been fatigued making the *same speech* so often!" "Ah!" said I, "never *the same speech*. Your administration furnished the most fruitful topics for discussion, and I had not gotten half through with you before the campaign closed." Van laughed heartily, and said he had not thought of *that*. He inquired if I ever told that *stud*-horse story upon him. "Yes," I replied, "once, to about five thousand people." "It took well," said he, "no doubt, for it is the best story in the world." The little fellow is busy making his arrangements for another trial. Let him come! I believe we can beat him, or any man of his party who has been spoken of.

Yours,
LETCHER.

(R. P. Letcher to J. J. Crittenden.)

FRANKFORT, June 21, 1842.

DEAR CRITTENDEN,—The old Prince is taking a pretty considerable rise everywhere, I can tell you. I guess he now begins to see the good of leaving the Senate,—of *getting off* awhile merely to *get on* better. He must hereafter remain a little quiet and *hold his jaw.* In fact, he must be *caged,*—that's the point, *cage him!* He swears by all the gods, he will keep cool and stay at home. I rather think he will be prudent, though I have some occasional fears that he may write too many letters; still, he is quite a handy man with the pen, and his letters have *some good* reading in them. Will Scott run upon his ticket as Vice-President? That matter ought to be understood very soon. Our people will move before long, and they would like to know what they are about before the work is begun. The Whigs were fooled too badly not to be particular another time. If Scott is the man of sense I think he is, he will not hesitate about the matter. Tyler, it appears from what Wise says, intends to veto the tariff bill, if it should pass! I wonder if he *hopes* to die a natural death? I rather think he wishes to render himself conspicuous by being hung. I should be sorry to say anything to wound your sensibilities, particularly as he is a friend of yours; but I am inclined to say he is the damndest rascal and biggest fool of the age. Hodges has returned full of wrath; he failed in getting an office. Charley Morehead is the man who is entitled to all the *damns* of the Whigs if a Loco is elected here. Tell John Russell to move himself home; he has been playing the game of cheating and deception long enough. Does he still board with Captain Tyler, or does Bob board with him? Order him off, and come home as soon as you can. I have the best assortment of good wines now in Kentucky, to say nothing of whisky and brandy, and nobody to drink a drop of it.

Your friend,
R. P. LETCHER.

(J. J. Crittenden to R. P. Letcher.)

SENATE, June 23, 1842.

MY DEAR LETCHER,—I owe you for two or three very interesting letters, and have nothing to pay you with. Captain Tyler and his sayings and doings are rich themes; but, then, he and they are so notorious that you are as well acquainted with them as I am.

He is supposed to be now pluming his wings for a new flight of treachery and folly. Rumors of changes and cabinets and measures fill the city, and are the subjects of our conversation in all companies. I believe that some such movement is in contemplation. Tyler cannot be insensible to the impotency and degradation of his present position, and may well conclude that any change must be for the better. He has injured the

Whigs deeply, and *therefore* hates them deeply. He does not hope for, and probably does not wish, any reconciliation with the Whigs; that is altogether impracticable. He must look, therefore, to the Locofocos, and his natural inclinations concur with the necessity of the case. His contemplated movements must, therefore, be made with the view of conciliating and coalescing with *them* or *some section* of that party. I think there cannot be a general coalition of that party with him, but that he may probably come upon terms with the southern branch of it; that is, with Calhoun and his tails, etc. The result of this would be a schism in the party very beneficial to the country. My wish is to see the Whig party rid of him—rid of the nuisance; and their true policy is to strip him of all disguise and compel him to appear in his true character of enmity and hostility. I think you may rely on it that the Whig party in Congress will act considerately and firmly. No public body, at least no previous Congress, were ever called to act under more circumstances of disadvantage and embarrassment. Thwarted and obstructed by the President, abused and reviled by the press, they have still toiled on in their patriotic course, and endeavored to serve their country in the midst of all this opposition and reviling. They are ever abused and slandered for imputed delay and negligence in the transaction of the public business, and they are thus abused by the President and the press, when he himself has been the main cause of all the derangement and delay that have occurred. I wish I could have been with you at the great Clay barbecue (I am opposed to the word "festival"). You may depend on it that Clay is going ahead like a *locomotive*. You will have heard of his nomination in Georgia,—a really popular and enthusiastic movement. In New York the Whigs will have no one but Clay; they are determined, ardent, and confident of success. I was surprised and delighted to find prevailing there so pure and noble a spirit. The Whigs of the city of New York are already acting with skill and efficiency, and pressing their operations and clubs throughout the State. They say they will have Clay, and no one but him; that they can and will give him the vote of the State. I believe them, for their spirit and energy give appearance of success.

I must make a little speech; so farewell, and God bless you.

Your friend,

J. J. CRITTENDEN.

ROBT. P. LETCHER,
Governor.

CHAPTER XV.

1842–1843.

Letters of Crittenden, Clay, Letcher, and Webster.

(J. J. Crittenden to Mr. Clay.)

Senate-chamber, July 2, 1842.

MY DEAR SIR,—I have learned here, from a source to be relied on implicitly, that at the meeting to be held in Pennsylvania, on the 26th of this month, for the nomination of a presidential candidate, it is intended to nominate General Scott, but with a declaration of their intention to support the candidate of the Whig party, whether designated by a national convention or other evidences of the choice and preference of that party. All these qualifications of their nomination are understood as having reference to and as providing for the event of your being the candidate of the party, which all seem to regard as a settled matter. It would be better for all parties that the Pennsylvania convention should at once and directly give you their nomination; and I have had conversations with some of Scott's most confidential friends to convince them of the correctness of my opinion, especially as it regarded Scott himself. Such a nomination, in the midst of so universal and ardent a sentiment in your favor, would place him in a very awkward, if not ridiculous, position before the world, and would, besides, expose him to much jealousy and prejudice. No one that I have conversed with dissents from this view of the matter; but yet it is doubtful if anything can be done to change this purpose of the Pennsylvania convention. It is most probable that their nomination will be given to Scott, but will be regarded by themselves and others as merely nominal, and, with the qualifications annexed to it, as virtually and substantially a nomination of yourself. I shall not cease, however, to attend to the subject and to give it, as far as I can, the best shape and direction. There is but one opinion here, and that is that you are the candidate of the Whig party,—the only man to be thought of; the people have already settled that question. I assure you I have never witnessed on any other occasion such a flow of public opinion as is now going on in your favor. Making all allowance for my own bias, I can say that the

(185) "

progress of this public opinion is such as to surprise both your friends and opponents. The influence of that public opinion is manifest; it decides the doubtful, encourages the timid, stimulates the bold, and alarms your opponents. All this I see around me. There is no longer any serious thought of a Whig competition for you. I understand that Scott has lost all hope, and I wish he could be saved from all further disappointment or difficulty on the subject; he is a good Whig and a good fellow, and will eventually support you heartily. It is not to be wondered at if, in the first moments of his disappointment, he should show some little impatience, and his wounded vanity not permit him to take the most proper or prudent course. In common with the rest of us, he has his portion of vanity, and that may well be excused on account of his other great and good qualities. I like him, and am sure he will do right at last. I have not conversed with him about this Pennsylvania convention or his purpose in respect to it. I have spoken freely with Preston and Archer, his most intimate friends, and left it with them to counsel him. Both of them fully agree with me as to the folly of bringing him into competition with you, and would be glad to see him *out of the whole affair.* The only question seems to be how he is to get out of it in the most respectable manner. Since I have been writing this, Evans, of Maine, came to my seat to tell me that he had just heard that the convention assembled in his State to nominate State officers had nominated you for President in a most enthusiastic manner. At my request, he has promised to write to you as soon as he receives a printed account of the proceedings. Be sure that you answer his letter; all our friends here would be flattered by your correspondence, and you must task yourself a little to please them. If we can only keep up the feeling that now exists, your election is certain. Tyler is one of your *best friends;* his last veto has scored us all well; it had just reached the convention in Maine, which nominated you and denounced him. It has also a fine effect upon our friends here, and will insure the passage of our tariff bill, with a reservation to the States of the proceeds of the public lands. Suppose Tyler vetoes that, what, then, shall we do? Shall we pass the tariff, giving up the lands, or adjourn and let all go together? Write me immediately in answer to these questions.

Your friend,

J. J. CRITTENDEN.

Hon. H. CLAY.

(J. J. Crittenden to Henry Clay.)

July 15, 1842.

MY DEAR SIR,—Our friend Botts is *passionately* resolved on impeachment of the President. I believe that the very fact of his taking such a lead in the matter has had the effect of checking or repressing, to some extent, the tendency that was apparent to such a result. Botts's ardor, and the strong personal feelings that are ascribed to him, alarm the more timid and prudent, and they do not feel safe or confident in following him in so responsible and delicate an affair. Besides, it is considered a little premature at present, when we have another *veto* impending. Botts is dissatisfied at not finding all the Whigs concurring with him, and, I am just told, has written to you on the subject. His discretion, you know, is the least of his virtues, and you should, I think, answer him very carefully and cautiously. He could hardly forbear to use your name and authority as a sanction for his course, and I should consider it as most unfortunate and injurious to have your name at all *mixed up* in this matter.

My feelings against Tyler are strong, but I doubt the policy of impeachment. He would be acquitted, and his acquittal might be considered a justification of his offenses by a country that now condemns him. A vote of a want of confidence amounts almost to an impeachment in all its moral consequences. We have just received intelligence of the election in New Orleans; it is most cheering, and will serve to increase the confidence of your friends, and to augment the *tide* that is now running in your favor.

Nothing has occurred to change or disturb my convictions that we shall pass the permanent tariff, with a reservation of the land fund to the States, and that Tyler will veto it. "Clouds and darkness" rest upon all beyond that. If our tariff friends from the North can be reconciled to it, we will, as the last alternative, pass a bill on Simmons's plan, with a duty of twenty per cent. on the home valuation. I received yesterday your letter of the 10th, and, as the merchants say, *contents* are *noted*. I have this moment seen our friend Abbott Lawrence, and happening to tell him I was writing to you, he *bids* me to say "that there is a sort of a *groundswell* going on in Massachusetts in your favor;" and as to the negotiation with Ashburton, in which you know he is engaged as a sort of auxiliary, he says " that though there have been great difficulties in the way, he sees light ahead, and hopes for favorable results in a few days." With the conclusion of this negotiation, I think it very probable, from what I hear, that Webster will retire from the cabinet, whether into private life or into some other office is more doubtful.

Heaven knows when we shall get away from here.   The last conjecture is that it will be about the 15th of the next month. That depends on contingencies.

Your friend,

Hon. Henry Clay.   J. J. Crittenden.

(Henry Clay to J. J. Crittenden.)

Ashland, July 16, 1842.

My dear Sir,—Your favor of the 9th is received.   You ask whether there may not be danger, in the event of another *veto* upon the permanent tariff, of some of our ardent friends of a tariff yielding distribution.   I hope not.   Acting together in the passage of the bill ; the indignation which another veto will excite; the public manifestation of disapprobation of the past, and the still stronger disapprobation which will be exhibited at the second ; the confusion which has been occasioned in the collection of the revenue by the late veto,—all these circumstances combined will, I trust, knit you together, consolidate your strength, and prevent dissension.   I think you cannot give up distribution without a disgraceful sacrifice of independence. The moral prejudice of such a surrender upon the character of the party, and upon our institutions, would be worse than the disorder and confusion incident to the failure to pass a tariff. Great as that disorder and confusion would be, it would be to give up the legislative power into the hands of the President, and would expose you to the scorn, contempt, and derision of the people and of our opponents.   The disorder and confusion would continue but for a short time, until Congress met again, or was called together, and then let them pass just such another tariff as he had vetoed.   The occasion calls for the greatest firmness.   Do not apprehend that the people will desert you and take part with Mr. Tyler.   They will do no such thing. When the veto comes back, the Locos will probably vote with the President ; *that* will identify them still further with him, and as, by their vote, they would enable you to pass the bill against the veto, they will have to share with him the odium of its defeat.   *But* if, in the contingency which has been supposed, some of our friends *should desert*, let them go ; they will find it difficult to sustain themselves against the storm they will have raised around their heads.   If they go they can effect nothing but by a union with the whole *Loco party*, and thus attempting to pass a good tariff without distribution.   Now, I suppose it will be impracticable to carry the whole Locofoco party, or enough of them, with the deserters, to pass such a tariff.   In my view of it, I think our friends ought to stand up firmly and resolutely for distribution.   The more vetoes the better now! assuming that the measures vetoed are right. The inevitable tendency of events is to impeachment; but nothing ought to be done inconsiderately, or without full consultation.

I was sorry, therefore, to see our friend Botts allow himself to be drawn out *prematurely* by Mr. Cushing. As to a vote of *want of confidence*, it would be a right thing if you will resolve to follow it up by more stringent measures. The idea of such a vote is drawn from English usage; and there, if ministers do not resign, the vote is followed by other more efficient proceedings. Here, John Tyler and John Jones would laugh at your vote if you stopped there. They would pass a vote of *want of confidence* in you. It would not do to move such a vote in the Senate, because it is the tribunal to try impeachment. It should be confined, *if moved*, to the House. I am afraid that you would not effect the object of a more thorough identification between the Locos and Tyler. They would go off upon the ground of its being irregular and unconstitutional, and would say that you *ought to impeach*. If a vote of "*want of confidence*" would be carried by the union of the great body of both parties, its effect would be very great. If it can be carried in the House without any splitting of our party, and *nothing* better *can be done*, I should think it desirable. You may show these views, if you think them worth anything, to the Speaker and your colleague, and General Green.

Your friend,

Hon. J. J. CRITTENDEN. HENRY CLAY.

(J. J. Crittenden to R. P. Letcher.)

SENATE, July 16, 1842.

DEAR LETCHER,—The Senate will adjourn in a few minutes, and I have determined to employ the interval in writing to you. You are a man of business, and a few words are enough for a wise man.

The permanent tariff bill, reserving the land fund to the States, will pass the House to-day or to-morrow. It will pass the Senate and will be *vetoed*. What then? I think we will then pass a bill in conformity to your compromise act, laying the duties at twenty per cent., etc. This will leave the distribution act unaffected. What more we shall do personal to Captain Tyler I can't say. Impeachments, votes of want of confidence, etc. are talked of, but it is hard to tell what may issue from the wrath— the just wrath—of Congress.

Webster will succeed, and in a few *days*, in concluding a treaty with Ashburton; so I believe from sure information. It is supposed that Webster will then retire from the cabinet, and then, or shortly after, it is probable that that illustrious body, the cabinet, will fall into a pretty general dissolution in some decided Locofoco firm.   So may it be.

We shall have stirring times here when Tyler's next veto is announced.   My great moderation and patience will then, I fear, give way, and explode in a speech.   The Senate has adjourned.   Farewell.

Your friend,
J. J. CRITTENDEN.

R. P. LETCHER,
    Governor.

(Henry Clay to J. J. Crittenden.)

ASHLAND, July 21, 1842.

MY DEAR SIR,—I received your letter of the fifteenth.   Botts has not replied to me.   If he should, I shall express to him my serious regret at that movement of his about impeachment.   It was, I think, ill timed and injudicious.   No such movement ought to be made, if made at all, without full consultation with friends.

I am not surprised at its tendency to repress the spirit of impeachment.   There is cause enough, God knows; but it is a novel proceeding, full of important consequences, present and future, and should not be commenced but upon full consideration, not of one mind only, but (and I dare say Mr. Botts has so considered it) of many minds.

Mr. Tyler will probably veto the tariff, and dismiss old Jonathan Roberts.   If he should do so, and Congress adjourns without settling the tariff, there will be a state of feeling among the people that may force Congress to impeach him when it reassembles.   In the contingency of his impeachment, I do not think that his acquittal by the vote exclusively of the Locos would have any bad effect.

In my former letter I wrote you what struck me about a vote of want of confidence, as a preliminary measure confined to the House.   I thought well of it, but as a definitive, final proceeding, without any ulterior measures, I was afraid it would not do much good.

We have lost the governor of Louisiana ; a committee of five gentlemen from that State, which they left on the 9th, dined with me yesterday, and they assure me that the result was owing entirely to the predominance of the Creole feeling and other local causes, and that there cannot be a doubt of the State being Whig, and for me.

Your friend,
H. CLAY.

J. J. CRITTENDEN.

(J. J. Crittenden to R. P. Letcher.)

SENATE, August 2, 1842.

DEAR LETCHER,—I have just received your letter of the 27th July. I will let you know when I shall be at home, but when it will be, I grieve to say, I cannot now tell. I have a hope, but it is only a hope, that we shall adjourn about the 20th of this month. I feel somewhat relieved to-day, having had, on yesterday, an opportunity of discharging a portion of my detestation of John Tyler. I am resolved that I will not in future allow any great accumulation of it to remain on hand, but will expend it gently upon him, from day to day, to the end of the session. This course will be necessary to my health in this hot season of the year. I go often to the Treasury to inquire about your distribution or land money. The answer is still, " The returns and accounts are not yet received and made out." I take pleasure in dunning them, and shall do it diligently.

We are now on the tariff bill. Bagby is drumming away, and makes some allusion to me. I must listen to him. He thinks while I am writing this letter that I am taking " *notes* on his speech," and has just said that he sees me taking notes. He is a bag of wind. Farewell.

J. J. CRITTENDEN.

R. P. LETCHER,
    Governor.

(J. J. Crittenden to Henry Clay.)

SENATE, August 3, 1842.

MY DEAR SIR,—Tariff bill is now under consideration in the Senate, and I hope we shall order it to be engrossed before we adjourn. So far we have succeeded in rejecting *all amendments,* as well those reported by our committee as those offered by our opponents. The bill is not in every particular as I could wish it, the duties being in some instances too high, as, for example, *our duty on bagging* of five per cent. the square yard. This is much complained of by our Southern opponents, and in truth I could wish it four per cent. But, upon consideration of circumstances, the exigency for money, the exigency of the times, and the delay and danger of sending the bill back to the House, we concluded, with the probability of a *veto* before our eyes, to take and pass the bill as it came to us. I think our determination was right ; there is nothing essentially wrong in the bill. We will carry it through without amendment, and have it before Mr. Tyler by Saturday night. Its fate with him is scarcely doubtful, though there are some who indulge the hope that he will sign it. So far as anything can be anticipated from such a man, he will most certainly *veto it.* My information *confirms* such an anticipation.   Mr. Adams is of opinion that, in such an event, we ought *at once to adjourn* without attempting anything more.   In that sentiment *some* of our ardent friends concur; *I do not.*   I think we should then pass Simmons's bill with a duty of twenty per cent. and immediately adjourn, and that, too, with a *determination* and agreement to disregard the threatened proclamation of the President to convene us instantly to supply him with revenue.   So far as I can learn, Tyler still retains all his delusion, malignity, and madness.   The treaty with England will be communicated on Saturday,—so I am confidentially informed by one of our foreign diplomatic friends.   There have been some difficulties in adjusting the Creole case not yet entirely settled, but give rise to no apprehension.

Your friend,
J. J. CRITTENDEN.

(R. P. Letcher to J. J. Crittenden.)

FRANKFORT, August 8, 1842.

DEAR CRITTENDEN,—I thank you for your letter of the 2d just received.   Do, for God's sake, *let out* all your wrath and gall and bitterness upon John Tyler before you come to Kentucky. Make haste and come home and be amiable all the time you have to spend with us.   I have not been very sweet-tempered myself for the last six or seven days; but, through the grace of God, I am getting a little better.   We shall have a few more Whigs in the legislature than I thought.   We shall have about fifty-five or sixty Whigs in the lower House, and seven or eight *pledged* fellows of the *Loco stripe pledged to vote* for Crittenden. *There is good reading for you!*   In my opinion, you need not have the slightest apprehension about your election.   Ben Hardin and John Helm may possibly try to figure in the game, but it will not amount to much.   I have neither seen nor heard from the old Prince very lately.   I am anxious to see what Webster will do or say when he leaves the cabinet.   If he has one grain of common sense left, he will give the *Tyler concern a hell of a kick* and fall into the Whig ranks and swear he is now and always was a true Whig.

Your friend,

Hon. J. J. CRITTENDEN.   R. P. LETCHER.

(J. J. Crittenden to Henry Clay.)

SENATE, August 12, 1842.

DEAR SIR,—We are in a state of great embarrassment here, and, as yet, no course has been determined upon to lead us through the confusion and difficulty resulting from the last veto.

It is difficult to adopt such a course as will satisfy those who are bent on resistance to the usurpations of Tyler and those who fear the effect of our adjourning without an *adequate tariff.* Our friends of the North seem to be very seriously and sincerely apprehensive that their constituents will be discontented to such an extent as to be fatal to their coming elections if we should adjourn without doing or attempting something more. We had several meetings on the subject with but little success, and are to have another this evening. In the midst of these differences of opinion a kind and conciliatory spirit prevails, and all agree that *union* is our greatest interest, and we will not allow that to be shaken in any event. This is the only conspicuous sign remaining in the dark prospect before us. To-morrow I may be able to write you more distinctly, and you may be assured that, whether wisely or not, we will act considerately. Mr. Adams is chairman of the committee and is preparing a report on the last veto. We look for an able and stirring report, and take care to stimulate him by letting him know that our expectations are high. The treaty with England was laid before us ; there has been no action or indication of opinion about it, but I presume it will be approved by the Senate.

Your friend,

Hon. H. Clay.   J. J. Crittenden.

(J. J. Crittenden to James Harlan.)

August 16, 1842.

Dear Harlan,—At the receipt of your last letter and ever since I have been constantly expecting so early an adjournment that I supposed you would prefer my retaining and bringing with me the certificates of stock, for which you wrote, rather than hazard their transmission by mail. Finding how much I have been mistaken, I regret that I did not at once send ; but as it can now not be long before our adjournment, I shall not think it safe to commit them to the mail, seeing that there will be so little difference in the time of arrival, and supposing that it cannot make any difference in the ultimate result.

I believe we shall adjourn during the next week, but all is uncertainty and confusion. While all the Whigs share in the indignation against Tyler's usurpation and despotism, sectional and particular interests connected with a tariff are drawing them in a different direction, and threatening us with divisions. Night after night have we held meetings and consultations with a view to harmonize in some course ; but I am sorry to tell you that we have not yet reached any such conclusion, and that I look forward to the issue with some apprehension. A general senti-

ment, however, is avowed by all to preserve the union of the
Whig party in any event, and in that it is to be hoped we may
find a remedy for the differences of opinion that exist as to the
course we ought now to pursue. Some are for giving up the
lands, others for passing such a bill as will not raise the question about the lands, and others again are for adjournment
without doing anything.

It is almost inconceivable how so paltry and impotent a being
as Tyler could do so much mischief; he is endeavoring to make
his apostasy the more paradeful and glaring, in order to recommend himself to the Locofocos. He is willing, for his acceptance by them, to pay the price of open shame and treachery,
and even on those terms offers himself somewhat in vain. For
they are really ashamed openly to take and avow him, though
they secretly incite and use him as a tool, as I believe.

We have not yet acted on the treaty with England. It has
not been much examined, but I presume that it will be ratified.

The elections in the West have somewhat disappointed us,
and especially that in our own State. The distresses of the
country are such, and originate in such causes, as seem to me
to entitle to lenient consideration those of our friends and
countrymen who are excited to some indiscretion, and the way,
as it appears to me, to prevent excesses, is to appeal to them in
a spirit of kindness and indulgence, and to grant all the relief
that is required, and that is warrantable and constitutional. By
a small, timely concession, we may avert, what may otherwise
probably turn out to be, the same miserable career that we ran
about twenty years. My anxiety on the subject induces me to
say perhaps too much. You, who are in the midst of the scene
and can look over the whole of it, will best know how this excitement for relief can be best tempered, and what I have said
you must regard as the private suggestions of a friend, who is
too far off, and so little acquainted with the exact state of things,
to decide upon it with any confidence in his own judgment.

Your friend,

To JAMES HARLAN, Esq.   J. J. CRITTENDEN.

(J. J. Crittenden to R. P. Letcher.)

August 18, 1842.

MY DEAR LETCHER,—I have only time write you a line.

I think now that we shall adjourn on Monday, according
to a resolution passed by the House and now before us.

There will be no tariff law; that seems to me to be pretty certain.

The last communication from the treasury on the subject of
your land-money is herewith inclosed. It *hurts* my feelings
very much to be dunning so good a man as Mr. Tyler. But

will not a man suffer for his country? Let the diligence of
dunning in this case answer the question.

In hopes to see you before long, I subscribe myself,

Your friend,

J. J. CRITTENDEN.

(R. P. Letcher to J. J. Crittenden.)

FRANKFORT, December 8, 1842.

DEAR CRITTENDEN,—I was called to the office to-night upon
a matter of business, and told my wife not to look for me back
before ten o'clock. My business is through, my fire is good,
and it's only nine o'clock. The idea occurred to me that you
would like to get a short letter from *old Kentucky*, so I give you
a few lines. I called at your house yesterday to inquire if you
were *dead* or *alive*, but got no satisfaction on either point. The
Yeoman is still upon your bones; I know that information is
quite agreeable to you. There is a long article in the morning
paper about the senatorial election. Turner never wrote that
piece; I will *bet two to one* that McCalla wrote it all, except a few
sentences penned by the D. All I have heard in regard to the
election of senator is favorable to you. Since you left, after
a few social gatherings, our town has become solitary and
alone. Colonel Johnson spent some time with me a few days
ago. *He talks well*, but how he will *act* remains to be seen. It's
all a mistake about his going for Clay next to himself for *President. He is for me*, after himself, for *he told me so e*xpressly,
and said, moreover, he did not care how soon they *put that* in
the papers. He says he will carry Pennsylvania *all hollo !* and
no mistake; he is happy in the prospect ahead, and feels confident of success. I told him he would have to hold very strong
cards to win the game against a *stocked pack :* he thinks his
cards strong enough. Ask Buchanan if the Colonel has any
chance for his State. I like Buck, and should be sorry to see
the Colonel take his own State from him. The plain truth is,
Buchanan is the cleverest man of all his party, and has the best
capacity, Van Buren not excepted.

Yours,

Hon. J. J. CRITTENDEN. R. P. LETCHER.

(Daniel Webster to R. P. Letcher.)

WASHINGTON, December 20, 1842.

MY DEAR SIR,—I received, this morning, your letter of the
23d. I assure you, my dear sir, I should be most happy to see
you and talk with you a good deal. I do not believe that in a
free conference we should differ very widely as to the causes
which have brought things to their present condition; but I am

much more doubtful whether either of us could invent a remedy. I have noticed, of course, what has taken place in Kentucky, not omitting the speeches, letters, etc. at the Frankfort barbecue. Very well! It would be affectation in me to pretend that some of these things, coming from the quarters they did, have not given me pain. They certainly have, while for others I feel nothing but contempt. But neither those which cause pain nor those which only excite contempt will be likely to move me from any purpose which I may entertain. I am glad you think favorably of the correspondence with Lord Ashburton. I send you herewith a copy of some parts of it. I wish it could be generally read in Kentucky, but I suppose that is hardly possible. I will add, my dear sir, that I retain my personal regard and good feeling towards you, never having heard of any personal ill treatment on your part, and not at all questioning your right, as well as that of others, to differ from me politically as widely as you please. Who thinks most correctly of the present, or who predicts most accurately of the future, are questions which must be left to be solved by time and events.

Yours very truly,

Governor LETCHER.   DANIEL WEBSTER.

(J. J. Crittenden to R. P. Letcher.)

WASHINGTON, January 13, 1842.

DEAR GOVERNOR,—I have this day received information of my re-election to the Senate; the majority has far exceeded my expectations. I know not what to say on this occasion; my heart is full, but not of words.

Better friends no man ever had, and to you especially I owe much; but, if the debt is to stand against me forever, I can never pay it off in *words*.

I have received all your letters, and most agreeable and satisfactory they have been to me. Your message is a very good one, and will be popular. It is prudent, wise, and temperate, and very prettily blended with some *tender* strokes of the "*ad captandum*,"—I mean no criticism,—just enough of that sort of coloring to give the whole a fair and glowing complexion.

Since the commencement of this letter, in the writing of which I have been interrupted, I have yours of the 10th inst., and one from Harlan, inclosing your certificate of my election. I suppose that in good manners I can say no less than "*Thank you, gentlemen.*" The result goes so much beyond my calculations that I am almost afraid there has been some conjuration about it. You have had about you, as I learn, sundry suspicious characters, such as Graves, Haws, Metcalf, Duncan, Pindell, etc., who, though without any seeming connections with you, have, as I suspect, been acting in some sort of concert with you, and under auspices———— My patriotism opposes all improper interference in such matters ; but, yet, as I would not be an accuser, and as I have nothing but *suspicion* against you all, I shall not consider myself bound *in conscience*, as Mr. Tyler would say, to decline accepting the commission which you have sent me. Indeed, I have rather made up my mind to banish all suspicious thoughts, and to consider my friends as the very cleverest fellows in the world, and the most competent, especially in the selection of a senator. Your old *friend* Buchanan has just passed through an awful time,—a *death-sweat*. His re-election was suspended by a single hair, and for one day, at least, he believed that he was to be beaten. *That* was a fearful day. The danger was occasioned by the same sort of combinations which threatened me at home. I comforted him and gave him all my sympathy, and in the most *disinterested manner* I denounced, for his sake, all coalitions designed to prevent the election of the man who was the choice of the party having the legislative majority. But Buck has escaped, and I am rewarded for my disinterestedness. We have exchanged congratulations.

My old friend Johnson has allowed himself to be drawn into the commission of a sad error. In the situation which he now occupies as a candidate for the Presidency, he ought not to have exposed himself to such a defeat ; it will be considered as ominous. I am very much disposed to concur in the suspicion that has been expressed to me, that some of the seeming friends who have urged him to this course, have really done so for the purpose of killing him off out of Van Buren's way. If the Colonel should have cause to believe this, I should think it would open his eyes a little. If the Van Buren-men have played this game upon him it was certainly very adroit, whatever may be said of its fairness. The greater probability, however, is, that it is nothing more than one of those blunders that the mistaken zeal of honest friends leads them to commit. The Calhoun-men are moved, "perplexed in the extreme," by the late letter of General Jackson, and the Philadelphians declare in favor of Van Buren. What they will do I don't know; they don't know themselves. I think they are strongly disposed to nullify that letter. Whether they will shrink from so *daring* a purpose remains to be seen.

There is one duty I must discharge before closing this short letter, that is, to send my most profound respects to Mrs. Letcher. The ladies have a right to interfere in elections. Even my *gag-law* does not touch their rights.

Your friend,
J. J. CRITTENDEN.

R. P. LETCHER,
Governor.

(J. J. Crittenden to R. P. Letcher.)

MY DEAR LETCHER,—I have received your several letters concerning the senatorial election, and last night your official certificate of its results in my favor. I do not intend to turn sentimental at my age, or, at any rate, to make professions; but to you and a few other friends in particular, and to the legislature of Kentucky in general, I do feel something more than a sense of obligation; it gives me pleasure to feel an affectionate sense of gratitude. Considering all the circumstances, my absence, my residence in the same little town with the other senator; the congregation, at Frankfort, of so many of our magnates who sigh for the place, and the presence of the sinister little party so adverse to me, and sustained by the favor of the federal administration, etc., I do think I may well be proud of the friends who could so signally triumph over all these difficulties and keep down any open opposition. Will some turn in the wheel of worldly events enable me at some time or other to do something in acquittance of these great obligations?

I have repeated consultations here with Sergeant on the subject of our application to the Pennsylvania legislature, and in respect to the most favorable legislation we could expect. In these matters I have been very much guided by him, and we have at length agreed upon a bill, and I start to-morrow for Harrisburg to try to get it passed. I shall touch at Philadelphia, on way to or from Harrisburg, and just feel the Schuylkill Bank a little, to see if there is any better disposition for an amicable settlement.

But for this business I should have returned home, and should now have been on the way, as I finished yesterday the last of my cases in the Supreme Court that will come on at the present term. But this business so encroaches upon the little time between this and the period that I must take my seat in the Senate, that I have abandoned all hope of seeing Kentucky till the adjournment of Congress. The disappointment is a severe one to me. Besides seeing my wife and children so soon, I had the liveliest visions of evenings spent at your house, with exchanges of Frankfort and Washington news, and a most unreserved denunciation of Tylerism and all its appliances and appurtenances. I can see *Old Master* stretched on the sofa, and you lecturing, and at least counting the *drinks* that Mason and I would take from your bottle. But, alas! all this must be postponed for at least three months. What a long three months! Indeed, it has seemed to me since the world began Time never went by so slowly as it has since the accession of John Tyler. Tyler and his cabinet still hold on together; but they are daily acquiring more and more contempt and odium, and

I think it impossible that they should hold out together much longer.

But I am about to become a politician of the most exemplary forbearance and moderation. Clay is in pretty good health and spirits, but I have no doubt he feels a secret melancholy at the thought of quitting the scenes in which he has been so long engaged. I think that I can sometimes perceive the gloom upon him; but his friends here with almost one voice agree that it is the right course for him. Harvey abandoned, as I have before stated, the idea of returning this month to Kentucky. I have written to my wife to set everything in order at home, and then to come on to Washington immediately with the first company that offers. Farewell.

Your friend,

R. P. LETCHER, J. J. CRITTENDEN.
    Governor, Ky.

(J. J. Crittenden to his wife Maria.)

WASHINGTON, February 5, 1843.

MY DEAR WIFE,—I have received your letter of the 28th; it renews to me the gratifying assurance that you are well, and gives me that delight which everything from your hand always does. Indeed, at the date of your letter all hands seem to have been not only well but *frolicking*. This is all very agreeable to me. I am glad to hear of Mr. Bullock's return in good health, and of the success of his mission. I shall not quarrel with you all for imputing the little indisposition of which I some time ago complained to my *drinking too much* on hearing the news of my triumphant election; but I must say it shows you all to be a very suspicious set and not overcharitable to be slandering a grave senator with such imputations. I think I have fully as good cause to suspect you of a little intemperance on the occasion. I certainly heard of your having a great carousal and a crowd of good and merry drinkers around you. I do consider my re-election, under all the circumstances, as the greatest and most honorable event of my life, and I rejoice at it the more because you have taken such an interest in it and derived so much gratification from it. I visited Mrs. Bayard last evening; she inquired for you. I never saw her look better or younger. I shall soon have the pleasure of seeing and being happy in the midst of you all.

I have this moment received two letters from Texas, giving me the afflicting intelligence that my son George was with Colonel Fisher in the late most unfortunate invasion of Mexico, and that he is, in all probability, now a prisoner. What is to become of him in such hands, God only knows.   I shall see the Mexican minister immediately and do all I can for his safety and release.

Farewell, my dearest wife.

J. J. CRITTENDEN.

Mrs. MARIA K. CRITTENDEN.

(J. J. Crittenden to his wife Maria.)

SENATE, February 28, 1843.

MY DEAREST MARIA,—I have just received your letter,—the last, you tell me, that I am to receive this session.   Then I am sure that I must go home very soon; for not to hear from you or see you is more than I can bear.   I am growing quite cheerful at the prospect of being with you so soon, and feel as if I was almost near enough to kiss you.   Friday is the last day of the session.   We have a great deal to do,—shall probably be in the Senate the whole of Friday night, and cannot be sure of starting homeward sooner than Sunday morning.   I hope you will excuse me for setting out on that day; expect me as soon as the journey can be performed.   Next Saturday week I shall, without accident, be at home.   For that evening let our friends of the legislature be invited to rejoice with us.   You know how to anticipate my wishes, and have done so exactly in your proposal to entertain our friends on that evening.   I shall be delighted to see the members of the legislature at our house.   To find you all well and the house full of friends, will make me happy.   My love to all, and to you, my dearest wife, a thousand kisses.

J. J. CRITTENDEN.

Mrs. M. K. CRITTENDEN.

CHAPTER XVI.

1843-1844.

Letters of General Winfield Scott, of Webster, Clay, Crittenden, and Letcher.

(General Winfield Scott to J. J. Crittenden.)

WASHINGTON CITY, April 5, 1843.

DEAR CRITTENDEN,—It is just a month to-day since you, Archer, and others turned your backs upon me, leaving me to my fate; and here is your first letter cruelly taunting me with the miseries of my isolation. In revenge, I have a great mind to turn *Tyler-man* and seek consolation in the pure circle about him. The run of the kitchen, as I have been cut off from his table since 1841, would be something. As he is everywhere organizing the *Swiss*, a now numerous body even in the United States, he may be glad to accept a "tall fellow"—a " proper man ;" and if I get the command of the guard, look out,—you can't *head me*—from the shoulders upwards, taller than your Botts. I shall begin under the good old second section to behead him and all the members of the cabinet except *Dan*, " the faithful among the faithless," and their abettors. "*Ego et rex*"—I and the Captain—will do the work thoroughly. I shall teach Wise that he is an ass, and Cushing that he is a stool. None of your bloodless reforms. Those whom I *turn out* shall be finally *turned in.* Dead men make no clamors. Did not you, at Mangum's supper, give me a lesson in despotism ? "Oh, the Father, how he held his countenance !" Oh, rare, "he did it like one of those harlotry players as ever I see." I shall imitate Macbeth : " Be bloody, bold, and resolute," until the whole mass of Whigs shall cry out for mercy. The age stands in need of an example. *I* am the man to give it,—I will bestride the narrow world like a colossus ! There's Archer, a "petty man," who of late did " walk under my huge legs and peep about," did no sooner reach Port Gibson than he writes, " Help me, or I sink !" and appoints me St. Louis, in May, to make the tour of St. Anthony's Falls, the lakes, etc. I have flatly denied him, *because* the Captain can't spare me. Preston, too, after much fond talk of you, has just desired me to bring Archer to his solitude; and here's a letter from Clinch tempting me with *bacon* and *greens* to his

(201)

end of the world.   As to Clinch, who is always talking about you, I have summoned him to receive judgment at the beginning of the next session.   Your eloquence shall not again respite him.   Besides the "*apple-brandy*," I owe him a grudge about the junction of "*them rivers.*"   Talking of cutting off heads, reminds me of your invitation to commit treason by promising to play the part of a silent accomplice; but he who plays at that game must be sure that he wins.

> " Treason never flourishes, what's the reason?
> When it flourishes, none dare call it treason !"

I have not seen the President but for five minutes last month, when I went to *say* that I was about to run away for a few days to New York on public business and to my house in Jersey on private business, and I have scarcely seen a member of the cabinet.   In this month they have committed rather more than the usual amount of *meannesses*.   Preston, in the letter before me, thinks this kind of *tape* rather more dangerous to our institutions than the open, ruffian violence of Jackson.   Removals and putting in relatives and *corrupt hacks* are the *order of the day*. Webster is gone east.   I learn from good authority that he has been in doubt whether to go to London or stay at home and run for the Presidency on the question of the assumption of State debts.   In one or the other position he hopes to become the *agent* of the European holders of American securities and make a million.   Can this best be done as President or minister ? That's the question !   He may therefore be expected to return. The new Secretary of War makes us already regret the old.

Upshur, it is said, is to go to the Department of State, and be *himself* replaced by Cushing.   Wise, I fear, will be re-elected, and our friend Botts beaten.   This I should greatly lament, for "we could better spare a better man"—or rather a *wiser*.   B. has great moral intrepidity, which the times call for.

Profit, I am told, is still here, but whether detained by sickness or waiting for his reward I know not.

I know not how to help your Missouri friend, who wants the charge of the hemp business, having no communication with the Secretary of the Navy.   I shall continue to turn the matter over in my mind, but with little hope of being able to do anything.

In a brown study I was brought up the other day all standing at your door in Jones's Buildings.   *Eight long months* more must elapse before we meet again.

You will see Webster's dispatch about the right of visit.   The *Madisonian* of to-day is even bellicose on the subject.   With respects to Mrs. Crittenden and Letcher,

I remain your friend,

Hon. J. J. CRITTENDEN.   WINFIELD SCOTT.

(General Winfield Scott to J. J. Crittenden.)

WASHINGTON, June 29, 1843.

DEAR CRITTENDEN,—I have just returned from a tour of special duty at the Military Academy, and find the accompanying letter, which I hasten to send you.

I see that (as they say of theatricals) you are "*starring*" in Missouri, in the same *troupe* with Benton! How is this? I shall have to cut your acquaintance or take the other tack and become a *Tyler-man*. I'll cut my throat first! Did you note how nicely I got off from swelling the pageant at New York, Boston, etc. by going to hard work at West Point? The President wanted me very much; but I spoke to him *of the importance of the duties in which I was engaged,*—and I told the truth. You have had a lucky escape, for I came very near setting out for Frankfort and Lexington yesterday. The Fayette Legion invited me to join them, but I was compelled to return here, and apologized to the Kentuckians. I shall never have another chance of seeing you under your own roof.

Hoping that you are taking care of your health and *pockets*, I remain, in haste,

Your friend,

Hon. J. J. CRITTENDEN.   WINFIELD SCOTT.

(General Winfield Scott to J. J. Crittenden.)

WASHINGTON, October 14, 1843.

MY DEAR SIR,—I dispatched a hasty note to you some days ago. You may remember what I said to you in the summer of the design to run Mr. Webster on Mr. Clay's ticket. The project has recently been revived in the *New York Courier and Enquirer*, and the Whigs in that city by resolutions have spurned the proposition. The *Richmond Whig* is equally indignant against the *Courier and Enquirer*. "Where am I to go?" the ex-Secretary may again piteously ask. I have no doubt there was some foundation for the report I formerly mentioned to you. We have had great success in Maryland and Georgia, upon which I felicitate you. In Philadelphia we have had a glorious victory. I have declined all invitations to public meetings,—the Bunker Hill, Fort Wayne, and some thirty others,— not wishing to divert a single Whig from the single candidate or to excite attention to my *humble self;* I understand, however, that certain newspapers still keep up my name. I have prevented the establishment of a new paper here with the same *partial views*. I wish to give a clear field, and God grant us success. Dick Johnson was here lately rather under the weather. He begins to think the *Locofoco leaders* will shuffle him out of the contest. He is gone North and East. I have no doubt he will gladly take the Vice-Presidency, and *that* will be the result. Of what the cabinet is doing, or design to do, I know nothing. I have not seen Mr. Tyler since the 4th of July, when I called. Upshur, I learn, has been writing certain bellicose articles in the *Madisonian* against England in relation to Texas. Clinch is with me for a day or two. We talk a good deal of you, the *Tems*, and the Withlacoochee. He will be back in January, when, if he does not abandon that *junction*, I shall have him shot under the former merited sentence. By the way, he brought some of Schley's brandy with him from Baltimore.

In great haste, most truly yours,

WINFIELD SCOTT.

Hon. J. J. CRITTENDEN.

(Daniel Webster to R. P. Letcher.)

MARSHFIELD (Mass.), October 23, 1843.

MY DEAR SIR,—I read your letter of the 2d instant not only with interest but with *emotion.* I believe every word you say, of your kind feelings and friendship towards me, which I am sure you believe I reciprocate fully and cordially.

In the first place, you are right in supposing that I must live and die, as I was born, a " Whig ;" as we have understood that term, and especially as we have understood it in the contest of 1840. He is a fool as well as a foe who supposes it possible for me to tread back the steps of my whole political career, and abandon those principles, the support of which has made me considerable in the country. I am as willing now as I ever was to exert my faculties for the continued support and further diffusion of those principles.

But, then, I have some degree of self-respect and some pride ; I shall certainly submit to no sort or degree of ill treatment, and such, I must confess, I think I have received. I seldom speak of myself or my affairs ; but, as you invite it, I will be frank. I think, then, that a certain party, or division of the Whigs, mostly in the West and South, have not extended, in time past, that cordial respect towards some of us, this way, which they have ever received from us. For instance, in 1836 there was no Kentucky candidate before the people; there was a Massachusetts candidate. *How did Kentucky act?* And, let me add, it was *Kentucky*, in the course adopted by her in 1836, that gave a new and unexpected direction to Whig preferences, *and kept her own favorite son from the place in which she wishes to see him.* I need not prove this; reflect upon it, and you will find it is just so. But let that pass. We all finally concurred in General Harrison's election. His death blasted our prospects, and we had another man, and another kind of man to deal with. The Whigs were immediately alarmed, but the universal cry was, "Let General Harrison's cabinet keep their places." I kept mine, and yet there are those who will never forgive me for it. The last conversation I ever had with Mr. Clay, he said, "I had great national objects, which I supposed I could answer by staying in the department; I was justified in staying." That was my own opinion. I had such objects, and I stayed till they were accomplished. You regret that I remained after the treaty *was completed*. My dear sir, when was the treaty completed? It was ratified at the end of the session of 1842. The laws for carrying it into effect had not passed, and I knew were to be opposed, as they were opposed. They passed, however, at the end of the last session; and then, and not before, the treaty was "*completed*."

I then drew up the papers for the China mission, a measure which had originated with myself, and then immediately resigned my office. Now, my dear sir, what is there to complain of in all this, supposing me to have been right in staying in the cabinet one hour after the other gentlemen left it?

There are other things : I did not approve of some acts of the Whigs in the called session of 1841. I did not approve of the rejection of Mr. Ewing's bank bill; I did not approve of the readiness, not to say eagerness, which was manifested in some quarters to have a quarrel between the Whigs and Mr. Tyler. I thought we ought to try, to the last, to hold him, as far as possible, to Whig principles and a Whig administration; for I was unwilling to lose *all* the great objects of the preceding contest. I lamented, therefore, the Whig manifesto of 1841, both in regard to its spirit and its topics.

In September, 1842, a proceeding took place at a Whig convention, in Boston, which I knew was aimed against me. Its object was to destroy my standing and character, politically, with the Whigs. This object I determined to defeat at all hazards, and all consequences; and, thank God, I did defeat it. I defended myself, and nothing more; and if what was done, *necessarily*, on that occasion, reached so far as to be detrimental to others, I am not answerable for that result.

And now, my dear sir, let me recall to your recollection a little the course of events, and the conduct of some leading Whigs. I remained in office under the circumstances already stated; I got through the negotiation with England, and it does not become me to say how important this was to the country, or whether it was well or ill conducted. But, one thing is certain, it never received a word of commendation from certain leading Whigs. They did not complain of its results; but they did not appear to think that, in the conduct and conclusion, there had been any *merit* worth speaking of. Very well; no man is bound to praise; praise and commendation must be voluntary. But, then, if to withhold approbation is no injury to be complained of, gross abuse, personal and political, is such an injury; and you know how freely that has been bestowed on me. You know how I have been attacked and vilified by such men as Garrett Davis, Botts, Jno. C. Clark, Rayner, and many others, in Congress, all of them being more especial friends of Mr. Clay; I say nothing of what has been done outdoors, or of the conduct of the scoundrel who publishes the leading Whig press in Kentucky.

And, I must add, that if any attempt has been made by anybody to check this course of atrocious abuse, in and out of Congress, such an attempt has never come to my knowledge.

I have now, my dear sir, spoken to you, of myself, quite as freely as I have spoken to anybody; I have done so with entire confidence in your friendship, and it is time, I believe, to take leave of the subject.

I wish well to the Whig cause, and am ready to make all reasonable sacrifices to insure its success. But those who expect to displace me from my position, will find, if they have not found already, that they have a work of some little difficulty. I verily believe there is Whig strength enough in the country to elect a President; but that object can only be accomplished by the exercise of much consideration, wisdom, and conciliation. We must have a hearty *union*, or the prospect is hopeless. That we must all be convinced of.

Our State elections are now going on as they should have gone on last year, with a studied abstinence from national topics. The result will be, as I believe, that we shall carry the State by a strong majority. Massachusetts may then properly speak on national subjects. At present, she must reckon herself among *Locofoco* States.

I shall be glad to hear from you, my dear sir, freely and fully as I write you. I go to Boston this week, at which place please address me.

With constant and sincere regard, truly yours,

D. WEBSTER.*

Gov. LETCHER.

---

* Two or three letters of Mr. Webster's to Governor Letcher have been kindly given to me by Mrs. Letcher, and I think they will be interesting in this connection.

(R. P. Letcher to J. J. Crittenden.)

FRANKFORT, November 30, 1843.

DEAR CRITTENDEN,—That you may not be disappointed, I tell you in the outset I have no news of any sort to interest you. The town looks like a deserted village; whether this is occasioned by your absence I will not undertake to say. We have, every now and then, a very good saddle of venison and a few jolly fellows around it,—some drinking, and others wishing to *drink*, but refraining lest they might incur the heavy penalties of excommunication from "*temperance privileges.*" I wonder how my friend General Scott would figure as a member of the temperance body? If he will apply for it, I will send him a commission as president of the anti-drinking club without delay. Let him have no false delicacy about the application. One of the merits of my administration is, to reward merit, though in obscurity. How do the political cards run now? The old Prince holds the honors, don't he? I see some signs of Calhoun's intention to run, under the "*free trade banner.*" Let him try his luck; he may do good—can do no harm. That old sinner declares and swears, I am told, that John Davis is the agent of the Yankee and English abolitionists, to raise an insurrection in the Western States, and that he is paid by the day for *services*. Shall he be put in the asylum at Lexington or Frankfort? Benton, I am told, called upon the old Sea Serpent on his way to Washington; that was, I suppose, to clear up the charge of a coalition with Clay. I think, after that, he might venture to visit Captain Tyler. Warmest regards to Mrs. Crittenden.

Your friend,

Hon. J. J. CRITTENDEN.   R. P. LETCHER.

(Henry Clay to J. J. Crittenden.)

ASHLAND, December 5, 1843.

MY DEAR SIR,—I received your favor of the 29th, on the subject of Texas, or rather its annexation to the United States. I had received a letter from Mr. Child, the editor of an abolition paper in New York, to which I returned no answer; not that I was unwilling to announce my opinion upon that subject, but that I did not think it right, *unnecessarily*, to present new questions to the public. Those which are already before it are sufficiently important and numerous, without adding fresh ones. Nor do I think it right to allow Mr. Tyler, for his own selfish purposes, to introduce an exciting topic, and add to the other subjects of contention which exist in the country. How is he to prevent it? Texas can only be annexed to the United States by *treaty* or by conquest. If the former, it is Mr. Tyler's duty —if he thinks it right to annex it—to conclude a treaty for that purpose, *if he can, and lay* it before the Senate.   Nobody, I presume, would propose to acquire it by war and conquest.   But, let me suppose that he limits himself to a simple recommendation of annexation without having negotiated any treaty for that purpose,—what could Congress do upon such a recommendation?   They could pass no act to effect it; he might as well recommend the annexation to the United States of Mexico itself, or of any other independent power.   Indeed, a recommendation of any other independent country would be less irrational than the annexation of Texas, because to Texas Mexico asserts a title which she is endeavoring to enforce by the sword.   We could not, therefore, incorporate Texas into the Union without involving the United States in war with Mexico, and, I suppose, nobody would think it wise or proper to engage in war with Mexico for the acquisition of Texas. We have, it is true, acknowledged the independence of Texas, as we had a right to do, for the sake of our commercial and other intercourse with Texas, but that acknowledgment did not extinguish, or in any manner affect, the rights of Mexico upon Texas.   What has the House of Representatives to do with the treaty-making power *prior* to its exercise by the President and the Senate?   Considered as a practical question, every man must be perfectly convinced that no treaty, stipulating the annexation of Texas, can secure for its *ratification* a constitutional majority in the Senate.   Why, then, present the question?   It is manifest that it is for no other than the wicked purpose of producing discord and distraction in the nation.   Taking this view of the matter, I think, if there be such a recommendation, it would be best to pass it over in absolute silence, if it can be done.   Should a discussion of it, in spite of your wishes, be forced, then, I think it would be better to urge some such topics as I have suggested above, and to treat it as a question with which Congress has nothing to do, and which has been *thrust* upon it by one who has neither the confidence of the nation, or either of the great parties in it, with the evident view of promoting his own personal interests by producing dissension, discord, and distraction.   If there be no formal application from Texas itself, it might be urged, that to discuss the question of annexing it to the United States would be derogatory to the respect due both to Texas and Mexico, and would violate the dignity and character of our own government.   I think, in some of the modes which I have suggested, or in some other which may present itself to our friends at Washington, the mischievous designs of Mr. Tyler may be averted.   Should, however, a question be actually forced upon you in such manner that you will be compelled to express an opinion *for* or *against* annexation,

I do not know what your view may be; but *I* should have no hesitation in voting *against it.* Here are some of my reasons:

First, the territory of the United States is already large enough. It is much more important that we should unite, harmonize, and improve what we have than attempt to acquire more, especially when the acquisition would be inevitably attended with discord and dissatisfaction. Second, it is wholly impracticable to accomplish the object of annexation, if it were desirable, for reasons already stated; and, in the third place, if Texas were annexed to the United States, the motive with those who are urging it would not be fulfilled. It would not now, or ever, give to the slaveholding section of the Union a *preponderating weight.* The other portion would continue to retain the ascendency, which would be ultimately increased by the *annexation* of Canada, to which there could be no objection if Texas were admitted to the Union. I might add that there is great reason to doubt whether Texas *could* be admitted consistently with the Constitution of the United States; but I do not dwell upon that point because of the force of the examples of Louisiana and Florida. Some six or seven years ago I addressed a confidential letter to a distinguished friend, communicating my opinion adverse to the annexation of Texas. I placed it upon the ground that we already had quite as much, if not *more*, territory than we could govern well; that I had no desire to see a new element of discord introduced into the Union; that it was far more important to the happiness of our people that they should enjoy in peace, contentment, and harmony *what* they have than to attempt further acquisitions at the hazard of destroying all those great blessings. I have no copy of that letter, but I hope it is in existence, and I will endeavor to procure a copy of it to be used hereafter if rendered necessary by the progress of events. I shall regret very much should the proposition come to a formal question. If the Whig party should in *a body* vote *in the affirmative*, such a vote would be *utterly* destructive of it, without the possibility of securing Texas. The best *use* to make of Texas, *perhaps*, is to hold out to our Northern friends that if by the unhappy agitation of the question of slavery they should *force* a separation of the slave from the free States, in that contingency the former would be prompted to strengthen themselves by the acquisition of Texas. Texas is destined to be settled by our race, who will undoubtedly carry there our laws, our language, and our institutions; and that view of her destiny reconciles me much more to her independence than if it were to be peopled by an unfriendly race; we may live as good neighbors, cultivating peace, commerce, and friendship. I think you will find there is not the smallest foundation for the charge that Great Britain has a design to establish a colony in Texas. Such an attempt would excite the hostility of all the great powers of Europe, as well as the United States. But odious as such a design on the part of Great Britain would be, as she would probably cover it under the pretext of emancipation, her conduct would not be regarded with so much detestation by *the civilized world* as would that of the United States in seeking to effect annexation. The motive that would be attributed to her, and with too much justice, would be *that* of propagating instead of terminating slavery. I send you this letter in its rough draught just as I have dictated it to my son John, who has acted as my amanuensis. When the message arrives I may write you again, if there is any occasion in that document for doing so. I am glad to hear of the faith which our friends entertain in our success next year; but I hope they will add good works, which I cannot help thinking important both in *religion* and *politics.*

I remain faithfully your friend,
H. CLAY.

Hon. J. J. CRITTENDEN.

(J. J. Crittenden to R. P. Letcher.)

WASHINGTON, December 10, 1843.

DEAR LETCHER,—I have received your letter and thank you for it.

The concern you expressed for that old gentleman who is so distressed about his son's banishment and troubled with such evil visions about John Davis's mission to the West is quite natural to one of your tender sensibility; and I am quite sorry that your charity should be disturbed by the doubts you entertain as to which of your *asylums* would be the properest receptacle for him. Something ought to be speedily done, for I understand he has been fighting lately almost in your presence, and if his distemper should take a belligerent direction, the danger might be great. I suppose you are now convinced, all your speculations or fears to the contrary notwithstanding, that Van Buren will be the candidate of his party. There is no doubt about it. All the developments that have taken place here prove it, and no question is any longer made about it. His friends have a clear majority in the House of Representatives, and the Calhoun men and all other malcontents sunk under their ascendency; though they had been plotting and threatening opposition, they did not, when the crisis came, dare to make it openly. They are now, I believe, ashamed of their tameness, and are revenging it by muttering their discontent, which I have no doubt is greatly increased, though to the world everything appears quite smooth and calm. Calhoun has no strength—no abiding supporters—out of South Carolina, and must soon be given up by the friends he has. When that time comes, I cannot tell where they will go. I think but few of them will support Van Buren, and I feel still more confidence that the better part will rally to Clay. They will have more confidence in the Whigs than in the Van Burenites, and I think we ought to manifest to them that ours is the liberal and catholic cause, and that all true men who come to its standard are received and treated according to their merits, —"that the latch-string is always out" and a welcome ready for them. The Whig press has been and continues to be very impolitic, and I may say ungenerous, in the hostile spirit with which it pursues Mr. Calhoun and his party. Cannot a wiser and a more liberal tone be given to it in Kentucky? Talk with Robertson on the subject; and if he concurs, as I am sure you will, he is the very man to give the right direction in this matter.

Tyler is very much incensed at the election of Blair & Rives as printers to the House of Representatives. He considers it as a sanction of all the abuse that the *Globe* has visited upon him. And so far he is right. He and his son Bob declare that the Democrats have insulted the President at every step they have taken during the session, and that if the contest must be between Van Buren and Clay they will prefer the latter. There is no doubt, I believe, that they are saying this, and much more, of anti-Van Burenism, as, for instance, "that the world cannot furnish a parallel of *the ingratitude* and treachery with which they have been treated by the Democratic party." But these gentlemen are at best very *unsartin*, and are now truly in a great passion. They are, thank Heaven, of no particular importance, and no calculation can be made about them. Webster is expected here about the last of the month. All that I hear about him is but confirmatory of the conclusions we formed at home,—that he wants to come back to the Whigs, that he will come back, and that he *must* come *back*.

Your friend,

R. P. Letcher,   J. J. Crittenden.
 Governor of Ky.

(R. P. Letcher to J. J. Crittenden.)

Frankfort, December 18, 1843.

Dear Crittenden,—Your letter of the 10th is received. You will get the *Commonwealth* to-morrow, and there you will see a hurried little article in regard to Calhoun and his friends. It will do pretty well for a beginning. Calhoun's friends feel *flat* and *foolish*, and *talk* and *look* like a slave who has been well chastised by his master, swearing he will be damned if he ever takes such another flogging without *hitting* a lick in return, and all the while looking around to see if his owner does not overhear his threats. Now, the plain matter of fact is, they are entirely too tame—*too submissive;* no reliance can be placed in such a bragging set of fellows.

However, cultivate their acquaintance,—they will surely come to the aid of the Whigs, particularly if their support is not needed. If we can do without their aid, they will be the most fiery, rampant fellows you ever saw or heard of. *I know the boys of old,*—the same fellows I served in Congress with for many years; but they come now with changed names. I am anxious to hear what Webster is about; what he says; how he looks, and what he will do. I think your idea about him is correct. I shall mourn over his downfall should he fail to come up to the mark.

I am rarely in town,—never, in fact, unless I go out to help some good friend to *eat venison.* That I am sure to do, being naturally a kind-hearted, obliging sort of fellow. Let me hear from you often.

Very hastily, your friend,
R. P. LETCHER.

CHAPTER XVII.

1844–1845.

Letters of Crittenden, Letcher, Clay, Buchanan, etc. etc.

(R. P. Letcher to J. J. Crittenden.)

FRANKFORT, January 18, 1844.

DEAR CRITTENDEN,—As I shall eat no dinner to-day I can take a moment to give you a line. *Why eat no dinner?* Because I shall give a large oyster-supper to-night to about forty, and of course I wish to have a good appetite. This legislature don't move to suit me at all,—there is no concert, no energy, no tact; therefore there will be no good results. Helm heads the Locos in his decisions and in most of his votes. I have never been in the House; see nothing of the members, except in large parties. A leader is wanted. Graves takes but little interest in the House; perhaps he is too modest to aspire to be a leader. Jake Swigert and others wish me to put you on your guard in reference to Hardin, the postmaster, saying there was a rascally intrigue on hand to *oust him.* Had you not better see Wickliffe about his illustrious kinsman, and endeavor to save him. I have not read Rives's letter,—*it will no doubt do to talk about.* I should like to see and hear what Calhoun can say why sentence should not be pronounced upon him. I still have my fears about *Van's* ability to *stand up,*—he is too weak to run, you may rely upon it; he is like Baillie Peyton's steer, which was so poor and weak it had to be *held up* to be shot. Mr. Crittenden will have, no doubt, a full report of the fair held last night. All I know is that a gentleman of your acquaintance *suffered severely* in the action. This thing of eating for a church is no light affair, I can tell you. I have been upon the decline ever since the fair opened.

Your friend,
R. P. LETCHER.

(R. P. Letcher to J. J. Crittenden.)

FRANKFORT, January 22, 1844.

DEAR CRITTENDEN,—You know I never complain; but I should like to suggest, in the most delicate manner, that you have all become exceedingly *silent* in and about Washington for

(213)

the last four weeks. What's the matter? Have you all turned Tyler-men? No, I should say not, as I see that the great "Prophet of Indiana" is rejected, and so is Henshaw. So far so good. Spencer, I suppose, will also be genteelly executed. If you can't get a good man, hold the place open for the next administration. My legislature is *no great things*, and I have very little reliance upon their sagacity or usefulness. The Locos have a leading control in everything, with the assistance of the Whigs, and I say it with the most perfect respect, take them altogether they are *a poor set of fellows*. They were afraid to give Dick Apperson his seat, though he was certainly entitled to it, lest they might *hurt feelings*. *You* may think I am writing you a letter, but I am not,—I am *now* talking to a fellow about a *fine* which he will have to *pay* to a *dead* and everlasting certainty. He is about closing his last speech, and when he gets through I have nothing further to say to you. What has become of Calhoun's *love*-letter? I am waiting with impatience to see it. Rives's letter takes very well in this county. Will Van Buren be the candidate? I fear not! Answer all these questions and a great many more which I have not time to put to you.

Good-by says my man, and good-by *says I.*

Your friend,
R. P. Letcher.

(Henry Clay to J. J. Crittenden.)

New Orleans, Jan. 24, 1844.

My dear Sir,—I received your favors of the 2d and 8th instant. The object of the latter is attained by the death of our excellent friend, Judge Porter, so far as respects a *vacancy*. I wish I could add that it would surely be filled by a Whig. That is very uncertain, although my hopes preponderate over my fears. A few days will supersede all speculation. I thank you for the information contained in yours of the 2d. If Mr. Tyler's present dispositions do not lead you to attach an undue importance to them, nor induce the Senate to confirm nominations which they ought to reject, they are not to be regretted. Among those nominations are Cushing's, Profit's, and Spencer's, the latter decidedly the most important of them all. Does any man believe these men true or faithful or honest? If Spencer be confirmed, he will have run a short career of more profligate conduct and *good luck* than any man I recollect.

My departure from this city I have fixed between the 20th and 25th of February, and my arrival at Raleigh 12th of April. I shall leave Mobile the 1st of March. I have appropriated about a month and a half for the tour of Alabama, Georgia, and South Carolina.

Your friend,
HENRY CLAY.

Hon. J. J. CRITTENDEN.

(J. J. Crittenden to R. P. Letcher.)

WASHINGTON, Jan. 28, 1844.

DEAR LETCHER,—I have just received your letter of the 22d instant, and am pleased to discover in it some evidence that a little neglect on my part in writing *has* had the effect of producing mortification and making you unhappy. This is quite flattering. But that poor petitioner! You were mad at not receiving one of my agreeable letters, turned your ill humor on him, and refused to remit his fine.

But now for your question. Calhoun's letter has no doubt been returned to him by his friends for reconsideration, because, as it is said, they thought it a little too strong or *harsh*. We *shall* soon have it, I suppose, in some form or other. His friends here give indications which satisfy me that they will prefer Clay to Van Buren. They have, however, been so much disappointed and thrown into such a predicament by the superior strength and management of the Van Burenites, that they seem hardly to know what to do or say. For the present, they are very cautious and stand on their reserved rights. Clay, I believe, will ultimately get the vote of South Carolina, if necessary to his election. Her public men will *have* a *hand* in the *contest*, and will be quite willing, I suppose, to take a share *in the crop*. They must be tired, it seems to me, of that pretension to superior purity, which in times past made them turn their backs on such contests and *throw away* their votes. Webster, you know, is here. He *called* to see me, and I returned the civility, and we are quite gracious, as much so as could be expected. We talk of the approaching presidential election as a *common concern*. He identifies himself with us, and says *we* ought to do *this, that,* and *the other,* and he has decided on his course, and will go with us in support of the Baltimore nomination, and he knows well what that will be. You may soon expect to see a manifesto from him in the form of an answer to some New Hampshire men who were good enough to ask him to be a candidate for the Presidency. It will answer the purpose well enough, but it is not in that lofty and magnanimous style in which, for his sake, I should have liked to see him take his station in the field. Rives's letter is a good one, and he deserves credit for it. He is in earnest, and means to act up to it. After a long withdrawal, he again attends our

Whig meetings and consultations, and evidently wishes to be considered *one of us*. The confidence of Clay's election is already producing *noble effects*. The *tide* is in his favor, and all the floating votes are turning to him. Van Buren is surely to be the *Loco* candidate; that is the settled *doom* of the party, and the authors of it could not, if they would, change it.

The abandonment of Van Buren now, or his withdrawal from the contest, would be the signal of dispersion and defeat to the party, so you need not make yourself at all uneasy lest he should withdraw. For my part, I should be very willing to see them make the experiment. Tyler, there is no doubt, is now chiefly hostile to the Van Burenites, and may probably give the Whigs a preference over them during the balance of his administration, but there is no anticipating his vacillations or where he will settle down. *We* will certainly do nothing to repel his preference; *we* will even do what we can to cherish in him any returning sense of kindness to the Whigs; but we intend also to hold on our course firmly and act our part in such a manner as to be satisfied with ourselves in any event that may happen. I think Porter will be rejected as Secretary of War, and Spencer, as Judge of the Supreme Court. This week will probably witness the decision in both cases. Wise has been nominated to Brazil, and will probably be confirmed. Many of the Whigs will vote for him from motives of kindness or policy, and some because they are satisfied with reducing him to so inferior a station. I have not determined myself what to do. I feel a repugnance at voting for him, and I do not like to vote in opposition to the friends who will vote for him.

Your friend,

R. P. Letcher, Governor, etc.   J. J. Crittenden.

(Henry Clay to J. J. Crittenden.)

New Orleans, February 15, 1844.

My dear Sir,—General F. Mercer has just arrived here from Texas, and brings intelligence which has greatly surprised me, but which, in fact, I cannot believe to be true. *It is in substance* that it has been ascertained by a vote in secret session, or in some other way, that forty-two American senators are in favor of the annexation of Texas, and have advised the President that they will confirm a treaty to that effect; that a negotiation has been opened accordingly in Texas, and that a treaty will be speedily concluded.

Is this true, especially that forty-two senators have concurred in the project? Do address me instantly, both at Montgomery, in Alabama, and Columbus, in Georgia, and give me such information as you feel at liberty to communicate.

If it be true, I shall regret extremely that *I* have had no hand in it.

> Your friend,
> HENRY CLAY.

(R. P. Letcher to J. J. Crittenden.)

FRANKFORT, March 13, 1844.

DEAR CRITTENDEN,—No. This is fact in regard to White's declension of the judgeship. It will wear the appearance of a mere connivance, a sort of strategy, on my part, to take time, etc. If I could have had the least intimation in advance of his change of opinion, I would have been ready for the occasion. But let it pass; no doubt there are some strong reasons why he should not leave his post. Squire Turner is in the field to fill White's vacancy. The disappointment which he will experience on the occasion is enough to break the heart of any man of your tender sensibility; and how do you suppose White can stand that? What about Virginia? I am afraid of the April elections; my strong impression is the State will go against us. There is this comfort in the matter, however: it may be the means of making Van Buren run the race. On this point I have always entertained strong fears. I can give you no town news. Oh, yes, I did hear that General Metcalf *pulled the nose* of a little fellow by the name of Green last Sunday evening. Let him pay his fine like a gentleman. I have already notified him not to look for any mercy from the executive, but to pay up promptly. He replied " that what occurred was *confidential*, and he hoped no trial would take place." When do you expect to be at home? I know the idea of an adjournment is distressing to you; but I want to know when you will be forced to come home.

> Your friend,
> R. P. LETCHER.

Hon. J. J. CRITTENDEN.

(Henry Clay to J. J. Crittenden.)

SAVANNAH, March 24, 1844.

DEAR SIR,—I arrived here on the 21st, and shall leave to-morrow morning. My reception everywhere, from Mobile to this place, has been marked by extraordinary enthusiasm. I have borne the fatigues of the journey better than I feared; indeed, I have nothing to complain of but a hoarseness produced by public speaking, into which I have been reluctantly drawn. I received at Montgomery and Columbus both of your letters relating to Texas, and I find that subject is producing great excitement at Washington. I have forborne hitherto to express any opinion with regard to it. I reserve for my arrival at Washington the consideration of the question whether it is not necessary to announce my opinions. I think I can treat the question very differently from any treatment which I have yet seen of it, and so as to reconcile all our friends and many others to the views which I entertain. Of one thing you may be certain, that there is no such anxiety for the annexation here at the South as you might have imagined. I take pleasure also in informing you that I have not seen one Whig during my journey who is not satisfied with the ground on which I place the principle of protection in connection with a tariff for revenue; and you may say to the senators from the South who belong to our party that they may with perfect safety and confidence vote against the fraudulent tariff which is working up in the House. I adhere to my purpose of reaching Raleigh by the 12th of next month, and of getting to Washington towards the end of April. I expect to pass by Columbia and Charleston.

Your friend,

Hon. J. J. CRITTENDEN. H. CLAY.

(R. P. Letcher to J. J. Crittenden.)

FRANKFORT, April 10, 1844.

DEAR CRITTENDEN,—You are so very much elated since the unexpected success of the Whigs in Connecticut, that you are entirely above writing to your *poor friends.* Never mind, the next news you hear will make you " laugh the wrong side of your mouth." I'll see then whether White and yourself will go off and *get confidentially* tipsy. Jeptha Dudley says, I am told, that when the full returns come in it will be seen that the Democrats have carried the State by a small majority against the combined fraud of the abolitionists, the Tylerites, and the *rascally coons.* Wait awhile; don't crow so soon; look out for complete returns. The *Yeoman* may possibly furnish you more accurate information than can be obtained from the Connecticut papers. However, upon a moment's reflection, I doubt whether the editor of that valuable journal is just now in a communicative mood. " Mr. Turner," said a young gentleman near the post-office door this morning, " can you tell me *how* the Connecticut elections have gone?" "*Damn* Connecticut," said he, " I neither *know* nor *care!*" I doubt from this whether the honorable gentleman will give you information on this point. What do you think of Virginia? I should be sorry for her to go with us at her spring elections, lest we should be deprived of the pleasure of beating that same *little fellow.* I have always been afraid he would "*slope off sorter*" before the day of the race. Don't let him get away,—hold him to the track. Is Buchanan happy now? What does he say? *How* does he look?

I wouldn't have been so *badly scared* about Connecticut as you were for *two* such States in fee simple. Now, take that. Adjourn your memorable Congress as soon as possible and come home. If you *must* get tipsy and will get tipsy, and nothing else will do, come home and I'll take a turn with you myself rather than you should fall into the hands of strangers. I did not see Benton when he passed through here. I regret it.

Your friend,
R. P. LETCHER.

Hon. J. J. CRITTENDEN.

(Henry Clay to J. J. Crittenden.)

RALEIGH, April 17, 1844.

MY DEAR SIR,—I transmit herewith a letter, intended to be published in the *Intelligencer*, on the Texas question. In my opinion, it is my duty to present it to the public, and in that *Badger,* the governor, and Stanley concur. I wish you to confer with Mangum, Berrien, Morehead, Stephens of Georgia, and any other friends you please about it. I leave to you and them the *time* of the publication, whether before or after my arrival at Washington. To slight modifications of its phraseology I should have no objections. I leave here to-morrow for Petersburg. I shall leave Norfolk, if I can, Wednesday.

Your friend,
H. CLAY.

(Henry Clay to J. J. Crittenden.)

PETERSBURG, April 19, 1844.

MY DEAR SIR,—I transmitted to you from Raleigh a letter, on the subject of the annexation of Texas, for publication. I observe with the greatest attention all that is passing in regard to it as far as it is visible to my eye. I feel perfectly confident in the ground which I have taken, and feel, moreover, that it is proper and politic to present to the public that ground. I leave *you* and other *friends* merely the question of deciding when my exposition shall appear. I cannot consent to *suppress* or unnecessarily *delay* the publication of it. I think it ought to appear not *later* than to-day or to-morrow week. I entertain no fears from the promulgation of my opinion. Public sentiment is everywhere sounder than at Washington. I should be glad to receive at Norfolk, if you feel authorized to send me confidentially, a copy of the treaty. I leave here to-morrow for Norfolk, from which I shall take my departure Wednesday or Thursday next.

Your friend,
H. CLAY.

Hon. J. J. CRITTENDEN.

(R. P. Letcher to J. J. Crittenden.)

FRANKFORT, Monday.

DEAR CRITTENDEN,—We have our troubles here, and they are not few. The Whig party is in the greatest peril and distraction,—no mistake. I am no alarmist, but a close observer of the times. There is a restless state of things in the Whig ranks which amounts almost to delirium. D—— has behaved outrageously; he has offered a resolution in the Senate nominating General Taylor for the Presidency. He promised not to do so, but it is done. This increases the distraction. The Senate will no doubt give it the go-by. It is unfortunate and inexpedient in every point of view. What is greatly needed is information from Washington. One word more: Dixon came to my house last night and said he had no doubt about his nomination, but he had doubts as to his election. He then proposed that I should request *you* to run. I refused. He said he believed he would write to you to that effect; said he had proposed to Graves that they should both *stand back*, which Graves refused. My object in telling you this is to afford you a chance in case he does write, to reply in such a way as your better judgment may dictate.

Your friend,

Hon. JOHN J. CRITTENDEN.   R. P. LETCHER.

(R. P. Letcher to J. J. Crittenden.)

FRANKFORT, May 10, 1844.

DEAR CRITTENDEN,—I have read your letter of the 4th with uncommon pleasure. *Yes*, I think the whole affair is now pretty well settled. Indeed, I never had any hesitation in believing most confidently that the second edition of the campaign of '40 would come out in '44 embellished and improved. You had a grand affair at the Convention in Baltimore, probably the most imposing spectacle that has ever been witnessed in America, and it is destined to have a great effect throughout the country. I am glad the *old Prince* is behaving handsomely in his travels and in his general deportment. The Van Buren party are really to be pitied; they change their man every day. Commodore Stewart, I understand, is their candidate *to-day;* to-morrow they will have another. Oh, how awfully they curse Benton! "Traitor, villain, rascal," are words of common use in connection with his name. Guthrie is sitting here reading a newspaper. I am too much of a gentleman to introduce a disagreeable topic of conversation, but I should like to hear him say a word or two about Texas and Van Buren. Well, let Charley W. *walk the plank*. I want to see him out of office; think he well deserves his fate if Tyler puts his foot on him.

The town is filled with lawyers, and the Whigs are the happiest rascals you ever saw. You might hear Jake Swigert laugh at least a half a mile.

Your friend,

Hon. J. J. CRITTENDEN. R. P. LETCHER.

(James Buchanan to R. P. Letcher.)

LANCASTER, July 27, 1844.

MY DEAR SIR,—I have received your favor of the 19th, and am rejoiced to learn that your distinguished friend has probably thought better of the publication. You have ever been a sagacious man, and doubtless think that James K. Polk is not quite so strong an antagonist as Andrew Jackson, and therefore that it would not be very wise to drop the former and make up an issue with the latter. If this had been done, it would not be difficult to predict the result, at least in Pennsylvania. The affair has worried me much, and yet I have been as innocent as a sucking dove of any improper intentions. First, to have been called on by Jackson as his witness against Clay, and then to be vouched as Clay's witness against Jackson, when, before Heaven, I can say nothing against either, is a little too much to bear patiently. I have got myself into the scrape from the desire I often expressed and never concealed, that Jackson, first of all things, might be elected by the House, and next that *Clay* might be his Secretary of State. It was a most unfortunate day for the country, Mr. Clay, and all of us, when Mr. Clay accepted the office of Secretary of State. To be sure, there was nothing criminal in it, but it was worse, as Talleyrand would have said, "it was a blunder." Had it not been for *that*, he would, in all probability, now have been in retirement, after having been President for eight years, and friends, like *you* and *I* (who ought to have stood together through life), would not have been separated; but, as the hymn says, I trust "there's a better time coming." You ask, Has Polk any chance to carry Pennsylvania? I think he has. Pennsylvania is Democratic by at least 20,000, and there is no population more steady on the face of the earth. Under all the excitements of 1840 and Mr. Van Buren's want of popularity, we were beaten but 343, and since we have carried our State elections by large majorities.

Muhlenburg, candidate for governor, is a fast horse, and will be elected; this will exercise much influence on the presidential election. But your people are in high hopes, and after my mistake in 1840, I will not prophesy. I was ignorant of the fact that any portion of the Democratic party were playing the part of Actæon's dogs towards me. I stood in no man's way. After my withdrawal, I never thought of the Presidency, and the few scattering votes I received in Baltimore were given against my express instructions. The very last thing I desired was to be the candidate. If they wish to *hunt me* down for any thing, it must be because I have refused to join in the *hue and cry* against Benton, who has been, for many years, the *sword* and *shield* of the Democracy. I differed from him on the Texas question, but I believe him to be a better man than most of his assailants, and I hope he will be elected to the Senate. I have delayed the publication of my Texas speech, to prevent its use against him in the Missouri election. It is not according to my taste or sense of propriety for a senator *to take the stump*, but I owe Muhlenburg much, and, if he should request it, I could not *well refuse*. I shall never say (as I never have said) anything which could give the most fastidious friend of Mr. Clay just cause of offense. As I grow older, I look back with mournful pleasure to the days of "Auld Lang Syne." There was far more *heart*, and *soul*, and *fun*, in our social intercourse *then* than in these degenerate days, but perhaps to think so is an evidence of approaching age. Poor Governor Kent! I was forcibly reminded of him a few days ago, when, at the funeral of a friend, I examined his son's grave-stone. To keep it in repair has been for me a matter of pious duty. I loved his father to the last. But away with melancholy. I have better wine than any man between this and Frankfort, and no man would hail you with a heartier welcome. When shall we meet again?

Ever your sincere friend,

To R. P. LETCHER.   JAMES BUCHANAN.

(J. J. Crittenden to Henry Clay.)

FRANKFORT, November 13, 1844.

MY DEAR SIR,—The intelligence brought to us this morning has terminated all our hopes, our suspense, and our anxieties, in respect to the presidential election. We now know the worst. Polk is elected, and your friends have sustained the heaviest blow that could have befallen them. You will, I trust, feel no other concern about it than that which naturally arises from your sympathy with them. You are, perhaps, the only man in the nation who can lose nothing by the result. Success could have added nothing to your name, and nothing I believe to your happiness. You occupy now, but too truly, the position described as presenting the noblest of human spectacles,—

> "A great man struggling with the storms of fate,
> And nobly falling with a falling State."

Business in the Federal court now hastens my departure. I will try to carry with me a heart as light as possible, but deeply impressed with the difficulties which *overhang* the country. It seems that we can only learn wisdom by suffering ruin, and I am tempted to leave the Polkites to dispose of the tariff among themselves. The people have preferred Mr. Polk, and are entitled to the benefit of his measures.

Very respectfully, your friend,

Hon. H. CLAY.   J. J. CRITTENDEN.

(Henry Clay to J. J. Crittenden.)

ASHLAND, November 28, 1844.

MY DEAR SIR,—I received your very kind letter written just before your departure for Washington. It is hardly necessary to say that I deeply sympathize with you, in consequence of the most unexpected and disastrous results of the presidential election. As to myself, it is of but little importance. But I deplore it on account of the country and of our friends. I had cherished the fond hope of being an humble instrument, in the hands of Providence, to check the downward tendency of our government, and to contribute to restore it to its former purity. I had also hoped to be able to render some justice to our enlightened and patriotic friends, who have been so long and so cruelly persecuted and proscribed. But these hopes have vanished, and it is useless and unavailing to lament the irrevocable event.

It will be more profitable to seek to discern the means by which the country may be saved from the impending dangers. I regret that they are not visible to me; still, it is our duty to the last to struggle for its interest, its honor, and its glory. And it is in that spirit that I venture to offer a few suggestions. It seems to me that the Whigs, or some of them, in Congress, would do well to have an early consultation, and to adopt some system of future action. We, I think, should adhere to our principles; for, believing in their wisdom and rectitude, it is impossible that we can abandon them. The recent election demonstrates that, although the Whigs are in the minority, it is a large minority, embracing a large portion of the virtue, wealth, intelligence, and patriotism of the country. That minority constitutes a vast power which, acting in concert, and with prudence and wisdom, may yet save the country. Then, there are the errors which we confidently fear and believe our opponents will commit in the course of their administration, an exposure of which must open the eyes of the people and add to the Whig strength. In your letter, you intimated an inclination to leave the dominant party free to carry out their principles undisturbed by the Whigs. I confess I am inclined to agree with you in that opinion; for, unless there is a partial operation and experience of the opposite systems of the two parties, I do not see how the country will ever settle down in a stable and permanent policy. As a general rule, I think that the dominant party ought to be allowed to carry out their measures, without any other opposition than that of fully exposing their evil tendency to the people, if they have such a tendency. Of course, I do not mean that members should vote contrary to their conscientious convictions, or to the will of their constituents; but I suppose that there are members, in both branches of Congress, who can vote in conformity with the will of their constituents without violating their own convictions, and thus leave the other party at liberty to establish its own policy. If that party should attempt to embody, in a tariff, just enough of protection on the one hand, and of free trade on the other, to secure its ascendency and farther to deceive and mislead the people, such partial legislation ought to encounter the most determined opposition. That is the course, I confess, which I most apprehend they will pursue. They will give protection where it is necessary to the preservation of their power, and they will deny it to States with whose support they can dispense.

There is a great tendency among the Whigs to unfurl the banner of the Native American party. Whilst I own I have great sympathy with that party, I do not perceive the wisdom, at present, either of the Whigs absorbing it, or being absorbed by it. If either of those contingencies were to happen, our adversaries would charge that it was the same old party, with a new name, or with a new article added to its creed. In the mean time they would retain all the foreign vote, which they have consolidated; make constant further accessions, and perhaps regain their members who have joined the Native American party. I am disposed to think that it is best for each party, the Whigs and the Natives, to retain their respective organizations distinct from each other, and to cultivate friendly relations together. If petitions be presented to alter the naturalization laws, they ought to be received and respectfully dealt with. There can be no doubt of the greatness of the evil of this constant manufacture of American citizens out of foreign emigrants, many of whom are incapable of justly appreciating the duties incident to the new character which they assume. Some day or other this evil will doubtless be corrected. But is this country ripe for the correction? and will not a premature effort, instead of weakening, add strength to the evil?

I perceive, in several quarters, a wish expressed that I should return to the Senate. I desire to say to you that I have not the remotest thought of doing so, even if a vacancy existed. I can hardly conceive of a state of things in which I should be tempted to return to Congress. My anxious desire is to remain during the remnant of my days in peace and retirement! Do me the favor to present me affectionately to all our friends in the Senate, and particularly to Messrs. Berrien, Bayard, and Rives, from whom I have received very friendly letters. I may write to them, perhaps, on some other occasion.

I remain faithfully your friend, and obedient servant,

H. CLAY.

Hon. J. J. CRITTENDEN.

(Thomas Corwin to J. J. Crittenden.)

LEBANON, November 15, 1844.

DEAR CRITTENDEN,—I have scarcely courage to address a line to a friend, but feel so disconsolate that I must inquire how the result of this election is received in Kentucky.

Much as I have distrusted public judgment on the merits of *great men*, yet I could not believe this last sin against the honest reason of man would be *actually* committed.

How does Mr. Clay bear himself under this last exhibition of ingratitude? Is truth, indeed, omnipotent? Is public justice certain? Is it only at the *grave* of a truly *great man* that the world opens its eyes to his real worth?

What is to happen? What will the charlatans do next? Will they repeal the tariff, and wage war on Mexico? or will they *pretend* to do this,—make a hypocritical effort and drop it, and complain that a Whig Senate or a Whig party prevented them?

Will they kick Calhoun out, and *then* in two years more make another bargain with him, and then deceive him for the *fifth* time? Pray tell me what we are to look for? I see it is said Van Buren is coming to the Senate. Will Mr. Clay decline all public concern?

Do let me hear about these things.

Your friend,

J. J. CRITTENDEN.   THOS. CORWIN.

(Henry Clay to J. J. Crittenden.)

ASHLAND, January 9, 1845.

MY DEAR SIR,—I received your favor of the 3d, and transmit inclosed a letter to Judge Story. I am not surprised at his disgust with his service on the bench of the Supreme Court. Among the causes of regret, on account of our recent defeat, scarcely any is greater than that which arises out of the consequence that the Whigs cannot fill the two vacancies in the Supreme Court. I see that they have *got up* Texas in the House, and I anticipate that some scheme of annexation will

be *cooked up* there.   Whatever fate may attend it in the Senate,
I think that the resolution of our friends in this body to leave
it to Mr. Polk is correct.   Among my fears, one is, that it will, if
annexed, disturb the territorial balance of the Union, and lead to
its dissolution.   Letcher, of whose silence you complain, bears
badly our recent defeat.   Time, the great physician, may heal
his wounds.   I sometimes have occasion to use another's super-
scription, and wish you would send me some half a dozen of
franked envelopes.

Yours faithfully,
H. CLAY.

CHAPTER XVIII

1845-1846.

Admission of Texas—Oregon—Letter to his Wife—Discussion in the Senate with
Allen—Letter of W. B. Leigh.

MR. CRITTENDEN said: I rise to address the Senate
with an embarrassment which I seldom feel in addressing that body. The subject under discussion is one of immense
magnitude, not only involving the question of the extension of
this Union but that of the preservation and duration of the great
charter, the *Constitution*, upon which this confederation rests.
I could have forborne the expression of my opinions had it not
appeared important to other senators to make known their views.
I am not willing to let my silence be attributed to any backward-
ness to avow my sentiments openly.

Mr. Crittenden then stated the principles of the joint resolution under consideration, and instituted an inquiry into the
grand powers of the Constitution upon which the action of Congress was now invoked. He proposed first to examine the arguments upon which it was assumed that the power granted in
the fourth article of the Constitution extended to the admission
of States, erected out of foreign territory or foreign States already formed. In pursuing this examination, he should confine
gentlemen who designated themselves par excellence strict con-
structionists to their own doctrine. He quoted the provision of
the fourth article that new States may be admitted by the Congress into this Union, and commented upon the construction
which alone should be the guide of legislation, and asked *how*
could the express grant be applied as the friends of annexation
applied it without opening it up to such a latitudinous construction as would be wholly at war with the nature of the
instrument in which it is found and the natural inference of
the intention of the framers of the Constitution. Can it be imagined by any candid and dispassionate mind,—a mind divested

of predilections to arrive at a foregone conclusion,—that if it had been contemplated by the framers of that instrument to authorize the admission of foreign States or foreign territory by act of legislation, they would have left such a vast and important power indefinite and hidden in mysterious expressions, wholly dependent upon construction and interpolation? To suppose this is to suppose what is contrary to all reason. Was it to be believed that the wise, jealous, and cautious men who weighed and deliberated upon the grants of power so long and so carefully would, if they intended that foreign States and foreign territory should be admitted by Congress at its discretion, have forborne the expression of their intention in clear and explicit terms which could not be misunderstood?

Mr. Crittenden reviewed at considerable length the arguments urged throughout this debate by the friends of annexation, commenting on each and dissenting from all, and in many instances insisting that gentlemen had wholly misapprehended the authorities upon which they relied. He did not intend to undertake the task of defining the exact line of demarkation between the legislative and treaty-making power; he agreed with the senator from Alabama, Mr. Bagby, "that there is a line." It would be sufficient for him to show that the acquisition of territory was confined exclusively to the treaty-making power. He quoted Justice Story's definition of the power to make treaties. It might be that some part or portions of the subjects enumerated by Justice Story may be regulated by law. Justice Story says the treaty-making power embraces the power of treating for peace or war, regulations of commerce or for territory. Did not, then, the treaty-making power embrace the case of acquiring territory? Mr. C. directed much of his review to the remarks of the senator from South Carolina, Mr. McDuffie. He quoted largely from the *Federalist* and authorities for the purpose of establishing his position that the power to admit new States into the Union was confined exclusively to the admission of States arising out of the bosom of the old thirteen States and territory in the neighborhood—*the neighborhood* meaning the territory belonging to the States, but out of the limit of the State confines. He next touched upon the limits of the treaty-making power, with a view of showing that, from their very nature and their possible effects upon our foreign relations, the power was lodged where it ought to be lodged, in the executive and the Senate; and he argued that the experience of the government before the adoption of the Constitution had proved the inconvenience and impropriety of exercising the power of Congress. He denied the position assumed by the senator from South Carolina that Congress has the power to declare war and make peace. *Where* was the power of making peace given to Congress by the Constitution? Would the senator tell him how Congress could make peace?

Mr. McDuffie.—Yes, sir, by disbanding the army and navy.
Mr. Crittenden.—That would not stop the war.
Mr. McDuffie.—He did not presume the executive and Senate would undertake to carry on the war after Congress disbanded the army and navy.
Mr. Crittenden.—No, sir; but that would be a very good time for the enemy to carry on the war. [Great laughter.]

In the course of Mr. Crittenden's remarks, he referred to Mr. Jefferson's opinions concerning the power of acquiring territory. He maintained that if it can be acquired by this government, it must be exclusively through the treaty-making power. It was admitted by the senator from South Carolina that territory might be properly acquired by treaty; but it was denied by him that the acquisition of it belonged exclusively to the treaty-making power. Now he (Mr. Crittenden) held that if foreign territory can be properly acquired by the treaty-making power, it is exclusively by that power and that alone in this government that it can be acquired. He admonished the Senate to *hold fast* to the Union *as it is,*—not to attempt expanding its territory,—not to risk anything by hazardous experiments. He denounced the idea of grounding any course of policy upon apprehensions of the grasping power of England. He feared nothing from England or any other power: his fears were of the destruction of our own constitution and institutions by novel and dangerous experiments. His objections to the annexation of Texas were founded upon public considerations; some of these were passing away,—they may yet be wholly removed. He feared at present this measure would disturb our foreign relations. It seemed to him unwise to act upon it now,—the people have not had an opportunity of expressing their will upon the subject at the ballot-box. The question was started for purposes of the presidential election since the people last appointed their representatives. Let the matter be postponed till the people can speak,—let its consummation be reserved for the incoming administration. To do this in an offensive way, at an improper time, and by unconstitutional means can excite nothing but hostility to the whole movement and its authors. This was a measure of the most vital importance to the country. Be patient and be just, and all may be well. The hand that grasps ambitiously, dishonestly, or unlawfully at the plunder of others, particularly when they are in a defenseless condition, is sure to be festered with the leprosy of dishonor and disgrace.

The question being taken on the motion of Mr. Berrien, Mr. Crittenden rose and said:

I wish to make a few remarks, and will not detain the Senate five minutes. According to the arguments which gentlemen on the other side had urged here, Congress has the power to admit new States into the Union, acquiring thereby not only the people, but the territory which they occupy. It is said that under the provision to admit new States Congress can admit foreign States; and if the argument of the gentleman from Mississippi (Mr. Henderson) is correct, this power has been exercised in several instances, and North Carolina and Rhode Island were foreign States, admitted by the same power that could admit Texas or Mexico. The gentleman had traced the history of their admission, and the Senate had learned from him that no law was passed for their admission,—that they merely signified their approbation of our Constitution, elected senators and representatives, who appeared in Congress and took their seats; and from that time these States acted as portions of our Union. The argument from this was, that we may do the same thing in regard to Texas. Now, I call upon the gentleman to say of what manner of use is all this legislation upon this subject. Let Texas make a republican constitution; let her appoint senators and representatives, and she has a right to come into this Union and participate in our legislation and all the affairs of the government. This is the argument of the gentleman from Mississippi: "North Carolina was a foreign State; Rhode Island was a foreign State; Texas cannot be *more* than a foreign State." This was the inference: let Texas do just exactly as they did, and the work is complete. The syllogism is perfect, according to the rules of logic. The whole fallacy consists in the utter groundlessness of the fact that these two States, North Carolina and Rhode Island, *were* foreign States. Let Texas read our history and the history of North Carolina and Rhode Island, and follow in their footsteps, and their senators and representatives may come here and take their seats by our sides. There was no occasion for her to ask for any law upon the subject,—none at all. " North Carolina and Rhode Island were foreign States ; Texas is a foreign State ;" and all that is necessary for her to do, according to the honorable senator, is to appoint her senators and representatives and come at once ! He who could imagine that North Carolina and Rhode Island were *foreign States,* might easily imagine, if his *imagination* was true to itself, that Texas was a domestic State. To him legislation did not appear at all necessary ; it would be derogatory to the rights of Texas, California, or any other State that had nothing to do but to send her senators and representatives here and become forthwith a member of the Union.

In the Senate, on 16th of December, 1845, the subject of advising the President to give immediate notice to Great Britain of the termination of the joint occupancy of Oregon Territory was under discussion. Mr. Crittenden saw no objection to the resolutions themselves, but he did not share in the apprehensions of the senator from Michigan, Mr. Cass, as to a *war.* The honorable senator, Mr. Cass, makes his inference as to war contingent upon the happening of other events,—upon the concurrence of other circumstances ; his conclusion to be complete requires other facts, such as that Great Britain will at the end of the year take hostile possession of the whole of Oregon. Mr. Crittenden thought it might be fairly inferred that such a course would lead to war ; and if Mr. Cass desired to make out a somewhat stronger case, let him suppose that Great Britain should land her forces and take possession of the city of Charleston, or Norfolk, or Baltimore. The meaning of the senator seemed to be that war would inevitably take place, *provided grounds* for war were hereafter supplied. Mr. Crittenden thought the diplomacy and wisdom of the country could certainly settle the boundary of a distant strip of territory without the shedding of blood ; it was no question of honor or national character. If we are to give the notice, let us give it to take effect *two years* hence. Let us not, like a spiteful landlord, limit our tenant to the shortest possible time, but give opportunity for reflection and negotiation. An insult between two high-spirited nations is a grave matter. This is a diplomatic question between the proper departments of this government and Great Britain. Theirs is the proper responsibility, and not one jot of that responsibility was he willing to abate. Of all the interests of the country *peace* was the mightiest. No fanaticism in politics must be suffered to guide the councils of a great nation upon so solemn a question, no little pouting, fretting, and strutting upon the stage; we have no necessity to go to war to make a character; we have a character to which we have a genealogical and historical title. It is the grand characteristic of a great nation that it vaunts not, boasts not of its power. Mr. Crittenden expressed great regret at the rejection of the proposition for arbitration. He did not know upon what right we exalted ourselves above all laws heretofore recognized amongst nations, and say that our territorial questions were to be placed above all arbitration. We had no ground upon which to base this mighty prerogative. The world has adopted a great code of pacification and acted upon it from the beginning. The choice of an *arbiter* is important. The administration may have good reason for rejecting the arbitration of crowned heads; but, thank God, they are not the wisest and best heads. What a glorious homage would this republic render to its own best principles by accepting the arbitration of a tribunal composed of men distinguished only for their talents, knowledge, and worth! This would tend to the elevation of the age. How majestic this spectacle to proceed from the hands of this free government! It would be worth more to us than all Oregon, if every inch had been awarded to us.

Mr. Crittenden regretted that this question had not been allowed to slumber; it would gradually have been settled by emigrants from the United States. It had been made the subject of party action and party declamation introduced in the Baltimore Convention by gentlemen met together for a party object. This is a mere question of property. Let us not be driven to war for a strip of territory. The child has seen the light who will behold one hundred millions of freemen in this land. *That* sought to be achieved to-day by arms will be ours to-morrow by natural inheritance. *We* are the great first-born of the continent. I smile with contempt at all the petty schemes of European ambition and Mr. Guizot's balance of power in our land. You have all no doubt heard of a memoir prepared and presented to the King of Prussia in which the author described the country, the bays, and rivers, and mountains, and stated that nature had raised a barrier against the dangerous usurpations of the American people by establishing on their borders the powerful tribe of Cherokee Indians, who would always keep them in check; nevertheless, the author thought the Americans in their wild ambition might seek to cross the Mississippi. Mark how our progress has outstripped the comprehensive views of this writer. Why show such eagerness of acquisition? Why pluck green fruit which to-morrow will fall ripe into our hands? Let us violate no right, and preserve our sacred Union, and all the rest is certain. From our lineage is to descend a race wielding a sceptre of imperial power such as the hand of emperors never grasped. I cannot doubt but that the President will do right. In my judgment, there is in the office of President a means of purification by which a man, whatever the medium of his elevation, becomes a new moral being. Providence has made him a leader in a part of that great march we are performing with giant steps.

(J. J. Crittenden to his wife Maria.)

SENATE, December 29, 1845.

MY DEAR WIFE,—I have received your letter giving me the agreeable intelligence that you are well. How happy I should have been to have been with you at your Christmas dinner.

My Christmas was a different one, a joyless and heartless one. Mrs. Webster has not been here this winter. Mr. Webster has gone for her, and we may expect her at the close of the holidays. I shall spend my New Year's day at Baltimore, being invited to attend Miss Johnson's wedding on that day.

At the late dinner at the President's, the lady Presidentess was the brightest object of the party. She of course occupied her place at the table, and I must say performed her part well and gracefully. I, at least, ought not to complain, for to me she was most polite.

I can't tell you how I long to see you. You are much inquired for here, and many wish to see you.

My love to all.   Your husband,

J. J. CRITTENDEN.

(General Scott to J. J. Crittenden.)

OFFICE, Saturday, February 14, 1846.

MY DEAR SIR,—Holding you to be duly indented to me,—that is, shipped and enlisted,—I send my orderly (a regular sergeant) with precise directions to move you up to my garrison this day, bag and baggage, without let or hinderance. Against him, a young veteran of three campaigns in Florida, what can you do, a mere civilian? No more than Sir Henry Vane and his mace-bearer against old Noll and his grenadiers. It is evident that you labor under some infirmity of purpose, some "*vis inertia*," which must be overcome by martial law—a touch of the second section *à la* Jackson, and the times stand in need of a wholesome example. It is for me to give it, and for you to submit. Therefore and wherefore, sir, I know you are to dine to-day with Corcoran (and so am I); you may as well then let the orderly get you a hack and store away in it trunk, books, and papers. He will take good care of all and deposit them in your new lodgings, where they will be safe, and *you too.* Backed as you are by that old veteran of the last war, it is possible that he may attempt a rescue. In that case I beg to admonish him that I will send down another detachment and move him up also; but if he (Cousin Vance) behaves well, and you come along, as you must, why, you may see him in your prison with your other friends,—not, however, oftener than six days in the week, nor more *than* six hours at a time. Such are the jail limits.

Yours according to behavior,

WINFIELD SCOTT.

Hon. J. J. CRITTENDEN.

(J. J. Crittenden to R. P. Letcher.)

WASHINGTON, March 9, 1846.

DEAR LETCHER,—I have received yours of the 27th of the last month, and upon my word I read it through and through, little as you seem to have expected such a grace. I am truly sorry to hear that Orlando's health and habits are so bad as you describe them; I think it is all due to my absence and the want of my good example. Your house was a bad house for drinking before I left home, and it is quite natural to infer that it has become worse since the restraints of my presence have been withdrawn. I will still hope I may be home in time to prevent fatal consequences, and before all your brandy is gone!

Well, well, your good luck does a little surprise me. What *a winning young man you* must be to convert Messrs. M. and G. into warm friends! Your solution of it is no doubt true. Hardin kept you, and you are indebted to him for these new friends. I should not wonder to hear next that Hardin and yourself are close confederates and friends, and that he is warmly for you in order to defeat the supposed hostility of M. and G. This is a rather prettier game than "*ride and tye*." Scott does seem to me to be happy. His prospects of the Presidency look bright to him; *that* makes him happy. Like the consumption, this ambition for the Presidency may be called a *flattering disease*. I believe I told you before that all you read or heard of nomination or recommendation of him as the Whig candidate at caucuses or dinner-parties was altogether unfounded,—the mere flummery and invention of letter-writers. But it is true that he rather seems to bear the palm here, and there is a more extensive *looking* to him than to any other. *As a party*, the Whigs stand uncommitted, and determined to avail themselves of the best selection that can be made when the time comes. We all think that if we are wise we can succeed in the next presidential election. Bitter dissensions are already manifested among our opponents; they are about equally divided in the Senate. They quarrel about what the President's sentiments and purposes are in relation to Oregon,—each interprets the "*oracle*" to suit himself, and each pretends to speak for him, while all are suspicious and jealous of him and of each other. They know that one side or the other is cheated and to be cheated, but they can't yet exactly tell which. In the mean time they curse Polk hypothetically. If he don't settle and make peace at forty-nine or some other parallel of compromise, the one side curses him; and if he yields an inch or stops a hair's breadth short of fifty-four degrees forty minutes, the other side damns him without redemption. Was ever a gentleman in such a fix? He might almost say like Satan, that "hell was around him." What a pity he hadn't such a friend as you to smooth down all his troubles and convert a few of these imprecators and swearers into friends! The Whigs, *poor* chastened race, are so far very quiet in the midst of the uproar,—they "*look innocent*," and say nothing. What can the poor creatures do but mourn over such troubles! But all this is not enough; our friend Buck not only comes in for his share of these common troubles, but has his own *particular* grief besides. He is for all Oregon,—he would not yield an inch "for life or death," and he is quite careful to *have* it told and known that he stands fixed on the *north pole*, right at the point of fifty-four forty. There may be some discretion in their valor. The hardest swearers are for fifty-four forty,—and he thinks, perhaps, by taking the same position he may escape more *curses* than in any other way. But what comes next? Why, he is charged with wishing to have a war in order to save the tariff for Pennsylvania and defeat his colleague, Mr. Walker, depriving him of all the glory of his free-trade bill lately submitted to Congress. If war comes, all know we can't think of reducing the tariff. Thus you see this unhappy dissension has penetrated even into the sanctuary of the cabinet, and may eventually drive Buck out of that *political paradise.* It being understood and agreed here that Walker is the ruling spirit in that council, I expect Buck is nearly ready to exclaim, " all is vanity and vexation of spirit." Scott already knows of the funeral eulogy you have prepared for him in case of his death, and I shall also inform him of the instructions you are preparing in case he should live to be a candidate, so that he may feel easy in the assurance that whether he *lives or dies* you will provide for him.

Your friend,

R. P. LETCHER,   J. J. CRITTENDEN.
      Governor.

(W. C. Rives to J. J. Crittenden.)

CASTLE HILL, March 9, 1846.

MY DEAR SIR,—I have seen with the greatest pleasure the lofty and courageous patriotism with which, in the spirit of peace, you have not feared to treat the question of Oregon from the moment of its warlike introduction by Colonel Polk. Your last speech on the subject has just reached us. I should do great violence to my feelings if I were not to tell you with what sincere gratification I have read it. Your bold declaration for peace, as the highest interest of the nation, will find a hearty response in the bosoms of nineteen-twentieths of the people. I can hardly conceive of such a hallucination as seems to have come over the dreams of some of our "grave and reverend seigniors," who, by their daily harangues, are seeking to *prepare the hearts* of the people, *as they tell us*, for war. One would suppose that when things had come to such an extremity as can alone justify the *ultima ratio*, the hearts of a brave and intelligent people would require no preparing for war by *the arts of oratory*. What is to become of all this singular and complex manœuvring of our modern Machiavel at the head of the government? It seems to me hard to foresee. But that they have gotten themselves into a narrow defile, between warring sections of their own party, with the solid phalanx of the public judgment arrayed against them,—a position from which no art can rescue them, retreat or advance being alike impossible or fatal,—admits, I think, of no question. Foreseeing that our friends in the Senate, from their high official position, would naturally feel themselves restrained in the expression of any unfavorable *judgment* on our boasted title to the whole of Oregon, I thought I would venture to say a word or two to suggest for consideration some doubts respecting the infallibility of our friend Buchanan's dialectics upon the old Spanish title. This question of right, by-the-by, though a very delicate one to discuss, lies at the bottom of the whole subject with the people. If they can believe our right *clear*, they will maintain it all *hazards*. I am not surprised that Mr. Polk is beginning to realize, at the hands of his own party, some of the consequences of his folly and duplicity in attempting to combine the braggadocio of speculation with the intended surrender of national claims. I hope you will so manage the subject in the Senate as to leave him exposed to all the inconveniences of his own position, while you do everything that is practicable to preserve the peace of the country. At all times, and very truly and faithfully

Your friend,

Hon. J. J. Crittenden. W. C. Rives.

In the Senate, on the 10th of April, 1846, Senator Allen, of Ohio, chairman of the Committee of Foreign Relations, made a violent speech on the subject of an amendment he had offered to a resolution of Mr. Johnson, of Maryland, on "giving notice to Great Britain." Mr. Allen lectured the Senate for not having passed the House resolutions, thought they should have yielded to the moral influence of the almost unanimous vote of the House; he charged the Senate with forgetting the interests of the country, and their own dignity, etc.

Mr. Crittenden's reply was masterly. The speech will be published entire in another volume, but I will give some extracts from it now, and also some letters, in relation to it, received at that time by him.

Mr. Crittenden.—I cannot suffer such imputations against the character and action of the Senate to pass unnoticed. What is the honorable gentleman's commission? Who authorizes him to assume here the air and tone of pre-eminence which so strongly marks his language when addressing the Senate? "Upon what meat doth this our Cæsar feed, that he hath grown so great?" Is it this petty office of chairman of the committee which warrants him in putting on these airs of authority, in assuming this predominance, and lecturing us as to our official duty? The Senate has just adopted a resolution, proposed to it by the senator from Maryland, Mr. Johnson, and the gentleman from Ohio characterizes it as a miserable, feeble, pattering, contracted, abject resolution.   Let me tell the gentleman he does not know this body, or the material of which it is composed.   There is another and more difficult lesson, which, I fear, the senator has got to learn, that is, to know himself.   I can tell the senator that the majority of the Senate and the humble individual who now addresses it, are as little moved by the dread of any responsibility, except that of doing wrong, as even the chairman of the Committee on Foreign Relations.   If the force of the gentleman's argument was to be measured by the extent and vigor of his manipulations, it would indeed be difficult to answer him.   I will not stand here to be rebuked, or to hear the Senate schooled or called to account by any such authority.   The gentleman undertakes to make himself the advocate and defender of the House of Representatives.   Who or what is the House of Representatives of the United States, that it stands in need of such an advocate?

The gentleman's advocacy of one of the Houses of Congress is equally an act of supererogation (shall I say of assumption?) with his rebuke of the other.   The gentleman tells us of the majority by which a certain resolution has passed another body, and brings that as an argument to govern and control us in our independent action.   When before did any member of this body tell us we were to be controlled by such majorities?   The gentleman informs us the " President will hide behind no bush." What does he mean?   Is his remark of that innocent kind of rhetoric which means nothing?   He calls upon us for *unanimity*.   Was the like ever heard?   A gentleman in a small minority calling upon us continually for unanimity!   Could the gentleman's comprehensive ingenuity point out no other mode of arriving at unanimity?   Suppose the gentleman should pack up, with all his dignities of chairman of the committee, and go over to the majority?   That would be some approach to unanimity; but no, we must come to him as the great standard-bearer, beneath whose banner alone all national unanimity is to be found.   Really, sir, I had supposed it to be possible that a man might have as much patriotism and as much bravery as even the senator himself, and not rally under that standard.   The gentleman seems to think he has an unanswerable claim to invoke our unanimity because, as he tells us, for many long years he himself on a great public measure stood *solitary and alone*.   He was then, I imagine, not quite so ardent in favor of unanimity.   But mark it, sir, such was the effect, such the influence of that magnanimous example, that now the Senate and all mankind have come to rally round the gentleman from Ohio.   True, he says it took five years to accomplish this.   Now, sir, will not the gentleman have magnanimity enough to allow us five years to resign our principles and convictions, and adopt his,—or does he demand instant submission, and is this his new doctrine of unanimity? The gentleman now tells us that he will vote against all resolutions; as we have not adopted his amendment, he goes against the whole. Well, sir, be it so; the gentleman's course may be a cause of great regret, he may consult his personal dignity by standing alone another five years and waiting in solitary grandeur till the Senate and House shall congregate around him— *Achilles in his tent!* Yes, sir, Achilles in his tent! I recommend the lesson to which I once before referred, " *Know* thyself." It is the wisest lesson any man can learn. Mr. President, I have no pleasure in this sort of animadversion, but I cannot and will not sit here and allow such language and see such airs of superiority and arrogance without making a reply.

(B. W. Leigh to J. J. Crittenden.)

RICHMOND, April 13, 1846.

MY DEAR SIR,—I am obliged to you for your letter of the 10th. I shall take care that its contents shall be made known to Mr. R. C. Wickham, whom I am sure they will highly gratify. I have seen the account in the newspapers of Mr. Webster's invective against Mr. Ingersoll, and of the course which Mr. Ingersoll has thought proper to take in consequence of it, or rather to revenge it, and the conduct of both has given me great pain, and that of the latter unspeakable surprise. I lament Mr. W.'s remarks, because they appear to me unsuitable to the dignity of Mr. W. and to that of the Senate, and altogether unnecessary to his own vindication, calculated to lower him and the Senate too in the opinion of the world, especially of the European world, where they will no doubt be reported. Not fit to be employed by such a man as Mr. W. against so weak an assault as Mr. I.'s really was. Why could not Mr. W., considering the charge against himself as repeated by Mr. Dickinson, on the authority of Mr. Ingersoll, have contented himself with saying, that on whose authority soever the charge was made, the facts on which it were grounded were a mere fabrication? I do not think the coarse abuse he heaps on the fabrication tends in the slightest degree to strengthen his vindication, and surely the floor of the Senate is not the proper place for the indulgence of such a temper as dictated Mr. W.'s remarks. I can only account for them upon the supposition that Mr. W. was informed of imputations made upon him by Mr. I. in conversation, similar to those he has since made in the House of Representatives. But what is to be thought of Mr. I.'s retaliation? To gratify his revenge, he goes to the

Secretary's office, inspects the papers relative to the application of the secret service fund, finds, *as he thinks*, matter to impeach the integrity of a former Secretary of State, and calls for the exhibition of the evidence. Mr. W.'s friends could not object without giving color to this charge; yet I am utterly amazed that his enemies in the House should consent to this call, that they should require an account of the expenditure of money which they appropriated for the very purpose of being expended without any account of the purposes to which it was applied. There is no longer a secret service fund! The call which has been made amounts in effect to *this*, and nothing more or less. Can the House think that it has a right to object to an improvident or even a wasteful use of the secret service fund, assuming that there has been such an expenditure, and that the present Secretary or the President of the party in power may use their offices to attack a former administration, or that there ought to be no such thing as a secret service fund? I dare say I think as ill of the late President Tyler as any reasonable man ought to think, but I should as soon suspect him of robbing a church of the plate belonging to its altars, as of embezzling or of being party to a corrupt use of the secret service fund. I do not suspect that there is the least possibility of truth in Mr. Ingersoll's charges; and that the House should lend its aid to the gratification of his revenge, so far as it has done in making this call, seems to me to justify the apprehension that it will go the length of giving its sanction to these monstrous charges. I fear Mr. W. is in great danger; he must depend upon the judgment of a furious and reckless party for acquittal from an accusation which assails his integrity and his honor as a man and a statesman. I infer from Mr. Ingersoll's speech that he has had the inspection of the papers in the Secretary's office relating to the expenditure of the secret service fund. Has Mr. Buchanan opened them to his inspection? If he has, what is to be thought of Mr. B.? Has he done so with the privity and by consent of the President? If so, what is to be thought of Mr. Polk? I cannot conceive of a greater crime! I wish you would tell me *how* the points are. I shall, for the country's sake, be rejoiced to see that he has got his information without the aid or connivance of the executive officers. I am grieved to see the resolution offered by Mr. Ingersoll to the Senate. His object is to get the means of *defending* the innocent. The end does not justify the means.

Your friend,
B. W. Leigh.

CHAPTER XIX.

1846.

ON the 12th of May, 1846, a message was received from the President on the subject of the Mexican war. Mr. Crittenden asked on what order General Taylor had acted in taking up his position on the left bank of the Rio Grande, and the clerk read an order, addressed to General Taylor, from the War Department, dated January 30, 1846. Mr. Crittenden said he was glad to see what he had before apprehended, that General Taylor acted under the authority of the government; he was an officer of great discretion and had full authority for what he had done; he regretted the events communicated by the President's message; he thought it was our duty to extend sympathy, comfort, and friendship to South America and Mexico in their struggles for liberty. In place of that, we had entered into war with one of those republics, our nearest neighbor; he deprecated it the more as the republic was feeble and impotent, her strength consumed by anarchy and revolution. The war being entered upon, however, defense was now a duty; that being done, it was our duty to find out *who* had brought about this most extraordinary state of things, who is responsible for the hostilities commenced, for the American bloodshed. The blood of the brave is not to be wantonly shed. Mr. Crittenden thought it our duty to settle our differences as soon as possible; we were so much mightier than they, that our condescension would be noble. This subject was worthy of a *special mission*. It would, indeed, be a great embassy. Take Henry Clay, Martin Van

Buren, the senators from South Carolina and Missouri,—one, two, three, or all of them,—and he believed they would make a just and honorable peace. By taking this position on the left bank of the Rio Grande, we had done all that could be done to wound the national pride of Mexico; we should try healing measures to remedy this state of things.

Mr. Crittenden did not think the emergency so great as some senators supposed; he had unbounded confidence in the officer commanding on the Rio Grande; believed that in forty-eight hours after the date of the last advices, it would be found that General Taylor had whipped the Mexicans, driven them across the river, and was in possession of the town of Matamoras. Mr. Crittenden said he would be glad to send a minister plenipotentiary along with the general, and hold out the offer of peace with every blow. On the fifth of June, it was stated that General Taylor had been enabled to meet and conquer the enemy, by being reinforced by troops called out by General Gaines. Mr. Crittenden rose, and said:

I deny this! Honor to whom honor is due. The brave little army under General Taylor deserves and shall have all the honor. Our glorious little army has won the glory and should enjoy it. It has been said that General Taylor was once in imminent danger of being attacked and *destroyed* by those terrible enemies, the Mexicans. I never believed he was in the least danger; I know the man; I was assured that, whenever General Taylor thought it necessary, he would drive the enemy across the Rio Grande, whip them, and take Matamoras. With regard to the insinuation made by Mr. Sevier, that General Scott had shunned the field of danger by idling his time away from the post to which his country called him, Mr. Crittenden denied that there was the slightest foundation for such charges. No! a braver soldier never met an enemy than General Scott; he was no idler, never shunned danger. How could he have reached the scene of war? He was not ordered there; he was compelled to wait for orders. Should he have rushed to the battle-field without law or orders? No, sir; he has given every evidence that he was willing to serve his country in any place which the government might assign him. I make no comparison between these brave soldiers; they are patriotic, brave, and tried. As for honors, for public thanks, what has not General Scott received for his long-tried services? Justice and patriotism, under the laws of the country, ever characterized his conduct. During these investigations, let us not forget that we live under a government of law and a Constitution. It has been said that the laws and Constitution are sometimes silent, or asleep. No! no! The Constitution never sleeps; it is dead when it sleeps; it is awake, day and night, and so may it be forever.

The following letters will explain the state of affairs at that time between the administration, General Scott, and General Taylor:

(J. J. Crittenden to R. P. Letcher.)

WASHINGTON, May 31, 1846.

DEAR LETCHER,—I received to-day your letter and Coombs's of the 26th inst. I have just written to him, and am determined to oblige you with a very short epistle. Coombs's *destiny* is evidently to be a general, though circumstances seem to struggle hard against it. His destiny must bear him through, and we shall yet hail him as a " military chieftain." I hope you did not fail to give him the "drink and the comfort" you promised. Indeed, it is a right hard case to exclude from this volunteer service all who aspire to any command above that of a regiment. Such persons are generally the most influential in raising forces, and their exclusion must tend to diminish the activity and zeal of the higher grades of our militia officers. I do not like it. It in effect takes from the States, or renders nugatory, their militia powers, and it is natural enough that the instincts of an old Kentuckian should be roused to some indignation; but still I don't approve of swearing, and especially swearing at Mr. Polk. I have not seen Scott since he read your letter. If he goes to the *wars*, I shall urge him to go by Frankfort; but he has lately been in a " sea of troubles" here with the administration, and, though it has calmed down, I do not think the waves have altogether subsided. Scott got into some nice questions with them,—wrote a *hot letter*, and was answered in kind, and told he was not to go to the Rio Grande. They have been since *mending up matters ;* but I suppose he will not be permitted to go, though it is not yet, I understand, absolutely settled and certain. Singleton's will case was to have been tried again this spring. Wolley promised to inform me of the result. Can you not give me the information?

Yours, etc.,
J. J. CRITTENDEN.

(General Scott to J. J. Crittenden.)

Thursday, June 4, 1846.

MY DEAR CRITTENDEN,—When the supplemental bill to the volunteer act of May 13, 1846, shall be disposed of, it is probable that Congress will take up one of the joint resolutions, that of the Senate, No. 26, or the one passed by the House, No. 34, presenting thanks to General Taylor. The second section of the Senate's resolution proposes a sword to be presented to the gallant and distinguished Taylor; that of the House is silent as to this or any other similar honor. Permit me to suggest that in all cases of thanks heretofore a gold medal (the highest honor) has been given to the commander of the army. Swords of honor are usually given to inferior officers under his command. In respect to the glorious victories of the 8th and 9th ultimo and the admirable defense of Fort Brown, I humbly suggest that a sword be given to the nearest male relative of each officer who fell on those occasions, or who may die of any wound there received. General Taylor has already been most justly rewarded, in part, with the brevet of major-general. It is probable that on the receipt of his detailed report of those victories, promised in his dispatches of May 9th, the President will be pleased to nominate other distinguished officers in the same victories for additional rank by brevet. Pardon this intrusion hastily made.

With great respect and esteem, yours truly,

WINFIELD SCOTT.

Hon. J. J. CRITTENDEN.

(General Scott to Hon. R. P. Letcher.)

WASHINGTON, June 5, 1846.

MY DEAR FRIEND,—It is always impossible to write a short letter to a friend, hence it has been impossible to write to you at all. Since about the 17th of May, including candle-light, I have averaged at my office table more than eleven hours a day amidst every sort of *vexation*, nay *persecution*, that you can imagine. On receiving the news of the passage of the Rio Grande by the Mexicans (the capture of Thornton's squadron), and when it was supposed Taylor's *two positions* were in great peril, the executive, as you may suppose, was in great alarm. Then it was (May the 14th) that I was told I should be sent with some twenty odd thousand twelve months' volunteers and a few additional regulars to reinforce Taylor and to *conquer a peace* in the heart of Mexico. The volunteers had just been authorized. I was needed here to make a thousand arrangements with the Secretary of War and the chiefs of the general staff, which could be made nowhere else and by nobody but the commander in constant contact with those persons, to distribute, to apportion, to settle rendezvous and routes, to regulate supplies of arms, ammunition, accoutrements, subsistence, medicines, means of transportation, camp equipage, and to raise the troops, have them properly organized, put in motion at the right time, and put upon the right points, etc. These objects necessarily occupied me here till about the 30th of May, being much of the time engaged in doing *besides* all the critical work of the Secretary *with my own pen.* It was my intention then, about the 30th of May, to have left this place, in order to see that all was in a train of rapid execution. I should have passed down the Ohio and the Mississippi, to see with my own eyes, or assure myself by correspondence, that all was going on rapidly and well, keeping a little ahead of the troops to change routes, destinations, etc., and finally arriving on the Rio Grande with such a cloud of reinforcements as would have insured the conquest of peace, perhaps this side of the city of Mexico, and have saved the honor and pride of (as I called him, even before his victories) the gallant and judicious Taylor. *This*, as I told all here (officially) from the first, could only be done by a cloud of reinforcements; I added, three days before I heard of any success, nay, when all nearly but myself believed his army in the utmost peril, that I should esteem myself the unhappy instrument of wounding the *just pride* of the gallant Taylor, who had *done well* and was understood to be *doing well*, if ordered to supersede him, *except as above*. In the mean time whilst so employed, day and night, about the 16th of May, as soon as it was known that I was to be sent to Mexico, Democratic members of Congress began to wait upon the President to remonstrate against me, on the ground—as is well known—that if I were sent I would certainly succeed, and that with success I would as certainly prostrate the Democratic party in 1848, and perhaps forever! The President is also known to *have* been embarrassed by these remonstrances, and to have faltered and apologized for having thought of me in the moments of alarm. It became necessary to devise means to supersede me. *Two* were resorted to about the same time, say May 19th and 20th. First, the Secretary of War, without consulting me, *stole* into the Senate's Military Committee (the 19th), in the absence of Crittenden, *the only Whig of the five*. He took with him a popular bill I had drawn for the better organization of the twelve months' volunteers. With the four Democrats of that committee he prefixed the first section, authorizing the President to add *two* major-generals and four brigadier-generals to the regular military establishment. One of each grade was designed to supersede me and Wool (who was here) in the command of troops against Mexico. It was avowed that all of these generals were to be Democrats. Seeing the bill in print the morning of the 20th, and knowing already of the Democratic clamors against me, "*I smelt the rat*," and immedi- ·

ately told the Secretary that I saw the double trick; first, to supersede me, and at the *end* of the war, say in six or eight or twelve months, disband every general who would not place Democracy above God's country. The same evening, having constant work, as above, and with the Secretary, I was lectured by him, or rather he *commenced* a lecture (no created man shall lecture me with impunity, except as a friend) about my employments here (one-third on his own peculiar work), instead of being off, "without waiting for reinforcements, to the Rio Grande and to supersede Taylor." He muttered something about impatience in the public mind (Democratic leaders were his public). His objects were evident,—the *objects* of those whom he diffidently attempted to represent in the *lecture.* To damn me with the army, and the *just men* out of it, for superseding Taylor *without reinforcements.* To damn me, when, on the Rio Grande, for inactivity, while waiting for two-thirds of the new army, probably eight hundred miles in my rear. To damn me, more certainly even with twenty odd thousand *new* troops, on account of unavoidable inactivity *during the rainy season,* beginning in June and terminating in September, months in which we all then believed, and still believe, it is impossible to carry on military operations to any advantage *much* beyond the Rio Grande; and, failing to drive me upon utter ruin, as above, he hoped to establish a quarrel with me, and to *damn me* for *not* going against the clamors of Democrats. Governor Marcy had not the spirit (he is not a bad man, but is deficient in *candor* and *nerve*) to say, General Scott is here executing indispensable preliminary arrangements, including much of my own peculiar work, which I could not do without his help; he as yet, though designated for Mexico, has received no orders to go. At the proper time I shall give him orders in the name of the President, when he will be off *fast enough.* Remember this was the state of things on the evening of the 20th of May, and that we did not hear of any success of Taylor till the evening of the 23d. His dispatches were received forty-eight hours later. Feeling that I was in the toils, and if not a *Samson,* that I was a man, and a *stronger man* than any of my *entrappers,* I flung, the next day, the 21st, a letter into the teeth of the poor Secretary (the mere tool in the hands of party), my employments and what had been my purposes, but in commiseration I suppressed the work I had done and had *yet to do* for him. I took care, however, that he should see and feel that I knew all their machinations. Suffice it to say, whilst I have continued to avow my readiness to go with the reinforcements necessary for the work to be done and to save the honor and pride of Taylor, I was told, May 25th, that I would not be sent to Mexico, but would remain in my office here. The glorious victories of Taylor, his brevet, his assignment to the command as *major-general* according to that brevet (which *I* contrived to effect), make it *now* impossible for any new major-general to *command him.* Such has been the glorious development of public feeling in his behalf that *he* may probably be the *one* new major-general to be added to the establishment. Even if not so, that enthusiasm will secure him in the continued chief command of the army against Mexico. The correspondence has been, and continues to be, grossly misrepresented by the Democrats here, and their newspapers elsewhere. Two members of the House have threatened to call for it; one of them was in the War Department a few days since, no doubt to consult with the Secretary on the subject. He was probably told that he would *catch a Tartar.* I have begged that no friend of mine would originate a call, but that all might join if the move came from the other side. The Democrats dare not call. Please keep me out of the newspapers. I write in great haste. You will see that I cannot take the friend of our friend Crittenden to Mexico. I have no power to help *anybody in any manner* here.

Always yours,
WINFIELD SCOTT.

Hon. R. P. LETCHER.

(A. Butler to J. J. Crittenden.)

BALTIMORE, June 15, 1846.

MY DEAR SIR,—I am apprehensive that General Scott has committed political suicide. The correspondence recently published was read to me during the day I spent with him. It was too late to arrest the mischief, the letters having already passed, or I would have advised striking out certain passages in his letters to the Secretary of War. His views as a military man are correct in relation to the period of commencing the campaign as well as his objections to taking the command out of the hands of General Taylor until the force on the frontier was augmented; and if this alone had been done, omitting the soup portion of the letter and the simultaneous fire against his front and rear, and the use of the phrase "*persons in high places,*" his letter would have been *unobjectionable.* As it is, public opinion sets against him very strong, and, worse than all, he is unmercifully ridiculed. I think it is Lord Chesterfield who cautions his son against a "*nickname.*" And now to the principal object of my present communication. On the subject of the next presidential election, the opinion uniformly expressed to me at Washington has been that you, *John J. Crittenden,* stand fairer as a candidate, with better prospects of success, than any other man of the Whig party. I quote to you the remark of the late Mr. Lowndes. In reply to an application to know whether he would be a candidate for President, he replied "that the Presidency of the United States was an office that should be neither sought nor declined," and I commend the sentiment to your consideration. Be silent, and leave your friends to pursue their course; *that is*, in no wise indicate a reluctance to being nominated. Your merits, talents, and services commend you strongly, and, in addition, your uniform amenity of character and general courtesy has earned you friends and secured you a support among members of the other party which I will undertake to say no other *Whig* possesses.

Your friend,
ANTHONY BUTLER.

On the 10th of July, 1846, a bill to reduce the duties on imports was under discussion. Mr. Crittenden opposed the whole measure and every part of it; was opposed to any decrease of the revenue when the utmost amount that could be obtained was required by the government. If the gentlemen on the other side were determined to pull down this great fabric by which American industry was fostered, they had no doubt the strength to do so. Samson pulled down the temple of the Philistines, and the result would be the same to them as it had been to Samson. He was opposed to all amendments; did not want to befriend the bill by making it a little better; was for bringing it *at once* to judgment with all its sins upon its head; wished it to receive that condign doom which it so richly merited. Mr. Crittenden thought such a state as the country now exhibited was never seen before. The administration had made a war that they might get back a peace after getting the country into a war which required all its resources; they reduce the duties to increase the revenue; they had been digging vaults and cellars and putting on locks and bars to keep the hard cash of the country, and now they were passing a bill to issue floods of paper money. Gentlemen were working diligently to fulfill the decrees of the Baltimore Convention. All these questions about free trade and sub-treasury and Oregon, etc., were but so many empty barrels set afloat on the stream of the late presidential election; they had answered their purpose, and ought now to be overboard.

As for the sub-treasury, he thought *that* was overboard. On the 1st of August, a bill for an "independent constitutional sub-treasury" was before the Senate. Mr. Crittenden declared it was an *old acquaintance* in the Senate. He thought if any measure had been ever rejected by the American people, it was this sub-treasury scheme. He wanted the old name retained, that the people might know it was the same thing forced upon them once before, which they quickly broke to fragments. The object of the bill in "*cabalistic phraseology*" was to divorce the government from the banks; its true object was to divorce the people from their government. This was tried once, and the people did not bear it well. If the gentlemen choose to dare their fate a second time,—well, be it so; let them take the consequences. Political life was not apt to make saints, but it has made many prophets, and the consequences of this measure might be safely predicted. We have authorized the government to issue twelve millions in treasury notes. *They* will help to augment the deposits in the treasury. There will probably be ten or twelve millions locked up in the sub-treasury. There may be more; but this is an old subject,—the bill must pass. There must be an *upper* as well as a *nether* millstone, or there will be no *grinding*. We have the *tariff*—we must have the sub-treasury. All we can do is to give the people warning. The people must decide whether the divorce of the people from the government *shall* or *shall not* be answered by a divorce of the government from the people.

(General Scott to J. J. Crittenden.)

WEST POINT, September 17, 1846.

MY DEAR SIR,—I send, to be read by you or any other discreet friend, copies of two notes. The Secretary's reply is vulgar and *cold-blooded*. Although I have not had a line from General Taylor himself, I have learned within a few days, through many channels, that he has *all along* expected and desired my presence; hence my renewed application. Being able to state his wishes, I scarcely doubted but that I would receive a favorable reply. But there is a project on foot, I suspect, at Washington, to withdraw Taylor and leave Butler in command. (See the *Union* of the 14th.) Of course General Butler is incapable of any machinations of *that sort*. The object of the party is to build him up *to run* for the *Presidency*, or second to Silas Wright.   I came here with chills and fevers, but am nearly well again.   Shall be absent from Washington, *in all*, nearly twelve days.   We shall have you back again.

I am yours faithfully,

Hon. J. J. CRITTENDEN.   WINFIELD SCOTT.

(General Winfield Scott to Secretary W. L. Marcy.)

HEADQUARTERS OF THE ARMY, WEST POINT,
September 12, 1846.

SIR,—In the letter I had the honor to address to you the 27th of May last, I requested that I might be sent to take the immediate command of the principal army against Mexico, either *to-day or at any better time* the President may be pleased to *designate*.   The horse regiments (twelve months' volunteers) destined for that army, being, I suppose, now within fifteen or twenty marches of the Rio Grande, and the season for consecutive operations at hand, I respectfully ask to remind the President of that *standing request*.   I do this without any hesitation in respect to Major-General Taylor, having reason to believe that my presence at the head of the principal army in the field (in accordance with my rank), is neither unexpected nor undesired by that gallant and distinguished commander.   A slight return of chills and fevers may detain me here with my family long enough to receive your reply.   Should the President yield to my wishes, a few hours in New York and Philadelphia would enable me to make certain arrangements, and save the necessity of a return to those cities from Washington.   I suppose it would be easy for me to reach the Rio Grande by the end of this month.

With high respect, I have the honor to be,
your obedient servant,

Hon. WM. L. MARCY,   WINFIELD SCOTT.
     Secretary of War.

(Secretary Marcy to General Winfield Scott.)

WAR DEPARTMENT, WASHINGTON,
September 14, 1846.

SIR,—I have received your letter of the 12th instant, and submitted it to the President.   He requests me to inform you that it is not within the arrangements for conducting the campaign in Mexico to supersede General Taylor in his present command by assigning you to it.

I am, with great respect, your obedient servant,

W. L. MARCY, Secretary of War.

Major-General WINFIELD SCOTT.

(General Taylor to J. J. Crittenden.)

HEADQUARTERS OF ARMY OF OCCUPATION OR INVASION, CAMARGO,
September 15, 1846.

MY DEAR SIR,—Your very kind and interesting letter of the 5th of June was duly received. The complimentary, and, I fear, too flattering manner in which you have been pleased to notice my services in this quarter has created feelings of no ordinary character, which are heartily appreciated but are difficult to describe, but for all of which I can truly say I am not ungrateful, and which are doubly gratifying to me coming as they do from one who holds, and has done so for such a length of time, so large a space in my friendship and esteem as yourself. From certain editorial remarks in the *Union*, as well as extracts of speeches made in the Houses of Congress, I must say I was not a little surprised at the course matters and things were assuming at Washington by those in power towards me, when it was supposed I was in great peril, from which, had I not succeeded in extricating myself, the administration and its friends were prepared to throw the whole responsibility on me. Mr. Sevier and the editors of the government paper, judging from what they stated (the first in the Senate, the latter in their paper), stood ready not only to deny, but had made up their minds to have sworn on the Holy Bible, had the executive required it, that I had received no order to take a position on the Rio Grande, before any court, civil or military, had I been arraigned before either to answer for doing so.

The capture of Thornton and his command was owing to his too great contempt of the enemy, in addition to his neglecting to obey my orders, both verbal and written, for which I deemed it my duty to bring him before a general court-martial, the result of which is not yet known. The affair in question, I observed from the papers, caused the greatest apprehension and most disastrous forebodings throughout the country, as well as no little dismay among the officers of the command; but I had no apprehension as to the final result, and continued, in a quiet way, to complete my arrangements, and with the blessing of Divine Providence and the discipline and courage of my command, more than succeeded in all my plans and designs.

The additional rank conferred on me by the President, in conjunction with the flattering and highly complimentary notices which have been taken, as well as communicated by several of the State legislatures, as well as by Congress, as regards my recent conduct and that of the army under my command, has been very far beyond what I expected or deserved, and however gratifying, I will not say it was less so in my case than it would have been in others under like circumstances; yet it was trifling to what I felt when I saw and read the bold, fearless, and confident statements (made by you in the Senate during the most gloomy period, as regarded my situation) expressing, in strong terms your confidence in my sustaining myself and the honor of the country, adding obligations which I can never repay, but which cannot be obliterated or forgotten. The promotion conferred on me, both brevet and general, was unexpected and unsolicited, connected as they were with the management of this war. I would have declined could I have done so with propriety. But under the circumstances in which I was placed in being assigned to so honorable, at the same time responsible, a position, I did not feel at liberty to decline it; and although prospects of success were, and are still, gloomy, yet I determined to go through one campaign, and to leave nothing in my power undone, which can be accomplished, to carry out the views and wishes of the executive in bringing about a speedy and honorable peace, at the same time with less prospect of advantage to the country, all things considered, as well as reputation to myself, than I could have wished.

The last order of importance I had then received from Washington was in February, while at Corpus Christi, dated in January, which was to move forward to take and maintain a position on the left bank of the Rio Grande, but not to cross it unless Mexico made war on us. I was, therefore, not a little surprised when about the 25th of July I was informed I had been selected by the President to conduct the war against Mexico with the brevet rank of major-general, which had been conferred on me, accompanied by a plan of campaign, the number and description of the troops to be employed, as well as many other details; and although differing in many respects in regard to it, particularly as to the number of volunteers, as being greatly too large for the means of transportation which is and can be procured in the country to make them available, or can be brought to it in any reasonable time. The first wagon or wheel-carriage, in addition to the limited means previously here for the use of the troops who accompanied me from Corpus Christi, has not reached my headquarters up to the present moment. Notwithstanding I anticipated many serious difficulties, yet I did not feel at liberty to decline the trust in question; and although I may not equal the expectations of the country as regards my successful operations against the enemy, I trust, however, my friends, at least, will give me credit for my zeal and exertions, which will be untiring, to put an end to the war. As soon as I found war was inevitable with Mexico, I made a requisition on the governors of Louisiana and Texas for a little upwards of five thousand men, to be brought into service for the longest time known to the laws in like cases; of equal numbers from each of the States,—not, as I informed the War Department and Major-General Gaines, to aid me in defending our soil, but to enable me to carry the war into the enemy's country. Instead of the two thousand seven hundred asked from Louisiana, double that number was sent me, besides a regiment of near one thousand strong from St. Louis and about the same number from Alabama, half of which was authorized by General Gaines. This force, in addition to the Texas quota, was more than could be used to advantage in this quarter. They were called out for six months. Before these or a part of them could be removed from near the mouth of the Rio Grande, the twelve months' volunteers commenced arriving at Brazos Island, and have continued doing so from time to time, until, a few weeks since, they amounted to sixteen regiments and one battalion, averaging seven hundred men each, the landing of which and their baggage, and removing it and their supplies, some fifteen or twenty miles, to the banks of the Rio Grande, the first or nearest place where wood and water fit for use could be had, has occupied much the largest portion of transportation to remove them from their place of landing to their place of encampment. While this was doing, Mier, Rionosco, and this place were occupied by small commands of regular troops as fast as I had or could get the means of doing so. While this was going on, it was determined at Washington that the troops from Louisiana brought into service under my call could not be legally held to serve beyond three months, and those from that State, Missouri, and Alabama, mustered in by authority of General Gaines, were illegally in service, and that they should be all discharged,—the first at the end of three months, the latter immediately, unless they would agree to serve for twelve months or during the war. This they declined doing, and, of course, they were sent to New Orleans and discharged. The whole had been removed from Brazos Island to the Rio Grande, and four regiments above Matamoras, expecting to concentrate them here preparatory to a move into the interior of the enemy's country. In this I was disappointed. The whole of the volunteers were brought out and landed near three hundred miles from where there was a probability of finding an enemy at the foot, or perhaps the table-lands, of the Sierra Madre, with a wilderness intervening of near half the distance, without bringing with them the means of removing, by land or water, a barrel of pork or flour, as well as being deficient in many other articles to render them comfortable and efficient. For want of the proper means to remove the men, a large portion of them are still occupying the first position taken on the Rio Grande, and will continue to do so for some time to come. I do not mention those things either by way of complaining or despairing. Be the obstacles what they may, I expect to overcome them and march into the heart of the enemy's country in the way you recommend, and will not only take but will occupy some of their principal towns and provinces until a peace is concluded between the two countries, if we can get supplies, or we will find honorable graves. I have with great difficulty and labor succeeded in getting here, near four hundred miles by water, from its entrance into the Gulf, up one of the most difficult rivers to navigate by steam known to our people, a large supply of ordnance, ammunition, forage, etc., besides between three and four hundred thousand rations, with the proper arrangements for keeping up the necessary supplies of every kind. One hundred thousand rations have been thrown forward to Lesalto, about half way between this and Monterey, where I am locating another small depot, and expect to leave here in six days for Saltillo, two hundred and fifty miles distant, by the way of Monterey, with six thousand men, two thousand five hundred regulars, the balance volunteers, which is the largest number we can get transportation for, and that for the most part pack-mules hired from the people of the country, where, if I succeed in reaching it, I contemplate, if there are supplies to be had in the country (even corn and beef), to throw up a strong fortified work, which can be defended by a small force, to bring forward to that point the largest force which can be fed there; after which I purpose to act as circumstances may seem to justify and warrant. On the contrary, if no adequate supplies are to be had at or near Saltillo, we must, as a matter of course, fall back within reach of our depot on the Rio Grande, concentrate at Brazos Island, and take Vera Cruz as soon as the season will permit, and march on the city of Mexico from that place. By referring to a map of Mexico, you will perceive Saltillo is a highly important position for concentrating a large force, which can be employed in cutting off all communication between several of the northern states and the capital, and where the necessary arrangements can be made for marching on San Luis Potosi and other important cities.

A revolution has recently taken place in Mexico. The principles on which it is based, or is to be carried out, are not fully known here. Some say the Federal party has come into power; others, that the people have put down the military; but I presume the principal actors hardly know or have any fixed object in view other than that of getting into power.

Certain it is, however, that Paredes has been put down, and is now, if he has not been murdered, in the hands of his opponents, and that Santa Anna has been recalled. How all this is to affect our present relations with that country, time must determine; but I trust the result will be favorable.

No one respects General Scott more than myself, and it would have been gratifying to me had he been assigned to duty in this quarter, which I had not only wished but expected would have been the case, in which event I would have taken his orders with much pleasure and given him every support in my power.

You must not, my dear sir, expect too much from me. You have but little idea of the difficulties I have had to contend with in consequence of so large a volunteer force having been thrown on my hands. The bad arrangements at Washington in addition to, if not a feeble quartermaster's department, an inexperienced one, and, instead of marching on Monterey, which I ought to have done more than two months since, I have been occupied, among other matters, in getting the volunteers removed to and encamped at the most eligible positions in regard to health, which I considered to be my first duty, as many of them, poor fellows, will fall victims, do what I can to prevent it in this latitude.

Let me assure you I have no political aspirations; my whole thoughts and wishes are now occupied in bringing this war to a speedy and honorable close. Let this be accomplished, and I will be perfectly satisfied, whether in a cottage or parlor. No one can appreciate your views and opinions as regards military matters more than myself, or the course I ought to pursue, which coincides fully with my own. But circumstances, over which I had no control, have prevented me from attempting what I wished and would have done under a different state of things. I have given you, in my crude way, the situation of affairs past and present in this quarter, which I hope you will be able to understand. The future must speak for itself, and I hope it will not be without interest. I hope to be in possession of Monterey and Saltillo as soon as our legs can carry us there. The troops have commenced marching for those places, and will not, I hope, be halted for any length of time on the way by the enemy. Should we reach those places, I will write you from the latter, if my life is spared and I am able to do so.

I have looked up the Hon. Mr. Pendleton's acquaintance, and find the 1st Regiment U. S. Infantry in good health and spirits; will see his company commander and know what can be done for him as soon as I have time to attend to such matters. I am interrupted every five minutes while writing, so you must make great allowances for blunders and blotting, etc., and take the will for the deed, as it is all most kindly intended.

Be pleased to remember me most kindly to your excellent

lady and every member of your family with and near you, as well as wishing you and them continued health and prosperity.

I remain your friend truly and sincerely,

Z. TAYLOR.

(General Scott to J. J. Crittenden.)

WASHINGTON, September 30, 1846.

DEAR CRITTENDEN,—I send herewith a copy of my letter to General Taylor, written four days ago. I wish I could send copies to Corwin, Morehead, Archer, and Burrow. Perhaps you may take the trouble to send the paper to them, beginning with Morehead. Probably you may soon hear that Jessup is on his way to New Orleans; he goes, *not* to take command, but to give a general superintendence to the business of the Quartermaster's Department at that city and on the frontier. The desire to *supersede* General Taylor with Patterson (which can only be done by recalling the seniors, Taylor and Butler), or with Butler, I know, through confidential private sources, *still prevails.* Taylor wishes very much to visit his family and property about the first of November. This fact I carefully withhold, and beg you to do the like, as, if known, the wish of the executive and the party would be instantly carried out. I should not know that you had reached home alive but for a short account I have seen of the grand *barbecue* near Frankfort. I am too proud to complain of neglect. Archer repassed this way improved in health. I think I am pretty clear of Tray, Blanche, and Sweetheart,—the little dogs and all, —who, since May, have been so eager to fly at my throat. And perhaps you might do well to imitate the example of that heathen who touched his *hat* to the fallen statue of Jupiter, saying, "Who knows but he may be *replaced upon his pedestal."* There's a taunt of vanity for you, and I add another,—

" True as the dial to the sun,
Although it be *not* shone upon."

I remain ever yours truly,

Hon. J. J. CRITTENDEN. WINFIELD SCOTT.

(General Scott to General Z. Taylor.)

WASHINGTON, September 26, 1846.

MY DEAR GENERAL,—Having had within a month several returns of chills and fevers, I went North, the 10th instant, to visit my family, and have returned nearly well. I find here your friendly letter of the 29th. Mine to you, of May 18th, required *no answer;* but, under the persecutions I had to sustain, —in part the result of my confidence in, and respect for, you,—I certainly felt a little hurt that you did not acknowledge, *or* cause to be acknowledged, that communication. The fact that, with the knowledge and approbation of the Secretary of War, I had written and dispatched that letter, *became*, in the controversy with the department, of great importance to me; hence my anxiety to have your acknowledgment, and hence the feeling that I had been neglected. Perhaps, under the persecutions alluded to, official and otherwise, I may have been too sensitive on the subject. Be this as it may, I never for a moment ceased to watch over your fame and interests with the liveliest solicitude, and I can assure you that even after hearing (May 23d) of your brilliant victories, that *watchfulness* was not unnecessary. By the 12th, public opinion in your favor had become powerfully developed in all quarters of the Union, and hence the instructions you received of that date, which I was desired to draw up; three or four days before it was still intended to *supersede you* and other *old generals* with a batch of six *Democratic* generals (see Colonel Benton's declaration in the Senate), which Mr. Marcy had asked for, May 19th. My first thought was to defeat the whole batch, *if I could*, leaving you *in command* by means of your new brevet, and get you assigned to duty accordingly; but, relying on the strength of public opinion, I was subsequently well pleased that the *batch* was reduced to one major-general and *two brigadiers*. The first place could not then be withheld from you, and the *second* and *third*, I hoped, from Worth and Harney. You have, however, since been in danger of being superseded, or recalled, in favor of Butler or Patterson. About the 7th, several leading Democrats waited upon the President, complained of your "*dilatoriness*," of your intention to throw the 'regulars forward, and to keep the volunteers (the better troops) in the background, that Jones and myself were sending to you more troops than you needed (except to aid you in that policy), that it was necessary to *build up* a reputation for Butler, in order to run him for the Presidency or the Vice-Presidency, etc. What reply the President made to this I did not learn; but that he himself, about the same time, had a wish to charge Patterson with the chief direction of the war in the field, I think I know with certainty, as well as the name of the individual (a Democrat) who defeated that wish for the time, on the ground that Patterson is a foreigner by birth, and the necessity of withdrawing the *two* senior major-generals. Having some knowledge of these machinations, and hearing of your liberal sentiments towards me through private letters from Colonel Taylor, Majors Thomas and Bliss to their friends, I addressed a letter to the Secretary of War, a copy of which I herewith inclose, together with his reply. You will perceive that there is nothing in the reply that precludes superseding you by placing Butler or Patterson in command. It is due to these generals that I should add, as far as

I know or believe, both are entirely innocent of any participation in these machinations. My hope and confidence remain firm that you will (as heretofore) defeat your enemies, both in *front* and in *rear*. All that I can do to give you that double victory you may rely upon. Candor requires that I should say while laboring under a sense of neglect on your part, I mentioned your silence, in a tone of *complaint*, to several common friends—all your *admirers*,—Crittenden, Morehead, Archer, and Corwin. Since I heard of your liberality towards me, about the 7th instant, I have written to these distinguished senators to do you justice.

In haste, very truly your friend,

To General Z. TAYLOR.   WINFIELD SCOTT.

CHAPTER XX.

1846-1847.

(Hon. Baillie Peyton to J. J. Crittenden.)

MONTEREY, October 2, 1846.

DEAR SIR,—This city capitulated on the 24th, after several days' hard fighting, and with the loss in killed and wounded on our side of five hundred men, among whom are some valuable officers, both regulars and volunteers. General Worth has immortalized himself in storming this city. He was detached with the second division of the regular army and Col. Hays's regiment of riflemen for the purpose of taking the city, occupying the Saltillo road and operating against the outworks and town from the west side. His success was complete; he performed a series of the most brilliant feats which will be classed with the brightest in our annals. Seven or eight battles won in the most splendid style, scaling heights, storming batteries, and forcing his way into the city, driving the enemy and his batteries before him in the streets. Worth's judicious conduct and noble and gallant bearing are the theme of universal applause. I had the honor of acting as one of his aids on the occasion, and no man could be near his person without becoming acquainted with the music of balls, with cannon, including grape, canister, and a whole orchestra of martial music. Now at some of the most emphatic of these notes *my horse* was a "*leetle skittish;*" but understand distinctly that I speak of *my horse*, and no other member of the family. General Worth has been so kind as to notice me in the handsomest manner. To this distinction I assure you I have very little claim. He requests me to tender to you his warmest regards, and to say that you must and shall be the President of the United States; that he has not fully made up his mind as to whether he will accept the office of Secretary of War, which he considers as tendered to him in advance. This depends much on your improvement in one particular—that is, in *dignity* and *distance;* he means to sustain all the pomp and circumstance of office himself, and cannot think of serving under a chief who is not up to the mark.

" Take him all in all," he is the high-combed cock of the army, head and shoulders above the crowd.

I have written out, at some length, my views of the operations under General Worth and sent them to New Orleans for publication. I was not altogether in favor of letting the Mexicans off so lightly; but when the thing was done by such men as Generals Taylor and Worth, I felt bound to sustain it.

Very truly your friend,
BAILLIE PEYTON.

Hon. J. J. CRITTENDEN.

(General Scott to J. J. Crittenden.)

WASHINGTON, October 19, 1846.

DEAR CRITTENDEN,—I am afraid you will exclaim, What, is a recess to be no holiday to me? for this is my third or fourth letter. Notwithstanding the three glorious days at Monterey, the terms of the capitulation came very near causing Taylor to be recalled; his standing with the people alone saved him. Mr. Polk, Mr. Buchanan, and some others of influence out of the cabinet argued that Ampudia and his army *were bagged;* that they could not have held out a day, if three hours longer; that a surrender as *prisoners of war* would have led to an early peace; that we have now to beat the same enemy again at the mountain pass (very difficult) between Rinconada and Los Muertos, thirty miles beyond Monterey, with such reinforcements as may arrive in the mean time from the interior; that Taylor (ignorant of our new proposition to treat having been rejected by the new Mexican government) was cheated into the abandonment of his first terms by the adroitness of Ampudia (and contrary to the instructions) to grant the armistice, etc. But, as I have said, notwithstanding the ardent desire to put Butler or Patterson in command, the *fear* of Taylor's popularity prevailed, and the *Union* was instructed to praise him. Perhaps Butler's wound may have aided this result. I know that minute inquiries *about that wound* were made of the bearer of dispatches, by two of the cabinet and Ritchie, who replied that Butler might not be able to resume the saddle in many weeks. Taylor's detailed report has not been received, and, indeed, nothing from him since 25th September; he makes *Worth* the principal *hero* of the occasion, which gives a lively joy to everybody, yet I fear he will not be breveted. I shall renew the application to that effect on the receipt of the detailed report. The armistice will be terminated by notice about the end of this month. No time will have been lost; for, under the impatience of the executive, the movement from the Rio Grande was premature. From the want of maturity in the arrangements, Taylor was forced to leave the great body of volunteers behind, and a respectable portion of the *regulars*. The Kentucky and Tennessee mounted regiments could not have reached the Rio Grande before the 10th, perhaps the 15th. For the want of this important force, Taylor and Henderson had to prevail on the Texan horse to engage for a second term, notwithstanding the Secretary's orders to discharge all volunteers for a term less than a year. They thus obtained a mounted force of some fourteen hundred men, including three hundred and fifty regular cavalry. But the Texan horse had already, on the 25th, become impatient to return home. The two regiments from Kentucky and Tennessee will be in time to replace them before the recommencement of hostilities. The cavalry will be of but little use in storming the difficult pass just beyond Monterey; but, in the plains beyond, they will be indispensable to protect our volunteer foot against the clouds of Mexican horse. Notwithstanding Santa Anna's fierce and unexpected letter, declining the *dictatorship*, I think we shall have peace before next summer. Two more victories at the pass of Rinconada and at Saltillo, with an evident capacity to continue the triumphant advance, will make him *sue* for peace, and sufficiently impress the nation to enable him to *dare* to accede to our terms,—the left bank of the Rio Grande and along the parallel of 36 from that river to the Pacific. *I* should be unwilling to claim an *inch* beyond these boundaries, but *suppose* the administration will be more extortionate in the case of continued successes. Friend Archer has written me two most abusive letters. He is angry with me (on old grounds) because I do *not* professedly and in fact *think*, *speak*, and *act* precisely as he directs. He crossed a *t* or dotted an *i* in your beautiful letter about the dissolution of the cabinet in 1841, and hence he always holds you up as a model of *successful docility*. If I would only put myself exclusively under his government, he would be the best friend in the world. As it is, he is a valuable one, for whom I have a very sincere affection. I inclose you a copy of my reply to his two letters, *half* jocose and *half* retaliatory. I deprecate his wrath, but I have also taken care to show him that he is not *invulnerable*. Show the copy to our friend Letcher, and please return it to me.

Yours sincerely,

Hon. J. J. Crittenden. Winfield Scott.

In October a resolution was offered in the Senate to increase the pay of the soldiers, especially the volunteers, engaged in the Mexican war, and also to grant a certificate of merit to every private soldier who distinguished himself. On this subject Mr. Crittenden made the following remarks:

Mr. President, I am not tenacious about the form of the resolution, but the substance is important. There were peculiar circumstances attending the service of our troops in Mexico, which, in my judgment, in the judgment of the people generally, render it proper that those troops should receive increased pay, especially the volunteers, who left their homes for the service with less experience of camp life and less ability to take care of themselves than the regular soldiers; they were entitled to receive an increased compensation. This resolution, however, was made to embrace the regular soldiers of the army as well as the volunteers. It is well understood that, owing to the character of the service, their expenses have been greatly increased. The resolution does not specify the amount by which it is proposed to increase their pay, and I think it just that this point should be left open to the judgment of the committee. I insist, however, on the propriety of some amount of increase.

The second branch of the resolution contains a provision which I am satisfied will meet with the cordial approbation of every one. Our officers who distinguish themselves receive an honorable reward for their services by brevet promotion; but the soldier may toil and dig and fight valiantly and perform the most heroic deeds without the possibility of signalizing his humble name. The resolution proposes that the committee shall provide a means by which this defect shall be remedied, by granting a certificate of merit to each private soldier who has distinguished himself, and that such certificate should not be a mere empty honor, but the holder should, in consequence of it, be entitled to some additional pay,—something to remind his companions that his country had taken notice of his services, humble as they were. I confess, however, that I have a decided preference for the form of the resolution. This is not a new subject to me. I think the prompt and unhesitating adoption of the resolution in its present form would be the most complimentary and honorable testimony which the Senate could bear to the army. I do not believe there is a nation in Europe which would not have honored with increased pay any army which had performed the same service. The British army in India had been very liberally rewarded for the services they rendered in achieving their recent victories over the Sikhs, and I believe a reward is usual in every victory won by the armies of the nations of Europe. Not only the privations to which the troops are exposed, not only the increased expenditure attending the soldier's life, but the meritorious and great services rendered justly claim an increase of compensation at the hands of the country. The resolution did not propose a permanent increase, but an increase only during the continuance of the war. I hope there is no diversity of opinion. I am unwilling to make it a subject of inquiry. Inquiry implies hesitation—doubt. I think the troops have a right to expect decision. Their conduct has been decided; so ought our sense of it to be. We should provide some consideration of honor as well as of emolument for the brave soldier who has hazarded his life equally with the officers for his country, though the eyes of the world rest upon the *officers* only. There is not an army in the world where a private soldier has not some hope of attaining a higher honor than in ours. That great soldier Napoleon made the star of the Legion of Honor to glitter on the breast of the humblest soldier as well as on that of the proudest marshal. This government can confer no such honor; it is not consistent with the institutions of our country. All that we can give is a mere certificate of honorable merit, which the brave soldier can hand down to his children with pleasing and grateful recollections. I am sorry that my friend from Florida takes such a view of the question; I had hoped a ready support for this resolution from him. I am sorry that his sterling democracy is alarmed by the creation of what he supposes to be distinctions in this country contrary to its laws. I think if the gentleman will reconsider the question, he will find no cause to fear lest this lead to a state of military despotism. The gentleman is willing to grant land to the soldiers or pay them out of the treasury, but not willing to give them any other kind or description of reward—no such token of approbation as grateful countries usually bestow upon meritorious services. How much more acceptable to the heart of a soldier is some lively token of the appreciation of his country than the mere mercenary recompense! I can find nothing in this proposition to justify the terrible apprehension of the gentleman. I regret that it is proposed to convert the question into a resolution of inquiry. No one has stopped to inquire whether our soldiers have taken Monterey or fought at Palo Alto or Resaca de la Palma. I hope the resolution will pass in its original form ; this will give it more weight and bring it home more pleasantly to those who are interested in it.

(General W. J. Worth to J. J. Crittenden.)

Saltillo, Mexico, December 28, 1846.

My dear Sir,—General Scott has written to me respecting your son. The young gentleman has not yet come within my reach. When he does, be assured I shall lay my hands upon him and look well to his interest. From present appearances, he may soon have chances to flesh his sword; then I have no doubt his blood will show itself. The enemy is very strong, numerically, in our front and within a few marches; whether to come here or observe Taylor, who is moving upon Victoria on the left, and perhaps strike his flank, "cannot yet be divined." During his absence I am under command of Major-General Butler. We have about five thousand men at and in supporting distance of this point, and quite indifferent what numbers they bring. The desert in front, *without water*, absolutely forbids a forward movement until the rainy season, which they say is not till June. They are operating on the wrong line, and from a base too remote. The inauguration of the President (*ad interim*) is highly belligerent, and his Minister of War smells of *sulphur;* but he of the finance says *he has not a dollar.* After a display of *heroics*, the President *leaves* it all to Congress—fifty-four forty or very like it. Shall we have peace?

Faithfully yours,

Hon. J. J. CRITTENDEN.   W. J. WORTH.

In the latter part of December, 1846, Colonel Alexander Barrow, senator from Louisiana, died very suddenly in Baltimore. Several of his intimate friends in the Senate were summoned to his death-bed, Mr. Crittenden among the rest. Colonel Barrow and himself had been warm personal friends for many years.

Both the colonel and his brother senators were aware of the immediate approach of death, and the final grasp of the hand and the sad words of farewell were very touching. With his last breath Colonel Barrow commended his two sons to his friends.

The funeral services took place in Washington; several addresses were made and warm eulogies pronounced. Mr. Crittenden had been requested to speak, and intended doing so. He rose and made several ineffectual attempts to control his voice. After uttering three or four almost inarticulate words, with his speaking countenance convulsed with grief and both eyes and voice filled with tears, he bowed low and took his seat. That this was more eloquent than any spoken words was manifested by its effect upon the brilliant audience. Such a scene was never witnessed in the senate-chamber; every eye was filled with tears, and low sobs were heard from every part of the room. The following letter from Senator W. J. Mangum is interesting as relating to this subject:

(Willie J. Mangum to J. J. Crittenden.)

WASHINGTON, December 31, 1846.

MY DEAR CRITTENDEN,—The scene of yesterday in the Senate, and the part you bore in it, have dwelt upon my mind, my heart, and my memory, the whole time, as it were, burned in *all* with a brand at white heat. You know me well enough to know that I never flatter my friends,—I have not flattered you. I will therefore say that the more I know of you, the more I respect and love you.

I would not exchange such a heart as yours, were it *mine* or my friend's, for one that the world would ordinarily call *good*, and for all your high and brilliant eloquence and undoubted abilities.

Could our excellent and lamented friend Barrow have witnessed the scene, his high and noble soul would for such a tribute have been almost willing to meet his fate, premature, as we short-sighted mortals regard it, for himself, for his family, and for his country.

Your friend,

To the Hon. J. J. CRITTENDEN.   WILLIE J. MANGUM.

(G. B. Kinkead to J. J. Crittenden.)

FRANKFORT, KY., January 2, 1847.

Hon. JOHN J. CRITTENDEN.

SIR,—I regret that I was disappointed in conversing with you on the subject of this letter before you left Kentucky, for it has been one of reflection with me and conversations with prudent friends for some weeks. I am, therefore, not acting rashly or without consultation with common friends; and from the nature of the subject, the motives which influence me, and the length of time since I first fell under your kindly notice, I trust and believe you will not consider me guilty of unauthorized freedom in addressing you.

I think it manifest that the present administration, from a variety of causes useless to enumerate to you, has made itself so unpopular as to break down all reasonable expectations that the party that placed it in power can elect its successor or prevent the candidate of the Whig party, whoever he may be,—with one exception,—from an easy triumph. That exception, in my opinion, and in the opinion of others of the Whig party worthy of much consideration, is no other person than Mr. Clay. And in thus frankly speaking I need hardly stop to vindicate to you, who have so long known me, from any suspicion of being discontented with the Whig party, its leading measures or men (a charge too often brought to terrify those who expresss themselves with freedom about that distinguished gentleman), or from having a disposition to erect my judgment and that of a few friends against the will of that party whenever it is uttered; nor will you suspect me of any improper feeling against Mr. Clay himself, from whom I never sought or was denied, or what in some natures is more offensive still, received a favor of any sort in my life,—whom from my earliest youth up I have supported and admired as becomes one man to admire another,—in whose hopes of success I have exulted, and in whose defeats I have felt deep and almost personal mortification; nor, to close my negations, do I look for or desire office from any President which I would not receive from Mr. Clay,—that is, I do not expect it of any.

I have thus been particular in denying all improper motives or feelings in connection with this subject because I know the habit has been in Kentucky to suspect the fidelity of any man to his party, or the singleness and sincerity of his motives, who believed and expressed the belief that that party could exist, or have any hopes of success, without Mr. Clay as its head. I confess for myself that for some time past, since his last defeat, the converse of this proposition has seemed to me to be true; and that the Whig party cannot exist, or with any hopes of success, so long as Mr. Clay continues his political aspirations. And instead of this opinion being an evidence of want of patriotism and sincere devotion to that party to which I have always belonged, I claim it as the highest I can present. I love that party too well willingly to see it dwindle into a faction, as it must become from a great party, by again supporting a man whom the people have so often rejected. I love the principles of that party better than I do any man; and I am sure I speak the sentiments of a large majority of the Whigs of the State when I say, I would rather take a certain triumph with another than to risk being, or rather to be certain of being, defeated with Mr. Clay.

And am I not right? Is the Whig party reduced so low, and its present leaders so unskilled, or its measures so complicated, that without Mr. Clay we can do nothing, and if he were dead we would be hopeless? Surely not so think the people, who, in the last few years, whenever Mr. Clay's name has been withdrawn, have manifested every disposition to sustain the Whig policy, but, with his name before them, have shown a willingness to forget their interest in his defeat. You should know better than I do, or any other in Kentucky; but, rest assured, should Mr. Clay again run for the Presidency he will be defeated, and the Whig party routed worse than ever, and scattered to the winds.

The facts and reason leading to this conclusion must strike

you and every other unbiased mind; and so strong is this conviction with many of the best men of the party, that they doubt even whether he will carry Kentucky. You know Kentucky, however, better than they or I do. I am satisfied she does not want him nominated again.

Under the circumstances, your friends in Kentucky are anxious, with your permission, to place your name before the people of the United States, and they grow a little impatient sometimes, when they think they see the road clear before you of all other obstructions but Mr. Clay, and your generous nature preventing you shoving him aside. Under your name they have confidence of success, because they feel that they can throw their souls into the conflict. I am no flatterer to you, but believe me, there is scarcely a precinct, in Kentucky at least, where men would not feel their bosoms beat for you as for a brother. And your very political enemies would feel themselves disarmed of their accustomed rage, because they would know you had no hoarded revenge to pour out against them, no vindictive and proscriptive feelings to gratify.

It is possible the body of the people, fascinated with the brilliant victories of General Taylor, would, at present, seize with more avidity on his name for the Presidency. But that is not a thing to change the action of Kentucky, or, at any rate, of your friends in it. A thousand casualties may befall General Taylor, and they desire to place you in a position which may be advantageous for all contingencies. They desire, unless you forbid it, to let the members of the legislature nominate you for the Presidency, and they know the people of Kentucky will stand by the nomination. They are unwilling to see you yield claims for the high place, which they acknowledge, to what they consider the selfish and vain ambition of another.

I have thus far expressed myself frankly to you, and I will do so once more. In searching for the motives which are stimulating your friends in Kentucky, I find them with others as with myself, not springing from expectations of office, or from any other unworthy source, but I feel great pleasure in giving my feeble approbation to the generous sentiments which, from your lips, impressed themselves on my boyhood's memory, to the enlarged and liberal views and magnanimous sense of justice which have compelled the admiration of my manhood, to the strong social nature, and warm and earnest eloquence which won alike boy and man. These I find the motives, and the expression of them the reward we seek in your elevation.

With sentiments of respect,
I am your obedient servant,
G. B. KINKEAD.

(J. J. Crittenden to G. B. Kinkead.)

WASHINGTON, January 10, 1847.

DEAR SIR,—I have received your letter of the 2d instant, and thank you for it. I may well feel some pride in the partiality and commendation of one known to me from his boyhood, and who is himself (I can say it in language of the simplest truth) esteemed and commended by all who know him.

I concur cordially with you in the patriotic sentiment, that *principles* are to be preferred to *men*, and that the triumph of a good cause ought not to be sacrificed or hazarded by the indulgence of any personal favoritism in the selection of a candidate. The selection of a candidate is a secondary consideration, and should be made with a due regard to all the circumstances that might render him more or less efficient in advancing the great cause that he represents.

And it is therefore that I think the nomination of a candidate for the Presidency ought to be forborne by the Whigs as long as possible, so that they may have the benefit of all intermediate occurrences, and all indications of the popular feeling and opinion to guide them in their choice, and may have the advantage of the last lesson that *time* can give them on the subject.

This is the general sentiment of the Whigs here. They think that it would be premature and impolitic for their party to bring forward, in any prominent or conspicuous manner, candidates for the Presidency at this time, or for some time to come; that those candidates would immediately become objects of attack by their political opponents, and enable the latter to divert the public mind from that attention to, and scrutiny of, the conduct and measures of the present administration, which is now bringing down daily condemnation upon it and the party that sustains it.

From all this you may readily infer my answer to your question, whether I am willing to consent that my Kentucky friends should place my name before the people of the United States as a candidate for the Presidency. I should very much regret it, and I do believe that such a nomination would be more prejudicial than favorable to the pretensions which you and other too partial friends are disposed to set up for me. My name, without the least agency on my part, has somehow or other gone abroad to the public in connection with the Presidency, and to an extent that has surprised me, and I find myself most unexpectedly set down in the grave list of personages out of whom it is supposed a President may possibly be made.

If there is any "conjuration" in my name, it will be found out as well without any formal nomination as with it. My opinion is, however, that no such discovery will be made. There will then be an easy end of the matter, so far as I am concerned, and my friends and I will be saved from any imputation of intrusiveness on the subject. In any event, it will be time enough to act next winter. By that time things will be developed, and we shall be able to see and act more clearly and understandingly. My opinion, my advice, my wish is that all action be postponed till then. I wish you to believe that I speak in all sincerity when I say that I not only feel no longing, no impatience, on the subject, but that I feel something more like alarm than gratification at being spoken of as a candidate for the Presidency. I do not know whether this indifference or shrinking results from my natural disposition or from the circumstances and relations towards others in which I have grown up. But if I was ever so anxious on the subject, if my feelings were ever so different from what they are, I should think it very bad *policy*, considered in that point of view only, that I or my friends should appear even to *push* Mr. Clay aside. I grieve to be obliged to concur with you that his present prospects seem to me to be discouraging and gloomy. But a change may take place. If not, he will not desire to become a candidate, and his mighty aid will be then freely and nobly given to any other that may be selected as the standard-bearer of his principles and his party. I think that such a deference and such a delay are no less due to him than required by sound policy.

In my anxiety to secure your hearty concurrence in these views, and to satisfy you that it is best to postpone any movement on the subject of the Presidency, I find that I have been very tedious, and this acknowledgment, I fear, will be considered as but a poor recompense to you.

Believe me to be very sincerely, your friend,

J. J. CRITTENDEN.

G. B. KINKEAD, Esq.

CHAPTER XXI

1846–1847.

Letter of General Taylor to Mr. Crittenden from Monterey, Mexico—Reply of Mr. Crittenden—Letter of James E. Edwards to Crittenden—Webster to Crittenden—Letter of Mr. Clay to Mr. Crittenden, inclosing J. L. White's Letter to Mr. Clay.

(General Taylor to J. J. Crittenden.)

MONTEREY, MEXICO, January 26, 1847.

MY DEAR SIR,—Your highly esteemed and very welcome and interesting letter from Frankfort of the 6th of November, favored by your son, Mr. Thos. L. Crittenden, was handed me on the night of the 25th ult. while on the march from this place to Victoria, the capital of the department of Tamaulipas, for which you have my sincere thanks, more particularly so for intrusting to my care my young relative, who I much fear, from the awkward and unpleasant position I have been placed in by those in high places, will be greatly disappointed in not having an opportunity to accomplish what he has made such great sacrifices to do, which was to have an opportunity to come in collision with the enemies of his country, as I have in a great measure been stripped of my command—laid on the shelf; or, in other words, I am ordered to act strictly on the defensive, or it is expected that I will do so; so that I need not expect again to see the enemy in force or in battle during the continuance of the present administration. But let matters and things fall out as they may, I shall take the best possible care of him as long as he is disposed to continue in the country, and hope to restore him, if not covered with scars and laurels, to his family and friends in at least excellent health, as well as being gratified at many of the scenes he will have passed through while in this country.

On the 10th of October I received, by Lieutenant Armstead, dispatches from the War Department informing me that copies of the same had been sent to Major-General Patterson, authorizing him to organize a force to move on Tampico, if I approved it, giving as a reason for commencing a correspondence with my subordinates on such subjects was to prevent delays, which might occur in consequence of the distance between General

Patterson and myself, which reason was futile and without foundation, as, in the first place, General Patterson could not move without I approved the measure ; and secondly, the distance between us could be readily overcome by express in twenty-four hours. As soon as the secretary commenced tinkering with my subordinates in my rear I was satisfied I was not to be fairly dealt by by that high functionary, and my suspicions have been fully verified. Again, on the 2d of November, I received by the hands of Major Graham, of the Topographical Corps, sent as an express, dispatches in answer to mine announcing the fall of Monterey, directing me to put an end to the armistice entered into with the Mexican commander, and to recommence hostilities with renewed vigor, when the same would have expired in five days by limitation after due notice was given to the enemy. This dispatch was followed by another brought by Mr. McLane, son of our late minister to England, directing me not to advance on San Luis Potosi, but to remain where I was and to fortify Monterey ; at the same time suggesting a descent on Vera Cruz, which they thought might be taken with four thousand men, presuming I could spare that number from the lower Rio Grande ; and, if I thought well of the measure, I could detach Major-General Patterson with the force in question on said duty. In reply, I informed the secretary that I thought not less than ten thousand should be employed on such an enterprise ; that but little should be left to hazard so far from reinforcements, supplies, etc.; but that if he would organize an efficient force in the States of six thousand men and send them to Vera Cruz, with the necessary means to carry on the most active operations against the city and castle, which ought to be done by the 10th of the present month, I would hold at or in the vicinity of Tampico four thousand men to join the six thousand, the whole to be under the command of General Patterson, or any other officer the department might designate. This communication was written about the 14th of November, to which I have, up to the present moment, received no answer, as well as to several other important ones.

Soon after sending the communication referred to, I received a private or unofficial letter from General Scott, stating he had addressed a memoir to the War Department on the subject of an attack on Vera Cruz, stating that it ought not to be made with a less force than ten thousand men, six thousand regulars, claiming the command of the expedition, which he did not expect would be given him, and objecting to its being given to Patterson on account of his being a foreigner. It appears, however, that he, General Scott, wormed himself into the same, which he effected, and which was determined on, on the 18th of November, when he proceeded to New York, from where he wrote me another private letter full of professions, in which he states he was on his way to this country, charged with important duties, which he did not feel authorized to disclose or communicate by mail, for fear his dispatches might fall into the hands of the enemy; that he had no officer at hand to send with them, etc., in which I have no doubt he was entirely mistaken; that he would leave New York for New Orleans on the 30th of November, expected to reach the latter place by the 12th of December, Brazos by the 17th, and Camargo on the 23d, when he would communicate with me fully by letter, as he did not expect to see me, and he might have very properly said he did not wish to do so; that he was not coming to supersede me, but would take from me the greater portion of my command, both regulars and volunteers, leaving me to act purely on the defensive until Congress could raise an army for me to command, which he hoped they would do by adding to the establishment some eight new regiments, and by large bounties would fill the ranks, so as to enable me to move into the enemy's country by May or June, and meet him somewhere in Mexico; all of which he knew was out of the question.

From the middle of November to the middle of December I was busily engaged in occupying Saltillo and Parras, when I left here for Victoria, for the objects I stated to you in my last communication, with about four thousand men, directing General Patterson to move from Matamoras with two regiments of foot and one of mounted volunteers, to unite with me at Victoria, leaving Major-General Butler with a respectable force in command here, General Wool at Parras, and General Worth at Saltillo; all to be under the command of the former when united, which was to be the case in the event of Santa Anna's moving on the latter place. On the night of the third day's march from here, when forty-five miles distant, I received by express from General Butler information that a dispatch from General Worth had reached him stating that Santa Anna was marching on Saltillo with a large force, asking reinforcements, in consequence of which I returned here by forced marches, passing Monterey the second day a short distance with most of the regulars with me, directing General Quitman to continue on to Victoria with upwards of two thousand volunteers and one battery of regular artillery, to form a junction with General Patterson, with orders to drive a body of the enemy's cavalry at and near Victoria, about fifteen hundred strong, across the mountains, which was done. The third day, and the next after passing this place, I received a letter from General Butler, who had proceeded to Saltillo, that the report of Santa Anna's movement was entirely without foundation, when I at once returned, and, after resting the command here one day, proceeded on again to Victoria, which we reached on the 4th inst. On the 24th, the second day after leaving here the last time, I received General Scott's private letter from New York, which I have already referred to, which was the only intimation I had received of said arrangement up to that time, when I did not consider it advisable to change any of my arrangements, but informed him by an officer sent to Camargo that I would await his orders at Victoria, which communication he received in due season. He reached Camargo on the 3d of December, and, as I was at Victoria, ordered General Butler to send down to Brazos, or the mouth of the Rio Grande, all the regular infantry and artillery serving as such, with two batteries of artillery, five hundred regular cavalry, and five hundred mounted volunteers,—the best to be selected by General Cox, premising that I had under my command seven thousand five hundred regular troops, a larger force of that description than has ever been under my orders at any one time, which fact he, General Scott knew, or ought to have known, as the prescribed monthly returns have been constantly furnished the department through the adjutant-general's office, to which he had constant access. The largest number of troops of that kind we have ever had here was about six thousand, and nothing like that number fit for duty; and at Victoria I received orders, after taking a sufficient escort to accompany me to this place, to send the balance of the command to join him at Tampico.

I must say that a more outrageous course was never pursued towards any one than has been in the present instance so far as I was concerned. I can but look on General Scott's course as marked by the greatest duplicity that he could have practiced. Mr. McLane, when here, stated to me that Mr. Polk informed him that great efforts had been made to have me relieved by General Scott, and stating among other reasons that I was anxious for General Scott to be sent here, and that I was determined or was very desirous to leave; that Mr. Polk stated in reply that I had never intimated a wish to be relieved by General Scott or to leave the country, and that he (General Scott) would not be placed in command. The same persons then proposed that Worth should be breveted and placed in command, which the President also refused to do, stating that I had fully carried out all the views and expectations of the department, and that if I wished and asked to be relieved, that General Butler would succeed me; authorizing Mr. McLane to say to me that I should not be interfered with. But it appears that General Scott not only knew the effect of a well-directed fire in the rear, but understands the proper mode of directing it with effect on others, particularly when aided by the Secretary of War and another individual in my front or neighborhood. But let it all pass; for, had General Scott claimed the command of the army as his right by seniority, and it had been granted him, and he had come out in an open and manly way and entered on the duties appertaining to the same, I certainly would have made no objection to the arrangement, but would have taken his orders, had I been placed in my proper position, and given him every aid in my power in carrying out his plans in accordance with the views and wishes of the department, or would have retired without a murmur if my services were considered of no importance : as some little relaxation would not have been unacceptable after having had my faculties, both mental and physical, completely on the stretch for more than a year and a half,—a large portion of which time has been passed in the saddle, with - out having passed one night in a house, or any other cover than a tent. What I complain of is in not being advised of the change which was to take place as soon as it was determined on at Washington, which would have been the case had the slightest regard to courtesy or decency been observed towards me; for in that case the murder of a young officer sent to me with important dispatches which fell into the hands of General Santa Anna, making him fully acquainted with the contemplated attack on Vera Cruz, as well as the limited force left for the defense of the conquered country, would have been prevented, and would have saved a portion of the troops here and myself a long and tedious march of more than four hundred miles, besides the expenditure of several thousand dollars; for had Mr. Marcy and General Scott come to the conclusion that their plans were not safe in my keeping, instructions might have been given to me to have suspended all movements of troops until the arrival of the latter; but it may be they thought the risk of their plans falling into the hands of the enemy, even if it turned out to be so, was less objectionable than it would be to have intrusted them to me. Their course would warrant such a conclusion.

As the department has withdrawn its confidence from me, whether with or without cause, the interest of the service, it appears to me, required I should at once have been superseded altogether or have been at once withdrawn from the country. Had I been disposed to be ill contrived, or even punctilious, I would not have turned over the troops or any portion of them to General Scott or any one else without an order from the Secretary of War, which order General Scott did not produce; in which course I would have been fully sustained by the regulations made for the government of the army. (See Article III. paragraph 15.) But it was sufficient for me to know the wishes of the President on the subject in question to do all in my power to carry them into effect; and have, therefore, withheld no one or thrown any obstacles in the way to prevent General Scott's complete success, even if compelled to fall back to the Rio Grande, preferring to be sacrificed rather than the expedition to or against Vera Cruz should fail, or even than it should be thought by the most censorious I had thrown any obstacles in the way of its complete success from any cause whatever.

Had General Scott, as I conceive he ought to have done, mounted his horse or got into a carriage and visited me at Victoria, or if he was not physically able to have done so, ordered or requested me to have met him at any point on the Rio Grande, where he could have at once ascertained the precise regular force under my orders, if he had neglected to inform himself on that point before leaving Washington, as well as to have discussed other matters connected with the further prosecution of this war face to face, it might, and in all probability would, have prevented some heart-burnings, as well as might have resulted beneficially, as far as some portion of the public service was concerned. But such a straightforward course did not suit, as he would necessarily have acted under great restraint, as he must have been constantly reminded of the intrigue concocted by him and Marcy, aided by the misrepresentations of a certain individual here, who has been promised a brevet of major-general, and to be specially assigned to duty with the same, for the performing his portion of the dirty work, in taking from me every battalion of infantry and every company of regulars or volunteers. But this will not prevent me, I trust, from doing my duty here and everywhere else as long as I continue in the public service. I have never asked for a command, and did not come here to serve myself, but the country; and when promoted to the high rank of major-general, which I neither asked nor expected, and charged with the management of this war, I informed the chief magistrate of the country, through the proper department, that I had great fears of not being able to meet his expectation, but would do all in my power to bring the war to a speedy and honorable termination, and would, at any time, turn over to another or lay down the command with more pleasure than I assumed it. No matter as to the course of General Scott, I truly and sincerely wish him success, notwithstanding one of the principal objects in getting up the expedition in question was to break me down, which I have been looking for ever since the surrender of the city of Monterey, particularly as so many persons had, contrary to my wishes, connected my name with the Presidency at the next election, which disconcerted and annoyed General Scott and other aspirants, who deemed it no doubt necessary to have me at once killed off. I regret to think of General Scott, and to express myself towards him to you as I have done, knowing, as I do, you are friendly to him, nor do I wish to destroy or even to shake the same; but I must think and speak of him, whenever I deem it necessary to do so, in the way I consider his conduct towards me warrants, judging from acts alone, not from words or professions.

It seems to me the expedition against Vera Cruz is a false move at this late season; nor will Santa Anna, if anything of a general, attempt the defense of the castle of San Juan; if the Mexican Congress determine not to negotiate, which I truly hope they will not do, but determine to carry on the war, Santa Anna will at once abandon the battle as soon as he is aware of the preparations made by us to take it; oppose the landing of our troops as long as practicable, falling back to the mountains, defending all the difficult passes through the same, and destroying the road, will so retard the progress of our troops that the vomito or yellow fever must drive us from the country, as it is more to be dreaded than one hundred thousand Mexican bayonets. I believe much the safest course would have been to have concentrated the whole force at Saltillo, which could have been made up to near twenty thousand effectives, and at once marched into the heart of the country and taken possession of the rich mining departments, where we would have found supplies of provisions and forage, and which must have compelled Santa Anna to have fought us on equal terms or to have thrown himself between us and the capital, if we had beat him, which we must have done, or if he had retired before us his army would have disbanded; in either case peace must have resulted, had there been a government to treat with. I should have suggested this course to General Scott had we met, if he had been invested with full powers, which should have been the case; for, although there might have been some, or indeed many, disadvantages in regard to the same, yet they would have been greatly overbalanced by health., etc., which would have enabled the command to act throughout the entire year.

Thomas wished to have gone on with that portion of the army to Tampico from Victoria, bound from thence to Vera Cruz; but I was not willing he should do so, as in that case he would have been running too great a risk among strangers as an amateur, particularly from the northers, and yellow and other fevers common to that part of the country. I considered him placed under my charge, and therefore have insisted on his remaining and living with me until he leaves the country; and should any chance for distinction offer he shall have the opportunity to embrace it.

The Kentucky volunteers were, by accident, or rather the Louisville Legion were, prevented from taking a more conspicuous part than they otherwise would have done in the battle of Monterey, particularly on the 21st, on account of their having been drawn up on the right of General Butler's division, near our battery of artillery; and when the general was ordered to advance and sustain the regulars then engaged in the town, I ordered one regiment to remain stationary and protect the artillery and for other purposes; the Kentucky troops were selected for that object purely on account of their position. Unless Santa Anna attempts to drive me from my present position, in which case I shall resist to the last, no matter as to the description or amount of my force, which I hardly expect he will do, the Kentucky troops shall have a full share of the work. McKee and his regiment I have the greatest confidence in; they are now in advance, which position they shall continue to occupy as long as they and myself continue to remain in the country.

On receiving the order at Victoria, which I considered a most outrageous one, I determined on the moment at once to leave the country, or rather to apply to do so; but on more mature reflection I have concluded to remain for the present, or until the department thought proper to relieve or supersede me in reality as well as in effect. In the mean time, if I can aid in bringing the war to a close I will take pleasure in doing so, with a perfect indifference as to who may get the credit of the same. On the subject of the Presidency, I am free to say, under no circumstances have I any aspirations for the office, nor have I the vanity to consider myself qualified for the station; and while I can say to you that while I would not refuse, perhaps, to serve and do the best I could, if the good people of the country should be so indiscreet as to confer that high station on me, at the same time could I reach the same by expressing even a wish to do so, I would never arrive at it. I had hoped, from the recent elections in several of the States, that some distinguished political Whig, yourself for instance, would be selected, and would be elevated to the office in question, and I consider the great cause in failing in bringing about so desirable an event will be, that there may, and will be, too many aspirants for the place among those calling themselves Whigs. Butler's division, with less than one thousand regulars, will compose my principal force; and I cannot precisely say what the first, or, indeed, what the latter, will number until General Scott leaves for Tampico or Vera Cruz. One of my greatest apprehensions is, that many of the volunteer officers and privates came here with the hope and expectation of gaining personal distinction by coming in contact with the enemy, and as soon as they understand they are barely to act on the defensive, with no hopes of a fight, they will disregard everything like instruction and orders, become dissatisfied, and will insist on being discharged to return to their homes; this state of things the officers of rank say they very much fear. I would much rather force extensive lines of an enemy, such as I have to look after with volunteers, than defend them with the same description of force. They must, the volunteers, have something constantly in prospect to excite them, keep them contented and efficient.

I much fear your patience will be exhausted before you get through this long and, I greatly fear, uninteresting epistle; if so, I must say to you, as I have on a former occasion, throw it aside, or in the fire, as you may think best, taking the will for the deed, as I can truly say it is kindly intended, admitting, at the same time, that I write under some excitement and constant interruption. Wishing you and yours uninterrupted health and prosperity, I remain truly and sincerely,

Your friend,

Hon. J. J. Crittenden, Z. Taylor.
United States Senator, Washington City.

P.S.—Just as I finished this, a report has reached here from Saltillo, sixty or seventy miles in front of this, where there is a considerable force stationed, that one or two companies of the Arkansas mounted men, under Major Borland, of that State, sent in advance, some fifty or sixty miles, to gain intelligence and watch the movements of the enemy, had been surprised and the whole captured; although it comes from an officer of high rank, yet I flatter myself it will prove erroneous.

Z. T.

(J. J. Crittenden to General Taylor.)

My dear General,—A few days before I left Washington, on my return home at the close of the session of Congress, I had the pleasure to receive your very welcome and interesting letter of the 26th of last month from Monterey.

The treatment you have received was certainly calculated to excite your discontent and resentment, and your friends, I may say, the whole country sympathize in your feelings.

The public seem very much disposed to put the harshest construction—the most sinister construction—on the conduct of the administration towards you, and of all concerned in it. I am not surprised that you have been discontented and excited on the occasion, but I am gratified to find that, notwithstanding your deep sense of personal wrong, you determined to remain in the service and to stand by your *country* until actually superseded, so that it may appear to all the world that your retirement was the act of the government and not your own voluntary choice. The *country* will appreciate your conduct and your services, and will reward them, whatever individuals may say or do. You and your reputation are under the best protection in the world—the protection of the people. You have deserved and acquired it by your services and your victories, and still further services and victories will strengthen and animate it. The public is not inattentive to your situation, and to the impotent condition in which you have been left. The perilous situation in which you are supposed to be placed with Santa Anna and an overwhelming force in your front, excites here the keenest apprehension and sensibility. Any disaster that should befall you will be visited with universal execration on the heads of those who have exposed you to the peril.

This place and the whole vicinity were thrown into the greatest excitement and agitation a few days ago by the fearful rumors that reached us that Santa Anna had marched upon you with overwhelming numbers, that your communications were cut off, and that you were engaged in doubtful and bloody battles. I send you with this a slip from the *Commonwealth*, a newspaper published here, announcing this intelligence. I have seldom seen such a burst of public feeling as it produced. You seemed to be the object of universal sympathy and concern. And every voice seemed to be raised against those by whom you had been left exposed to such inevitable dangers. They were ready to believe that it was impossible for you to defend yourself against such odds, and that you had been blindly, if not willfully, sacrificed.

The greatest anxiety still prevails, and will continue until further intelligence is received to clear away our fearful doubts and apprehensions. We wait for further intelligence with the utmost impatience.

I must confess that I feel the greatest uneasiness when I consider your situation and the great numerical superiority of your enemy, and the desperation that compels and forces that enemy to the conflict. But still my confidence, perhaps unreasonable, prevails over my fears, and makes me say that you will defend yourself and be again victorious. God grant that it may be so, and that our next intelligence from you may convert all our fears into rejoicings and triumphs. I must tell you, however, that the public mind is full of the forebodings of evil. If these should prove true, the blame will not be laid on you. You will be considered as a victim, and others will be held responsible. But if out of all these difficulties and perils you shall be able to come victorious, what a victory it will be, and how it will fill the heart of the nation with exultation! I will indulge that anticipation to the last.

I think, general, as you do, that the administration is very blamable in its conduct towards you. It has been wanting, as it seems to me, in that courtesy, respect, and confidential communication and consultation with you that were due to you and to the public service. But perhaps this may have been the result of inadvertence only, — a blamable omission merely,—without any intention of disrespect or offense. I hope that it may be so, and that you may be willing at least to admit that construction to prevail, unless something shall occur to render a different course necessary to your own vindication.

I should exceedingly regret any controversy between you and General Scott, and hope that it may be avoided, unless it becomes necessary for your defense and your honor. I hardly think it can become necessary for any such purpose. You need no defense, and your reputation having become part of the *country's* fame, the country will take care of it. My views in all this, I must confess, are not limited only to your military position.

Yours,
J. J. CRITTENDEN.

(James G. Edwards to J. J. Crittenden.)

BURLINGTON, IOWA, March 4, 1847.

DEAR SIR,—In accordance with instructions, I take great pleasure in forwarding to you a resolution, which was unanimously adopted by a large Whig meeting, held at the capital of Iowa, on the 22d ult. I have delayed forwarding the resolution until I could furnish you the proceedings in detail, which you will find in my paper, the *Hawk Eye*, of this date.

Resolved, That inasmuch as we have been deprived of our representation in the Senate of the United States by the unconstitutional refusal of the Locofoco party of Iowa to consent to an election, we therefore commit the interests of the people of Iowa, in the United States Senate, to the kind care and keeping of the Hon. John J. Crittenden, of Kentucky, and Hon. Thomas Corwin, of Ohio.

With heartfelt feelings of admiration for your undeviating attachment to the Whig cause, as well as for your virtue and patriotism,

I am, dear sir, your most obedient servant,
JAMES G. EDWARDS, Ed. *Hawk Eye*.

(Daniel Webster to J. J. Crittenden.)

WASHINGTON, April 6, 1847.

DEAR CRITTENDEN,—My son Edward is a captain in a regiment of Massachusetts volunteers, and has arrived at Rio Grande with two or three companies under his command. In the course of events, I hope he may arrive at General Taylor's headquarters. My own acquaintance with General Taylor is slight, and I have thought that you might be willing to inclose Edward a note of introduction, to be presented to General Taylor when he shall meet him, or to be forwarded, in case he should find it convenient. Edward's first desire will be, of course, to go on that he may see active service, and not remain passive. His command consists of fine fellows, quite well drilled and disciplined for the time. I believe they are as well inclined to follow as to lead, where something is to be done. General Taylor is certainly a most remarkable person. He has shown himself not only superior to his enemies, but far abler and wiser than his superiors at home. I admire his prudence, judgment, and modesty as much as his coolness and bravery. In my opinion we have had no such military man since Revolutionary times. Your son gave us an hour while here, for which we were greatly obliged to him. There were about as many of us putting questions to him *all at once* as there were men in buckram upon Sir John Falstaff.

Truly and cordially yours,
DANIEL WEBSTER.

The following letters from Mr. Clay to Mr. Crittenden, and the letter from J. L. White, which Mr. Clay inclosed to Mr. Crittenden, explain themselves.

These letters show the commencement of that coolness between Mr. Clay and Mr. Crittenden, and the causes that led to it, which arose about the time of the nomination of General Taylor for the Presidency, and continued until a short time before Mr. Clay's death. I regret that I could not obtain Mr. Crittenden's reply to Mr. Clay's letter of the 21st of September, 1847. I found, by a letter from Mr. White to Mr. Crittenden, that Mr. Clay had forwarded Mr. Crittenden's reply to him. I made an application to Mr. White's executors for the letter, but did not succeed in obtaining it.

No event of Mr. Crittenden's public life, relating to him personally, distressed him so much as his alienation from Mr. Clay.

(Henry Clay to J. J. Crittenden.)

ASHLAND, September 21, 1847.

MY DEAR SIR,—I think it due to our mutual friendship, and the candor and confidence which have ever existed between us, that I should afford you an opportunity of perusing the inclosed letter.   I need not say that I do not indorse any of the conjectures and reflections affecting you which it contains.   You will give to it such consideration as you may think it merits, after which, be pleased to return it to me.

Your faithful friend,

H. CLAY.

(Letter of J. L. White sent by Mr. Clay to J. J. Crittenden.)

MY DEAR SIR,—I should have made one of the New York party who visited you at Cape May had I been in the city when it left, but at that time I was absent in Indiana and Kentucky. My desire to see you was stronger than ever, because I hoped to learn something of the cause of the movement in your State by leading Whigs in behalf of General Taylor.   That Mr. Crittenden should lend himself to it was, to all your friends here, a subject of regret and disappointment; yet I had a lingering hope that his object was not to go ultimately for General Taylor, but temporarily to divert public attention from yourself to him, and thus create an opinion among our opponents that you would in no event be a candidate.   Such a hope was natural, knowing, as I did, Mr. Crittenden's former devotion to your interests. My recent visit to the West has destroyed it, and unless he has acted in the matter with your knowledge and approbation, he has separated himself from his friends, in this region, without warning and, I fear, without just excuse. *Is it possible that he had such approbation?* and has the recent movement in Kentucky been made after consultation with you, and approved by you? I do hope you will inform me on these points, if it is not asking too much of a *not very old* but as an undeviating and unchangeable a friend as you ever had or now have.

My visit to Kentucky convinced me that there was, among the controlling spirits of the Whig party, little or no interest felt for General Taylor out of Kentucky.   If our friends in it would remain quiet, the flame kindled for him, with the aid of his incessant correspondence, would soon be extinguished, and the entire mass of the Whig party, excepting only Webster, Seward, Weed, Greeley & Co., with whom we can dispense, would again rally for their first love.   Will not the Whigs of your State preserve a neutrality at present, or are they demented?   My desire is simply to ascertain if the Whigs of your State are acting with your concurrence.

I remain, as ever, your sincere friend,

J. L. WHITE.

(Henry Clay to J. J. Crittenden.)

September 26, 1847.

MY DEAR SIR,—I hasten to acknowledge the receipt of your letter, and to relieve your mind from any impression that I shared in the views taken, in regard to the next presidential election, by Mr. White. Repeatedly, whilst I was recently abroad and since I have returned home, such statements in respect.to your course have been made to me. I thought I understood you. I find I did, and to all such inquiries I make representations of your conduct substantially corresponding with your own account of it.

Your friend,
H. CLAY.

CHAPTER XXII.

1847-1848.

THE three following speeches I have thought proper to introduce here rather than in the volume of collected speeches. They do not so much indicate Mr. Crittenden's patriotism or political views as his humanity and large-hearted charity for the suffering poor, his love for and confidence in his friends, and his prompt courage in defending them and battling for a just recognition of their rights.

Mr. Crittenden.—Mr. President, it appears to me, from the character of this resolution of thanks to General Taylor, that there is a feeling existing against the general, arising, no doubt, from that sort of party spirit which has interfused itself through everything and with which all persons are more or less imbued. I think a subject of this nature should be treated irrespective of party. As the leader of the forces of the country, General Taylor had nothing to do with party; he was above all party; he sought for no party approbation—desired only the approval of his country. I believe, if it were known how little General Taylor busies himself about politics, parties, or political operations, how exclusively devoted he is to the service of his country, the knowledge of the fact would shield him from every unkind suspicion.

General Taylor is not a political partisan, much less is he *actuated* by that sort of spirit which seemed to have given complexion to this resolution. The whole country has received the intelligence of the gallant achievements of our little army, under the leading of General Taylor, with proud satisfaction, mingled with surprise at the singular success which has attended these operations. Conducted under circumstances of extreme difficulty and embarrassment, I believe they are not surpassed by anything which has ever occurred in the history of the world. Now, when the councils of the country are called upon to express the public gratitude inspired by these great achievements, why should they give room to that sort of spirit which prompts them to look for some circumstance to dim the lustre of these great achievements? Why qualify the expression of their approval in such a manner as to make it doubtful in the opinion of the world whether it was not the intention to cloud the glory of his renown and drug the very cup of thanks they are holding to his lips? It is not usual to inquire, after a great victory has been won, whether, if managed in some other way, the battle could not have been better fought. It is surely enough that victory has been gained, without regard to the order of battle, whether gained by the superior exertions of the centre, or of the left wing, or of the right. General Taylor has done *all* that was expected, has evinced the skill of an accomplished general, and the courage and valor of a perfect soldier. Why, then, strive, with a critical eye, to grasp at some little circumstance in order to convey a sentiment of disapproval? I do not impugn motives. I speak of the interpretation which will be put upon the resolution by the world. It bears evidence upon its face that they do not approve the armistice. What can they know about the armistice which would enable them justly to determine whether it is a subject of approval or otherwise? Some gentlemen whom I have heard converse upon this subject seemed to entertain the expectation that General Taylor, with his slender forces, exhausted by a three days' battle, should have rushed upon thousands of their intrenched adversaries and forced them to an unconditional surrender. Would any of those cavilers have so acted?

At the close of the battle, General Taylor had about five thousand available troops. Was it to be expected that those brave fellows, after three days' fighting, should rush, bayonet in hand, upon the enemy, nine thousand in number, strongly fortified, and make them prisoners? It is an easy matter to talk of such deeds by our firesides; but I venture to say that the opinions of Worth, Davis, Henderson, and General Taylor are of more value than the judgment of any man, or men, who did not participate in the battle. In regard to the armistice, what could have been done more than had been done if the armistice had not been agreed upon? For two months, at least, after such a battle and victory the army could have done nothing, whilst the armistice would have the effect of paralyzing the enemy during the time of its continuance. The fact of assenting to an armistice proves General Taylor to be a man of sound judgment as well as humane feeling; it gave him time to obtain supplies and restore the vigor of his own little army, and afforded to the women and children of the beleaguered city time to escape the horrors which would attend the sacking of a town by a triumphant soldiery.

Military men are the best judges of these matters ; they stand upon the point of honor; they are trained to that sentiment; they *live* and *die* for honor, and appreciate, above all other things, the honors conferred upon them by their country. What, then, would they think of this obliterated compliment,—this uncertain mark of approbation ? How would such a compliment be received by an army after winning such a battle ? What will the people think when it is perceived that senators are endeavoring to qualify the matter so as to go against or for General Taylor according as the tide of war or politics might turn ; ready to take a sort of neutral position ; to take shelter under the armistice, and to vote approval and disapproval at the same time? Such resolutions should be not only a reward for past good service, but an incentive for further achievements and further victories. Will this be so ? The next time they fight, the next time they accomplish a brilliant victory, what thanks will they expect ? If an expression of approbation is of any value it must be free and unrestrained,—free as the rain from heaven. The compliment, if qualified, is turned to dust and ashes. The senator from Alabama seems to entertain an impression that striking out this proviso would imply some censure or disapprobation of the President of the United States, who disapproved the armistice. Now, I think the gentleman unduly sensitive on that point. I do not see how such a construction can be given it. General Taylor might have had reasons unknown to us which induced him to make that capitulation ; while, on the other hand, the President may have had purposes which were unknown to General Taylor and which justify him in disapproving it. The conduct of both may be reconcilable, and both may be right.

No one can undertake to say that that battle was managed with the skill of a Washington or a Napoleon; but it was conducted with skill enough to accomplish a great purpose and achieve a great victory. For this the country rejoices, and we return thanks. I am not thoroughly acquainted with military history, and have listened with respectful attention to the senator from Alabama, who says there has never been an instance of a conquered army leaving a conquered city as the Mexican army left the city of Monterey—with arms in their hands—after dictating the terms of their capitulation. I agree with the gentleman in this; my slight reading does not furnish a similar case. Nor do I know of any case where seven thousand, eight thousand, or nine thousand troops, in good training, in the heart of a city, with cannon, and equipped and provided with all the destructive means of warfare, —a city in which every house is a fortress, — had surrendered to five thousand and agreed to march out between the files of the enemy,—taking with them nothing but their clothes and side-arms,—leaving their ammunition and all public property behind. Now, how did Santa Anna regard this? As a triumph? If all that we hear can be relied upon, Santa Anna has those officers in custody, from Ampudia down, and they are to be tried for cowardice. It would, indeed, be a singular state of things for us to be disapproving the conduct of our general in permitting the officers to go out, and Santa Anna should be trying them for cowardice for going out! Enough has been done to entitle our soldiers to our unqualified thanks; they have shown themselves to be brave and patriotic. General Taylor had no purpose but to serve his country to the best of his power; he and his little army had done great things; their exploits are to form part of the history of this country, and the Senate is forming material to enable others to detract from the value of those services,— authenticating records by which the historian may blemish our military glory. I hope this will not be done! This victory is more dear to the American heart because it is crowned with the wreath of humanity. General Taylor has shown not only courage and skill, but also humanity,—humanity to women and children. This armistice is sanctioned not only by the laws of nature, but by the laws of God. To have acted otherwise would have been to commit most sacrilegious murder, for which there would have been no defense. Thank God, this capitulation had been *distinguished* not more by courage than by humanity.

(In Senate, February 26th, 1847. Relief for the suffering poor of Ireland.)

Mr. Crittenden.—Mr. President, I rise in accordance with a notice given on a former day to introduce this bill for the suffering poor in Ireland and Scotland, but before making this motion I beg leave to make a few remarks. The whole world has heard of the calamity which has fallen on these countries, of the scarcity and famine which prevail there. I do not rise with an empty parade of words to impress the picture of a famishing people upon the minds of this honorable body. I wish only to discharge what I consider a solemn duty. As representatives of the people it is our duty to carry out their views, as they have been presented to this body. The calamity is no ordinary one. It is not the result of idleness or folly on the part of the people. It is one of those inscrutable dispensations of Providence to which we are as nations one and all liable, and in which we should be one and all interested. The depth and extent of the calamity is known to the whole world, and the whole world must feel for the sufferers. It may be asked, is it any duty of ours to attempt to relieve their sufferings, to interpose our charity? I think it is. Our liberality as a nation has been exhibited in cases by no means as appalling. The bill which I have drawn up is in the language of the bill passed in 1812 for the relief of the people of Venezuela suffering from the effects of an earthquake. That bill was approved May 8th, 1812. It was introduced by a committee, of which Mr. Macon was chairman. The character of Mr. Macon is well known. From his ceaseless vigilance he was called the watchman of the committee. The bill passed by the unanimous vote of the House of Representatives, and I notice among those voting for it the names of Randolph, Richard M. Johnson, and Mr. Calhoun. It does not appear that there was any opposition to it in the Senate, and the bill appropriated fifty thousand dollars. In that case it was but a partial calamity, arising from an earthquake. No great national famine seemed to sweep the people from the face of the earth, and yet the case presented a sufficient motive for the exercise of our national sympathy. How much more appalling and widespread is the evil now appealing to our charity! The people of Venezuela were of a different race, yet they were men, and the appeal came to us, and though connected only by the tie of a common humanity, we interfered for their relief. But who are the sufferers at this time? They are our kindred, bound to us not only by a common humanity, but by a more intimate bond of brotherhood. We are, to a great extent, the descendants of the people of Ireland, the kindred, the offspring, of Irishmen, and every day the tie is strengthened and endeared by emigrants coming to our shores to become one with us. This famine fills the world with the voice of lamentation. Are we not bound as men and Christians to listen and respond? I think we are. So far as the constitutional argument is concerned, with the voice of suffering ringing in my ears, and this precedent before me, I lay down all objections at the feet of charity. But we are under other obligations to incite us to this deed of mercy. Our happy land is crowned with plenty, surpassing in fertility and abundance anything known in the history of nations. Do not these rich blessings lay an obligation on us? "From him to whom much is given, much will be required." We must render obedience to the great law of humanity. It would be strange, indeed, if our Constitution was so fashioned as to interdict the exercise of Christian charity, when the hearts of the people prompt them to offer such assistance as is now proposed. It would look as if the Constitution was set up in opposition to the commandments of our religion, and laying down rules for the government which repealed the laws of heaven—the law of the King of kings. No sir, no!

Every consideration of high, moral, and political character calls upon us to meet this question in a liberal spirit. There are other incentives almost as strong and as high as those to which I have referred. What will be the influence of such an example? What a spectacle will it be for the people of the world to see one nation holding out her hands full of plenty and pouring joy and consolation into hearts now sick with sorrow and into desolate and famine-stricken homes! Can you imagine any moral spectacle more sublime than this? Hitherto the hands of the nations have been red with each other's blood; national hearts have been without sympathy and without charity. Thank God, it is not so now. Governments have been converted to Christianity and have learned that the great source of human happiness consists in peace and amity among nations. The day is coming when nations will be bound together in a common brotherhood, and war, if not extinguished and forgotten, will be less frequent, and will only arise from overwhelming necessity. There is nothing more noble than to give, to the extent of our ability, both food and raiment to the naked and the hungry. We should be proud of the opportunity. The people everywhere are moved to act generously. From Boston to New Orleans, the heart of the nation is alive and panting with the spirit of charity. The villages emulate the cities in the exhibition of the noblest sympathy with the sufferers. In giving this national bounty, we but follow the impulses of the national heart; we act within the pale of our duty when we undertake this great work; we can do what individual charity cannot do. I would not give the national reputation of such an act for ten times the appropriation proposed. I would not do this with ostentation, but unobtrusively; I would not herald it with the sound of trumpet and call the attention of the world to our charities, but I would have it done effectively. I have introduced a clause to authorize the President to send out a national vessel under a national flag to the British government, carrying the national contribution, a present from the government of a people rejoicing in plenty to another government, whose people are suffering from a national calamity. What a glorious spectacle to see these floating instruments of death,— their decks no longer frowning with implements of destruction, but wafting substantial evidences of a nation's good will to the afflicted! Such exhibitions would mark the onward march of benevolent civilization, brighten the intercourse between nations, and speak the longing aspirations of the people

of all climes for the advent of a holier and happier day. Yes,
sir, I would have this offering of our sympathy and fraternal
feelings for the generous sons of Erin and Scotia borne to them
under our national flag; I would have all the world honor and
love and welcome that flag, not only as it is now known, as the
flag of valor, but I would broaden its stripes and brighten its
stars by making it the welcome messenger of generosity and
humanity.

(J. J. Crittenden to A. T. Burnley.)

WASHINGTON, January 8, 1848.

DEAR BURNLEY,—I received your letter of the 12th of last
month with the pleasure it always gives me to hear from you.
Our friend Duke has been somewhat mistaken in respect to occurrences at Lexington. I have no recollection of saying to
Mr. Clay what he supposes me to have said, and what I think I
did not say. My sentiments in relation to Mr. Clay, General
Taylor, and the Presidency have not been concealed. *I prefer
Mr. Clay to all men for the Presidency;* but my conviction, my
involuntary conviction, is, that he cannot be elected. That
being my belief, I thank God that He has given us, in the person of our noble old friend General Taylor, a man who can be
elected, if Mr. Clay cannot. In these few words you may read
all my opinions and feelings,—you may read me and the whole
subject. I am apprised that the mere fact of my belief that Mr.
Clay could not be elected (though expressed only to his friends)
has drawn upon me the suspicion and jealousy of some of them.
Mr. Clay, I trust, is of too noble a nature to admit of any such
feeling, or to doubt the sincerity of my friendship because of
my regard for truth and candor. I should consider myself as
dishonored—I should consider myself a false and treacherous
friend—if I should advise or say that Mr. Clay could be elected
when I believe the contrary. Such a course might suit a *flatterer*—not a friend. My relations with Mr. Clay have been personal and peculiar. I feel myself honored by them, and they
are precious to me. I hardly know what sacrifice, consistent
with honor, I could refuse to make to them. You may well
imagine how much, under all these circumstances, I am constrained and embarrassed. I endeavor to be as prudent and
quiet as I can until the present difficulty shall have passed by,
as soon it must. I did not till lately believe that Mr. Clay
desired to be regarded as a candidate. I knew that he was not
even willing to be a candidate except under circumstances which
showed clearly that it was the *general* wish of the people, and
that his election was certain. It was manifest to me that this
state of things had not occurred, and hence I concluded he

would not wish or even consent to be brought forward; but his information and his view of the state of public opinion are different from mine. I have every confidence in him that he will do right when he is rightly informed. He is now at Baltimore, on his way to Washington, and he will have full opportunity here of seeing, hearing, and deciding for himself. Since my arrival in Washington I have not sought, indeed I have rather avoided, inquiry and conversation with members and others on this subject; but I have heard members say, that though Mr. Clay *had* many warm friends among them, they did not believe there was a single one would desire and advise him to become a candidate under present circumstances. General Taylor has some very active, zealous friends among the members, and the almost universal tendency is plainly and strongly towards him. There is evidently a general impression that he is to be the President, and that itself becomes a powerful cause of success. Mr. Clay's oldest and most eminent friends in Congress and out of 'it, in this part of the country, believe that he cannot be elected, and are, therefore, adverse to his being a candidate. But, for the present, his position in respect to it keeps them in suspense. As soon as they are relieved from that they will be prepared to take an active and energetic part for General Taylor. In the mean time they are all anxious that all excitement and collision between friends of Clay and Taylor should be carefully avoided; that they regard as a primary policy. This is as good a view as I can give you in the limit of a letter (already too long) of the state of things here. Some might suppose that I am inclined to make out a case against Mr. Clay, when I am only endeavoring, at your request, to give you a true and candid statement.

For this and other reasons I desire you to consider this letter confidential, and its contents not to be spoken of in connection with my name. I inclose you a letter for my son in Mexico. It may be a great relief to my brave boy George to know that the President has declined to accept his resignation. He is indebted for this to his gallant conduct displayed in the battles near the city of Mexico. The interest that has been felt and expressed for him by the most eminent men here may well excite his pride and furnish new motives for action. My friend Conrad, formerly one of your Louisiana senators, left here a few days since for New Orleans. He is a good Whig, and a gentleman. I expressed to him the wish that he would become well acquainted and place himself on terms of friendship with Baillie Peyton and yourself. Receive him kindly and with confidence,—he is to be relied on. He has intelligence, honor, and spirit. When you meet him receive him with open hand and heart, and, if necessary, you may say at my request. There is coming rapidly a *time of great scarcity* of money and great embarrassments in the currency and business of the country. All prominent men here most skilled in finance are of that opinion. Indications and symptoms of its approach are already operating and visible. I pray you to be *warned in season.* Collect your debts; avoid liabilities.   Your friend,

A. T. BURNLEY.   J. J. CRITTENDEN.

Some time in January, Hon. Mr. Foote, of Mississippi, during a debate in the Senate on the Mexican war, charged Mr. Clay with using political arts for the purpose of promoting his pretensions to the Presidency.   Mr. Crittenden interrupted him with the following remarks:

Give me one moment, sir. I have had the honor of knowing Mr. Clay, of calling him friend, and being called friend by him for the last twenty-five years. I think I know him, and I can venture to assure my honorable friend from Mississippi that there is no man in this country more incapable of the practice of any ignoble act than he is,—that he would not accept the Presidency at the price of any arts practiced by him.

To his renown the Presidency could add but little; he will adorn a bright page in the history of this country.   Then, sir, when the passions and prejudices of party shall be hushed, his will, indeed, be held by all Americans the " *clarum et venerabile nomen,*" a name honorable and illustrious, which, combined with the names of his great and distinguished opponents, will, with their blended light, illuminate and illustrate the annals of our country through all time.   I regret, then, sir, that, in the course of these animated remarks (and much, I know, escapes us in the heat of debate which we would willingly retract), a passage should have occurred which may, perhaps, be construed more seriously than was intended.   I can assure the gentleman that whatever information he may have received to the contrary, Mr. Clay has practiced no art,—neither the art of the mesmerizer, the magnetizer, nor the politician to promote his pretensions to the Presidency.   The highest official honors could add but little to his name.   Office, in itself, is but an ignoble object of ambition. Mr. Clay has ever had the higher object of serving his country; he is incapable of any art to circumvent, to obtain, any object; he has used no means which the honorable senator from Mississippi, Mr. Foote, would, in the exercise of his nicest judgment, condemn.   I make this appeal kindly and respectfully in vindication of a private citizen and my friend now absent, and represented here, however unworthily, by myself.

(Wm. Ballard Preston and others to J. J. Crittenden.)

WASHINGTON, February 28, 1848.

HONORABLE JOHN J. CRITTENDEN,
  SENATOR FROM KENTUCKY.

We have heard this day with regret that you have accepted a nomination from your State as the Whig candidate selected by them for the office of governor of Kentucky. We, the Whig members from Virginia, are deeply distressed that such acceptance will deprive the Senate of the United States of the services of one who has rendered his country such signal and distinguished services in that exalted station. The present is a crisis which demands the experience, wisdom, moderation, and courage which has so long rendered you conspicuous, and now, in your person, commands the confidence and judgment of an immense portion of your countrymen. We therefore request that should it not be wholly incompatible with your own views of public duty, that you would not resign your present station as senator until the great and impending issues which are before the Senate for decision are disposed of. We say to you in sincerity, and in view of the true glory of our common country, that we regard your presence in the Senate of the United States as of the very highest importance.

With sentiments of profound respect and regard, we are your most obedient, humble servants,

WM. BALLARD PRESTON, of Va.,
W. L. GOGGIN,
JNO. S. PENDLETON,
AND. S. FULTON.

It will, perhaps, be remembered that there were two *Allison letters;* they were signed by General Taylor, addressed to his brother-in-law, Captain Allison, and published throughout the country. In September, 1848, Mr. Crittenden received a letter from General Taylor, written at Baton Rouge, in which he says: "In consequence of the intentional misrepresenting of the meaning of several of my letters, or parts of my letters, which have been given to the public by my enemies to prove a want of consistency in my course in regard to the Presidency, particularly one I wrote to Mr. Pringle, of Carolina, accepting the nomination tendered by the Democrats of that city, I deem it necessary, in order to place such matters right before the public, to address a letter to Captain Allison, which you must have seen, and which, I hope, will meet your approbation." This letter was soon followed by another letter to Captain Allison The first was greatly discussed, and the last produced a great sensation. It was, in fact, the political platform upon which General Taylor was supported throughout the country, and it was written by Mr. Crittenden. I had heard from several sources that it was written by Mr. Crittenden in the Hon. Alex. H. Stephens's room at Washington. I wrote to him on the subject, and he has given me permission to use his reply as I may think best. I have concluded to publish it, as it contains a history of the affair.

(Hon. Alexander H. Stephens to Mrs. Coleman.)

LIBERTY HALL, CRAWFORDSVILLE, GA., October 13, 1870.

DEAR MRS. COLEMAN,—Your letter was received this morning. I am glad to hear that your work is so nearly finished. General Taylor's *second* Allison letter, I am quite sure, was written, in substance at least, by your father. He, Mr. Toombs, and myself were then living together, occupying one house in Washington. Major Bliss visited us from General Taylor. We were all earnest advocates of General Taylor's nomination for, and election to, the Presidency. It was, upon consultation, thought best, as General Taylor had had but little to do with politics, and was not very conversant with the public measures likely to enter the canvass, that an outline of such issues as should be presented, both for nomination and election, should be prepared and sent to him by Major Bliss for his consideration and announcement, if it met with his approbation. After a thorough understanding and agreement between your father, Mr. Toombs, and myself about all the points proper to be presented in such a paper, *he*, your father, undertook the drafting of it. He did not read it to us when it was finished, but told us the substance of it. Major Bliss set out that night, with the paper, to General Taylor. In a few days this second letter to Major Allison made its appearance in the newspapers. It embodied in substance what had been agreed upon as proper to be said by General Taylor, and what your father told us he had written. This general statement of facts connected with it you may make any use of you may think proper.

Yours most respectfully,

Mrs. ANN MARY COLEMAN,   ALEXANDER H. STEPHENS.
Baltimore, Maryland.

(J. J. Crittenden to Orlando Brown.)

SENATE-CHAMBER, March 25, 1848.

DEAR ORLANDO,—I was shown, this morning, a letter from a confidential friend of General Taylor, from which I infer that he was about to write to you a letter intended for publication, expressing, probably, some political opinions, and especially in respect to the policy which we ought to observe towards Mexico, and the indemnity we ought to insist upon. That letter states that he *would* have indemnity, and TERRITORY for indemnity. Though this is the manner in which the letter-writer expressed himself, I am persuaded that General Taylor *would not so* express himself. This is a point in our present politics of exceeding delicacy, and in regard to which there is a great deal of sensitiveness, particularly in the New England States. You will see Mr. Webster's speech published in the *Intelligencer* of this morning, in which he takes such very decided ground against the *acquisition* of *territory*, or against such acquisition as might form *new States*. I may say that I almost *know* he would not be opposed to the establishment of the Rio Grande, up to New Mexico, as the *boundary of Texas*, and thence (excluding New Mexico) to such a parallel of latitude as would, when pursued to the Pacific, include the harbor of San Francisco. But if General Taylor was to say in general terms that " he *would have indemnity* and *territory* for indemnity," it might fairly be construed that he meant to include in that indemnity all the expenses of the war, and to *coerce* that indemnity in territory, *regardless* of its *extent*. Such a declaration, on his part, would put him, as you will perceive, into *direct conflict* with the opinions of Mr. Webster and the feelings and prejudices of the New England States,—a position much to be avoided at this crisis. I know that such is not General Taylor's true meaning, and I am persuaded that he has not and will not so express himself in his contemplated letter to you. If, however, he has done so, it was probably the effect of carelessness and inadvertence, and I would advise, by all means, that you write to him on the subject, and return his letter for *revision* before publication. Another reason for this course may be, that when it was written he did not know of our treaty with Mexico. Whatever General Taylor may say in reference to public questions, ought to be, in general terms, relating to *principles* rather than to *measures* and *avoiding details*. His opinions (as I believe them to exist) in regard to a peace with Mexico, might be sufficiently expressed in some such manner as this: That peace between the two republics was greatly to be desired, that the honor of our country had been fully vindicated by our victories, that the fallen condition of Mexico ought to prompt us to magnanimous moderation and forbearance towards her, and make us careful to exact nothing beyond the just measure of her rightful claims, and a satisfactory establishment of a boundary for Texas; that for the satisfaction of those claims we ought to accept, *if* more convenient and suitable to Mexico, such limited cessions of territory as *might give us* a boundary, including the harbor of San Francisco, without incumbering us with a useless extent of territory, that might embroil us with disturbing questions at home. This would cover the whole case without entering into detail. Out of it, with your *good pen*, you could frame something that would do, and for that *contingent* purpose have I made these suggestions. It is important to General Taylor that all should go smoothly on this subject, so that we may avoid all disadvantage, if it should so turn out that *he*, and not Mr. Clay, should be finally selected as our candidate. Things have been so badly managed among us that, with all *our prudence*, we may find it no easy matter to elect either of them.

Your friend,
J. J. CRITTENDEN.

CHAPTER XXIII.

1848.

IN SENATE, April 6, 1848.

MR. CRITTENDEN.—Mr. President, I wish to occupy the attention of the Senate a few moments, rather because I differ from some of my friends than with the expectation of enlightening the Senate. Some gentlemen have supposed that the Senate of the United States have no power to express, and ought not to express, the congratulations of the American people to the French government in the form of this resolution. I do not consider that there is any question of power involved. We express an opinion, a sentiment, that is all. Surely this is a right belonging to every individual. Is the Senate of the United States the only body in Christendom which is to be paralyzed on the occurrence of such scenes,—to stand as a sort of *caput mortuum* in the midst of the civilized world? No, sir; we have a right to do this. It is said that we ought to delay our congratulations, that enough has not yet been accomplished to enable us to pronounce judgment. I concur in that we are not in a condition to pronounce a final judgment; but the question now is, Has not enough occurred to make us rejoice, and offer congratulations to France and to the world? If we are to wait until all the consequences of the revolution are known to congratulate them, when will that time come? The youngest man here will not live to see that day. The conseqences for good or ill will extend beyond our time. This is one of the great events of the world, full of mighty consequences to mankind. There is no exaggeration in this thought. It is the greatest movement in civilized and social life which has occurred within our knowledge, one of the signs, and marks, and wonders of the times. It excites the hopes, and fears, and tremulous anxiety of mankind. I have my fears, but my hopes preponderate. This is a mighty work to be accomplished, requiring a degree of virtue, intelligence, and experience which is rare, in

the midst of alarmed Europe. The French have made this great
experiment in the midst of hostile crowns and principalities. I
hope that the God of truth and liberty will be with them in this
mighty trial, and that they are destined to be successful.
Whether this revolution is to form the basis, to be the proximate cause, of a great amelioration in the condition of mankind,
I know not; I cannot anticipate.

But however that may be, of one thing I am satisfied: its
ultimate consequences cannot but be for the good of humanity.
Who can say of the French Revolution of 1792, with all its
carnage, and tumult, and the terror which it spread throughout
the world, that from all that horror and blood good has not
accrued to mankind?

The earth and the sea have covered up the victims of that
revolution. They are no more; but the great principles of
liberty involved in that contest have lived to expand and spread
abroad among mankind. A new world of intellect has been
opened; a new sense of freedom has been spread throughout
the civilized universe. The ideas and principles to which it
gave size, though for a time seemingly trampled on by the iron
heel of tyranny, *yet live.* So will it be with this revolution.
Gentlemen imagine this to be nothing more than a temporary
ebullition of popular feeling, and prophesy that it will go down
in *crime* and disaster. This may be; but it has already shown
to the world the power of public opinion. There is an established government, with its army of a hundred thousand men
at the command of the reigning sovereign,—a sovereign who
has been firmly seated on the throne of his ancestors for seventeen years, who traces back his royal descent for centuries,—
suddenly finding its ramparts broken down, and by what?
Not the power of a mob under temporary excitement. No, sir,
but by a great and majestic feeling. pervading the whole mass of
the people. That feeling took from the sword of his army its
edge. The *ultima ratio* of kings was here at an end. A moral
change was proclaimed by a power which is above all thrones,
greater, more exalted, more irresistible, than all their impreg-
nable ramparts and fortifications. The change is strange and
grand! The mighty movement of the people, produced by a
deep sense of what was due to themselves, is to be applauded.
Sir, I congratulate them! France may have to go through
many disastrous convulsions before she attains her great aim—
the establishment of a system of free government. I wish I
could believe that this revolution is to be the proximate cause.
I am not confident that it is so; but I have hope. It cannot be
otherwise than productive of good. For this we congratulate
France, and bid her God speed!

About this time a bill was introduced in the Senate proposing to authorize the judges of the Supreme Court to hold a second term in the course of the year. Mr. Crittenden thought the accumulation of business in the Supreme Court rendered this necessary, and made the following remarks in favor of it:

Mr. Speaker, I shall only occupy the Senate a few moments. I regret that gentlemen have chosen this occasion, so important in itself, for the purpose of debating questions and principles which, according to my judgment, are not included in the subject under consideration. To what purpose is it to debate the question as to the political character of the Supreme Court of the United States—to debate the question whether it was best to appoint the judges in the manner prescribed in our Constitution, or to change that Constitution and make them elective? Where is the necessity of inquiring into the nature and extent of the jurisdiction of the court on this occasion? Where the propriety of inquiring into the individual or collective competency of the judges? This bill does not touch the subject in regard to any principle or question involved in it as a system. It takes the court as it stands, as it is legally and constitutionally established, without change or alteration of its jurisdiction, and simply proposes—what? That because of an inconvenient accumulation of business in the Supreme Court of the United States, rendering it impossible for that court to dispose of the business in less than two or three years, a remedy should be applied to obviate the evil. And what is the remedy? The bill simply proposes to authorize the judges of the Supreme Court to hold a second term in the course of the year besides that to which they are now limited. Now, what principle is involved in this? If I understand the arguments which have any application to this subject, gentlemen would have no objection to this measure if they did not apprehend that it was intended as a wedge— the commencement, as they express it—of another system, having for its object the suspension of the judges of the Supreme Court from all duty in the Circuit Courts, confining them solely to their duties in the Supreme Court. They imagine this, and refuse to apply the proposed remedy for an acknowledged ill.

They speak of the danger of the remedy! Let us examine it. The bill provides for a single year. According to existing laws the next term of the Supreme Court will commence on the first Monday in December next. We are now in the first week of April; four months of the year have expired. The three corresponding months of the next year will be occupied by the court in the transactions of its business, so that the whole peril of the proposed measure lies in the compass of eight months. But, forsooth, if we *indulge* the Supreme Court (for gentlemen seem to regard it as an indulgence) by granting them permission to come here and dispatch the business of the court in that period, great danger is to arise, a new system is to grow up, a new principle is to be evolved, which is to relieve the judges of the Supreme Court from all other duties except those belonging to the Supreme Court, and other serious political consequences will result. I apprehend no such evil. There is not a senator here, so far as I can judge from the opinions that I have heard expressed, who is willing to change the present system so far as to separate the judges from the Circuit Court and limit them to the Supreme Court. The Senate, then, has the issue and consequences in its hands, and, I ask, what solid ground is there for apprehension? Is there any danger that the senator from Arkansas will be, even in these revolutionary times, so perfectly revolutionized in his opinions as to come back prepared to reverse all his opinions which he has expressed to-day. Why, sir, are we afraid of ourselves? It is supposed that this is a bill for the relief of the Supreme Court. Relieve them from what? It relieves them by requiring them to hold a term of the Supreme Court and discharge all the arduous duties of their office. Are these labors less expensive to them than traveling on their circuits would be? I apprehend not. But relief, it is obvious, is not the purpose of this bill. The honorable senator is apprehensive that some cases may not be tried according to law; that some admiralty cases may be delayed to the tremendous and incalculable detriment of all parties; and we hear also of appeals to the Circuit Courts. Now, litigation may be infinitely more active in the part of the country where the honorable senator practices his profession so much more profitably than I do; but in my section of the country there has not been in twenty years twenty cases of appeal from the District to the Circuit Courts.

As to the Spanish pirates, the gentleman will agree with me that our entire coast is free from such pestilence. The keeping a felon out of the penitentiary for a few months is the only possible contingency that may occur. Such a case may occur. Some petty robber of your mails, or something of that sort. It seems to me that the honorable senator's mind is a little fevered on this subject; that he does not view it with calmness and discretion, which usually characterize his labors as chairman of the Committee on the Judiciary. I apprehend that he has allowed his mind to run off from the consideration of the particular subject before it to other questions not at all involved in it. His mind is evidently prejudiced. He apprehends that the judges, consulting their own experience, had suggested this bill as a proper remedy for the existing evil, and that *that* is a sort of Nazareth from *which* no good can come. But, *as* my friend from New Jersey has said, who so well qualified to suggest a remedy as the judges of the courts? I do not know that they have suggested this plan; but admitting it, I desire no prejudice against the measure on that account. The judges are competent. I desire the decision of the Senate,—to their judgment I shall bow with all the deference to which it is entitled.

(Henry Clay to J. J. Crittenden.)

ASHLAND, April 10, 1848.

MY DEAR SIR,—I transmit you inclosed a copy of a note, the publication of which I have authorized.

I can add nothing to the reasons which it assigns for the course which I have finally felt it my duty to adopt, but I shall be most happy if they meet with concurrence of your judgment.

I am faithfully your friend,

The Hon. J. J. CRITTENDEN.   H. CLAY.

(J. J. Crittenden to Henry Clay.)

WASHINGTON, May 4, 1848.

MY DEAR SIR,—I had the pleasure to receive your letter, inclosing to me a printed copy of your published note of the 10th of the last month, announcing your course and determination in respect to the ensuing presidential election. I hope it may turn out for the best ; *but* you are apprised of my opinions and apprehensions on the subject, and though so much less competent than yourself to judge, I must confess that I still retain the same impressions. It has all along seemed to me that there was not that *certainty* of success which alone could warrant your friends in again presenting your name as a candidate. The whole subject of the presidential election is becoming more and more perplexed. General Taylor's two letters of the 20th and 22d of the last month, which you will have seen, have reached here. No certain judgment, I suppose, can yet be formed of their effect. The public press has not been heard on the subject. I have conversed with but few about it. I understand that these letters have produced considerable sensation here, that of the 22d being entirely satisfactory and mitigating, to a great extent, the discontent produced by that of the 20th. The declaration contained in the latter, " that he would not withdraw from the canvass even if yourself or any other was nominated by the national convention," was received here with great surprise, and though not inconsistent with the grounds taken in his previously published letters, it seemed to give quite a shock to the Whigs. It was regretted by us all. What will be the result of the position thus taken by General Taylor I am at a loss to conjecture. It makes the future still more impenetrable and dark, and I cannot contemplate it without despondency. General Scott, as I learn, begins to be much spoken of as a candidate, and his friends are said to be making preparations to press and sustain him strongly in the national convention. I know nothing of the extent of these preparations or of the grounds on which his friends rest their confidence. So far as I can see or judge, it appears to me that the general can have no great strength of his own in the convention, and that his nomination can only take place (if at all) in consequence of the conflict of other interests.

Upon the whole, it seems to me that the political prospects before us present only a troubled scene, from the contemplation of which we can derive no pleasure.

That you may be saved from, or pass through, that scene in safety and honor is the sincere wish of your friend,

J. J. CRITTENDEN.*

Hon. HENRY CLAY.

(J. J. Crittenden to his son George B. Crittenden.)

SENATE-CHAMBER, April 14, 1848.

My DEAR GEORGE,—Before this reaches you, I hope you will have received your commission as major of your regiment, which I sent you through the State Department, addressed to General Butler. I have also the great satisfaction to inform you that in a long list of brevet nominations for distinguished services lately made by the President, you have the honor of being *breveted* as major. These nominations have not yet been acted on by the Senate, but will doubtless be confirmed. I can hardly express, my dear son, the gratification I feel at these honors won and obtained by you. You have won them fairly; take care and *wear* them worthily. I am *honored in my sons*. Their *honors are mine*, and as dear to me as life. To enjoy them fully I must feel secure in them. I have not yet received a line from you. I have looked long and anxiously for a letter. We are looking anxiously for news from Mexico,—for intelligence from our commissioners, Sevier and Clifford. May it be news of peace, and may that peace soon restore you to us. You

---

* *This* is supposed to be the last letter ever addressed by Mr. Crittenden to Mr. Clay. Circumstances growing out of General Taylor's nomination and election produced an alienation between them. During Mr. Clay's last illness there was a cordial reconciliation, and Mr. Clay expressed to his son Thomas, on his deathbed, the warmest affection for Mr. C., and his approbation of his course throughout. I am indebted to the kindness of Mrs. James Clay for this and other letters of Mr. Crittenden to Mr. Clay.

may not have heard that I was lately nominated as candidate for governor of Kentucky. I was *constrained* to accept it, and shall return to Kentucky in the early part of June.

Farewell, my dear son.

J. J. CRITTENDEN.

Major G. B. CRITTENDEN.

A public dinner was tendered to Mr. Crittenden on the occasion of his retirement from the Senate, by a large number of his friends in Congress and a number of the citizens of the District. This compliment may be said to have been impromptu. Almost every member of the Senate in the city, and a large number of the members of the House of Representatives, without distinction of party, united in the invitation.

No similar mark of respect was, perhaps, ever offered to any public man with more readiness and sincerity. The dinner was given at the National Hotel, Mr. Senator Mangum presiding, assisted by the Hon. J. S. Pendleton and the Hon. Robert Toombs, of the House of Representatives. The toast to Mr. Crittenden, expressive of affectionate respect and warm admiration, was responded to by him in eloquent and affecting terms. The following is the correspondence which preceded the banquet:

WASHINGTON, June 12, 1848.

To THE HON. J. J. CRITTENDEN.

The undersigned, a few of the many friends whom you have made in the course of your distinguished career as a public man, having heard that you were about to leave Washington immediately, in obedience to the call of the great State which has honored you so long, and in honoring you has so much honored herself, beg that you will remain long enough to receive at their hands a slight testimony of their confidence, respect, and esteem, and they will also add, of their sincere regret that any circumstances should at this time make it necessary that you retire from a "theatre" on which you have enacted, and by all the qualifications of a statesman and a patriot are able to enact, so useful and so eminent a part. They purpose that you will remain long enough to dine with them on such a day and at such an hour as may suit your convenience.

D. WEBSTER,	A. P. BAGBY,	A. C. GREENE,
W. P. MANGUM,	SYDNEY BREESE,	JOHN BELL,
W. L. DAYTON,	A. FELCH,	WM. UPHAM,
J. M. MASON,	D. S. YULEE,	J. C. CALHOUN,

S. M. Downs,	C. G. Atherton,	Jefferson Davis,
D. W. Lewis,	J. McP. Berrien,	Simon Cameron,
H. Johnson,	Thos. Corwin,	John A. Dix,
J. A. Pearce,	Reverdy Johnson,	D. S. Dickinson,
J. R. Underwood,	Thomas J. Rush,	J. D. Westcott,
Solon Borland,	A. P. Butler,	W. K. Sebastian,
J. M. Niles,	R. M. T. Hunter,	D. R. Atkinson,

On the part of the Senate.

J. S. Pendleton,	M. P. Gentry,	E. B. Holmes,
R. Toombs,	John Freedly,	W. Hunt,
W. B. Preston,	J. E. Holmes,	T. Butler King,
R. W. Thompson,	John Strohm,	E. Embree,
George G. Dunn,	G. N. Eckert,	D. M. Barringer,
T. S. Flournoy,	E. Therrill,	Daniel Duncan,
P. T. Sylvester,	J. Collamer,	R. C. Canby,
J. W. Houston,	John Dickey,	M. Hampton,
E. C. Cabell,	John Crozier,	O. Kellogg,
Green Adams,	J. G. Hampton,	T. L. Clingman,
James Pollock,	L. C. Sevier,	John W. Jones,
T. A. Talmadge,	A. Stewart,	Caleb B. Smith,
Th. P. Campbell,	A. H. Stephens,	Samuel F. Vinton,
George Ashmun,	J. R. Ingersoll,	J. W. Farrelly,
R. C. Winthrop,	Aylett Buckner,	W. Nelson,
J. B. Thompson,	D. Rumsey,	D. B. St. John,
W. Duer,	P. W. Thompkins,	Joseph Grinnell,
A. S. Fulton,	W. L. Goggin,	John Gayle,
R. C. Schenck,	Garnett Duncan,	A. Lincoln,
J. C. Roman,	J. W. Crisfield,	C. S. Morehead,
W. T. Lawrence,	B. G. Thibodeaux,	John L. Taylor,
John Blanchard,	William Cocke,	

On the part of the House of Representatives.

W. W. Seaton,	W. H. Aspinwall,	G. C. Washington,
John Carter,	W. A. Parker,	John E. Shell,
Henry Chauncy,	R. C. Weightman,	D. F. Slaughter,
Dan. F. Delaney,	M. St. Clair Clarke,	T. L. Smith,
	Charles Morgan,	

Citizens of Washington.

(Mr. Crittenden's Reply.)

Senate, June 12, 1848.

Gentlemen,—I have received your most kind letter and invitation of this day's date, in which you are pleased to express your regret at my intended resignation of my seat in the Senate of the United States, and request that I would postpone my departure from Washington "long enough to dine with you on such a day and at such an hour as will suit my convenience."

This most unexpected mark of your kindness and regard does me too much honor. Your commendation, gentlemen, is praise indeed; it is far, I know, beyond any merit of mine. But yet I take it to my heart as a testimony of your personal regard; I will treasure it as a most precious treasure, and it will grow in my memory as long as memory shall last.

I have no language in which to make you suitable acknowledgments. I will only ask you to believe that I receive this testimony of your "confidence, respect, and esteem" with a heart full of feeling, which I know not how to express.

I have only to add that I accept with pleasure the invitation to dine with you. The necessity of my speedy departure from the city obliges me to name to-morrow.

I have the honor to be, with great respect, your obedient servant,

J. J. CRITTENDEN.

To Dan. Webster and others of the Senate; Hon. J. S. Pendleton and others of the House of Representatives; W. W. Seaton and others of the citizens of Washington.

CHAPTER XXIV.

1848.

(From the Weekly Commercial Journal of Pittsburg, June 24, 1848.)

IT having been announced that Mr. Crittenden would address
our citizens last night, a large yard in the rear of the hotel
was crowded at an early hour to its utmost capacity.

Mr. Crittenden appeared upon the platform and was greeted
with loud applause. Mr. Forward rose and said he had great
pleasure in introducing to the meeting the Hon. J. J. Crittenden,
of Kentucky. (Loud and continuous applause.) From the
prominent part which this eloquent and able gentleman had
taken in the advocacy of interests especially near to us, his name
has become as familiar to us as household words.

After Mr. Forward sat down, the cries for Crittenden! Crittenden! were absolutely deafening, and when he rose the welkin
rang with shouts and cheers.

Mr. Crittenden said he wished he could address the meeting
in a style to justify the highly complimentary introduction he
had received from Mr. Forward, or that he was as well able to
instruct and entertain his fellow-citizens as that distinguished
gentleman. " Could I address you with his ability, the utmost
measure of my ability would be filled. Fellow-citizens, I hope
no one will believe me guilty of the presumption of desiring
the people of this great city to be called together for the purpose of hearing an address from me. I received an invitation
by telegraph, and promised Hampton I would be here.

"The great topic now agitating the public mind is that relative
to the presidential question. The chief executive magistrate of
this Union occupies a position which extends over the whole
country and into all the departments of government. The two
great parties have met in convention and selected their candidates and made their nominations. The Whig Convention has
nominated General Zachary Taylor. Preceding this nomination there existed, as there always will upon such occasions,
great difference of opinion among the Whigs as to who should

be their candidate. It was not possible that the wishes of all could be gratified; but the convention was composed of delegates from all sections of the Union; they compared their opinions, and General Taylor's nomination was the result of the free and full interchange of their views. The only virtue these conventions can have is to unite us. The National Whig Convention of Philadelphia has nominated General Zachary Taylor for President of the United States, and he is presented to us as our candidate by all the forms known to us in such cases. I now propose to examine somewhat into the qualifications of General Taylor for this high office, and the *traits* which recommend him for it. In the first place, I know General Taylor personally. What objection can be made to him? What objection is made to him by his opponents? I have heard no impeachment of his character as a soldier or a man; but his qualifications for the office of President have been called in question. I do not myself think that mere military talents and renown qualify a man for exalted civil stations any more than I think that great civil talents qualify a man to command an army. It is sometimes the case, however, that those who wield the sword bravely in the defense of their country are also endowed with the qualifications of statesmen, learned in civil duties, and submissive to the Constitution and laws of their country. What is the foundation of the belief that the possession of high intellectual powers is the great qualification necessary for an aspirant to the presidential office? After all, the heart of a man is the best qualification,—a heart that is honest and faithful. Gratitude will keep such a heart in the right path, and under the rule of such a man we could not be in danger. None of our Presidents have ever failed through want of intellect. The failure of our administrations (where they have failed) have been through want of heart, and not of head. A man with a sound American heart and a good common understanding is what is wanted, and with such we are secure against treachery and danger. An honest man is needed, and honest men are not so scarce as is sometimes supposed. We have an anecdote of an old philosopher who, when asked why he walked in daylight with a torch, replied, that he was searching for an honest man. Well, gentlemen, I think the people of the United States have found what the old philosopher searched for,—they have found an honest man in Zachary Taylor. They have not needed to carry a torch to find him,—his character is a torch, lighting up and showing an honest man. That torch flames so high that all the world can see it, and the earth and the heavens are filled with its light. A word as to General Taylor's political principles, and to the attempts of politicians to investigate his character. No man was more universally recognized as a Whig among his personal acquaintances than General Taylor. I know him to be a Whig. He has said (and if there is a man living who would not tell a falsehood that man is General Taylor), 'I am a Whig, but not an ultra Whig!' If he had been near a place of election in 1844 he would have voted for Mr. Clay. This brave man has spent his life in camp,—in distant places,—where the service of his country called him. He has kept his mind free from the bitter animosities of a party politician. While actuated by all the leading Whig principles, he has no unkind feelings towards those who differ with him. *Whigs* and *Democrats* have fought under his orders side by side,—equally fighting, shedding their blood, and conquering under him. How could it be possible for him to regard the one with less favor than the other? How can General Taylor give place to any of those little animosities of the petty politician? How could the old hero be bound by paltry party ligaments, inducing him to favor one more than another of those who fought under him, bled under him, and to whom their old general is alike the object of obedience and affection? This, my fellow-citizens, is the school of General Taylor's politics. 'I have seen Whig and Democrat bleed together in the cause of their country,' said General Taylor; 'and if I am President I will proscribe no man. I would as soon turn my back upon a friend or run from a Mexican as proscribe any man for an honest difference of opinion.' General Taylor, though he took no degree in college, is a reading man; he is familiar with history, ancient and modern; he is a student of Plutarch,—he is one of Plutarch's men! In worth, in modesty, he is equal to any of Plutarch's heroes, and as an American I am proud to proclaim it, and to claim him as my countryman!

"When General Taylor commanded the army in Texas, he was ordered to advance to the western boundary of Texas. The honest old soldier had sense enough to perceive that it was not his business to decide as to where this line lay, and he made the cabinet tell him that which they had not distinctly decided among themselves. When asked by the cabinet to take a position on the Rio Grande, he did so, and commenced the campaign. Let any one who doubts General Taylor's capacity examine the history of this campaign, and let him say if he can discover one solitary fault, one thing which was omitted, but which ought to have been done, or one thing done which ought to have been omitted.

"The government—never friendly to him—had found fault with him for the capitulation of Monterey; but the officer who carried him the reproof of the War Department has said that, as a military man, he would have preferred the honor of that capitulation to the glory of General Taylor's previous victories. This officer was Major Graham, one of the most accomplished men in the American army. Major Graham carried the rebuke of the War Department, composed in the midst of peace, safety, and luxury in the White House, to the brave old soldier who was fighting in the mountains of Mexico. Graham says he watched the old man's countenance as he read the letter: no sign of anger or emotion was visible. After reading it calmly, he said, 'I am sorry my conduct has not met the approbation of the President, and that the government condemns my course.' 'General,' said Graham, 'the people do not condemn you.' 'I would have taken Monterey,' said General Taylor, 'with a high and bloody hand, but it would have cost me the lives of five hundred more of my men. I did not care about the Mexicans; I could whip them at any time; what I wanted was the town. The President does not understand the matter, or the reasons for my conduct. I had my cannon and my supplies to bring up, and my lines of communication to establish and secure. While I affected to grant the enemy time, I was really securing it for myself.' This is the only objection I have heard against General Taylor; and public opinion and military critics have long since decided that in his favor. (A voice from the crowd, "I know another objection: he never knows when he is whipped.") I think you are mistaken there, too, my friend. General Taylor has never been whipped, and I don't think he will live long enough ever to be whipped.

"To command an army of ten thousand men in a foreign country, scattered over a large space, requires talents and genius. General Taylor has done this successfully, and I think we may fairly conclude he has the ability necessary to be our President. General Gibson, of Washington, told me a circumstance relating to General Taylor which is well worth repeating. You all know General Gibson; at least you all ought to know him. A Pennsylvanian, he is not only an honor to his State but to the Union. I have passed through times in Washington when almost everybody's integrity was questioned, but in all times General Gibson's name stood crowned for truth and honesty. Well, speaking of General Taylor, he said to me, 'I know him well; we were in the same regiment; I was one grade above him, and so we kept on in the service together, the promotions of one keeping pace with the promotions of the other. We have served together on nineteen courts-martial, and we always selected Taylor to draw up the opinion of the court and the report of the proceedings; he was the best writer among us!' By a rare combination General Taylor is not only a conqueror in war, but he is eminently a friend of peace. Said he, ' If I could restore peace to my country, and put an end to this bloody war, I would go with pride and pleasure to my farm and spend the balance of my life in retirement.'   A warrior, a hero in the hour of battle, when the battle is over this lion becomes a lamb.   Not only in America, but in Europe, has he established our fame as a warlike and martial people, and yet he is always the advocate of peace.   His soldiers love him—all love him; and the military critic, when in looking over all his campaigns, cannot point to a single error of commission or omission.

" In all his career, so far as I am informed, General Taylor never put his hand to a death-warrant of a soldier for execution under military law; he rules his army by affection, and not through fear.   How great must be the satisfaction of the brave old man, when he reflects, The enemies of my country fall before me, but my hand is free from the blood of any of my fellow-citizens !

" A remarkable instance of his reluctance to sentence men to death is related of him as occurring after the battle of Buena Vista.   When the battle was over, two deserters were brought to him who had been taken fighting among the Mexicans.   One might suppose that in such a case he might be expected to give way to feelings of vengeance.   Between five and six hundred of his soldiers lay bleeding on the earth; but the battle was over; he thought there had been enough blood shed.   The thirst of conflict was over, and the feelings of humanity prevailed. If acknowledged as deserters, these men must be put to death; but Taylor could not do this.   ' No, no,' said he, ' these men were never my soldiers; they never belonged to my army; drive them back again to the Mexicans, to the tune of the Rogue's March !'   (Loud laughter and great applause.)

"No man ever questioned Taylor's honesty.   A short time since General Twiggs said to me, ' There is not a man in the world who can look five minutes in Taylor's face and make a dishonest proposition to him.'   A private soldier in the army would refer a difficulty with a major-general to General Taylor with the certainty that he would receive from old Zack the most absolute justice."

After a few words descriptive of the battle of Buena Vista, Mr. Crittenden proceeded to say: " I mean no disparagement to any other general in the army,—many of them are great men; but I do not believe there is another officer in the army who could have fought that battle ; or, if so, who could have won it. (Loud and continued applause.)

" And now, since he has returned home, I hear nothing of him except his going up and down the river visiting his friends. Why, there can't be a wedding in the neighborhood without his being present. (Loud laughter and applause.) They follow him about like chickens. He moves about talking to the farmers, for he is as good a farmer as any of them; and if he should visit Pennsylvania, although he could no doubt learn something from you, he would not fail to give you also some instruction.

"General Taylor's habits are of the simplest kind. His fare was only that of the common soldier; so that no man could say he endured more than his general. No general in the American army was ever so loved, so obeyed, so fought for; no sentry, no guard, was around his tent; any private soldier might enter it, and if the general was not occupied he would sit down and talk kindly with him about his family and home. During all the months of his service in Mexico he never slept in a house,—the tent was his home, in the midst of his men. There is a soldier for you; there is a citizen for you.

"And this man,—so pure, so plain, so upright,—as ready with a tear for the sorrows of a friend as with a blow for an enemy, would he not make a real, genuine, old-fashioned Democratic President? ("Yes, yes;" and loud applause.) Not a spurious, partisan Democrat, but a real Democrat? Would not his election be a new light over our fading Democracy? Do you not think, my friends, that our Democracy has been falling to the rear a little in the sere and yellow leaf? Have not abuses crept in, from the long continuance of power in the same hands? I make no allusion to any individual. Are we not gradually getting into our government too many little aristocratic notions? (A voice, "It all comes of the loaves and fishes.") Yes, my friends, there is a good deal in that, too. One set of Presidents have held power a long time,—I mean a set of Presidents professing the same political principles,—and in this long continuance of power in the same hands abuses must have crept in. But, my fellow-citizens, I have already detained you too long, and I must now conclude."

Mr. Crittenden was about taking his seat when he was prevented by a perfect tempest of shouts, "Go on — go on — go on! give us a little more grape," etc.

"Well, my countrymen, I will make a few more remarks, but they must be brief. I wish to say a word on one subject in regard to which there is a good deal of feeling in this section of the country. It is objected to General Taylor that he is a Southern man and a slaveholder. Why are these local distinctions made? I am a Kentuckian, but I thank God I can take you Pennsylvanians by the hand and call you brother. Separated by State boundaries, under different State governments, there is still a bond of union,—the Constitution of the United States, which binds us all into one great country. I am proud and thankful to call you all my countrymen. Providence never allotted to any other people such a country as ours. Rome, when she had desolated half the world, and tinged every streamlet and river with blood in her career of conquest, never possessed half the power that you possess or will possess. That power is for extending liberty to millions yet unborn, and your influence to every portion of the inhabited world. If we but hold together—this and greater will be our lot—we will go on increasing to incomprehensible, indescribable greatness. Over all this wide domain, stretching from the Pacific, four thousand miles distant from us, to the shores of the Atlantic, we are, and can be, one great people, speaking the same language, and governed by the same laws. I know not for what purpose we may be reserved, but so far our progress has been unexampled in the history of the world. Let us not, then, speak of a Northern man, a man from the Middle States, or a Southern man,—what matter where he is from so he is *the man* to serve our purposes and work out our destiny? We are none of us Kentuckians, none of us Pennsylvanians, we are all Americans! (Loud cheers.)

"General Taylor is called a Southern man. Well, in Kentucky, we call ourselves Western men. Let us inquire where General Taylor has passed his life,—in the South, in the North, in the West. For forty years he has lived in his tent, for forty years he has been covered by the glorious stars and stripes. Is not this answer sufficient to silence all those objections? He has lived where his country's interests called him, and is he now to be questioned as to where he comes from? (Applause, "Hurrah for old Zack!") General Taylor has said, I will proscribe no man for difference of opinion: which of you, who now hear me, will proscribe him?

"Will you proscribe him,—the gallant, warm-hearted, kind, truthful old soldier, the great warrior, the kind neighbor, the skillful general, the good husband, the good father, and good citizen? Will you proscribe him, the indulgent master whose slaves are always most happy when his duties allow him to return among them? ("No—no—no!") I have always supposed you Pennsylvanians to be particularly susceptible to the claims of high military qualities. I saw it in the days of Jackson. I have remarked it on many other occasions. I have a sort of superstitious belief about me, a certainty, I may say, that when General Taylor's character and achievements shall be known among you, a generous enthusiasm in his favor will sweep your State from the Delaware to your utmost mountains. (Continued applause.)

A voice, " What about Fillmore ?"

"I know him well. He is an excellent man, and man of great ability, honesty, and sound principles; he aided materially in the construction of that bill of which you Pennsylvanians think so much,—the tariff of 1842.

" I have dwelt but little on the politics of General Taylor, but there is one subject of which I will speak, as it touches closely your interests here. You, my friends, may be called the Spartans of America. The old Lycurgus, in order to prevent luxury and avarice among his Spartans, made iron money their circulating medium. You in Pittsburg, by your enterprise and industry, have done the same thing. You are workers in iron, and you have made your iron money. If in your business you need some little aid, some little protection from your government, and Congress shall pass a law giving it to you, it will receive no obstruction from General Taylor's veto.

" I will add one more remark, gentlemen. If the tariff laws do not afford sufficient protection for you, they soon will. There is no evil without some good accompanying it, and even this evil of one hundred and eighty-five millions of debt growing out of the war with Mexico will result in some good. To meet this debt, the taxes on importations must be exorbitant, and the tariff, of course, increased. Providence has given us great advantages, and I see not why they should not be used for the benefit of our own people. Is it not lawful for us to enjoy these advantages? In Europe, with its crowded population, industry is enslaved; with us, industry confers independance and wealth. If we throw open our doors to foreigners, sleep with them, and make them as our own countrymen, is it not lawful for us to protect ourselves against the pauper labor of the old world? It is surely the duty of each nation to protect its own citizens, and the world is best managed when this system is most closely adhered to. General Taylor says that he thinks all this legislation should be left to Congress. When Congress passes a tariff law it is not the business of the President to veto it. If you elect old Zack President, —and we are bound to do it,—you will have an honest, humane man. And you can point him out the old world, ruled over by kings, some of them almost idiots, others despots, and say, Here is a *man!* look upon our President,—a man whom you cannot buy, whom you cannot sell, whom you cannot scare, and who never surrenders!"

When Mr. Crittenden sat down, the cheering was tremendous. Three cheers were given for John J. Crittenden with a will which made the mountains ring.

(Thomas H. Clay to J. J. Crittenden.)

MANSFIELD, June 24, 1858.

MY DEAR CRITTENDEN,—I received on yesterday a copy of your speech, delivered in the Senate of the United States, corrected by yourself, on Kansas and the Lecompton question, which you did me the honor to inclose to me.

It was my intention to have written to you before this to express to you my thanks and gratitude for the able, patriotic, and conservative course you pursued during the late session of Congress; not that the opinions of as humble an individual as myself could avail you anything, but I thought that a proper veneration for my father's memory demanded this from me. I am satisfied, as you observed in your speech on last Monday evening, that, had he been living, he would have pursued a course similar to that which you adopted.

Why should you regard the denunciations of the Southern Democratic press? Was not he, throughout his career, assailed by it with the charge of abolitionism? When did public virtue and patriotism ever escape its detractions?

If the Black Republican party eschews sectional issues, and have become national and conservative in their action, whilst the Democratic administration manifests itself as corrupt and imbecile, why should not all true Americans unite with it to cleanse the Augean stable at Washington, and to purify the country from this baleful influence?

With my best wishes for your continued health, and with the highest regard,

I am truly your friend,

The Hon. J. J. CRITTENDEN.   THOS. H. CLAY.

(General Zachary Taylor to J. J. Crittenden.)

NEW ORLEANS, July 1, 1848.

MY DEAR SIR,—Your highly esteemed and interesting letter of the 11th ult., in relation to my nomination as a candidate for the Presidency at the coming election, by the National Whig Convention, which recently assembled in Philadelphia, reached me a short time previous to my leaving Baton Rouge for this place. However much I might have felt gratified, which was not a little, at the distinguished honor done me by that talented, pure, and patriotic body, yet, when I first received information of my nomination, I must say that I felt nothing like pride or exultation at the same, which may be owing to my reluctance in embarking in the canvass and doubts as to the propriety of my going into the high office in question, which seem to grow stronger as the time approaches when it is possible I may have to do so. Perhaps another cause may have operated on me in connection with the above, which is on account of Mr. Clay's feelings of disappointment and even mortification at the course matters and things took, and resulted, in the convention, which, from his age and temperament, I fear he will not bear with the greatest philosophy, or even with that resignation and magnanimity which should be displayed on such occasions. But, I hope for the best. Without regard to my personal wishes or pretensions to the high office in question (for which I have none), I very much regretted Mr. Clay permitted his name to be brought before the country as a candidate for the Presidency, which, I make no doubt, he was overpersuaded to do by many false friends; but as he did so, if there had been anything like a certainty in his being elected, I would have been much more elated on hearing of his nomination than I felt when my own was communicated to me, or since then, notwithstanding the warm congratulations I have received on my success from many warm friends,—yourself among the number,—which was greatly enhanced in value by the regret you felt at the defeat of an old and dear friend. If I could place him in the presidential chair, on the 4th of March, 1849, I would gladly do so. At the same time, I deem his election, even had he been the nominee of the convention, entirely out of the question; nor do I believe his real friends, on that account, wished to have seen him again in the field, as they were satisfied, had that been the case, it would have resulted in saddling the present party in power on the country for another term of four years, and, in all likelihood, until our institutions were utterly destroyed, or nothing left of them but their name. In that light I must view them should the nominee of the Baltimore Convention be elected, which is not unlikely will be the case. But the Whigs must contest that matter to the utmost, and if our fair fabric of government is to be pulled down and destroyed, they, the Whigs, must do all they can to prevent it. The question by the convention was not who ought to be elected, but what Whig could be elected and arrest the downward tendency of our institutions. I have not language to express in appropriate terms the distinguished and high compliment done me, more especially for the manner in which it was paid by that enlightened assembly, in which there were so many fathers of the land. That they should, in a state of high party times like the present, growing out of the management of our national affairs, have nominated me, an humble individual, personally unknown to but few of them, as a suitable candidate for the highest office in the gift of a great and free people, and, in fact, to rule over them, is an honor I did not expect or deserve, and for which I felt, when notified of the same, more grateful and elated than I know I shall do, even if the good people of the country should carry out what the convention has recommended by placing me in the presidential chair,—an honor I shall never forget, for which I am truly grateful, and which I will try to continue to deserve. I have not yet received official information of my nomination by the convention, but expect daily to do so. When I do, I trust my letter of acceptance will meet the approbation of my friends.

Previous to the receipt of your letter, I had a conversation with a very discreet friend in regard to the nature of my reply in acknowledging the receipt of the communication informing me of my nomination, and it was thought best to make it *very brief*, barely referring to the high honor done me without attempting to define my position, leaving that to be judged by what I had already written. It was with great pleasure I learned that you coincided in this opinion. I have never intimated my intentions to retire at the end of four years, should I be elected to that office; nor shall I do so, but will leave the subject to future consideration, although there is but little doubt I would gladly retire at that time to private life. I have never intimated who would form my cabinet; it will be time enough to do so after I am elected. I have said more to you on the subject than I have to any one else; indeed, I have but in one instance alluded to it, to Colonel Davis of the Senate before he left Mexico, and only to him that, in the event of my election to the Presidency (which I did not then expect), my cabinet would be composed entirely of Whigs. That I will be visited by many designing individuals to draw from me expressions by which they can assail me, as well as others who will write to me under the mask of friendship to draw from me some opinions which they hope to use to my injury, there can be no doubt. Such I hope to disappoint, as I will be as cautious as possible with all such persons and everything connected with them. There is a certain class which neither vigilance nor prudence can guard against, therefore they must be *endured*,—such as a celebrated Doctor B., who repeats conversations which he says occurred between us without ever having seen me, made up without the slightest regard to truth, but whose high character for veracity was vouched for upon the floor of the House by such men as Brown, of Mississippi, McClernand, of Illinois, and Henly, of Indiana. Things in this respect must take their course, and we must make the best of them. I came to New Orleans to meet the volunteers who are rapidly arriving from Mexico. I am happy to say they are, for the most part, in excellent health and spirits, being delighted at the prospect of returning to their

families. The Kentucky regiments have not yet reached here.
I hope they will do so before I shall be under the necessity of
leaving the city. I am very desirous of seeing them, particularly my friend and cousin, your son Thomas, who, from last
accounts, was in excellent health, which, I hope, he will long
continue to enjoy. While I regret your having to quit the
Senate to canvass the State of Kentucky for the office of chief
magistrate, I sincerely hope you will conduct the same in a way
calculated to improve, instead of injuring, your health. Your
life is of too much importance to your friends, family, and country to be endangered. Having recently been assigned to the
command of this division of the army, I deem it most consistent with my position to enter quietly on my duties, remaining
in this section of the country until after the election, leaving it
to my friends to attend to my political affairs, in whose hands I
consider them safe ; at any rate, I am willing to abide the issue,
and most cheerfully acquiesce in the result.

Wishing you and your family health and prosperity through
a long life, I remain with high consideration of respect and
esteem. Say to Mr. O. Brown that I have profited not a little
by his judicious advice ; it *is not* and will not be forgotten. In-
terruptions are frequent,—I scarcely know what I have written.

Your friend, truly and sincerely,

ZACHARY TAYLOR.

Hon. J. J. CRITTENDEN.

In 1848, Mr. Crittenden, in obedience to the wishes of the
Whig party, resigned his seat in the Senate of the United States
and became a candidate for governor of Kentucky; he was
elected without difficulty. Governor Powell was his opponent,
and a speech made in Versailles during the canvass was considered one of his finest efforts. Of this speech a correspondent of the *Commonwealth* said :

When Mr. Crittenden rose to reply to Mr. Powell, his manner
had undergone a great change; he was roused by the remarks of
his competitor. The genius of the debater—the keen, dexterous,
pungent debater—was up; his countenance wore that expression, half comic, half sarcastic, midway between a smile and a
sneer, with which benevolence curbs and half conceals scorn,
and which a soul, naturally kindly and generous, flings, like a
graceful and delicate veil, over unbounded powers of raillery and
ridicule. Nature has conferred upon Mr. Crittenden, among
other gifts, some of the highest qualities of an actor, and a comic

actor. It requires all his dignity to retain within just limits his perceptions of the ludicrous and his exquisite powers of mimicry. The weapons of his wit, if wielded by malignity, would suffice to kill. In his hand, however, and guarded by fraternal charity, they are used as instruments of defense and chastisement; he never strikes at a vital part or aims a mortal blow. No one can report Mr. Crittenden literally and do him justice,—the look, the peculiar accent, and half-mocking pronunciation would be wanting. In this speech, however, all was courtesy; stimulated by the delight of the crowd, he felt himself pursuing this jesting vein too far, suddenly checked himself and said, " But this is badinage," and resumed the air and manner of the great statesman.

When Mr. Crittenden rose, he spoke of Woodford as the *heart* of Kentucky, and of Kentucky as the *heart* of the *Union*, and of the ties which bound his own to " *this heart of hearts.*" He alluded to his birthplace and his present position with graceful propriety, with a taste, a delicacy, a beauty, a *tenderness* of which, I think, *he alone* is capable. To attempt to report him is always grossly unjust, unless you could use words as colors and paint the expression, the tone, the action, and, above all, the countenance. Mr. Crittenden said, sixty years before, he had been a nursling there, in Woodford, in what was then a *canebrake.* Since then what revolutions had swept over the beautiful face of the country where he was born, lovely in its original wilderness, still lovelier, perhaps, under the forming hand of taste, art, and culture! He stood now upon the spot where he had set out, his starting-post and goal. A child of Woodford, and *proud of his nativity.* In discussing the presidential question, Mr. Crittenden said that Mr. Powell claimed a great advantage for his candidates over General Taylor because they had principles—*printed principles*—and a platform to stand upon, and poor old *Rough and Ready* presented himself, his naked self, on foot, without printed principles, without any platform. Mr. Crittenden said there was great convenience in these printed principles and candidates *made to order!* " These creatures of the type and press could be made to suit circumstances—new editions could be struck. Does the gentleman really think it is in the power of a Baltimore Convention to manufacture principles for this country? The principles which guide a man's understanding and control his actions are discoverable by an observation of his whole life, and the result is more or less correct according to the variety and severity of the circumstances under which he has been called to act. Tried by this test, has General Taylor no principles? Is he just, is he faithful to his word, is he brave, does he love his country, has he been clothed with power and accustomed to high command, has he been placed in subordinate stations? How did he demean himself to his superiors? Has he been surrounded with dangers, pressed with enemies, clothed with supreme command, with thousands of his fellow-men dependent for life and safety upon the steadiness of his nerves? How has he borne himself throughout? Has he seen battle, has it been his stern duty to direct the murderous charge and gaze on fields of slaughter? *How* did he lead? Did he blanch from the helm when the wind blew highest? Did his spirit sink or soar as the whirlwind swept over him? Has victory perched upon his standard? When flushed with triumph, and fresh from the bloody conflict, with what *countenance* did he regard the vanquished? Let his long, and honorable, and glorious life answer these questions. Is there not principle involved in justice, truth, courage, and patriotism? Can a committee manufacture these things? Imagine, if you please, gentlemen, that in 1789 a committee of politicians, a little squad of party organizers, who had figured at county meetings, had called upon General Washington to know if he would sign their *printed principles* and become their party candidate. Figure to yourself the shades of Mount Vernon,—the lawn, the trees, the heights, where still stands, in simple majesty, the hero's homestead, unchanged, since last its walls resounded to his tread, the whole river, which spreads itself out there, like a broad mirror, to receive and fling back, as if in grateful pride, the image of the most beautiful and affecting scenery in the world. Surround, steep yourselves in the very genius of the spot, and then, in the cool, summer evening, in the portico which looks to the east, dedicated to his solitary musings, seated with thoughtful brow and capacious eye, bending its deep, tranquil gaze upon the stream he loved so well, behold the grand, the awful form of the Father of his Country. Imagine the little squad, with their printed platform, signifying to General Washington that he should be the nominee upon condition *that he would sign.* They enter, fearless and unblushing, with their printed principles. With a grave politeness and a dignity which never through life deserted him, a dignity which was with him in death, when he turned his face to the wall, in conscious pride, that the last agony which convulsed and distorted the hitherto heroic calm of his features might have no witness, he rises to receive this committee of his countrymen. Imagine the explanation! See the grand face, long used to veil emotions, never apt to kindle under light or transient excitement.

The face of the hero remains fixed, rigid, impressive.   Imagine the long-gathering storm now concentrated on that Olympian brow ; then look at the committee!"   At this point the crowd burst into one long, loud roar of applause which drowned the residue of the sentence.*

(J. J. Crittenden to Orlando Brown.)

MADISONVILLE, July 27, 1848.

MY DEAR SIR,—I had time only to write you a very hasty letter, and without much consideration, from Russellville, and since then I have been so whirled along that I have hardly had time to think.

There is a mystery to me as to the source from which it is pretended to derive information as to the contents of a letter of mine to Mr. Anderson.   I have not the least recollection of having written a letter to any other Anderson than Mr. Lars Anderson.   He is a friend and gentleman, perfectly incapable of betraying confidence or of doing any other dishonorable act ; and, besides, I cannot be more confident of anything that depends on recollection than that I have never written to him or any one else any letter of which that extract you sent me formed a part.   I send you in this a statement in the form of a letter, to which you will please to prefix the name of any of your editors, and have published, if you deem it proper so to do ; and I presume that it will be proper, unless Mr. Anderson has in the mean time given such a contradiction as will be entirely satisfactory, or unless you shall have learned, what I do not believe possible, that any letter of mine to Anderson contains any careless expression that could at all warrant the statement contained in the extract you sent me.   I am as certain as I can be of anything that that extract is a fabrication or perversion.   But yet I would desire to act with all the caution of a man more tenacious of his truth than of his life.

It may be, and that seems most probable, that some forgery has been resorted to, and, to detect it, the production of the original letter may become necessary, in order to determine the genuineness of the handwriting.

---

* This speech is given entire in the volume of speeches now in preparation. Mr. Crittenden's official acts during the two years he was governor of Kentucky were local in their character; but portions of his messages to the legislature, 1848-1849, have a general interest, and will be given here.   After General Taylor's election to the Presidency, he visited Mr. Crittenden at the Government House, in Frankfort, and offered him choice of the cabinet appointments.   Mr. Crittenden thought it most consistent with his honor and dignity to decline, and remain in Frankfort.

Do not believe for a moment, from the caution I manifest, that I have the least idea that I ever wrote that extract or anything equivalent to it. I am most confident that I did not, and, unless something has been disclosed that satisfies you I am mistaken, I place the inclosed at your discretion for publication. As far as I can now see, it will be proper to publish it.

J. J. C.

1848–1849.

(J. J. Crittenden to A. T. Burnley.)

HENDERSON, July 30, 1848.

DEAR BURNLEY,—I have received your letter of the 21st inst. and the one which preceded it a few days. I was, indeed, astonished at the imputation to me of the "Anderson letter." I knew that I had never thought, spoken, or written of Mr. Clay in the terms or spirit of that letter. On the other hand, I could scarcely conceive of the audacity and depravity of such a *forgery*. It was a dark mystery to me. You have seen my contradiction of the genuineness of that letter and its exposure, which I rejoice to say has been more prompt and complete than I had even hoped for.

This affair and the subject of your first letter, which is connected with it, has made me sick at heart, and has too greatly excited me. I am ready for *peace* or *war*, and will certainly submit to nothing that encroaches on my honor or independence as a *free* man and a Kentucky gentleman. I have been a true friend,—I will not be checked and rated like a bondman. And there is another thing I will not submit to : I will not make excuses or explanations on compulsion, or to gratify or appease the unfounded or voluntary irritation of anybody. I feel that I am more sinned against than sinning. I believe that Mr. Clay cannot, will not, give his countenance to the course that I understand some of his friends about Lexington are pursuing towards me. As to their votes, I care nothing ; I want no vote grudgingly given. The contradiction and exposure of the Anderson letter may, I suppose, be considered as disposing of the villainous letter of the Washington correspondent of the *Herald* which you sent me ; but there is one statement in that letter which I am hardly satisfied to pass by without a contradiction.

(322)

It is this: "Mr. Crittenden still declares, I understand, to the friends of Mr. Clay, that he was anxious for that gentleman's nomination." I was not anxious for the nomination of Mr. Clay, because I did not believe that he could be elected, and it is false that either before or since the nomination of the Philadelphia Convention I ever declared that "I was anxious for his nomination." I did not wish it, because I believed his defeat would be inevitable. I told him this in substance, and with all the candor of sincere friendship. I regretted deeply that he permitted his name to be used before that convention. When late, and contrary to my wishes and expectation, he expressly permitted that use of his name, I from that time endeavored, as far as I could, to refrain from taking any part or agency against Mr. Clay in respect to the nomination. My feelings prompted to this forbearance, and I think I acted up to it. This was a matter of feeling with me, and there were moments when those feelings were conflicted with by a sense of duty and other periods when I thought it quite probable that Mr. Clay would not be General Taylor's most formidable competitor in the convention. However others may please to interpret my course, I did not consider that I was exerting my influence as against Mr. Clay. But enough of all this for the present. I have given you but an imperfect sketch; it will enable you to understand my general motives and course in respect to this presidential question. I have given it for your private satisfaction. On Tuesday, I will be in Louisville with all the expedition I can.

Your friend,

A. T. BURNLEY. J. J. CRITTENDEN.

(Abbott Lawrence to Hon. J. J. Crittenden.)

BOSTON, September 18. 1848.

MY DEAR SIR,—I have your letter of the 10th, and regret to say I am obliged to employ an amanuensis in consequence of inflammation of the eyes. With regard to our political condition in New England, I feel entire confidence that General Taylor and Fillmore will carry Vermont, Connecticut, Rhode Island, and Massachusetts. We have some chance of including Maine. The letter of General Taylor of the 4th of September is a noble production: *that*, with the letter to Captain Allison, embraces everything that any reasonable Whig can desire. The composition and sentiment of those letters would have done honor to the framers of the Constitution, or to General Washington himself. I ask nothing and want nothing more from General Taylor; he is the man raised up by Providence at this important period of our history to administer the government of this great country.

We have had many obstacles to overcome in this State; we have been in a false position for the year past, and are just now dissipating the fog under which we were enveloped by the action of one man who has lately given some poor, faint praise to the pure and elevated candidate for the Presidency and the Whig party. We look with anxiety to the action of your great *man* in Kentucky. I cannot but hope that he will have the magnanimity, for the sake of his *own honor*, the happiness of his old friends, and the good of his country, to come out boldly and fearlessly in favor of General Taylor. I took the liberty, last week, to write to him ; and as for us, I was able to place before him his true position. It was a plain statement, which I hope will be received with the same candor in which it was written.

In regard to my own position, I feel most sensibly the importance of the coming election. I propose to spend and be spent in the cause. As soon as my eyes permit, I will abandon all business of a private character, and give myself up entirely to the important business of the country and the election of General Taylor. I have already made engagements to address the public, and so far as writing, speaking, and paying, my friends *will not find me wanting*.

Pray let me hear from you, and believe me, always, your friend,

ABBOTT LAWRENCE.

Hon. J. J. CRITTENDEN.

(Henry Clay to James Lynch, A. H. Bradford, etc.)

ASHLAND, September 20, 1848.

GENTLEMEN,—I have received your official letter as members of the Whig Democratic General Committee of the City and County of New York, and I take pleasure in answering it. Never from the period of decision of the Philadelphia Convention against my nomination as a candidate for the Presidency have I been willing, nor am I now, to have my name associated with that office. I would not accept a nomination if it were tendered to me, and it is my unaffected desire that no further use be made of my name in connection with that office. I have seen, therefore, with regret, movements in various quarters having for their object to present me as their candidate to the American people. These movements have been made without any approbation from me. In the present complicated state of the presidential election, they cannot, in my opinion, be attended with any public good, and may lead to the increase of embarrassments and the exasperations of parties. Whilst I say this much without reserve, I must, nevertheless, add, that I feel profound gratitude to such of my warm-hearted and faithful friends as continue to indulge the vain hope of placing me in the office of chief magistrate of the United States, and that I neither think it just nor politic to stigmatize them as *factionists* or by any other opprobrious epithets. Among them I recognize names which have been long distinguished for ability and devotion to the Whig cause and for ardent patriotism. You advert with entire truth to the zeal and fidelity with which the delegation from New York sought in the Philadelphia Convention to promote my nomination as a candidate for the Presidency. I am most thankful to them, and shall ever recollect their exertions with profound gratitude. And here, gentlemen, I would stop, but for your request that I would communicate my views. This I shall do, briefly and frankly, but without reluctance and regret. Concurring entirely with you that the peace, prosperity, and happiness of the United States depend materially on the preservation of Whig principles, I should be most happy if I saw more clearly than I do that they are likely to prevail. But I cannot help thinking that the Philadelphia Convention humiliated itself, and, as far as it could, placed the Whig party in a degraded condition. General Taylor refused to be its candidate; he professed, indeed, to be *Whig;* but he so enveloped himself in the drapery of qualifications and conditions that it is extremely difficult to discern his real politics. He *was*, and *yet is*, willing to any and every nomination, no matter from which quarter it might proceed. In his letter to the *Richmond Republican*, of the 20th of April last, he declared his purpose to remain a candidate, no matter what nomination might be made by the Whig Convention. I know what was said and done by the Lousiana delegation in the convention; but there is a veil about that matter which *I* have not penetrated. The letter from him which, it was stated, one of that delegation possessed, has never been published, and a letter on the same subject, addressed to the Independent party of Maryland, has, at his instance, been withheld from the public. It was quite natural that *after* receiving the nomination he should approve the means by which he obtained it. What I should be glad to see would be some revocation of the declaration in the *Richmond Republican letter before* the nomination was made. On the great leading measures which have so long divided parties, if he has any fixed opinions they are not publicly known. Exclusively a military man, without the least experience in civil affairs, bred up and always living in the camp, with his sword by his side and his epaulets on his shoulders, it is proposed to transfer him from his actual position, as second in command of the army, to the chief magistracy of this great model republic. If I cannot *come out* in active support of such a candidate, I hope those who know anything of my opinions, deliberately formed and repeatedly avowed, will excuse me. To those opinions I shall adhere, with increased instead of diminished confidence. I think that my friends ought to be reconciled to the *silence* I have imposed on myself. From deference to them, as well as from the strong objections which I entertain to the *competition* of General Taylor, I wish to lead or mislead no one, but to leave all to the unbiased dictates of their own judgment. I know and feel *all* that can be urged in the actual position of the present contest. I entertain with you the strongest apprehensions from the election of General Cass, but I do not see enough of hope and confidence in that of General Taylor to stimulate my exertions and animate my zeal. I deeply fear that his success may lead to the formation of a mere personal party. There is a *chance*, indeed, that he may give the country a better administration of the government than his competitor would; but it is not such a *chance* as can arouse my enthusiasm or induce me to assume the responsibility of recommending any course or offering any advice to others. I have great pleasure in bearing my humble testimony in favor of Mr. Fillmore. I believe him to be able, indefatigable, industrious, and patriotic. He served in the extra session of 1841 as chairman of the Committee of the two Houses of Congress, and I had many opportunities of witnessing his rare merits. If you deem it *necessary*, you may publish the first four and the last paragraphs.

With great respect, I am your friend and servant,

HENRY CLAY.

JAMES LYNCH, A. H. BRADFORD, etc.

(W. P. Gentry to J. J. Crittenden.)

HOME, Nov. 20, 1848.

DEAR CRITTENDEN,—Since the presidential contest has terminated in the election of General Taylor, men begin to speculate about coming events. It is assumed that you will be offered, and will accept, the position of Secretary of State. A conversation held with you, makes me doubt if you will accept that position. I perceive there exists a public opinion as to the influence you will exercise over General Taylor, which will hold you responsible, in a great degree, for the acts of his administration, especially in respect to appointments for office. Aspirants to executive favor will expect to enlist your influence; those who *fail* will *curse* you, and those who succeed will soon persuade themselves that their own superior merit needed no fictitious aid to secure that result, and they will forget to be grateful. If you decline to take the helm, and the vessel of state should sail before prosperous gales into a harbor of safety, *others* will claim the glory,—if *she founders*, the blame will fall upon you. Your friends will say, Crittenden did not hold the rudder, and *is not responsible*. Your enemies will answer, he might have held it, but would not; he launched the ship, but would not trust himself with her amid the storms; he gave the vessel, with its rich freight, to the winds, and selfishly sought safety for himself on shore. As you cannot escape the blame if misfortune comes, would it not be wiser to take the responsibility, *dare all dangers*, and guide the ship through the storms and breakers that are *obviously ahead?* Placed as you are, this appears to be the wisest course, but I do not presume to advise; you have doubtless considered seriously, and with lights to guide you to proper conclusions which I do not possess. I write for the purpose of advising you of some small dangers on this part of the political ocean. Having gone to sea, I suppose I had as well stay upon water to the end. You have not forgotten that in this State a portion of the Whig party made powerful efforts to defeat the nomination of General Taylor, and that when those *monster demonstrations* at New York and Philadelphia, in favor of Mr. Clay, sent the idea abroad that he would be the nominee, they made a vigorous effort to make this State change front. This produced a collision, or trial of strength, between the *Taylor Whigs* and the Clay Whigs; the struggle was animated and vigorous. Aided by the talent of our old Captain, we triumphed completely. Our defeated friends were sore under the defeat. The victory won, we sought to soothe them by giving them posts of honor under that standard they had labored to cleave down, and by our united exertions we carried that standard to victory. Some of the prominent Clay Whigs referred to are supposed to maintain *very friendly relations with you*, and I am informed that some of them have been so silly as to boast, that although originally opposed to General Taylor, they will control all questions of executive patronage pertaining to Tennessee THROUGH YOUR INFLUENCE. This is offensive to the original friends of General Taylor, and anything which may seem like a realization of it would create towards you unappeasable resentment with those who can wield a larger influence than the boasters *referred* to. Let me, then, advise you to do nothing or promise nothing to support the idea that your influence can be obtained for the accomplishment of any such purpose. Let it be understood that you *stand* inflexibly aloof from such questions. I want no favors for myself, and do not know that I shall desire to control any questions of that kind for my friends.

My advice to you is founded upon the conviction that any interference of the *kind* alluded to for *the persons* alluded to would permanently injure your popularity. I confess also that I feel a personal resentful unwillingness to see men who did all in their power to prevent the nomination of General Taylor, insolently assuming, in the very moment of his election, to control his administration *through you. Beware of them!*

Your friend,
W. P. GENTRY.

(Alexander H. Stephens to J. J. Crittenden.)

WASHINGTON CITY, December 5, 1848.

DEAR SIR,—When will you be with us to fill the cup of our rejoicing to the full? We want you here, above all things, and *you must come.* The session opened to-day with a pretty full attendance, and we had the *longest message* ever before made by any President. I would not be surprised if Ritchie should say in the morning that it is the *ablest.* You will, however, *see* it, if you do not *read it.* I think Judge Collamer made a good criticism upon it. Some member said "it was like a lawyer arguing a point *after it was decided.*" Collamer said "it was rather like a lawyer in one of the courts who, upon being reprimanded for arguing against the opinion of the judge, replied he was not rearguing the case, *but damning the decision.*" Polk seems to be damning the decision. The best spirit seems to prevail among our friends, and the tone and temper evinced in all quarters argues well. General Taylor will doubtless be annoyed with applicants for office, but the prevailing spirit here is that of discretion and moderation. Some men are busy making a cabinet for him, but they are not the men who had any sympathy with the Taylor movement. The real Taylormen *are all right*, all disinterested. They look upon the late most glorious achievement as a public deliverance, and not a party victory with no other advantages but the acquisition of a few spoils for the faithful. They look for greater and higher objects—for reform in the government, and not bounties and rewards for partisan services. All they desire is for General Taylor to keep all managers and cliques at a distance, and after the maturest deliberation to select for his cabinet men of ability, wisdom, prudence, moderation, and purity. They have full confidence in the correctness of his judgment in the matter. With his administration is to commence a new era in our history. "Old things have passed away, and all things are to become new." The *tone* and *temper* here is all right, it will only require to be kept so when the *press* from without becomes strong. I repeat, *you must be here.* Your friends demand it, the friends of General Taylor demand it, and the *country demands* it,—I need not be more *definite* or more *emphatic;* and you will allow me to say that I am not without my apprehensions of some mischief in case your senatorial election should take a particular turn. *That* ought to be averted if it can be done. I may be wrong in my *conjectures*, and I am fully aware that *you* will *think that I am*, but I will nevertheless be candid and frank in telling you my apprehensions. More *danger* to the success of General Taylor's *administration* is to be feared from that source than all others. You must bear with me, I tell you. I *fear* this is so, and I am not often mistaken. I wish I was acquainted with some of the leading men in your legislature, I would put them on *their guard.* It is important that no blunder be committed, and I know it will require firmness to prevent it. This is a crisis which calls for decision. After hostilities have commenced, it is too late to *pay compliments.* Toombs is not here, nor Pendleton, nor Duncan. Preston is here, and so is old *Truman*, as we familiarly called our late field-marshal, and with their zeal, knowledge, good sense, and sound judgment I know you are *acquainted.* I need not add, therefore, that their efforts are to keep *all things* in good order until *old Zack* himself shall arrive on the field. You see I still scribble with the left hand; I trust, however, you can make out to understand what I mean.

Yours most respectfully,

Hon. J. J. CRITTENDEN.   ALEXANDER H. STEPHENS.

(J. J. Crittenden to Moses H. Grinnell.)

FRANKFORT, December 9, 1848.

DEAR SIR,—I received this morning your letter of the 2d inst. inclosing Mr. Draper's note to you.

It is quite natural that some public curiosity and interest should be felt in respect to the formation of General Taylor's cabinet, and the press in its impatience circulates all sorts of rumors and gossipings on the subject.

The rumor that Mr. Draper has heard of my being authorized by General Taylor to offer the Treasury Department to Mr. Abbott Lawrence is without any foundation or color of truth.

You, sir, I readily believe, are one of the disinterested friends of General Taylor, who, wanting nothing, desire only to see his administration just and successful. You may be satisfied that his course will be marked with prudence, firmness, and decision. I do not suppose that he has even made up his own mind as to the individuals who are to compose his cabinet. He will do that, I have no doubt, with care and deliberation. My firm impression and belief is that he is far from commitments, and will come into office more non-committed than any President we have had since the days of Washington.

It need not, I think, be feared by his friends that he will entangle or encumber himself with promises of office; he is too wise and prudent for that. I know nothing of his general course except as I infer it from his published declarations and from the opinion I entertain of his character.

Like you, sir, I desire only to see him preserve such a course in his administration as will redound most to the advantage of the country and to his own honor. That course I believe he will preserve, and I trust that we shall all have cause to rejoice in his success.

Very respectfully your friend,

J. J. CRITTENDEN.

MOSES H. GRINNELL, Esq.

Mr. Crittenden resigned his seat in the Senate and was elected governor of Kentucky in 1848, and the following extracts are made from his first message to the legislature of Kentucky:

FRANKFORT, KY., December 30, 1848.

Gentlemen of the Senate and House of Representatives,—In obedience to the provision of the Constitution requiring the governor, from time to time, to give to the General Assembly information of the state of the Commonwealth, and to recommend to their consideration such measures as he shall deem expedient, I will now proceed to address you briefly on the topics that appear to me to possess the most general interest. And here permit me to state that, in contemplating the peace, plenty, and security with which the Creator has blessed our people, the first impression of the mind and impulse of the heart should be of gratitude and praise to Him for the happiness of our condition. He has given to us a country having the advantages of a vigorous climate and a soil of unsurpassed fertility, and placed within our reach the natural means of greatness and prosperity. We have but to use these gifts with thankfulness and wisdom to insure a glorious destiny to the inhabitants of our favored land. Nor should we, on an occasion like the present, when the General Assembly will be called upon, in the course of their deliberations, to prepare the way for a new order of things, be unmindful of the obligations we are under to the wisdom and virtue of those who have gone before us, who framed for us a system of government and laws so well adapted to the genius and wants of the people for whom they were enacted, and which have for so many years afforded the amplest protection to the rights and liberty of the citizen. To the benign influence

of their wise and patriotic legislation we owe much of that character that constitutes the pride of every Kentuckian, causing
him to feel that there is something honorably distinctive in the
name, and attaching him, by the institutions of his country and
the force of early association, to the great principles of republican government. The strength of our form of government is
in the truth of the principles upon which it rests. Those principles are the liberty and equality of all before the law, and in no
State or country have those ends been more thoroughly attained
than in ours. Ours is, indeed, a glorious past, and that should
be an example and an encouragement to us to endeavor so to
shape the future that it may truly be said of us that the republic
sustained no damage at our hands. The article of the Constitution that makes it the duty of the executive to see that the
laws are faithfully executed, whilst it is among the most important of the functions of that officer, is happily one that he is
rarely called upon to exercise in any forcible manner. There is
such a judicious distribution of powers to the various departments, and the legislation of the country has been marked by
so much justice, temperance, and moderation, that there is an
habitual respect and obedience paid to them, and anything like
opposition to the laws by individuals or by organized resistance
is almost unheard of. Undoubtedly there are imperfections
incident to all legislation, and it must, in the nature of things,
sometimes happen that the laws are unequal in their operation.
Should such be the case, it will not escape the attention of the
people's representatives, and they will be the first to apply the
corrective.

The people having expressed their will in the legal and constitutional mode for a convention to frame a new constitution,
it will become your duty to pass such laws as are necessary to
carry their wishes into effect, and I would recommend an early
action on that subject.

The important question of a change in the fundamental law
of the land was wisely left to the determination of the people
alone, and they have, in two consecutive elections and by an
increased majority at the last, voted for the call of a convention.
They have exercised their high prerogative in a manner that
augurs favorably for its ultimate issue. We have seen them
assemble without violence, excitement, or tumult, expressing
their will with the calm dignity of freemen too well acquainted
with their rights to bring them into contempt by an unseemly
manner of asserting them. The extraordinary unanimity of
the vote proves beyond controversy that the question rose high
above party or ephemeral considerations, and it is to be hoped
that this lofty spirit will prevail unto the end. When the people

speak, the voice of faction or of party should not be heard. Parties rise and fall with the exciting topics of the day, and catch their hue from the schemes of their leaders. But constitutional law is the ægis of a whole people, and those who are called upon to frame it should never forget that their labors are to affect not only the present but future generations. The people of Kentucky should remember that their old constitution has been to them the shadow of a great rock in a weary land; that it has protected them in the midst of strong excitements and the most embittered party conflicts; and that it had the power to do this because it was not the work of party, but of patriotism and political wisdom. I have no fears myself as to the issue of the approaching convention. I believe that it will be guided by a wise and temperate spirit, which, whilst it avoids all rash innovation, will at the same time, by its prudence and wisdom, satisfy that public opinion which called it into existence and trusts so much to its hands.

Under the auspices of our State governments to take care of our domestic concerns, and of the general government to guard our national and external rights, we may confidently look forward to a future full of everything that can gratify the hearts of a civilized and free people.

It is in this general result of the operation of the American system of government that the States feel and know that they are important parts of a great whole; and that they have other cares, interests, and duties which claim their attention beyond those that are merely local and peculiar to themselves respectively. If we could act in the right spirit, and under the influence of proper sentiments, we must habitually contemplate ourselves and our State as members of the great national Union. It is in and by that Union that we are known among the nations of the earth. It is in that Union that we are respected by the world. And under the joint protection of the government of the Union and the government of the States, we have the amplest securities that patriotism and wisdom can furnish for freedom and prosperity. The union of the States is not only indispensable to our greatness, but it is a guarantee for our republican form of government. With the preservation of that Union and the Constitution by which it is established, and laws by which it is maintained, our dearest interests are indissolubly blended. An experience of near sixty years, while it has confirmed the most sanguine hopes of our patriotic fathers who framed it, has taught us its inestimable value. Its value will be above all price to us so long as we are fit for liberty, and it will fail only when we become unworthy of it. No form of government can secure liberty to a degenerate people. Kentucky, situated in the heart of the Union, must and will exercise a powerful influence on its destiny. Devotion to the Union is the common sentiment of her people. I do not know a man within the limits of the State who does not entertain it. We all feel that we can safely rely upon a Union which has sustained us so triumphantly in the trials of peace and war; and we entertain no fears from those who have a common interest in it with ourselves. The paternal feelings with which we regard them, and the filial reverence we ourselves have for the link that binds us together, give us strength in the faith that they cherish the same bonds of brotherhood, and will practice no intentional injustice towards us. We can have no better security for our rights than that Union and the kindred feelings that unite us with all the members of the Confederacy. If these sentiments ever cease to prevail, I trust that Kentucky will be the last spot from which they will be banished. Errors and even abuses may occasionally arise in the administration of the general government,—so they may in the administration of all governments,—and we must rely upon public opinion, the basis of all republican governments, for their correction. The dissolution of the Union can never be regarded—ought never to be regarded—as a *remedy*, but as the *consummation of the greatest evil that can befall us.*

Kentucky, devoted to that Union, will look to it with filial confidence, and, to the utmost of her might, will maintain and defend it. We let no meditations or calculations on any sectional or other confederacy beguile us to the point of weakening our attachment to the Union. Our relations and our attachments are with and to *all the* STATES; and we are unwilling to impair them by any entangling engagements with a *part.*

We are prouder of our rank as a member of the United States than we could be of any sectional or geographical position that may be assigned us. We date our prosperity as a nation from the adoption of the Federal Constitution. From the government that it established we have derived unnumbered blessings, and whatever of evil has occurred in its administration bears no proportion to its benefits.

In proof of the foregoing sentiment we may appeal to our past history. We have seen measures of national policy which we consider of vital importance to our welfare perish in the conflicts of parties; and other systems, deemed by us inimical to our best interests, prevail. Yet we did not falter in our allegiance to our common government, but waited with patience for the development of the conclusion to which a majority of the whole nation would ultimately arrive after a calm survey and experience of what would best promote the public good.

The administration that is now drawing to a close was not called into existence by the vote or the wish of a majority of the people of Kentucky. Many of its most important measures have not been such as we desired to see enacted. Yet it has met with no other opposition than a manly expression of an honest difference of opinion. And when war was declared with Mexico, notwithstanding the opinion that prevailed that it might have been avoided by wise statesmanship, still Kentucky responded to the call of the President, not halting to debate the necessity of the war, but finding in the fact that it was declared by the constituted authorities of the nation a sufficient claim of her patriotism. She has come out of that war with an increase of glory, being behind none in advancing the honor of the national flag ; and to our brave volunteers, who gained for us that proud eminence, the thanks of the State are due. If such has been her action through the past, may we not safely promise that the administration of General Taylor will receive a cordial support from the State of Kentucky? The veteran patriot, who has been just chosen to administer the government of the United States, was brought to Kentucky an infant in his mother's arms. He was here reared to that vigorous manhood, and with those sterling virtues, that have sustained him through a long period in his country's service. There is, therefore, a natural reason for our confidence and attachment.

But he comes into his high office with the avowed purpose of endeavoring to carry out the principles and policy of Washington, and this should commend him to the affections of the American people. It will be his aim to soften, if he cannot extinguish, the asperities of party strife,—to give to the government its constitutional divisions of powers, as they were designed to be exercised by its framers, and to make the Congress of the United States the true exponent of the will of their constituents.

Under such an administration, guided by such principles and motives, the people of the United States seem to have the best assurance of their liberty and of all the blessings that good government can bestow. These relations have been alluded to in no partisan spirit, but in the hope that we at last see the dawn of an era ardently desired by every lover of his country,— when the discordant elements that have so long disturbed the public repose will give place to more fraternal feelings, and the pure patriotism of the Revolution prevail in every American heart. But in the midst of our bright prospects and high hopes, it becomes us to acknowledge our grateful dependence upon that Supreme Being without whose favor all schemes of human happiness are in vain, and without whose benediction the wisdom and exertion of man can accomplish nothing truly great and good.

J. J. CRITTENDEN.

December 30th, 1848.

(R. Toombs to J. J. Crittenden.)

WASHINGTON, D. C., January 22, 1849.

DEAR CRITTENDEN,—We have been in trouble here for the last month about this slavery question, but begin to see the light. I am anxious to settle it before the fourth of March. The longer it remains on hand the worse it gets, and I am confident it will be harder to settle *after*, than before, the fourth. We have, therefore, concluded to make a decided effort at it now. This morning, Preston will move to make the territorial bill the special order for an early day, which will bring the subject before us. We shall then attempt to erect all of California and that portion of New Mexico lying west of the Sierra into a *State* as soon as she forms a constitution and asks it, which we think the present state of anxiety there will soon drive her to do. This will leave but a very narrow strip, not averaging more than fifteen or twenty miles, between this California line and the Rio Grande line of Texas. This Texas line the Democrats are committed to and some of our Northern Whigs. Corwin, etc., say, if that line is established, they will vote this strip to Texas. I think we can carry *this*, or something like it. The principle I act upon is this,—it cannot be a slave country! We have only the point of honor to serve, and *this* will serve it and rescue the country from all danger of agitation. The Southern Whigs are now nearly unanimous in favor of it, and will be wholly so before the vote is taken. We know nothing of General Taylor's policy, but take it for granted he would be willing to any honorable settlement which would disembarrass his administration from the only question which threatens to weaken it. If you see any objections, write me immediately, and we will keep ourselves in a condition to *ease off* if it is desirable. I have a strong opinion in favor of its propriety and practicability, and with a perfect knowledge of the *hopes*, *fears*, cliques, and combinations of both parties. I do not hesitate to say *now* is the best time to force it to a settlement. We have completely foiled Calhoun in his miserable attempt to form a *Southern party*. We found a large number of our friends would go into the wretched contrivance, and *then* determined it was best to go in ourselves and control the movement, *if possible*. We had a regular *flare up* in the last meeting, and at the call of Calhoun I told them briefly *what* we were at. I told him that the union of the South was neither *possible* nor *desirable* until we were ready to dissolve the *Union*. That we certainly did not intend to advise the people now to look anywhere else than to their own government for the prevention of *apprehended evils*. That we did not expect an administration which we had brought into power would *do* an act, or permit an act *to be done*, which it would become necessary for our safety to rebel at; and we thought the Southern opposition would not be sustained by their own friends in acting on such an hypothesis. That we intended to stand by the government until it committed an overt act of aggression upon our rights, *which* neither *we* nor the country *ever* expected to see. We then, by a vote of forty-two to forty-four, voted to *recommit* his report. (We had before tried to *kill it directly*, but failed.) We hear that the committee have whittled it down to a weak *milk-and-water* address to the *whole Union*. We are opposed to any address whatever, but the Democrats will probably outvote us to-night and put forth the one reported, but it will have but two or three Whig names. Don't think of *not* coming into the administration. There is but one opinion here as to its necessity.

Yours truly,
R. TOOMBS.

J. J. CRITTENDEN.

CHAPTER XXVI.

1849.

(J. Collamer to J. J. Crittenden.)

WASHINGTON CITY, January 30, 1849.

DEAR SIR,—I have summoned resolution to write to you, and you know it will be done with confidence and frankness; so forgive my presumption. First, then, the great topic here is the cabinet of General Taylor. Now, sir, among the very few things generally conceded on this subject *is this:* that you *will be* and *ought to be* consulted on this point by General Taylor. I trust this may be so, and that he and the country may have the advantage of your judgment and knowledge of men on this occasion. Next, sir, I desire to say distinctly that the Whigs of Vermont have desired and expected that you would be Secretary of State, and I think the Whigs of the Union, or at least a large majority of them, participate in this desire. I would add that if in the cabinet you should be at the head of it, to sustain your public and political position. I regard *this* as a national demand, more imperious than any local claims Kentucky can have upon you and paramount thereto. Such are my views, but I never volunteer my unasked advice; nor do I regard my views of any great value; but in this case I express them because I think the public opinion coincides with mine. I, however, frankly acknowledge that I should not have written this letter but for another matter, which relates to myself. You know, sir, I am utterly incapable of soliciting any man, even yourself, to sustain me for an office; but I have a favor to ask which comes *so near it* that I have great reluctance to state it. Last summer and autumn the very decisive and active course I thought it necessary to take in Vermont in relation to the election of General Taylor exceedingly exasperated the Free-Soil party, and they, holding the balance of power in the House of Representatives in the State, prevented my election to the United States Senate. Before the adjournment in November, at a convention of the Whig members of the two Houses, they unanimously recommended me to General

Taylor for the office of Attorney-General. This was without my knowledge. That recommendation has been sent to General Taylor. Now, sir, I do not mention this matter with any view to press such appointment or to expect it; for though I think the claim of Vermont as the only uniform Whig State in the Union, and in which no cabinet appointment was ever made, is very great, yet I suppose no such appointment will be made, especially as the State presents such a candidate. I have, however, a favor to ask. You perceive my situation. I desire that my recommendation by the State may not be to my disparagement and injury. It seems to me that if both this recommendation and myself are disregarded, myself entirely overlooked and the claims of Vermont are attempted to be met by the appointment of *other men* to *other places* by private influence, it will, undoubtedly, be to me a *matter* of *direct personal injury* and reproach. Now, sir, I solicit the exercise of the influence which all ascribe to you to save me from this. In short, sir, if anything of value is to be offered to Vermont, should it not be offered to me?

I am, sir, very respectfully, your obedient servant,

J. COLLAMER.

(J. J. Crittenden to A. T. Burnley.)

DEAR BURNLEY,—Your letter by Swigert reached me yesterday at Mrs. Innis's, where I now am, and you will receive this to-morrow after due consultation with Letcher, who is embraced in your invitation to the Mammoth Cave. As to the cigars, you have acquitted yourself well! Letcher would have taken them all if you had not assigned him *a part*. I do not know what Letcher may think of it, but he is reputed a wise man, and I must, therefore, believe he will concur with me in regarding your proposition to go to the Mammoth Cave as a most strange and wild fancy. Go to the cave! travel three long summer days to get there, and as many to get back, and for what? There is no medical water to restore or invigorate health. Thomas tells me that you promise venison and salmon every day for dinner. That's a "*fish story.*" I know better. You are more likely to get both at the Blue Licks; but the cave,—the cave itself,—the Mammoth Cave is the attraction. There is a deathlike coldness in the idea that may have some charm for people who come panting from the tropics, and who have lately felt that it was better to be buried alive than to endure the burning sun. It must be some disorder of the mind that thus misleads you, and from which I trust the temperate climate you are now in will soon relieve you. For my single self, if I was standing at its mouth, I would not again enter its infernal *jaws*.

I had rather make my explorations on the surface of the earth, in the free air and open light of heaven; I have neither ambition nor curiosity to be thrusting myself into places that were never intended for living men, nor anything better than dragons or reptiles. My seven senses altogether can't comprehend the pleasure of leaving " the warm precincts of the cheerful day" to stumble and grope about in the Mammoth Cave, making its everlasting darkness hideous with miserable glimmering, smoky torches. I would greatly rather have descended with *Æneas* into the infernal regions. *There* a man might indeed *see sights:* here the utmost of his achievements would be to see, perhaps catch, a *poor, little blind fish* that says to him as plain as a fish can speak, "What a foolish thing it was to come so far for such an object." No—no—no, sir, you will not get Letcher and myself into that cave, but if like sensible men you would rather live in society than be buried in a cave, and will go to Harrodsburg or Blue Licks, *we are your men.* Don't let Dr. Croghan hear one word I have said *against caves.* If I could fancy *any cave* it should be his, *because it is his.*

P.S.—Well, I have consulted with Letcher. I find to my surprise that he does not agree with me altogether as *to caves.* Indeed, he says *"he has a passion for caves,"* and has constrained me to consent to suspend a final determination, and to hear an argument from you on the subject. Letcher desires an argument, and if you can remove the objections we will change our decision and go to the Mammoth Cave. Bring Alex. Bullitt along to the argument.

Your friend,
J. J. CRITTENDEN.

(Jefferson Davis to J. J. Crittenden.)

SENATE-CHAMBER, January 30, 1849.

MY DEAR GOVERNOR,—I have been long intending to avail myself of your kindness by writing to you; but you know the condition of a senator during the session of Congress, and may be able to estimate the condition of a lazy man thus situated. It is, I hope, unnecessary for me to say that my sympathies have been deeply enlisted in the case of Major Crittenden, and, what is more important, my conviction is complete that he has been unjustly treated. You know Mr. Polk, and your view of the manner in which he should be dealt with, as shown by your letters, has very closely agreed with my own. Worried by his hesitation, I have called for the proceedings in the case, and if he holds out, it is a case in which the weaker goes to the wall. I think I will beat him, and so you may say in confidence to your gallant son.

My boy Tom, in which style I hope you will recognize Colonel Crittenden, has been discreet and, I think, efficient in a cause where feeling might have warped the judgment of an older man. I regret exceedingly to see that Mr. Clay is to return to the Senate. Among many reasons is one in which I know you will sympathize—the evil influence he will have on the friends of General Taylor in the two houses of Congress. Many who would have done very well in his absence will give way in his presence. This will also introduce a new element in the selection of the general's cabinet. It must be composed of men of nerve and of no Clay affinities.

One instance to illustrate my meaning: Berrien, of Georgia, though well enough without Clay's shadow, would not do under it. You see that I disregard Mr. Clay's pledge to support the administration; he may wish to do so, but can his nature reach so much? The Englishman, Baker, who came from the Rio Grande to draw pay, mileage, and a year's stationery, as a member of Congress, is here, with recommendations from legislatures for the post of Secretary of War. What would General Taylor say to such impudent dictation and indelicate solicitation? L. Butler King wants to be Secretary of Navy. You know the little Yankee, Andrew Stuart, wants to be Secretary of Treasury—the man who proved wool to be a vegetable. I hope you will talk fully with General Taylor; he knows very little of our public men personally, and will have very little opportunity to observe them after his arrival.

Clayton is true, and talks right. Has he the necessary nerve? How would Binney, of Philadelphia, do for the Treasury? As Lawrence is not a lawyer, and is a manufacturer, how would Mr. Lawrence do for Navy? How would Gadsden do for War? How will a Postmaster-General be selected? The general will need you, and I hope to see you here. Loose and hurried as my remarks are, written in the midst of much "noise and confusion," you may, from intimate knowledge of all I have treated of, unravel what would be unintelligible to one less informed.

Your friend,
JEFFERSON DAVIS.

(J. J. Crittenden to O. Brown.)

FRANKFORT, July 3, 1849.

MY DEAR SIR,—Your letters of the 23d and 27th of the last month were anxiously expected, and read with great interest; and yesterday your telegraphic dispatch was received, announcing your acceptance of your new office. You have now become the great *sachem*, and I have no doubt will demean yourself like a proper chief. You have but to take hold of your office earnestly, and all its exaggerated difficulties will vanish before you. It can be no great matter for you, and to comprehend all your official duties, you will then feel at ease. And master of your house, you can order and execute as you please, and with but little trouble, if you have such subordinates as you ought to have. Knowing your capacity, I desire to see you do justice to yourself in your present office, so as to show yourself capable of higher and greater things. And these I anticipate for you without the least pretension to prophecy. Without anything the least personal or selfish in the wish, I hope you will avail yourself of all opportunities of cultivating the acquaintance, the friendship, and the confidence of General Taylor. I desire this for your own sake, for his sake, and for the sake of the country. Such relations with him will be honorable to you, and will, I am certain, be useful to him. His prepossessions are all in your favor, you stand with him as the representative of his great bulwark, Old Kentucky, and he will be glad to have some one with whom he may *talk* outside of the cold, formal limits of the cabinet. That's as *natural* as the desire to break out of prison. You are exactly the man to occupy that relation with him, all circumstances favor it, and nothing but negligence, or something worse, will prevent your falling into that position.

He is a noble old patriot who deserves to have disinterested and faithful friends to soothe and assist him, and I know that you will be such a friend.

Indeed, I have had a sad time since you and the boys left me. It seemed as if all my *light* had gone out. But yet there was a ray from within that was constantly breaking from the clouds to cheer me and to brighten my thoughts. I had advised you all to go. It was good for you to go. And the brightness of your prospects, and of the skies above you, reflect a sunshine upon me. I shall flatter you by telling you how much we all miss you; how much the town misses you; and how much we inquire, and speculate, and talk about you. Letcher seems to be widowed by your departure. In walking together by your house, a few evenings past, he, the practical man, grew poetic, and insisted that your vines, plants, and trees seemed to droop and mourn your absence. Your absence has been an actual grief to me. Missing you in the office day by day, I feel as if my office, "my vocation," was gone. I am glad that you are where you are, and yet grieved that we cannot have you here. There are many peculiar reasons why none of your friends here can lose so much, or miss you so much, as I—but I will not grow too serious or gree-vi-ous on the subject.

The emigrants deducted, our little town remains just as you

left it. I haven't felt like more than half a governor since you left. I have succeeded, however, in getting a very clever fellow, Joshua H. Bell, to take the office of secretary. He has written me that he would be here to-day. And it is quite necessary he should be, as from the last days of June, when your resignation was entered, there has been an interregnum, and will be till his arrival.

By the intelligence which you and Thomas gave us from Washington, we have set it down as certain that Letcher is to have a mission, and most probably that to Mexico. As to what you say of my friend, General W. Thompson, I had heard about the same through a letter from Thomas, with whom also Thompson had conversed, and to about the same effect I received a letter from himself on the day that your last reached me. Fearing that Thompson might think that I had brought about the collision and competition between him and Letcher, I wrote to him immediately on the receipt of Tom's letter, expressing my regret at the competition; that the object of Letcher's friends was to obtain a mission for him, not caring as to what mission it was, and that if it was the wish of the administration to confide to him the mission to Mexico, that Letcher's friends and I would undertake to say Letcher himself would willingly waive any preference he might have for that mission, provided there should be given to him either the mission to Berlin or St. Petersburg. I wrote this not only to acquit myself with Thompson but to place the responsibility where it ought to rest, or at least to throw it off my own shoulders. The truth, I suppose, is that the administration cannot well give one of the first-rate missions to South Carolina after the disposition of other offices which it has made; and not being able to give one to my friend Thompson, are explaining away his disappointment as well as it can be done. That does not concern me; but I do not wish to appear to have gotten up the rivalry between Letcher and Thompson, and to be chargeable, of course, with the disappointment of one of them.

Letcher's spirits have evidently improved greatly under the influence of the letters of Thomas and yourself; and we all congratulate ourselves on the certainty of his success. We shall hold you not a little responsible for the mission to Mexico, Prussia, or Russia. And I don't believe Letcher cares a pin which. But, by Jupiter, I wonder at my own disinterestedness! I am wishing good offices for all my friends here and aiding in getting them,—offices which will carry them far away from me. I shall then be left solitary and alone, and what is to become of me? You stand in need of no lessons from me. Just be yourself and follow your own natural bent and character, and all will be right. Be not jealous of the "Satraps;" be respectful and give them all due deference and honor upon the proper occasions, but show no anxiety to seek or avoid them. Let old Zack be the rock on which you build,—that is the proper position for you,—and all the "Satraps" will soon seek you.

Clayton is a noble fellow; he may have faults and imperfections, but still he is a noble fellow. I want to hear that you are good and confidential friends. You must try and break down the barrier that seems to divide Bullitt from the administration. Between the editor of such a paper and the President and cabinet there ought to be an unreserved communication. It used to be so in old times. There was hardly a day in the administration of Mr. Jefferson, Mr. Madison, and Monroe that the editor of the *Intelligencer* did not visit the President just to hear what he had to say and to imbibe the spirit of the administration. It ought to be so again. Tell Bullitt that his paper is still too much on the *defensive*. He does not show forth old Zack enough, his plainness, his integrity, his patriotism, and that therein lies the hostility of old Ritchie and that whole breed of politicians. These are all mad with the people for electing him. Old Ritchie, for instance, is mad to the amount of ten to twenty thousand dollars annually that has been taken from this old feeder in the treasury. These are the gentlemen that are making all the outcry against old Zack, and they, to conceal themselves and their "private griefs," affect to represent and speak in the name of the Democratic party. I would take the ground that the *people* of that party honored and reverenced old Zack, and that it was the *partisans* only who live on party warfare and its plunder that were abusing and making war on him; that he was emphatically the people's President and not the President of office holders and of Mr. Ritchie. And to illustrate all this, I would signalize Mr. Ritchie's case,—show how he was fattening on the spoils, how he had been cut off from those spoils by the people's President, and what good cause he had to be mad with the people and old Zack for all this. But Bullitt, I think, will soon bring all this right.

You must hold on to your office for a time at least, and let me know all that is going on at Washington.

Your friend,

O. Brown, Esq.   J. J. Crittenden.

P. S.—Buckner's district is doubtful; but I think you may be confident that we will send you eight Whig representatives at least from Kentucky.

J. J. C.

(John M. Clayton to J. J. Crittenden.)

WASHINGTON, July 11, 1849.

MY DEAR CRITTENDEN,—Letcher will be appointed Minister to Prussia or Mexico as soon as your Kentucky elections are over, and *so you may tell him.* He understands me, and when he returns *you* must go in his place. Tell him I *try to do* as he says *I should do,* "have winning ways;" but if I am *kind* in manner to some men, they take occasion to construe *that* into a *promise* of *office.* The President says that it has now come to such a pass that if he does not *kick* a man down-stairs he goes away and declares he *promised him* an office. You never wrote a more sensible letter in your life than that in which you gave me your lessons in diplomacy. I agree with you in everything, and you will see *by-and-by* that I have sent an agent to recognize the independence of Hungary on the first favorable indication. The agent (at present unknown) is Dudley Mann, *now in Paris.* The same policy (sympathy with the advance of republican principles) will characterize all my course, if the President will allow me. On this subject do you write to me to give me a loose rein. Some of my colleagues (*who are noble fellows*) are somewhat young and tender-footed. We must keep up with the spirit of the age. Preston got it into his head that our "Sir John Franklin expedition" was like Mason's *Dead Sea* expedition, and so his *department* defeated us, by holding the matter under consideration until it was too late to do anything. My mortification has been extreme about the failure of it, especially as the British Parliament and the Royal Society received the intelligence of the President's intention to send out the expedition with applause absolutely enthusiastic. It was a pretty feather in the President's cap, and *lost* by the opposition of the navy. Oh, if you could see what a fine letter the "*Lady Franklin*" sent me in reply to the one the President wrote to her, and what a jewel of a letter I was preparing in reply to it! But, alas! we were blown *sky-high* by the navy after the President had ordered them to prepare the expedition. Many here blame the old Commodores Smith, Warrington, etc., the committee to whom the matter was referred, and who reported that we had not a ship in the navy *fit to go.* These old commodores are all behind the age. The spirit of progress ought to be ours. We must keep up or be distanced. Our friend Collamer is behind; he is a glorious fellow, but *too tender* for progress. He has been often indeed at his wit's end, frightened about *removals* and *appointments,* but I cry courage to them all and they will go ahead, *all,* by-and-by! Taylor has all the moral as well as physical courage needed for the emergency. I know Brown; he is at first sight a *trump*—"the *king* if not the *ace.*" Your son

Thomas has gone to Liverpool as happy as a lord. I had to recall Armstrong; he refused to resign. If you will come here and take my office I will give it up to you with pleasure, and with a *proviso* to stand by you all my life. I have not had a day's rest for nearly five months. The honor of *serving* the man I now *serve* is the only reward I can offer you. *That* is indeed *an honor.* I have never met with a man who more justly deserved the respect and devotion of his friends and of all good men. Tell Letcher I am willing to be *hung* if this administration *fails.* Letcher has, in a letter to me, *sworn* to *hang me* if it does.

Remember me kindly to Letcher. I mean to instruct him gloriously. He shall know a *thing or two.*

Faithfully your friend,

Hon. J. J. CRITTENDEN. JOHN M. CLAYTON.

CHAPTER XXVII.

1849–1850.

Letters from J. Collamer, Crittenden, and Letcher—Extracts from Crittenden's Message to the Legislature of Kentucky in 1849—Letters of Crittenden to Letcher and Thomas Metcalf.

(Hon. J. Collamer to J. J. Crittenden.)

WASHINGTON CITY, July 14, 1849.

DEAR SIR,—I have before me your letter of the 9th inst., frankly expressing your feelings of dissatisfaction at my apparent neglect of your recommendation of Dr. Alexander as local mail agent at Louisville. Many persons were recommended, and Russell had many leading men for him, including the member Mr. Duncan. Alexander had no paper on file, but your letter, that would have been very potent with me. In this state of things I received charges enough against Pilcher for his removal. The President having made his own selection for postmaster, then handed me a line addressed to me, but which had been inclosed to him, signed J. S. Allison, recommending the appointment of Russell as agent, and as being most desired at Louisville. The President expressed to me his desire that I should follow the recommendation of Captain Allison. This I regarded as *law* for me. I am *but a subaltern*, and obey, but it seems that in so doing I must lose all the personal attachment and respect of those whose respect I value. It seems to me that even in this matter I have done no wrong, nor have I deferred your wish to anything but what I regarded as imperative upon me.

Respectfully, but *afflictedly*, yours,
J. COLLAMER.

I should be pleased to send my respects to Mrs. Crittenden, but I hardly think they would be at present well received.

J. C.

His Excellency J. J. CRITTENDEN.

(J. J. Crittenden to Orlando Brown.)

FRANKFORT, July 26, 1849.

DEAR ORLANDO,—I learn from your letter to Letcher that you are becoming better reconciled to Washington. The few

(346)

first weeks there would be the *dead point* in your transactions; after that you will have formed new associations that will make all go smoothly. With Burnley and Bullitt for your associates, you have a great resource, and may be a mutual relief to each other in the troubles of your *common exile.* Whatever may be your intention as to resignation, it is best to say nothing about it for the present. It may weaken your position at Washington without doing you good anywhere. I hope to see you a cabinet minister before the expiration of *old Zack's* term. Give my commendation and my thanks to Bullitt, and tell him he has now got the *Republic* up to the right *temperature;* he must keep it as *hot as a furnace* till the *Union* is purged in " liquid fire." *Old Zack* must be kept constantly in view as the *people's President,* and the rage of Ritchie & Co. must be attributed to its natural cause—their exclusion from the domination and spoils they have so long indulged in. *Old Zack* is trying to manage things for the good of *the people,*—Ritchie & Co. trying to get back to the days when the office holders managed things for their advantage and *fed fat* on the public treasury. Old Zack is the people's man, and old Ritchie the champion of the late office holders; the issue is, whether the people shall rule by *their man,* or whether old Ritchie shall be able, by misrepresentation and defamation, to put down the people's administration and take possession of the premises as their own. It is easy to perceive that you feel some distrust of the cabinet and some apprehension of *its success.* This is a contagious feeling with you, Burnley, and Bullitt, and your association keeps it up. I am anxious to see you all *cured of this disorder.*

Yours,
J. J. CRITTENDEN.

(J. J. Crittenden to Orlando Brown.)

FRANKFORT, September 5, 1849.

DEAR ORLANDO,—I start for the Estell Springs to-day, and I am constantly finding little last things to be done that have been before neglected.

A Mr. Harrison, of Greenupsburg, in this State, is very anxious to obtain an office. Application was some time ago made for an Indian agency for him, and I write on his behalf. I have since received a letter from him, suggesting that his application had been too limited; that if he could not get an Indian agency he desired some other equivalent office, and requested me to write again in his behalf. You know Mr. Harrison, I believe. I think you were in my room when he first visited me on this subject. My impression is that he was a sort of Democrat who became a zealous Taylor-man.

He is a good-hearted, worthy man, and very competent to the duties of any such office as he solicits. If you find an opportunity of doing anything for him, I pray you to do it.

I have received your letter of the 29th ult., but have not time now to reply to it further than to say that I am glad you have got your hands to a work more worthy of them than the ordinary drudgery of office. Insist, if it be necessary, on having it all your own way, and take responsibility so far as to make it your own work. Give up in no essential point without an appeal to old Zack. There is no necessity for you to stand in awe of any secretary. And where anything important and good occurs to you, insist on it independently, and, my life upon it, the President will back you. Bate not your breath for ministers. Your tenure is as good and strong as theirs. They will know it, and you will be the more respected and appreciated by them, if they are as smart as they ought to be.

Your friend,

ORLANDO BROWN, Esq.   J. J. CRITTENDEN.

(R. P. Letcher to J. J. Crittenden.)

WASHINGTON CITY, November 17, 1849.

DEAR CRITTENDEN,—This letter is headed, as you perceive, with a word calculated to inspire the expectation that something of much interest is to be communicated. Not exactly so, —but as yet I know not *what* I may say, what guesses I may make, what apprehensions I may express in regard to the present and the future. Things are terribly amiss, out of sorts, out of joint, in this quarter. There will be a change in the cabinet, sooner or later, to a dead certainty! I can't cheat myself in this matter, though I have tried to do so.

Clayton is in great trouble, poor fellow. I am truly distressed for him. I have seen but little of him for five or six days. The truth is, it gave me pain to see him, and as I had not the heart or courage, without being specially invited to do so, to say all I felt, all I thought, and all I know, I purposely kept away, merely telling him when he needed a *doctor* to send for me. I scarcely know how to begin to tell you the whole story, and, in fact, it would be too tedious and laborious to attempt a narrative in detail. His misfortune is, that every man in the cabinet *wants him out.* These letters, which you see published in the *Herald*, telling the secrets of the administration and foreshadowing its policy, have rekindled a flame which had been almost extinguished to the highest point. For the last twenty-four hours, without saying a word to any human being *but two* of the cabinet, my efforts have been directed to prevent (right in the face of Congress) an open rupture—a ruinous rupture. All I hoped to accomplish was to endeavor to inspire prudence in action and wise forbearance. Possibly I may have had some slight agency in pouring a little oil upon the troubled waters; but the storm is bound to come, it is only a question of *mode* and *time*. My opinion in regard to Mr. Clayton's holding on to his place has totally changed since I got here. His position is such that it is altogether impossible for him to be useful to the administration. There is no mistake, no doubt, about it whatever, and if he gives me half a chance I mean to tell him what I think, as sincerely as I would tell you or my brother, under similar circumstances. Clayton don't know, don't see, the abyss before him! General Taylor has said nothing as yet,—in truth, is unacquainted with all the facts connected with the case, but they *mean* to tell him. They charge and say *that they can prove* that Mr. C. made that clerk write the communication which you saw in the *Republic* denying the authenticity of his *Herald* letter. Well, as I said to one of the party (very much excited), "suppose he did. What of it? Had he not a perfect right to call upon any man who had slandered him and ask him to do him justice?" But say they, "This letter that rascal wrote was by the knowledge and with the consent, and even by the request, of Mr. C., and *this* we can *prove*." I don't believe that! What is to occur, and when it may occur, the Lord only knows. All I say is, that something will occur before long. I would not be surprised if it happens in two hours. I will use every effort within my power to see that what is done shall be done decently and in order. I was consulted with for two nights past, until two o'clock in the morning, in case of a vacancy in the State Department, as to *who* ought to be the appointee. My opinion was given just as truly and candidly as if upon oath, and you are at no loss to understand what that opinion is, though your wife would like me none the better for it. I think I may venture to say from what I know and from what I learned from one of the distinguished parties concerned, that the whole of the cabinet would *pull together* upon this point. I give you this gentle hint that you may think about it, and if the contingency arises, don't *refuse* till you see me. I don't know when I can get away. I am in a whirlpool; perhaps I may be here ten days. I am most sincerely damned impatient to get away,—not meaning to *swear* in your presence. I am unhappy in my mind. The cabinet are now in session. I trust they may break up in harmony. I have not had a good night's sleep since I got here. The hours for *close chat* in this city are from eleven to two at night. *That* don't suit me. There are many reports on the street of the resignation of the cabinet; none of which are true. Nobody wishes to resign, unless it be Clayton. More to-morrow.

Hastily, but sincerely, your friend,

R. P. LETCHER.

(Extract from Governor Crittenden's Message to the Legislature of Kentucky, December 31, 1849.)

The preceding remarks have been confined to the domestic affairs of our own State; but as nothing that concerns the *Union* can be alien to us, I am unwilling to close this communication without some reference to our relations and duties to the Constitution and government of the United States. This seems to be made more imperatively my duty by the deplorable agitation and political excitements which have recently been but too manifest in the proceedings of one branch of Congress, and which, if they do not threaten and endanger the tranquillity and integrity of the *Union*, have excited solicitude for its safety. The Constitution of the United States was made by the whole people, and no compact among men was ever made with more deliberate solemnity. Inviolable respect and obedience to that highest law of the people, in all its consequences, is the bounden duty of all. While it confirms all our State institutions, it unites us for national purposes as one people, one GREAT REPUBLIC. It is in that *Union* alone that we exist as a *nation* and have our bond of brotherhood. From it, as from a rich fountain, public prosperity has streamed over our whole land, and from the base of our great national republic a spirit has gone forth throughout the world to quicken and raise up the oppressed, to teach them a new lesson of freedom, and, by pointing to our example, show them the way to self-government. The heart of man must swell with conscious pride at being the free citizen of such a republic. Dear as Kentucky is to us, she is not our whole country. The Union, the whole Union, is our country; and proud as we justly are of the name of *Kentuckian*, we have a loftier and more far-famed title—that of *American citizen*,—a name known and respected throughout the world, and which, wherever we may be, has power to protect us from the despotism of emperor or king.

As a party to the Constitution, Kentucky, interchangeably with the other States, pledged herself to abide by and support that Constitution and the Union which it established. If that pledge were her only obligation, it ought to be inviolable. But the seal of Washington stamped upon it, the thousand glorious recollections associated with its origin, the benefits and blessings it has conferred, the grander hopes it now inspires, have day by day increased our attachment, until the mere sense of plighted faith and allegiance is lost in proud, grateful, and affectionate devotion. I can entertain no apprehension for the fate of such a Union. The approach of any danger to it would be the signal for rallying to its defense,—the first moment of its peril would be the moment of its rescue. I persuade myself that there will be found in Congress, on the exciting subject which has given rise to the late agitation and alarm, a *wise forbearance and a wise patience*, that will secure us from danger; and that the very men who, in the heat and contention of debate, have spoken most boldly the language of defiance and menace to the Union, will not be hindmost in making sacrifices for its preservation. The Union has further security in the parental care and guardianship of its present illustrious chief magistrate; and far above all other securities, it has the all-powerful public opinion and affections of the people.

To Kentucky and the other Western States in the Valley of the Mississippi, the Union is indispensable to their commercial interests. They occupy the most fertile region of the world, eloquently described by a celebrated foreigner as "the most magnificent abode that the Almighty ever prepared as a dwelling-place for man." These States, already populous and productive, are rapidly increasing, and in no long time must become the most populous and productive portion of the United States. They are remote from the sea, and to enable them with any advantage to dispose of their boundless production and purchase their supplies, they will require the use of all the channels and avenues of commerce, and of all the markets, ports, and harbors from Boston to New Orleans. Under our present *Union* we enjoy all these facilities, with the further advantage of a maritime force capable to protect, and actually protecting, our commerce in every part of the world. Disunion would deprive us, certainly, to some extent, and most probably to a great extent, of those advantages and of that protection. I cannot enlarge on the subject. A moment's reflection will show the ruinous consequences of disunion to the commerce of Kentucky and the other Western States. The most obvious considerations of interest combine, therefore, with all that are nobler and more generous, to make the Union not only an object of attachment, but of necessity to us. Kentucky is not insensible to the causes which have produced so much sensibility and irritation with her brethren of the Southern States, nor is she without her sympathies with them. But she does not permit herself to harbor one thought against the Union. She deprecates disunion as the greatest calamity; she can see NO REMEDY in it,—none, certainly, for any grievance as yet complained of or to be apprehended. Kentucky will stand by and abide by the Union to the last, and she will hope that the same kind Providence that enabled our fathers to make it, will enable us to preserve it. Our whole history has taught us a consoling confidence in that Providence. It becomes us, as a people, to acknowledge with gratitude and thankfulness the many signal proofs we have received of divine goodness, and to invoke the Great Ruler of events for a continuation of his favor, humbly acknowledging that without his aid the labors of man are but vain.

J. J. CRITTENDEN.

December 31, 1849.

(R. P. Letcher to J. J. Crittenden.)
WASHINGTON, November 26, 1849.

DEAR CRITTENDEN,—Things look better upon the surface for the last few days; the elements are in much less commotion; and it may be that the storm indicated will pass away for the present. But it will come, I fear, certain and sure some day. The message is made up. It was finished last night, but may possibly undergo some little pruning. I have not seen but will probably be asked to hear it read, and invited to make such commentaries as I think proper. It was intimated that the general *might probably* desire *this*. No news. Breck got here last night on his way North. *Benton* is here. I had quite an agreeable and satisfactory chat with him this morning. He said, "Sir, you must not go away until the meeting of Congress." I was utterly opposed to staying so long, and am so still. General Taylor *looks well, acts well*, and Judge Breck called to see him, and was perfectly charmed. He says "all hell can't *beat him* in the next race." Orlando is mighty busy with his Indians. I have hardly seen him for four or five days.

Your friend,

Hon. J. J. CRITTENDEN.   R. P. LETCHER.

(J. J. Crittenden to O. Brown.)
FRANKFORT, January 14, 1850.

DEAR ORLANDO,—It has been so long since I received a letter from, or written one to, you that I hardly know where or how to recommence our correspondence. I suppose I must, as the lawyers say, begin *de novo*.

I have read about two columns of your official report about your red brethren, and expect to read the residue at the first leisure moment. I congratulate you on the many compliments it has received from the public, and I now especially congratulate you on your deserving all those compliments.

Old Zack's message is characteristic. It is marked with a noble resolution and simplicity that must commend it to every sound head and heart in the nation, and its whole matter and manner make it a model and monument.

The reports of the Hon. Secretaries are excellent, and such as ought to bring honor and strength to the administration.

I must say, however, that I differ from our friend the Secretary of War on two points of his report—namely, the *mode* of increasing the army, and the *exclusive* employment of the topographical corps in superintending all the works of improvement for which Congress may make appropriations.

As to the first, I should have preferred the raising of *new regiments* to any extent that increase of the army was necessary, thereby preserving the old policy of keeping our little army in such a *form* as to admit of great expansion in time of need under its old and experienced officers. The officers of our army may be considered as reduced in force and number by all those who are now, and who must be, stationed anywhere on the coast of the Pacific, for they are so remote as to be incapable of any co-operation with our forces on the Atlantic. I think, therefore, that the old policy ought to have been adhered to. And with me, it would have been a recommendation of this course that it would have afforded the President the opportunity of giving military appointments to some of the gallant fellows among our volunteers and temporary troops who distinguished themselves in the Mexican war.

My objection on the other point seems to me to be still stronger. Why give to the "topographical corps" *by law the exclusive* or *any exclusive* direction and superintendency of the public works of improvement?

Why not leave the President and his cabinet to make, according to their discretion, selections of proper superintendents? The administration must at last be responsible for the due execution of the works, and it seems to me that the choice of the agents to be employed is a part of their proper duty and patronage, and ought not to be surrendered. I see no propriety requiring such self-denying ordinances. Some of those works would require the science of the topographical corps, and then the President would employ them as a matter of course. But in other works, such as clearing out our rivers, this *science* would not be necessary, and the President should be left free to choose competent employés among his friends who did not already enjoy the benefit of public office.

I am opposed to this *monopoly* of the topographical corps for reasons public and private, general and particular. Such a monopoly would confer the *means* of great political influence, and opportunities for exercising it. How far officers of that corps might be disposed to use that influence I do not know.

But should any of them be disposed to use it, the greater probability is that it would be used against the administration, as probably every officer of that corps has received his commission from its political opponents. I by no means intend any disparagement of that corps, but am arguing only from general and natural causes. Now, though I do not desire to see any of the President's appointees playing the part of partisans, or appointed for any such purpose, I would not, on the other hand, have him and Mr. Crawford voluntarily surrendering the power of appointing their friends, and voluntarily exposing themselves to the inimical influences of those who may be their enemies. I say, therefore, that I do not see the justice or policy of giving to the topographical corps, in this instance, the *exclusive legal preference* which the secretary's report seems to concede them. I am not very conversant about such matters, and may not understand correctly the extent and import of that report, but, as I do understand it, it would exclude our friend Russell, and cut him off from any competition for the superintendency he formerly had over our river improvements. Pray let me know if that would be its effect, and if so, intercede with our friend Crawford, and tell him that Russell understands the navigation of our rivers better, and knows better how to improve it, and especially how to remove snags, than all his topographical corps together; and furthermore, that all they could do would be criticised and complained of, while all that he would do, even though not quite so well done, would, from a fellow-feeling, be praised by his fellow-boatmen. Attend to this matter, and do all that is possible to secure Russell in his expectations and hopes of being restored to his old office and employment.

Our legislature, as you know, is now in session, with nothing very interesting as yet before them, unless it be the various resolutions that are occasionally exploded concerning you Washington people and Federal affairs, disunion, slavery, etc. All these will no doubt be eventually reduced to the standard of a sound discretion and a sound patriotism. There is evidently among the members of the legislature a good deal of dissatisfaction with the late convention and the constitution they have proposed to the people. Yet it remains doubtful whether any serious opposition will be made to its adoption. I am led to believe that it would not be difficult to raise an opposition that would be very formidable, if not fatal, to the new constitution.

Our little town is very quiet, and stands just where it did and as it did when you left us. It is at this time covered with one of the deepest snows I have seen for a long time. It has been snowing for about eighteen hours. Letcher, you know, has left us, and has left a sort of darkness behind him, which we cannot entirely dissipate.

I see that my old friend Cass is threatening him in the Senate, and rebuking the love of office. That is well. The old gentleman, as is very natural, having been surfeited with office, wonders that anybody can have any appetite for it. I hope there can be no danger of Letcher's rejection.

The two most important events of the last month were fights between David Humphreys and Philip Swigert and between Cates and Hodges; pretty well matched in both cases, and no damage done. Both, indeed, have resulted fortunately; the first led to a prompt settlement of an old quarrel, the compromise of an old lawsuit, and the reconciliation of the parties; in the other, the affair has been so far arranged that the parties when they meet are to meet as friends, and peace is established again throughout our borders.

And now, unless this long letter should be considered as a grievance and drive you into a dissolution of our Union, I shall expect a very long answer, for you can tell a great deal that I want to hear.

How do you and old Zack get along together, and how does the old general bear himself amidst the storm of opposition in Congress? Who have you become acquainted with among the members of Congress? Are Toombs and Stephens among the number? How comes on the cabinet generally and in the particular, etc.?

But first in order and above all these mere public concerns, how is your household? Do you intermeddle much in politics? How is Burnley, who has not written to me since we parted?

Your friend,

Orlando Brown, Esq. J. J. Crittenden.

(R. P. Letcher to J. J. Crittenden.)

Norfolk, Sept. 6, 1850.

Dear Crittenden,—*Here* I am, and here I have been for seven long days, waiting, in the first place, to have Tom Corwin's canoe repaired, and in the second place, for more favorable winds. It is hoped we may embark to-morrow, but the Lord only knows how this may be. It would take a man of your amiable disposition to bear with Christian meekness and patience all I have borne since I left home. I have not been quite equal to it, and you know well that, next to yourself, I am decidedly the best-natured fellow living. I was forced to leave Washington without having the pleasure of an interview with the President. I regret it exceedingly. I was anxious to hold a confidential chat with him on two or three matters of much interest. But, to rid myself of the constant, eternal, and ungodly *importunities* of some folks who were always at my heels dogging me, I felt ready to jump into the raging sea to get out of their reach. I shall use every exertion to accomplish the object of my mission, but I must tell you my hopes of success are by no means as strong as I could wish. Mexican affairs are in the most terrible disorder. My advices from that quarter are full. I wanted to see you before I left, but you were too happy in the mountains to tear yourself away. I wrote to Bob Crittenden, if he were not profitably employed, and could contrive to have his expenses paid to Mexico, *to call over there* in a month or so. For the sake of the Lord, the Virgin Mary, and all the saints, write to me. A poor man in Mexico feels unhappy in his mind without letters. Be kind enough to offer my warmest regard to the President, and tell him if it be in the power of mortal man to accomplish the objects he has so much at heart in Mexico, I intend to do that thing.

Your sincere friend,
R. P. LETCHER.

(R. P. Letcher to J. J. Crittenden.)

MEXICO, Feb. 5, 1850.

DEAR CRITTENDEN,—Here I am in this great *bell-ringing city*, and hardly know how to employ myself. Calls upon calls, of a civil and business character, have worried me down to such a degree that I have refused to see anybody else this blessed saint's day. I can't write, I can't read, I *won't think*, and I can't sleep. In this state of half existence I will make a poor attempt to write you a sort of a letter, but it seems like writing to a man in the moon. I hope you won't see it, and lest you should, I sha'n't tell you how I feel in this ungodly city. You would laugh me to death, should we ever meet again, if I were to tell you the *half* of what I have experienced since I was fool enough to leave home. All I am willing to confess is this, if any man wants to know exactly how well he loves his wife, his friends, his country, and *the town of Frankfort in particular*, let him take a sea voyage over the renowned Gulf of Mexico, and then over the mountains in a stage with eight mules, and sometimes ten, in the team, running ten miles an hour *at that*. Then let him be called the *American minister*, let him be worried day and night by distressed, moneyless claimants, and if he is not brought to a knowledge of the truth by this process I should pronounce him an original fool. There have been more falsehoods told about this city, in some respects, than about all the rest of God's globe. The city and the surrounding country is beautiful ; the valley of Puebla is also a delightful country :

but such a poor, wretched, miserable people are nowhere to be found upon the face of the earth; four-fifths of them, at least, are beasts of burden, and most of the residue are destitute of moral principle. No gentleman can live here for less than ten or twelve thousand a year; everything is dear; butter a dollar a pound. No article of diet cheap, except beans. I have seen but few of the great men. My audience takes place day after to-morrow. Between ourselves, *in confidence*, I must get away from here soon. I wrote to Clayton a private note, to obtain leave of absence for me in May. I want you to write him a line to the same effect. If I am not hemmed in by the vomito and yellow fever, I wish to go home for my family, even if I *must come back.* I won't go away if the interest of the country is to suffer by it; but it won't suffer. I don't know where I shall go,—one thing is certain, I don't mean to lay out all my salary in chickens and butter, *that's a fixed fact!* I think you might make a speculation in those articles if you would bring on a cargo. You will never know during your natural life anything about the charms of home until you take a trip to Mexico,—so just come over here and learn *wisdom.* I am the smartest man now living in the whole world, and " *no mistake."* But I have suffered terribly in obtaining such a valuable education. I haven't heard one word from home since I left. If you are a Christian man, write to me. There are at least one hundred and fifty bells now ringing, and have been ever since four o'clock this morning. I don't know the name of the saint who causes all the fuss.

Your friend,
R. P. LETCHER.

Hon. J. J. CRITTENDEN.

(R. P. Letcher to J. J. Crittenden.)

MEXICO, March 4, 1850.

DEAR GOVERNOR,—Mr. Walsh, my secretary of legation, will hand you this line of introduction; he will spend a few days in Frankfort to ascertain if all his lands in Kentucky have been fully administered upon. Mr. Wickliffe, he tells me, was his executor. My private belief is that he won't find very much left after his executor is paid and satisfied. Mr. Walsh is on his way East; his health is bad, and spirits worse. I thought it just to let him go. I care nothing about work in this country. In fact, it is my only recreation. I want to get off from here in May. It is better *for effect* that I should be absent three or four months. Not one syllable have I received from Kentucky since the blessed hour I left. Now make the calculation! How much is it worth—in other words, what would you take—to cross the Gulf in a great *square trough*, and then travel three hundred miles by land in a small stage, be three thousand miles from home, and remain three months without hearing one word? Will you take all my salary? If yes, then it's a bargain; but you must pay *charges*. *One charge*, to bring my carriage from Vera Cruz, two hundred and fifty dollars *"right smack bang!"* bringing horses, seventy-seven dollars,—that's cheap. I don't complain about *bills;* not at all, but give you a few items in case you wish to take the bargain. I wish I was a doctor, and could be called in to a few cases in this country; somebody would suffer. Don't ask me how I look, how I feel, or what I think. Take it for granted I look wise. I send you a small pitcher dug out of the ruins of this place; no doubt of its antiquity. I am determined to curtail every possible expense within my power. To come here and be miserable, and make nothing, would be a hard case. "*No, sirree*," you don't catch a weasel asleep. I am *robbed* a little bit every day; but they sha'n't rob me of all my salary. If my horses turn out well I expect to get eighteen hundred for them. If I can get away upon a leave of absence for four months, I *guess* I could save *right smartly*.

Ah! my dear fellow, I thank you—I thank you for your letter of the 24th of January,—the first tidings from home since my arrival in this distant region. Your letter was handed to me just as I was about to sit down to dinner; it was twilight. I sprang from the table and ran out to the door to get light enough to read it. Oh, you have no sort of conception of the excessive delight I experienced on reading it! I had made up my figures this morning that in *nine days*, if I heard nothing from home, I should be a *maniac* to a dead and everlasting certainty. Your letter and one from my wife, received at the same moment, have saved me from that terrible misfortune. And what a rascally letter it is, *after all!* I don't see how it had the impudence to travel in company with my wife's letter. Her letter told me of her gloom, melancholy, despondency, and misery in consequence of my absence. Yours tells me of her *gayety*, cheerfulness, happiness, and good looks by reason of the same thing. What a contrast!

But I won't quarrel with you, *nohow*, I was so rejoiced to hear once more from old Kentucky. No time to finish my letter; my boy Sam will be off in a few minutes.

Your friend,
R. P. LETCHER.

(J. J. Crittenden to Governor Thomas Metcalf.)

FRANKFORT, March 25, 1850.

MY DEAR SIR,—I have received and perused with great concern your letter of yesterday, and hasten to relieve your feelings and my own as far as I can by an immediate reply. You do me but justice in supposing me incapable of betraying or deceiving so old a friend as yourself. I am, indeed, incapable of deceiving any man intentionally, and my nature would revolt from the betrayal of one whose friendship I have valued and cherished so long as I have yours. For our friend Orlando Brown I would answer as for myself. It was during the last fall that, at your written request, I addressed a letter to the Secretary of War recommending your grandson, young Campbell, for appointment as one of the cadets at West Point. You were anxious for his appointment, and I felt a sincere pleasure in contributing all I could to your gratification. I accordingly recommended him zealously, and urged his appointment not only on account of his own qualifications but on account of his hereditary claims and the great consideration that was due to you, your wishes, and your *public services*. A prompt acknowledgment of that letter was received from the War Department, which I made known to you. I do not remember whether, when I wrote that letter, I was apprised that there was or was about to be a vacancy for a cadet from your district; nor do I recollect whether I recommended your grandson in general terms as a person that ought to be appointed, or specifically for a district appointment or one of the presidential appointments. In all this I was no doubt guided by your letter requesting my recommendation. I will write immediately for a copy of my letter, and will send it to you that you may see how earnestly I recommended your grandson. Some time after all this a friend stepped into my office (then *generally thronged*) and requested me to write a recommendation of a young Mr. Lashbrook for a cadet appointment. Upon his representation I did so, and without the least thought or apprehension that he and your grandson were seeking the same place or that there was any competition between them. Had such a thought ever crossed my mind, I should never have recommended young Lashbrook. No consideration would have induced me knowingly to recommend any one in opposition to your grandson; besides, I had no motive to do so disreputable a thing. I had no personal knowledge of young Lashbrook and was under no special obligation to his father. My letter in his son's behalf passed at once from my mind, and would probably never again have been remembered but for your late letter and the untoward circumstances that now recall it to my recollection.

The whole case, I suppose, is this : I have inadvertently given a letter in favor of young Lashbrook and produced an effect that I never contemplated.   It is as though I had shot an arrow which, missing the mark it was aimed at, wounded a friend, an old and valued friend.   I regret it most deeply; nor can that regret be altogether removed by my confidence that you will not attribute what has happened to any design or ill intention on my part.   There will still remain the regret of having fallen into a blunder.   I am not willing to make the painful addition to that regret of supposing that my letter in favor of Lashbrook was the cause of his being preferred to your grandson, for there was also my more earnest letter in favor of your grandson. But I will say no more on this most unpleasant subject, and can but hope that my explanation will be satisfactory to you. It will gratify me to receive a line from you as soon as your convenience will permit,—my feelings are much disturbed by this matter.

Your friend, etc.,

Governor Thomas Metcalf.   J. J. Crittenden.

CHAPTER XXVIII

Letter of Charles S. Morehead—R. Toombs to Crittenden—Letters of Crittenden to Letcher.

(C. S. Morehead to J. J. Crittenden.)

WASHINGTON, March 30, 1850.

MY DEAR SIR,—I received your letter of the 19th inst., for which I am very much obliged to you. All that is done here is so fully detailed in the daily papers that I need not attempt to give you an account of it. We are proceeding slowly with the debate on the absorbing topic growing out of our territorial acquisitions. I begin to believe that the whole question will be satisfactorily settled by admitting California as a State and making territorial governments for the residue of the country without the *proviso*. I regret, however, to state that we can hope for very little, if any, aid from the Whigs of the North in the House. I do not know one man that we can certainly count. There were eight or ten who promised to go with us, but I have reason to believe that the cabinet influence has drawn them off. Ewing and Meredith have evidently much feeling on the subject. Clayton, Crawford, Preston, and Johnson, I understand, will go for territorial bills. It is understood that General Taylor himself would be glad if such bills can be passed without the proviso, and would prefer such a settlement to the *non-action* policy. I cannot, however, speak from any personal knowledge on this subject. I have no doubt, however, as to the four members of the cabinet I have named. Indeed, it is indispensably necessary that it should be settled on this basis. There is not one single man from any slaveholding State who would agree to any other settlement, and I fear the very worst consequences from any attempt to force through the California bill without a full settlement. Fifty members, under our rules, can prevent the bill from being reported from the committee of the whole, where it now is, to the House. But I believe we have a decided majority for such a settlement as the South demands. There are twenty-nine Democrats from the North pledged to go with us. McClernand, from Illinois, has prepared a bill upon general but private consultation, embracing all the points of difference, and will offer it as a substitute, in a few days, to the California bill. If General Taylor would take open ground for a full settlement, we could get ten or twelve Whigs from the North. I believe he only wants a suitable occasion to do so. I never have in my life had so deep and abiding a conviction upon any subject as at this moment of the absolute necessity of a settlement of this whole question. I am pained to say that I fear that there are some Southern men who do not wish a settlement. We have certainly something to fear from this source, but they are so few that I think we can do without them.

The cabinet, as you might well imagine from the present state of things, receives no support from any quarter. John Tyler had a corporal's guard who defended him manfully, but the cabinet has not *one* man that I can now name. Each member of the cabinet has a few friends, but I do not know one man who can be called the friend of the cabinet. I apprehend that they are not even friendly to each other. You may have noticed in the *Union*, if you ever read it, a charge against Ewing for having allowed a very large claim in which Crawford was interested personally to the extent of one hundred and seventeen thousand dollars. It turned out that Mr. Ewing had nothing to do with it; that Whittlesey reported that there was nothing due, and Meredith, in accordance with the opinion of the Attorney-General, allowed it. Now, Ewing, if I am not mistaken (but conjecture on my part, I acknowledge), through his friends is attacking Crawford for having a claim acted on in which he was interested while a member of the cabinet. Upon the whole, I am clearly of opinion that there is but one safe course for General Taylor to pursue, and that is to reconstruct his whole cabinet. I am perfectly satisfied that he cannot carry on the government with his present ministers. Your name and that of Winthrop and of Webster have been spoken of as Secretary of State in the event of a change; but if I had to make a full cabinet I could not do it satisfactorily to myself. I am inclined to think that Mr. Webster would like to be Secretary of State, not from anything I ever heard him say but from occasional remote intimations from his friends. Just at this time his appointment would be exceedingly popular in the South. I wish most sincerely that you were here. We are altogether in a sad, sad condition. There is no good feeling between Mr. Clay and General Taylor, and I am afraid that meddling and busybodies are daily widening the breach. I keep entirely aloof, taking especial and particular pains to participate in no manner whatever in the feeling on the one side or the other. I hear all, at least on one side, and try always to reconcile rather than widen the breach. I have sometimes, however, thought that a want of confidence in me resulted from the fact of my being his immediate representative. I may be mistaken—probably am; it may arise altogether from a less flattering consideration. At all events, I have never been able to converse *one minute* with the President upon politics without his changing the subject, so that when I see him now I never, in the remotest manner, allude to political matters.

March 31st. Not finishing my letter last night, I have to add this morning the news, which you will no doubt hear long before this reaches you, of Mr. Calhoun's death. He died this morning at eight o'clock. I do not yet clearly see what effect his death is to have on political events. He was firmly and, I suppose, honestly persuaded that the Union ought to be dissolved. I understand that he has prepared a paper showing that the only salvation of the South is by disunion. It is said to be a very strong and dangerous argument, placing the whole matter upon the ground that there can be no security for our property by any other possible or attainable means, and that the South has all the elements of unbounded prosperity without the Union; while with it it is fast assuming a mere provincial character, impoverishing itself to aggrandize the North. I do not, of course, know that this rumor is true, but I believe it is. This was the purport of a conversation he held with Mr. Toombs a few days ago. He told him he would not live this session out, and that he must leave to younger men the task of carrying out his views. A pamphlet has recently been published in Virginia calculated to do much mischief. It is an argument for disunion with an array of pretended facts, which, if true, or if not shown to be unfounded, I think would produce a very great effect. Mr. Clay told me that he thought it the most dangerous pamphlet he ever read.

Our Northern friends are blind, absolutely blind, to the real dangers by which we are surrounded. They don't want to believe that there is any danger, and in general they treat the whole matter as mere bravado and as scarcely worth notice. I concur this far with them, that it is *utterly impossible* formally to dissolve this Union, and it never will be dissolved by any convention or by any declaration of independence. The dissolution must precede these things if it ever does take place. The fear I entertain is of the establishment of mere sectional parties, and the commencement of a system of retaliatory local or State legislation. You may have seen that this has been already recommended by the governor of Virginia. If the slave question should not be settled, there is scarcely a Southern State that will not pass laws to prevent the sale of Northern products by retail in its limits. The decision of the Supreme Court, in the case of Brown *vs.* Maryland, declaring the unconstitutionality of taxing the imports of another State, contains some dictum of the right of a State to tax such imports after they have become incorporated with the property of the State. The whole proceeding would doubtless be a violation of the spirit, if not the letter, of the Constitution. But what is it that men will not do when smarting under real or imaginary grievances? You may think that I am inclined to be gloomy, but I do most solemnly believe that disunion will ensue, and that more speedily than any man now has any idea of, if there should be a failure of an amicable settlement. You cannot be surprised, then, that my whole heart and soul are engaged in the effort to bring this about. I feel as you do about the Union, as I know that Kentucky does, and it *must* be preserved at the sacrifice of all past party ties. I am perfectly sure, from the most mature and calm consideration, that there is but one way of doing this. The North must give up its apparently determined purpose of making this general government assume an attitude of hostility to slavery. We cannot prevent individual agitation and fanaticism, but I think we have the undoubted right to ask that a common government shall not, in its action, become hostile to the property of a large portion of its own citizens.

Mr. Clay sent for old Mr. Ritchie, and had a long and confidential conversation with him upon this subject. The tone of the *Union* is evidently changed since that time. You may have noticed that he speaks much oftener in favor of union than he did. This is not generally known, and of course I do not wish it spoken of as coming from me. I have written you a long letter, which may occupy some of your dull moments at Frankfort. I wrote to your new Secretary of State some time ago, which he has never answered. I hope in the enjoyment of his new honors he has not forgotten his old friends.

I remain very truly and sincerely your friend,
C. S. MOREHEAD.

(R. Toombs to J. J. Crittenden.)

WASHINGTON, April 25, 1850.

DEAR CRITTENDEN,—I have been thinking for several months that I would write to you, but as I did not wish to annoy you with disagreeable intelligence, I deferred it, hoping that events would open up a better prospect for the future. That expectation has not yet been realized. "It were a tale too long" to detail all the blunders of the cabinet, which have brought the Whig party to the brink of ruin; but of the special question upon which their policy has nearly estranged the whole Whig party of the South it is proper to give you some brief hints, that you may understand our position. During the last summer, the government, with the consent of the whole cabinet, except Crawford, threw the *entire patronage* of the North into the hands of Seward and his party. This was done under some *foolish idea* of Preston's, that they would get rid of a Northern competition for 1852, as Seward stood for 1856. The effect of this was to enable Seward to take the entire control of the New York organization, and force the whole Northern Whig party into the extreme anti-slavery position of Seward, which, *of course*, sacked the South. I knew the effect of this policy would certainly destroy the Whig party, and perhaps endanger the Union. When I came to Washington, I found the whole Whig party expecting to pass the proviso, and that Taylor would *not veto it*, that thereby the Whig party of the North were to be built up at the expense of the Northern Democracy, who, from political and party considerations, had stood *quasi* opposed to the proviso. I saw General Taylor, and talked fully with him, and while he stated he had given and *would give* no pledges either way about the proviso, he gave me *clearly* to understand that if it was passed he would sign it. My course became instantly fixed. I would not hesitate to oppose the *proviso*, even to the extent of a dissolution of the Union. I could not for a moment regard any party considerations on the treatment of the question. I therefore determined to put the test to the Whig party and abandon its organization upon its refusal. Both events happened to defeat this policy; it was of the first importance to prevent the organization of the House going into the hands of the Northern Whig party. I should have gone to any extent to effect that object,—they foolishly did it themselves. Without fatiguing you with details, my whole subsequent course has been governed by this line of policy. I have determined to settle the question honorably to my own section of country, *if possible*, at any and every hazard, *totally* indifferent to what might be its effect upon General Taylor or his administration. In the course of events, the policy of the cabinet has vacillated *to* and *fro*, but has finally settled upon the ground of admitting California, and *non-action* as to the rest of the territories. Seward and his party have struck hands with them on this policy, but Stanly is the only Southern Whig who will stand by them. I think it likely the course of events may throw the whole of the Southern Whigs into opposition,—such a result will not deter us from our course. We are willing to admit California and pass territorial governments on the principle of McClernand's bill; we will never take less. The government, in furtherance of their stupid and treacherous bargain with the North, are endeavoring to defeat it; with their aid we could carry it, as more than twenty-five Northern Democrats are pledged to it. They may embarrass us, possibly may defeat us, but our defeat will be their ruin. The cabinet have intense hostility to Mr. Clay, and I think it likely *we*, and the country, will be greatly benefited by the feud, inasmuch as it makes Clay the more anxious to conform to the interests of his own section and of the Southern Whigs, and this the rather because the government has the whip hand of him (through Seward) with the Northern Whigs. The Senate's committee will, I think, agree upon propositions which will pass; this can only be defeated by the want of common sense and common prudence on the part of Mason, Butler, and others of that "*ilk*" in both houses of Congress, and the efforts of the *administration.* But as to the latter it is but candid to say that they have little power, either for good or evil. For some reason, wholly unaccountable to me, the Northern members of the cabinet are universally *odious*, even to the Northern Whigs. Clayton is a dead body tied to the concern. Johnson is honorable and clever, but without wisdom. Preston is speculative, and, what is worse, has no sentiment in common with the section which he represents. Crawford alone is true and faithful to the honor and interest of our section, and the late scene about the Galphin claim is an effort of men in the service of government to drive him out. He is the last link that binds a majority of the Southern Whigs to the government, and I have no doubt but they will soon make it inconsistent with his own honor to remain there. I have thus given you a brief outline of men and parties in the government. I have said nothing of General Taylor; my opinion is that he is an honest, well-meaning man, but that he is in very bad hands, and his inexperience in public affairs, and want of knowledge of men, is daily practiced upon, and renders him peculiarly liable to imposition. I think there has been a studied effort to alienate him from his original friends, and that it has been eminently successful; time will show that he and not they will suffer most by that alienation. Morehead is now making a good speech at my back, and has perhaps, to some extent, destroyed the continuity of my narrative. Let me hear from you.

I am truly your friend,
R. TOOMBS.

(J. J. Crittenden to A. T. Burnley.)

FRANKFORT, April 29, 1850.

DEAR BURNLEY,—I reached home last night, and found a letter from our friend Orlando Brown, which explains somewhat the causes for which you have been called back to Washington. I trust that you will be able to reconcile all differences and difficulties, and give a right direction to things. It is important to the country, to the administration, and to the interests of the friends that are engaged in the *Republic*, to whom I am greatly attached.

From what I understand, it is a settled matter that the cabinet is to remain unchanged, and I think you will agree that but little good could be expected from any imaginable new cabinet that could be formed in the midst of the present tumult and discord in the political world, increased by the disruption of the present cabinet. What remains, then, for those who, though dissatisfied with the cabinet, are the friends of General Taylor and his cause, but to yield up that dissatisfaction, and for the sake of old Zack and his cause to go thoroughly to the work in their support? I would not have a gentleman for any consideration to concede his honor or his independence; but still, in public life, where the opinions and feelings of many must be consulted and conciliated, there is a necessity for many concessions. It is a false and unwise pride that would refuse these concessions where they relate to mere questions of expediency or opinion, and are necessary to that union and harmony without which nothing good or great can be accomplished in public affairs. Your own good sense and your generous feelings of attachment to General Taylor would have suggested to you all that I have or could say on this subject, and it is only out of my great solicitude that there should be no break between the President and the *Republic* that I have written at all. I trust you will do all you can to prevent any such break.

I shall feel great impatience and anxiety till I hear from you.

Your friend,
J. J. CRITTENDEN.

(J. J. Crittenden to Orlando Brown.)

FRANKFORT, April 30, 1850.

DEAR ORLANDO,—On my return, last Saturday, from Louisville, where I had been spending some days, I found your letter. I perused it with the most painful interest. My heart is troubled at the discord that seems to reign among our friends. Burnley will be in Washington when this reaches you, and with his good sense and his sincere devotion to General Taylor will be able to settle all difficulties about the *Republic*, and give to it a satisfactory and harmonious direction. The editors of that paper are the friends of General Taylor, and if his cabinet is not altogether what they could wish, they ought, for his sake and the sake of his cause, to waive all objections on that score. Concession among

friends is no sacrifice of independence.   The temper to do it is a
virtue, and indispensable to that co-operation that is necessary
to political success.   I do not, of course, mean that any man, for
any object, ought to surrender essential principles, or his honor;
but in this instance nothing of that sort can be involved.   The
utmost differences of the parties must consist of personal feelings, or disagreements in opinion about expediencies.   If even
an old Roman could say, and that, too, with continued approbation of about twenty centuries, that he had rather *err* with Cato,
etc., I think that we, his friends, one and all of us, ought to
give to General Taylor the full benefit of that sentiment, and
strengthen him thereby to bear the great responsibility we have
placed upon him.   Cato himself was not more just or illustrious
than General Taylor, nor ever rendered greater services to his
country.   When I read your account of that interview, in which
he uttered the indignant complaints extorted from him by con-
tumely and wrong, I felt, Orlando, that scene as you did, when
you so nobly described it,—my heart burned within me.   It is
not with such a man, so situated, that friends ought to stand
upon niceties, or be backward in their services.   The men of
the *Republic* will not, I am certain.   They are men of the right
grit, and I assure myself that all will be amicably arranged and
settled with them.   The course pursued in Congress towards
General Taylor and his cabinet will, I think, react in their favor,
and out of the very difficulties that surround him he will triumph,
as he has triumphed before.   This is my hope and my faith.
The committees intended to persecute and destroy, will
strengthen and preserve, the cabinet, and the slavery question
settled, the friends that it has dispersed will return to the
standard of old Zack.

I am sorry that you intend to resign your office so soon.   I
am satisfied that you are useful to General Taylor, and that
your leaving Washington will deprive him of a great comfort.
There must be something soothing in escaping occasionally
from the stated and formal consultations of the cabinet and in-
dulging in the free and irresponsible intercourse and conversation of a trusted friend.   Who is to succeed you when you
resign ?   Every one, I believe, feels some particular concern in
his successor, as though it were a sort of continuation of himself.   If you have not committed yourself otherwise, I should
be pleased to see Alexander McKee, the clerk of our county of
Garrard, succeed you.   You know him, I believe.   He is the
near relation of Colonel McKee, who fell at Buena Vista, a man
of business and a bold and ardent friend of General Taylor.   If
you are willing and will advise as to the time and course, he
will probably visit Washington and endeavor to obtain the

office. Let me hear from you on this subject. I think you will yet be offered the mission to Vienna, and that you ought not to decline so fine an opportunity of visiting the Old World.

It seems to me evident that the slavery question must now soon be settled, and that upon the basis of admitting California and establishing territorial governments without the Wilmot proviso. If this fails, great excitement and strife will be the consequence, and all will be charged, right or wrong, to the opposition of the administration to that plan. In the present state of things, I can see no inconsistency in the administration's supporting that plan. It is not in terms the plan recommended by the President, but it is the same in effect, and modified only by the circumstances that have since occurred. General Taylor's object was to avoid and suppress agitation by inaction, and by leaving the slavery question to be settled by the people of the respective territories ; but the temper of the times was not wise and forbearing enough to accept this pacific policy. To promote this policy, General Taylor was willing to forego what, under ordinary circumstances, would have been a duty, the establishment of territorial governments. But what has since happened, and what is now the altered state of the case? The agitation which he would have suppressed has taken place, and, instead of the forbearance recommended by him, a course of action has been taken which must lead to some positive settlement, or leave the subject in a much worse condition than it has ever been. Here, then, is a new case presented ; and it seems to me that the grand *object* exhibited in the President's recommendation will be accomplished by the admission of California and the establishment of territorial governments without the Wilmot proviso. The prime object was to avoid that proviso and its excitements by inaction ; but any course of action that gets rid of that proviso cannot be said to be inconsistent with the object in view. The only difference is in the means of attaining the same end, and that difference is the result of the altered state of the subject since the date of the President's message. In the attainment of so great an object as that in question, the peace and safety of the Union, it will, as it seems to me, be wise and magnanimous in the administration not to be tenacious of any particular plan, but to give its active aid and support to any plan that can effect the purpose. I want the plan that does settle the great question, whatever it may be, or whosesoever it may be, to have General Taylor's *Imprimatur* upon it.

I shall expect letters from you with impatience.

Your friend,

To O. BROWN. J. J. CRITTENDEN.

(R. P. Letcher to J. J. Crittenden.)

MEXICO, May 6, 1850.

DEAR CRITTENDEN,—Ah, my dear governor! not quite so fast. You have pulled trigger a little too quick. There is no discrepancy between my speech and my letters. What a man says in his official capacity is one thing, and what he has a right to say in his private capacity is quite another thing,—it's all "as straight as a gun-barrel." *I spoke for the United States*, and am in no way responsible for what I said as *an advocate;* mind, I *appeared as counsel.* I reserve my defense till my return. If Clayton is a tender-hearted man, he will give me leave to return in October. I could not go now if I had leave, because of the crowd of business,—because, also, of the vomito. I am surprised, disappointed, and mortified exceedingly to hear that you are all taking the rounds, eating and drinking just as merrily and as happily as if I were with you. It is too bad, really. Had the good ship Walker been cast away, sure enough I don't believe it would have made a single *swallow less*, particularly of the *liquids*, among the whole squad of you. What a prolific topic of reflection does this furnish to one of my tender sensibilities, whose vanity had prompted him to suppose his absence would make a *vacuum* in the social circle that time itself would hardly ever fill up! Nobody died of a broken heart, nobody shed a tear, nobody lost a meal, or even a drink,—in fact, *increased* their drinks when it was fully believed I was food for the sharks in the Gulf of Mexico; and if this *had been so*, by this time the whole matter would have been *utterly forgotten.* Well, all I can say is, my friends can stand trouble and loss better than any other man's friends *living.* A noble set of fellows they are! I am as *bad off* as Orlando Brown was in Washington, when he took it into his head that the Frankfort people were glad he had left, and asked me to tell him candidly how it was. I told him he was right, and the only fear was that he might possibly come home. I am not altogether happy in my mind, but I don't wish my rascally friends to know that, they might think it was on that account,—not a bit of it! My depression is owing to the deep interest I feel for my country. Write to me often, write me the longest sort of letters. The Prussian minister just called to take a last farewell. A noble fellow he is! It was quite a *tender scene.* I shall miss that man more than any human being in this city. I have had one of Bob's and Harry's hams boiled, and I eat it *twice a day*,—no eating three times a day in this country. Bankhead and his wife are here; they are more broken down than any couple I know. I am distressed to look at them.

Your friend,
R. P. LETCHER.

HON. J. J. CRITTENDEN.

(J. J. Crittenden to Orlando Brown.)

FRANKFORT, May 18, 1850.

MY DEAR SIR,—Your letter of the 9th inst. was duly received, and, by the telegraph, we already know that all you taught me to expect has come to pass. The *Republic* has changed hands, and Mr. Hall has succeeded the former editors. It is to be greatly regretted that there should be any motive or cause for such a movement. Not that Mr. Hall is not very competent and worthy, but the regret is that there should have been any disagreement between the retiring editors and the administration. I had hoped that Burnley's mediation might have reconciled all differences, and that our friend Bullitt's known attachment to the President would have made him forego all his objections to the cabinet. The extent of his objections I do not know, nor do I mean to blame him, for I am very certain that he has acted from honest convictions and motives. But I must say, at the same time, that for myself I am not sensible of any objections that require such an opposition to the cabinet. Indeed, I doubt very much whether General Taylor could select another cabinet of more ability, or character, or personal worth. But I do not mean to make comments on the subject. The storm that has just passed by will be followed, I hope, by that calm that usually compensates for its ravages; and I trust that we shall yet see the administration emerging successfully from the difficulties that now surround it.

I shall be delighted to see you at home, but this is overcome by the absolute sadness I feel at your quitting old Zack at such a time, when, perhaps, he most requires the comfort and assistance of your society and counsel. I received Robert's letter yesterday. You may tell him so, and his children and all are well. I have not another word to say about his affairs and solicitations at Washington. Under a *first impulse* I said and wrote much more than I ought. Hereafter he can only have my good wishes, and must depend on himself. I must not be mixed up with any office-seeking for my own family.

I have written to our friend Mr. Richard Hawes, apprising him of your views and wishes, and inquiring whether he would be willing, in the event of your resignation, to accept your present office. I have not yet received his answer, but I anticipate, from many conversations with him, that he will not accept it. If he will, he is the very man, and the man of my choice. Without much acquaintance with Mr. Alexander Mc-Kee, I had formed a kind opinion of him, and supposed, from information, that he was very much a man of business. In a conversation last winter, I mentioned that it was not expected by your friends that you would continue long in office, and suggested to him the vacancy as one that would very well suit him. But little more was then said on the subject, and nothing since has passed between us about it. I am told that he went through the place a few days ago, on his way to the East, but he did not call on me, and I know not his object. I have heard that his thoughts have been turned of late towards California, and an office at Washington may not now be desirable to him; and in the present uncertainty I have no more to say about it. He is not apprised of what I lately wrote to you in his behalf.

I wish that before you leave Washington you would especially take it upon yourself to have something clever done for our friend, Mr. George W. Barbour, a senator in our General Assembly from the Princeton district. You recollect him, I hope. He is a fine-looking, high-spirited, and noble-hearted fellow,—a lawyer by profession, and of fair capacity. He is poor, and too modest and proud to seek for office, though he wants it. He is an ardent and *thorough Taylor-man.* Now, what can be done for such a man? I have undertaken to be his intercessor, and have written in his behalf time and again to Clayton, and perhaps to others, but, so far, have not got even any answer relating to him. A chargé-ship to anywhere in South America would be very acceptable to him; so would a judgeship in any of our territorial governments, or the office of secretary in those governments. Now, this is a wide range; there are many offices in it, and mighty few such clever fellows anywhere as Barbour. The place that that fellow *Meeker* was slipped into, and ought to be slipped out of, would suit poor Barbour exactly, and he is worthy of it. I have told Barbour that he must be patient, and that I was certain something would, sooner or later, be done for him. It begins to be the " later," and nothing is yet done. The last alternative is to try and get you to make up this business and do something in it.

Your friend,

O. Brown, Esq.   J. J. Crittenden.

P.S.—I can do nothing more with Clayton in Barbour's case but quarrel with him, and that I don't want to do,—first, because he is a stout fellow and might whip me; secondly, I like the fellow.   J. J. C.

(J. J. Crittenden to Orlando Brown.)

Frankfort, June 7, 1850.

Dear Orlando,—I returned last Sunday from Indianapolis after a week's absence. Nothing could exceed the kindness and hospitality which attended me throughout the State. The receptions and honors with which they endeavored to distinguish me were almost overwhelming to one so plain as I am and so unaccustomed to such ceremonies and distinctions. I feel that

I owe to Indiana and her governor a great debt of gratitude. In that State there is very little political abolition, and, with a strong and patriotic feeling for the Union, there is mingled a particularly fraternal kindness and affection for Kentucky. The prevailing sentiment there is for a compromise and amicable settlement of all the slavery question. The plan suggested in General Taylor's message was spoken of frequently as most acceptable, but I think they would be satisfied with Mr. Clay's bill. In my speech at Indianapolis I spoke of *old Zack* as the *noble old patriot* in whom the country might have all confidence, and, without discriminating between the various plans that had been proposed, I expressed my hope and confidence that they would result in some form of amicable adjustment. The occasion required me to avoid, as far as possible, the appearance of partisanship or party politics; but it was *due to my heart* to give old Zack a *good word*, and I did it. I felt it a duty, too, to talk right plainly to them about abolition and the mischiefs that its meddlesome and false humanity had brought and was tending to bring upon the country. I went so far as to advise those who, from tenderness of conscience about slavery, could not acquiesce in what our fathers had done, and could not reconcile themselves to the Constitution of the United States and the performance of the duties it enjoined, *to quit the country*, etc. All this seemed to be well received except, as I learned afterwards, by some half-dozen abolitionists out of a crowd of as many thousand. The convention is in session, and I have scarcely time to steal a moment to write to you.

Well, you have resigned. It makes me *glad*, and it makes me *sorry*; *glad* that you are coming back to us,—*sorry*, that you are leaving General Taylor. The difficulties that are surrounding him only tend to increase my sympathy and zeal for him, and I retain my confidence that the storm will rage around him in vain, and that his firm and resolute integrity and patriotism will bear him through triumphantly. There is one *peril* before him that is to be carefully avoided, and that is the *peril* of having thrown upon his administration the responsibility of defeating the *bill* of the *committee of thirteen* or any other measure of compromise. It has appeared to me that the principal questions of the slavery controversy might have been disposed of more quietly and easily on the plan recommended by the President; but the people are *anxious* for a *settlement*, and comparatively indifferent as to the exact terms, provided they embrace anything like a compromise; and it seems to me that any concession or sacrifice of opinion as to the *mode* ought to be made to accomplish the *end*. It is not necessary to enlarge upon this subject. General Taylor's message is the *foundation* of all their plans in this, that it *avoids* the Wilmot proviso; all the rest is the mere *finish* of the work. *My whole heart* is bent on the success of General Taylor. I know that he deserves it, and believe he will achieve it. Tell Robert his little girls are gay as birds, and are continually dragging me into the garden to pull *strawberries* with them. I have taken poor Bob's disappointment quite to heart; but let that go.

Your friend,
J. J. CRITTENDEN.

(J. J. Crittenden to A. T. Burnley.)

July 19, 1850.

DEAR BURNLEY,—I returned from Louisville last evening, where I was suddenly summoned a few days ago to attend the sick and, as was then supposed, dying bed of my son-in-law, Chapman Coleman. I left him much improved, and, as the doctors induced me to hope, out of danger, though still quite ill. This absence delayed the receipt of your telegraphic dispatches, in which you ask me if I will accept the office of Attorney-General, and say that it is important I should answer immediately. A little reflection will show you the difficulty of answering this communication with the telegraphic brevity of a " yes" or " no." Indeed, I find much of the same difficulty in responding to you in any mode. You are upon the spot, and with a nearer and better view of the condition of things. You give me no intimation of your opinions or wishes; nor do you give me to understand that the inquiry was made at the suggestion or by the authority of the President or any other official. I must therefore understand it as more an inquiry of your own, in order, perhaps, to enable you and other friends to press me more effectually for the office. If this be the object and purpose, I could not answer you affirmatively without in substance seeking the office for myself. That I am not willing to do, either in form or substance, directly or indirectly. I would not for any consideration subject myself to the imputation of endeavoring to force or solicit my way into the cabinet of Mr. Fillmore. There are stations that can be neither agreeably nor usefully occupied except by persons having the personal good will and confidence of the President. My relations with Mr. Fillmore have always been of the most agreeable and amicable character, and I hope they may continue so. It seems to me that if he pleased to desire my acceptance of the office of Attorney-General, the most proper course would be for him to tender it to me; and that the most proper and becoming course for me would be to wait till it was tendered. The tender would then be most honorable to both parties, and certainly most gratefully received by me. I feel that before such an offer it would be indelicate in me to say that I *would* or *would* NOT *accept.* You will appreciate all this without any explanation, and so I shall leave the subject. There is no confidence, Burnley, that I fear to repose in you; and if it should appear to you that there is too much of reserve in this letter to be used towards an old and well-tried friend, I wish you to understand that it is intended to apply to the subject only, and to keep distinct and clear the line of conduct that I sincerely desire to pursue in relation to this matter.

My situation now is not exactly what it was when I declined an invitation to go into the cabinet of General Taylor; and to you, as my friend, my personal friend, I may say that my impression is that I should accept the office if tendered to me; but I will have no agency in seeking or getting it; nor do I wish my friends to place me in any attitude that can be construed into any such seeking; nor do I wish them to give themselves any trouble about the matter. If the offer of the office comes freely and without solicitation, then it comes honorably, and may be taken the more honorably. I think you will now understand me fully, and I have only to add that I am always your friend,

J. J. CRITTENDEN.

To A. T. BURNLEY, Esq.

CHAPTER XXIX.

1850–1853.

(J. J. Crittenden to his daughter A. M. Coleman.)

FRANKFORT, July 23, 1850.

MY DEAR DAUGHTER,—Doubly near and dear to me in your affliction, I do not know how to address you, or to express my sympathy in your great calamity. You will find, my child, in your own heart and in your own reflections the only real consolations. If, as I believe, this life is but a state of preparation and probation, *happiest is he* who, having done his duty like a man and a Christian, is soonest relieved from it. You have every reason to be assured that such is the fortunate lot of that husband of whom death has deprived you. That very excellence, which you mourn the loss of, will become a source of comfort and consolation to your heart. The death of your husband has placed you under great responsibilities, and left you many duties to perform. Turn, then, courageously to the performance of those duties, and in their performance you will find strength and consolation. You will feel, too, the high and pleasant consciousness that you are thereby best gratifying and manifesting your respect and devotion to the memory of your husband. He has enjoined it upon you to take his place in respect to your children, and to be to them as a father and mother also. You will, I know, consider this a sacred duty, and will not abandon it by giving yourself up to unavailing grief. I had intended to go to Louisville, to-morrow, to see you, but, upon consultation with Harry, it is decided to be best to postpone my visit for about a week; *then*, perhaps, I may be more serviceable to you than *now*. Your mother will probably accompany me. Farewell, my dear child.

J. J. CRITTENDEN.

Mrs. A. M. COLEMAN.

After the death of General Taylor, Mr. Crittenden accepted

the office of Attorney-General, under Mr. Fillmore, appointed July 22, 1850, and remained in that office till the close of Mr. Fillmore's administration in 1853.

The following is his opinion as to the constitutionality of the fugitive slave bill, given September 18, 1850:

CONSTITUTIONALITY OF THE FUGITIVE SLAVE BILL.

The provisions of the bill, commonly called the fugitive slave bill, and which Congress have submitted to the President for his approval and signature, are not in conflict with the provisions of the Constitution in relation to the writ of *habeas corpus.*

The expressions used in the last clause of the sixth section, that the certificate therein alluded to "shall prevent all molestation" of the persons to whom granted, " by any process issued," etc., probably mean only what the act of 1793 meant by declaring a certificate under that act a sufficient warrant for the removal of a fugitive; and do not mean a suspension of the writ of *habeas corpus.*

There is nothing in the act inconsistent with the Constitution, nor which is not necessary to redeem the pledge which it contains, that fugitive slaves shall be delivered upon the claim of their owners.

Attorney-General's Office,
September 18, 1850.

Sir,—I have had the honor to receive your note of this date, informing me that the bill, commonly called the fugitive slave bill, having passed both houses of Congress, had been submitted to you for your consideration, approval, and signature, and requesting my opinion whether the sixth section of that act, and especially the last clause of that section, conflicts with that provision of the Constitution which declares that "the privilege of the writ of *habeas corpus* shall not be suspended unless when, in cases of rebellion or invasion, the public safety may require it."

It is my clear conviction that there is nothing in the last clause, nor in any part of the sixth section, nor, indeed, in any of the provisions of the act, which suspends, or was intended to suspend, the privilege of the writ of *habeas corpus,* or is in any manner in conflict with the Constitution.

The Constitution, in the second section of the fourth article, declares that " no person held to service or labor in one State, under the laws thereof, escaping into another, shall, in consequence of any law or regulation therein, be discharged from such service or labor, but *shall* be delivered up on claim of the party to whom such service or labor may be due."

It is well known and admitted, historically and judicially, that this clause of the Constitution was made for the purpose of securing to the citizens of the slaveholding States the complete ownership in their slaves, as property, in any and every State or Territory of the Union into which they might escape. (*Prigg* vs. *Commonwealth of Pennsylvania,* 16 *Peters,* 539.) It devolved

on the general government, as a solemn duty, to make that
security effectual.   Their power was not only clear and full, but,
according to the opinion of the court in the above-cited case, it
was *exclusive,*—the States, severally, being under no obligation,
and having no power to make laws or regulations in respect to
the delivery of fugitives.   Thus the whole power, and with it
the whole *duty*, of carrying into effect this important provision
of the Constitution, was with Congress.   And, accordingly, soon
after the adoption of the Constitution, the act of the 12th of February, 1793, was passed, and that proving unsatisfactory and
inefficient, by reason (among other causes) of some minor errors
in its details, Congress are now attempting by this bill to discharge a constitutional obligation, by securing more effectually
the delivery of fugitive slaves to their owners.   The sixth, and
most material section, in substance declares that the claimant
of the fugitive slave may arrest and carry him before any one
of the officers named and described in the bill; and provides
that those officers, and each of them, shall have *judicial* power
and jurisdiction to hear, examine, and decide the case in a summary manner,—that if, upon such hearing, the claimant, by the
requisite proof, shall, establish his claim to the satisfaction of
the tribunal thus constituted, the said tribunal shall give him a
certificate, stating therein the substantial facts of the case, and
authorizing him, with such reasonable force as may be necessary, to take and carry said fugitive back to the State or
Territory whence he or she may have escaped,—and then, in
conclusion, proceeds as follows: "The certificates in this and
the first section mentioned, shall be conclusive of the right of
the person or persons in whose favor granted to remove such
fugitive to the State or Territory from which he escaped, and
shall prevent all molestation of such person or persons by any
process issued by any court, judge, magistrate, or other person
whomsoever."

There is nothing in all this that does not seem to me to be
consistent with the Constitution, and necessary, indeed, to redeem the pledge which it contains, that such fugitives "shall be
delivered up on claim" of their owners.

The Supreme Court of the United States has decided that the
owner, independent of any aid from State or national legislation,
may, in virtue of the Constitution, and his own right of property,
seize and recapture his fugitive slave in whatsoever State he
may find him, and carry him back to the State or Territory from
which he escaped.   (*Prigg* vs. *Commonwealth of Pennsylvania,*
16 *Peters,* 539.)   This bill, therefore, confers no right on the
owner of the fugitive slave.   It only gives him an appointed
and peaceable remedy in place of the more exposed and inse-

cure, but not less lawful mode of self-redress; and as to the fugitive slave, he has no cause to complain of this bill,—it adds no coercion to that which his owner himself might, at his own will, rightfully exercise; and all the proceedings which it institutes are but so much of orderly, judicial authority interposed between him and his owner, and consequently of protection to him, and mitigation of the exercise directly by the owner himself of his personal authority. This is the constitutional and legal view of the subject, as sanctioned by the decisions of the Supreme Court, and to that I limit myself.

The act of the 12th of February, 1793, before alluded to, so far as it respects any constitutional question that can arise out of this bill, is identical with it. It authorizes the like arrest of the fugitive slave, the like trial, the like judgment, the like certificate, with the like authority to the owner, by virtue of that certificate as his warrant, to remove him to the State or Territory from which he escaped, and the constitutionality of that act, in all those particulars, has been affirmed by the adjudications of State tribunals, and of the courts of the United States, without a single dissent, so far as I know. (*Baldwin, C. C. R.* 577, 579.)

I conclude, therefore, that so far as the act of the 12th of February, 1793, has been held to be constitutional, this bill must also be so regarded; and that the custody, restraint, and removal to which the fugitive slave may be subjected under the provisions of this bill, are all lawful, and that the certificate to be granted to the owner is to be regarded as the act and judgment of a judicial tribunal having competent jurisdiction.

With these remarks as to the constitutionality of the general provisions of the bill, and the consequent legality of the custody and confinement to which the fugitive slave may be subjected under it, I proceed to a brief consideration of the more particular question you have propounded in reference to the writ of *habeas corpus*, and of the last clause of the sixth section, above quoted, which gives rise to that question.

My opinion, as before expressed, is that there is nothing in that clause or section which conflicts with or suspends, or was intended to suspend, the privilege of the writ of *habeas corpus*. I think so because the bill says not one word about that writ; because, by the Constitution, Congress is expressly forbidden to suspend the privilege of this writ, " unless when in cases of rebellion or invasion the public safety may require it;" and therefore such suspension by this act (there being neither rebellion nor invasion) would be a plain and palpable violation of the Constitution, and no intention to commit such a violation of the Constitution, of their duty and their oaths, ought to be imputed to them upon mere constructions and implications; and thirdly, because there is no incompatibility between these provisions of the bill and the privilege of the writ of *habeas corpus* in its utmost constitutional latitude.

Congress, in the case of fugitive slaves, as in all other cases within the scope of its constitutional authority, has the unquestionable right to ordain and prescribe for what causes, to what extent, and in what manner persons may be taken into custody, detained, or imprisoned. Without this power they could not fulfill their constitutional trust, nor perform the ordinary and necessary duties of government. It was never heard that the exercise of that legislative power was any encroachment upon or suspension of the privilege of the writ of *habeas corpus*. It is only by some confusion of ideas that such a conflict can be supposed to exist. It is not within the province or privilege of this great writ to loose those whom the *law* has bound. That would be to put a writ granted by the law in opposition to the law, to make one part of the law destructive of another. This writ follows the *law* and obeys the *law*. It is issued, upon proper complaint, to make inquiry into the causes of commitment or imprisonment, and its sole remedial power and purpose is to deliver the party from " all manner of *illegal* confinement." (3 *Black. Com.* 131.)   If upon application to the court or judge for this writ, or if upon its return it shall appear that the confinement complained of was *lawful*, the writ, in the first instance, would be refused, and in the last the party would be remanded to his former *lawful* custody.

The condition of one in custody as a fugitive slave is, under this law, so far as respects the writ of *habeas corpus*, precisely the same as that of all other prisoners under the laws of the United States. The " privilege " of that writ remains alike to all of them, but to be judged of—granted or refused, discharged or enforced—by the proper tribunal, according to the circumstances of each case, and as the commitment and detention may appear to be legal or illegal.

The whole effect of the law may be thus briefly stated : Congress has constituted a tribunal with exclusive jurisdiction to determine summarily and without appeal who are fugitives from service or labor under the second section of the fourth article of the Constitution, and to whom such service or labor is due. The judgment of every tribunal of exclusive jurisdiction where no appeal lies, is, of necessity, conclusive upon every other tribunal ; and therefore the judgment of the tribunal created by this act is conclusive upon all tribunals. Wherever this judgment is made to appear, it is conclusive of the right of the owner to retain in his custody the fugitive from his service, and to remove him back to the place or State from which he escaped. If it is shown upon the application of the fugitive for a writ of *habeas corpus*, it prevents the issuing of the writ; if upon the return, it discharges the writ and restores or maintains the custody.

This view of the law of this case is fully sustained by the decision of the Supreme Court of the United States in the case of Tobias Watkins, where the court refused to discharge upon the ground that he was in custody under the sentence of a court of competent jurisdiction, and that that judgment was conclusive upon them. (3 *Peters*.)

The expressions used in the last clause of the sixth section, that the certificate therein alluded to "shall prevent all molestation" of the persons to whom granted " by any process issued," etc., probably mean only what the act of 1793 meant by declaring a certificate under that act a sufficient warrant for the removal of a fugitive, and certainly do not mean a suspension of the *habeas corpus*. I conclude by repeating my conviction that there is nothing in the bill in question which conflicts with the Constitution or suspends, or was intended to suspend, the privilege of the writ of *habeas corpus*.

I have the honor to be, very respectfully, sir,

Your obedient servant,

J. J. CRITTENDEN.

To the PRESIDENT.

This eulogy, pronounced by Mr. Crittenden while filling the office of Attorney-General of the United States, upon Judge McKinley of the Supreme Court, the day after his death, is eminently worthy of a record in his life. Mr. Crittenden's generous appreciation of the virtues and talents of his friends is well known. Certainly no loftier encomium was ever pronounced upon a wise and righteous judge than this. Nothing could be added and nothing taken from it without marring its classic beauty.

PROCEEDINGS IN RELATION TO THE DEATH OF THE LATE JUS- TICE McKINLEY OF THE SUPREME COURT OF THE UNITED STATES.

At the opening of the court this morning, Mr. Crittenden, the Attorney-General of the United States, addressed the court as follows :

Since its adjournment yesterday, the members of the bar and officers of the court held a meeting and adopted resolutions expressive of their high sense of the public and private worth of the Hon. John McKinley, one of the justices of this court, and their deep regret at his death. By the same meeting I was requested to present those resolutions to the court, and to ask that they might be entered on its records, and I now rise to perform that honored task.

Besides the private grief which naturally attends it, the death of a member of this court, which is the head of a great, essential, and vital department of the government, must always be an event of public interest and importance.

I had the good fortune to be acquainted with Judge McKinley from my earliest manhood. In the relations of private life he was frank, hospitable, affectionate. In his manners he was simple and unaffected, and his character was uniformly marked with manliness, integrity, and honor. Elevation to the bench of the Supreme Court made no change in him. His honors were borne meekly, without ostentation or presumption.

He was a candid, impartial, and righteous judge. Shrinking from no responsibility, he was fearless in the performance of his duty, seeking only to do right, and fearing nothing but to do wrong. Death has now set her seal to his character, making it unchangeable forever; and I think it may be truly inscribed on his monument that as a private gentleman and as a public magistrate he was without fear and without reproach.

This occasion cannot but remind us of other afflicting losses which have recently befallen us. The present, indeed, has been a sad year for the profession of the law. In a few short months it has been bereaved of its brightest and greatest ornaments. Clay, Webster, and Sergeant have gone to their immortal rest in quick succession. We had scarcely returned from the grave of one of them till we were summoned to the funeral of another. Like bright stars they have sunk below the horizon, and have left the land in widespread gloom. This hall that knew them so well shall know them no more. Their wisdom has no utterance now, and the voice of their eloquence shall be heard here no more forever.

This hall itself seems as though it was sensible of its loss, and even these marble pillars seem to sympathize as they stand around us like so many majestic mourners.

But we will have consolation in the remembrance of these illustrious men. Their *names* will remain to us and be like a light kindled in the sky to shine upon us and to guide our course. We may hope, too, that the memory of them and their great examples will create a virtuous emulation which may raise up men worthy to be their successors in the service of their country, its constitution, and its laws.

For this digression, and these allusions to Clay, Webster, and

Sergeant, I hope the occasion may be considered as a sufficient excuse, and I will not trespass by another word, except only to move that these resolutions in relation to Judge McKinley, when they shall have been read by the clerk, may be entered on the records of this court.

(R. P. Letcher to J. J. Crittenden.)

MEXICO, October 20, 1850.

DEAR CRITTENDEN,—Mr. Marks, a gentleman of respectability and intelligence, has just signified to me that he *sets out* for Washington City in a few hours. I give you a brief letter. Attend to him and introduce him to Mr. Webster. He is quite intimate with the government, and has been for many years the confidential friend of some of the leading members of the cabinet. Mr. Webster's amendments to the treaty were received about ten days ago. I have succeeded in getting the whole of them adopted, with the exception of two. Marks can tell you all about it. *They* never can be carried, if tried, to the day the great *judgment-gun* shall be *fired.* I have tried every argument, every persuasion, every threat, to prevail upon the cabinet to accept these two amendments *in vain.* In fact, I tried very hard to have these amendments inserted in the original treaty for three months. I believe I could prevail upon these folks to cede the whole country to the United States sooner than agree to these modifications. I won't trouble you with these matters. *Unhappy* as I am here, anxious as I am to return home, I will not quit my post till the end of this treaty is seen. I have some reason to believe Mr. Webster is not satisfied with my negotiations in regard to this treaty. This fills me with the deepest concern. It is utterly impossible for Mr. Webster to know and see things in this country as they really exist. Under all the circumstances, I know it was right to sign that treaty; I care not *who* may think to the contrary. Mr. Webster shall have a chance of appointing some one in my place who suits him better. I have worked hard since I have been in this country, and expect but little thanks; but I don't deserve censure or reproach. I don't mean to utter a word of complaint against Mr. Webster, or to say to any one else what I have said to you, unless it becomes necessary in my own defense, and then I'll say a *damned deal.* The truth is I feel a little desperate, and as cross as —— at the idea of being *reproached.* Damn the treaty; it's opposed by all the foreign influence, by the opposition party, and by all the moneyed and commercial men of this country in solid column. The newspapers have openly charged me with forcing the government to make it. They have charged me with the *crime* of controlling

this government as I please.   The foreign ministers talk in the
same way.   So I am, you may well imagine, worried to death,
and get no thanks for it.   If anything whatever occurs, which
in your judgment should render it proper for me to resign, *you*
are fully authorized to file my resignation at any moment.   All
I care about is to see the end of this treaty, and then my mission shall be at an end through *the grace of God.*

Good-by to you.

R. P. LETCHER.

Hon. J. J. CRITTENDEN.

(R. J. B. to J. J. Crittenden.)

LEXINGTON, Nov. 23, 1850.

MY DEAR SIR,—More than a year ago our friend Garrett Duncan made application to the President and to the Secretary at
War for a cadet's warrant at West Point for my oldest son.   He
did this spontaneously as an act of personal regard, and perhaps as some expression of his sense of things of other days.
I had other friends whose influence might have aided him;
but in the same spirit that actuated him, I told him I would
do nothing; so that if he succeeded, he should have all the
gratitude of the lad and all the pleasure of the good deed.   He
failed.   But the President and the Secretary both promised to
put the lad's name on the list, and held out strong hopes, if not
a certain assurance, of his appointment a year from that time,—
to wit, *now.*

Now, my dear sir, if this appointment can be had, I shall
be very glad; my boy will be gratified in the strongest and
almost the earliest wish of his heart, and I trust the country
may be gainer thereby in the end.   The lad is now a little past
sixteen years of age; he is a member of the Sophomore class at
Danville, and is of robust constitution, fine talents, and earnest,
firm, and elevated nature.   It is to gratify *him* in a strong, nay,
a vehement, passion that I desire this thing.   For myself I never
did, never will, solicit anything from any government.   The
ancestors of this lad, paternal and maternal, have done the
State some service.   You know all about all I could with propriety say.

If there is any impropriety in my thus addressing you, I pray
you to excuse it; if there is none, and this thing can be accomplished, it will be only another proof of your goodness and
another ground of the grateful and affectionate friendship of

Yours ever,

R. J. B.

Hon. J. J. CRITTENDEN.

(R. J. B. to J. J. Crittenden.)

LEXINGTON, KY., April 12, 1851.

DEAR SIR,—You may, perhaps, recollect that I was inconsiderate enough to address a letter to you during the last winter on the subject of a warrant to West Point for one of a numerous family of sons, under circumstances which I erred, perhaps, in supposing were somewhat peculiar, and with claims upon the country, personal and hereditary, which I no doubt greatly overrated in my desire to gratify the ardent wishes of a beloved child.

I was not fortunate enough to receive any answer to that letter; and although the application was warmly supported by both the senators from this State and several members of Congress from this and other States, being myself without political influence, it failed, as I ought to have foreseen it must. I feel it to be due to you and to myself to say that I regret very much having, in a moment of parental weakness, committed so great an error, and by this declaration atone, at least to my own feelings, for the only instance, through a life now not very short, in which I have asked from any one anything for myself or any member of my family. Praying you to excuse what I so much regret, I am, very respectfully,

Your friend and servant,

Hon. J. J. CRITTENDEN. R. J. B.

(J. J. Crittenden to R. J. B.)

WASHINGTON, April 21, 1851.

SIR,—Your letter of the 12th inst. was received yesterday, and read with painful surprise. It is marked with such a spirit of rebuke and irritation that I hardly know how I ought to understand or reply to it. You have almost made me feel that any explanation under such circumstances would be derogatory. But, sir, suppressing all these feelings, and preferring *in this instance* to err, if at all, on the side of forbearance, I have concluded to address you a calm reply and explanation of the subject that has so much irritated and excited you.

Know, then, that I did receive the letter you addressed to me last winter requesting my assistance in procuring for your son the appointment of cadet in the Military Academy at West Point.

All such appointments, except ten, are so regulated by law that they must be made, one from each congressional district, on the nomination and recommendation of the representative of that district.

There was no vacancy in your district, and, of course, the

only hope for your son was to obtain for him one of the ten extraordinary appointments at the disposal of the President. The power of conferring these is understood to have been given to the President for the benefit of the sons of officers of the army and navy, and especially of those whose fathers had perished in the service of their country; and although these appointments have not, in practice, been always confined to this description of persons, their claims have been generally favored and preferred. The number of such applicants has been greatly increased by the Mexican war, and their competitors from civil life are still more numerous.

From this general statement may be inferred the uncertainty and difficulty of procuring one of these appointments.

In the winter of 1849 and '50 I had, at the instance of my old friend, Gabriel Lewis, of Kentucky, very earnestly recommended a grandson of his to General Taylor for one of these appointments. He did not get it, and it was then determined by his family, with my advice and my promise to give what assistance I could, to renew or continue his application for another year, and I had, accordingly, again recommended him for one of the appointments that were to be made this spring.

Such was the condition of things and such my situation and engagement when your first letter was received. Notwithstanding all the difficulties in the way, I was not without the hope of serving you, for the sole reason, perhaps, that I wished to do so, and wished to obtain the appointment for your son. To learn something of the prospect of success, I conversed several times with the Secretary of War on the subject. He could only tell me that no selections would be made, that the subject would not be considered till the time had arrived for making the appointments, and that the number of applicants was very great, amounting to hundreds,—I think he said fifteen hundred.

I ought, perhaps, to have acknowledged the receipt of your letter and have given you all this information; and most certainly I would have done it if I had had the least apprehension of the grave consequences that have followed the omission. It did not occur to me that any punctiliousness would be exacted in our correspondence.

But, besides all this, and to say nothing of the daily duties of my office, and my almost constant attendance upon the Supreme Court, then in session, I had nothing satisfactory or definite to write. I waited, therefore, willing to avail myself of any circumstance or opportunity that time or chance might bring forth to serve you and to procure an appointment for your son as well as for the grandson of Mr. Lewis. I could find no such opportunity—no opportunity even for urging it with the least hope of success.

The appointments have all been recently made, and, with few exceptions, confined to the sons, I believe, of deceased officers, to the exclusion, for the second time, of the grandson of my friend Lewis, who has been on the list of applicants for two years, with all the recommendation I could give him.

I should have taken some opportunity of writing to you on this subject, even if your late letter had not so unpleasantly anticipated that purpose.

This, sir, is the whole tale. It must speak for itself. I have no other propitiation to offer. I am the injured party. When you become conscious of that, you will know well what atonement ought to be made and how it ought to be made. Till then, sir, self-respect compels me to say that I will be content to abide those unfriendly relations which I understand your letter to imply, if not proclaim.

I can truly say that I have written this "more in sorrow than in anger." I have intended nothing beyond my own defense and vindication, and if I have been betrayed into a word that goes beyond those just limits and implies anything like aggression, let it be stricken out.

J. J. CRITTENDEN.

LEXINGTON, KENTUCKY, May 3, 1851.

Hon. J. J. CRITTENDEN.

DEAR SIR,—I regret very much to perceive by your letter of the 21st ultimo that you considered my letter to you of the 12th April wanting in proper respect to you, and prompted by irritation on my part. I retained no copy of that letter; but, assuredly, I know very little of myself if it contained the evidences of either of those states of mind.

For the first time in my life I had condescended to solicit, from any human authority, anything, either for myself or any member of my immediate family, though many hundreds of times I have done what I could for others. It was particularly distressing to me that I had been seduced into such a position by the extreme kindness of an old personal friend (Mr. Duncan), as I explained in my first letter to you, and, by some ridiculous notion, that the present administration might consider itself any ways connected with that of General Taylor, so as to feel disposed to fulfill any expectations it may have raised.

Unless my memory deceives me, my first letter, making the application, intimated to you that I was not sure it was proper in me to write you such a letter, and asked you to excuse the impropriety, if indeed one existed. Such, I remember well, was the state of my mind, and I think I expressed it. The only notice ever taken of that letter, by you, is the allusion to it in your letter before me. What took place in the mean time may be uttered in a sentence, and need not be repeated here.

Under all the painful, and to me altogether unprecedented, circumstances of a very humiliating position, I thought it due to you to express my regret at having implicated you, in any degree, in such an affair by my letter of application to you; and I thought it due to myself to express to you, under such circumstances, my regret at allowing myself, in a moment of parental weakness, to embark in a matter which, in all its progress and its termination, was especially out of keeping with the whole tenor of my life and feelings. If my letter, to which yours of the 21st April is an answer, expresses more or less than these things, it is expressed unhappily and improperly. If, during the progress of the affair, you had judged it necessary or proper to have treated it differently, or had had it in your power to do so, I should not have been more bound to feel obliged by any other or further service than I am now bound to feel obliged, by such as your letter informs me you were good enough to render me, under circumstances which, it is now obvious, must have been embarrassing to you, and which, if I had known, I would have instantly released you from. But all this, as it appears to me, only the more painfully shows how inconsiderate my first application to you was, and how needless it was for my subsequent expression of regret for having made it to be taken in an offensive sense.

The sole object of this letter is to place the whole affair on the footing which, in my opinion, it really occupies.

Certainly I had no right to ask anything of the sort I did ask at your hands. But assuredly having been weak enough to ask it, and having, in the course of events, had full occasion to perceive that weakness, I had the right without offense to express sincere regret for what I had inconsiderately done,—to the needless annoyance of yourself and others,—and to the wounding of my own self-esteem.

Permit me, in conclusion, to say that altogether the most painful part of this affair, to me, is that I should have given offense to a man who, for nearly if not quite thirty years, I have been accustomed to regard with feelings of the greatest esteem, admiration, and confidence, and for whom, at any moment during those thirty years, I would have periled everything but my honor to have served him; such a man will know how to appreciate the workings of a nature perhaps oversensitive and overproud, in the midst of unusual and oppressive circumstances. If not, it is better to forget all than lose our own self-respect.

As to Mr. Fillmore and Mr. Conrad, strange as it may seem

to you, I would never, under ordinary circumstances, have asked either of them for any favor whatever. I rather considered myself asking you and Mr. Clay and Judge Underwood and Judge Breck and a few other old friends to whom I brought myself to the point—not without great difficulty—of saying what I did. This may seem very absurd to you; perhaps it is so; it is nevertheless the truth; and most certainly I did not suppose that any administration of which yourself and Mr. Clay and Judge Underwood and Judge Breck were avowed, if not confidential, supporters, would, under the entire circumstances of this case, have it in its power to refuse so paltry a boon; and after seeing the published list of successful applicants, from which alone I learned the fate of my application, I saw still less reason to comprehend such a result. As to yourself, three particulars separated your case from that of the other friends I have named: 1st. I loved you most, and relied most on you. 2d. I the most distrusted the propriety of writing to you, on account of your connection with the cabinet. 3d. From you alone I had no word of notice; and for these two last reasons, the more felt that an explanation was demanded of me as due both to you and myself.

If you have had patience to read this letter, it is needless for me to say more than that I still desire to be considered your friend.

R. J. B.

END OF VOL. I.

9 783337 278502